MONUMENT AT LANDING

JEFFRY DWIGHT

MONUMENT AT LANDING
A science-fantasy novel by
Jeffry Dwight
The Sundering Saga, Book Two

The Book of the Ship
(restricted section)

"Oft evil a fair face dons, the simple to deceive and the wise to beguile."

—Monkish Aphorism

"Arrogance blinds clever people to the obvious fact that some actions are intrinsically wrong; it also lets them elevate rationalization over rationality. Reason is a tool as easily misused as language itself."

—Justinian Pontifex

"Nothing will ever remain as faithful to you as your gravestone."

—Abbess Siobhan

"What will future generations remember of me? Not that I recognized the duplicity of the muria, but that it took me so long. We will never leave this planet. I accept responsibility for that."

—Captain Leonais

CHAPTER ONE

I SURMOUNTED the last hill separating Maran's hidden valley from the flatlands and forests of Colonial Plain. I stood for several minutes to rest my bad leg and catch my breath, then pushed myself around a boulder and scanned for danger. I heard a bird's call, short and piercing, quickly repeated from several directions. I sighed, but didn't turn back. This was the fifth time in the last month they had discovered me. It was probably time to deal with them instead of retreating.

I had no desire for conflict, but I didn't fancy being the subject of a protracted hunt, either. I decided to wait them out and learn who had been stalking me so patiently for so long. The whistles—badly disguised bird song—took on urgency and grew nearer.

Within minutes, twenty-five riders cantered through the woods toward me from three sides, ducking branches and avoiding undergrowth. They had clearly been scattered throughout the forest, waiting for me without knowing precisely where I would emerge. The same charms that precluded them from finding the valley itself also prevented me from sensing them before I climbed up. I found the situation annoying. Things would be so much easier if I could scan the area before exposing myself.

I stood patiently, my back against the boulder, until the riders surrounded me, their horses champing and pawing at the soft ground. They wore the livery of the King's Guard, silver-braided dark blue coats covering lighter blue underneath. I quickly counted armaments to divine their intent. Only one carried a crossbow, but had it uncocked and slung at the side of his saddle. All had sheathed swords, and a few had longbows over their shoulders. I noted several hunting bows as well, but none drawn. They rode with the easy assurance of veterans, but their eyes held only curiosity, not belligerence. The riders farthest away led packhorses laden with supplies. They were clearly a search party, not a hunting party, but well equipped to deal with any trouble that might arise. I breathed a bit easier, and nodded affably by way of greeting.

"Lord Grey," said the captain, urging his horse a few paces forward. He rested his right hand on the pommel of his saddle rather than the pommel of his sword. I took his posture as a gesture of good will—or at least peaceable intent. I guessed him to be in his mid-forties, a bit older than most of the others, with the leathery skin that spoke of a life spent mostly outdoors. His face was narrow, and his eyes sparkled with intelligence.

"You have the wrong man, good fellow," I said in a cheerful voice. "I'm no one's lord."

He squinted at me for a moment. "White hair and skin, tall, gaunt, a scarf around your head to hide your eyes, and a withered left arm. I think we have exactly the right man. Do I need to check for a missing ear?"

I sighed. "What does Ashe want from me?"

"The *king*," he said, stressing the title, "instructed us to guide you to court, my lord. No doubt, he will tell you in person what he wants. We've been quartering these woods for weeks now. How did you manage to escape our search?"

"Signposting a hidden retreat rather defeats the purpose. And, should I step back around this boulder, you could scour the forest forever without finding me again."

The captain tugged at his beard and regarded me closely, trying to gauge my intentions. "Likely true," he said at length, "but since we *have* found you this time, will you allow us the honor of escorting you?"

"I don't belong at court, and it's too far. I have a game leg. Making me walk to Jappa is purposeless cruelty. I'm only here to find herbs for my wife. She thinks we need rosemary and lemon balm. Kindly take your soldiers and leave me in peace."

He looked confused. "Lemon balm, lord?"

"It's a kind of plant. Useful for many things."

"Yes, lord," he said, "I know what it is. Just not why you would consider the search for herbs more urgent than a summons from the king."

I smiled faintly. "You haven't met Maran. A whim from my wife far exceeds the authority of royalty. Jappa is weeks away. My leg precludes a long journey, and I must return to Maran today."

"You needn't walk, lord. We have spare horses. We can redistribute the packs to free one for you. And our destination isn't Jappa. King Ashe is holding court at Landing just now."

"I don't ride," I said, more harshly than I intended.

The captain swung neatly out of his saddle and bowed. "Then you may sit my horse," he said, "and I shall walk before you to ensure your safety. A pleasant day's outing, no more, even at a walking pace. Please think of us as an honor guard rather than soldiers."

"Thank you, but no. I don't ride horses, even if led by a gallant and courteous captain. You've done your duty. Tell Ashe you found me, but that I refused the summons."

"My lord," he said, ducking his head apologetically, "we were instructed to bring you at any cost." He lifted a gloved hand, and two of his riders dismounted. Neither reached for weapons or showed hostility, but they advanced steadily in my direction.

I stiffened, twining a breath of god-winds around my right hand. "Ashe gave you my name and description, but did not warn you? How embarrassing. I am beyond your compulsion." I flicked my fingers, letting loose a small whirlwind directed against the ground. Dirt, pebbles, and twigs flew through the air, flapping all their cloaks, making the horses shy, and temporarily blinding the soldiers. As the riders frantically fought with their mounts and tried to rub the grit from their eyes, I closed my fist to subdue the winds.

"A small demonstration," I said when everyone had quieted, "of the least of my protections. Take your horses and go away. My wife is due to give birth very soon, and I cannot leave her side. Give my apologies to the king."

The captain stood his ground, though the rest of his troop backed their horses. "The king did indeed warn me, lord, but he also sent a message, should you prove reluctant to answer his summons."

"Your name, sir?" I asked.

"Benlyn of Sallas."

"Sallas?" I mused, memories flooding me. "I've passed through there." I didn't mention that my journey had been mostly at night, flitting from shadow to shadow to avoid the Archon's soldiers. "You're a long way from home, Benlyn. Tell me the message."

He closed his eyes in the manner of a courier trained to recall verbatim, and recited: "The monks have agreed to open their secret books, but only in your presence. The need for your counsel is urgent."

"Those were Ashe's exact words?" I asked sharply.

Benlyn nodded. I considered the message for a second, then cursed silently to myself. Ashe had known I couldn't resist. Aloud, I said simply, "I'll come, although I've never been on a horse before. You'll have to help me up and find some way to keep me in the saddle."

"The king said you knew how to ride."

"Not horses. Never mind. I'll manage with your help."

Benlyn made a circular gesture with his fist, and his company lined up in neat columns. The two men afoot remounted and joined the formation. Benlyn beckoned me to approach, and I limped forward. "He is a warhorse, but gentle enough if I lead him. We will not go at a pace to unseat you. Allow me to assist, lord."

He showed me where to put my boot, and boosted me up. We set off at a sedate walk, the soldiers following. I had no idea what to do with the reins, so I left them alone. Instead, I held onto the saddle horn.

"Did the king say anything else?" I asked, after a minute's riding convinced me I wasn't in imminent danger of falling off. At a walking pace, the horse's movements were surprisingly smooth. We soon gained a small road, and progress became even easier.

"No, lord. I am not privy to his councils."

"I haven't seen Ashe for nine months. Has he fully recovered from his wounds?"

"He has, lord."

"Stop all that lording, man. Just call me Grey."

"Yes, lord."

I leaned forward so I could glimpse the side of his face. Did a small smile lurk there, or was he unaware of his response? I let it go, and turned my mind to the riddle Ashe had used to draw me. On the one hand, I was not surprised that the hierophants had finally yielded; on the other, the timing made little sense. I had expected their capitulation either months ago, or not until I banged on the monastery doors and forced the issue. Why would they require me to be present? The entire point of getting their secret records was to share them with the entire world. I sighed, resigning myself to wait until Ashe could explain.

The crisp air hinted at autumn, and red-gold tinged nearly half the deciduous trees. The sun, unhindered by branch or leaf after we gained the road, provided a pleasant warmth. I gradually relaxed my death grip on the pommel and began to trust the horse. Our path led through a thickly wooded area of old growth, but its width easily accommodated the double-column of riders. Heavy traffic over the years had worn deep ruts down the center.

"Rumor says the king has had dealings with elves," ventured Benlyn after some time had passed with only the thud of hooves and jingle of tack to accompany us. "I've never seen one."

"Few have. Fewer still have lived to tell the tale. But don't call them elves. The proper name is muria. They are the descendants of the First Colony, but are no longer human. And yes, the king has met more than one. Why do you mention it?"

He turned, walking backward for a moment so he could study me. "Curiosity, lord, nothing more, except to pass the time. I hoped for information. Are elves—pardon, muria—as capricious and dangerous as people say?"

"They are dangerous, yes, but not capricious. They move to a different rhythm than humans, and never do anything without a reason. If we encounter one of the muria, I advise keeping your distance."

"But you, lord? You understand them?"

I unwound the scarf and let him see my eyeless sockets. He immediately spun on one heel to face forward again. "I'm sorry to have asked," he said.

I rebound my eyes and let a minute pass before answering. "No one understands the muria, unless they choose to explain themselves. Even then, the price of dealing with them is high, with no guarantee that their explanations will make sense. They are *different.*"

"Yes, lord."

"Can this beast go any faster? At this pace, it will take all day to reach Landing."

Benlyn shook his head. "If you are not a rider, lord, you would find a trot painful after a few minutes, even if I rode behind you in the saddle. Faster gaits would also risk throwing you. If we had known, we would have made other arrangements. In another three miles or so, after clearing the woods, we will reach a Justian road, which will be flat ship's metal underneath, providing easier passage. I can send a few of my company at a gallop to fetch a carriage or a wain. You could then—"

"Wait!" I called, interrupting him. My spine tingled, and the hairs on my neck and forearms lifted. Despite the sunshine, I suddenly shivered. "Tell your troops to stop, and then get me off this damned horse."

Benlyn responded to the urgency of my tone. Without asking questions, he signaled for a halt, and the company arranged themselves in a protective posture behind us, facing outward, swords drawn. Five horses sprinted ahead to protect the front of the line, and two sidled up on either side to interpose themselves between the trees and me. I was impressed with their efficiency and discipline.

Once in place, the riders quieted their mounts and held still. Only bird song and the scampering of squirrels disturbed the silence.

"Lord Grey," said Benlyn after a minute, "we perceive no danger. We are alone."

"You only think so. Get me down."

"Do you fear ambush, lord? This is an unlikely spot."

"Nothing that mundane. Get me down!"

Benlyn shrugged. "Disengage your right foot from the stirrup, and lean left toward me. I'll take your weight."

I did as instructed, and he reached up to drag me safely from the horse's back. His grip on my withered left arm was painful, but I paid no attention. All of my concentration focused on the road ahead of us. A deep dingle lay nearly a mile ahead, off to the left. The forest track swung far south to avoid it. We were still a good distance from the Justian road, but the rutted path we followed through the trees seemed clear and mostly level. I would have no trouble walking it.

"Stay here. Don't follow me. And put the swords away," I told him. "This isn't a danger you're equipped to fight. There's something ahead on the left." I limped forward past the horses posted in the vanguard, Benlyn at my side. "This is far enough," I said. "Wait for me here. I walk the last mile alone."

"My lord!" Benlyn protested. "Do you not need a guide?"

"I'm only blind to the obvious," I said with a hint of bitterness. "I can see the trail well enough."

"Then what shall I do?"

"As you're told. Await my return. Better yet, take your men ahead, until the road curves back. I'll take the straight path and rejoin you on the far side."

With that, I limped onward, following the road until it started curving away from the hollow. I pushed my way into the underbrush on a course that would eventually intercept the dingle. The way got easier when I found a deer track going roughly the right direction, but I had to abandon it before long. No animal in its right mind would head toward the emanations arising from the depths of the dingle. I kept alert, mostly for roots that might trip me. There was little chance of ambush here, and it was impossible to lose direction. The chief danger lay in falling and breaking my leg.

Benlyn caught up with me near where the level ground started crumbling and falling steeply toward the bottom of the hollow.

"My lord, the king charged me with your safety," he said.

"Can't you feel it?" I pointed ahead toward the dingle. "Something unnatural waits down there. I intend to investigate. This is my line of work, not yours. You should wait with your company."

"Are you saying there is danger, lord? I feel nothing," he said stoutly.

"Then why is your hair standing on end? I don't need your protection."

"Nevertheless, lord."

"You're braver than you look," I said, mentally reappraising him. Even here, at the lip of the hollow, the emanations from below were palpable. I didn't know what lurked at the bottom, but I had a good guess. It was no place for ordinary humans. And Benlyn clearly felt it already. His hands trembled, his face had gone pale, and sweat beaded his brow. Yet he stood his ground. I measured his blanched features against his insistence on accompanying me, and decided to let him make his own decisions. "Your courage exceeds your good sense," I told him, "but I can't stop you from following. Come along, then."

The ground sloped sharply down, and I kept my balance by bracing myself on tree trunks. As I descended, the branches met overhead, and the cold grew ever stronger. My boot heels dug into the deadfall, sending showers of dirt and old leaves tumbling ahead of me. Benlyn followed, but fell further and further back. I found a stream and used it to ease my passage. At length, I reached the bottom, and found the clearing I had expected. The stream, joined by dozens like it from all sides of the dingle, emptied into a small, startlingly clear pond. There must have been an underground exit, for the water was only a few feet deep, though the streams trickled in continuously.

The noise from Benlyn's descent had stopped about halfway down. He was close enough to see the clearing and its contents. "Lord Grey!" he called.

"Yes, it's a dolmen," I called back. "Either bide where you are, or climb back up to the top. There's no shame either way."

"I'll wait for you near the top, and move my troop to the far side to wait. Surely you don't intend to enter the circle?"

I didn't answer him, and shortly I heard him scrambling back up the steep incline.

I focused all my concentration on the standing stones. Most dolmens were built on hilltops, or level high ground, to avoid flooding. A ring of twelve neatly cut and dressed bluestones encircled the pond, menhirs standing approximately six feet apart and reaching at least twenty feet high, with intact lintels capping them. As I passed the boundary, the cold grew more intense, but I sensed no tomb guarded by the megaliths, and there was no king stone at the center. Nevertheless, I felt the latent power from the ring. I flicked the nearest menhir with my thumbnail, and multicolored bands of lights, like streamers or bangles, filled the hollow. They arose from the stones themselves, arching high overhead to create a dome of pulsating energy. A chime, deep and sonorous, emerged from underground, sending ripples across the pond. I quickly extinguished the lights, letting the power sink back into dormancy.

Unlike any dolmen I had encountered before, this one seemed to stand alone, unconnected to the continent-spanning network of faerie mounds. I moved to the pond, knelt, and tasted the water. It was bitter, rife with minerals leached from the surrounding soil and stone.

I stood up, wiping my hand on my trousers. I had rung the front doorbell by bringing the dolmen briefly to life; now I awaited an answer.

"You came," said a timorous young voice. "We didn't dare hope."

"Show yourself," I replied. "You cannot be muria, not here, and the nina no longer speak. I did not think any human would dare cross the boundary." When there was no reply, I repeated, "Show yourself," and added, "let there be amity between us, whatever you are."

"Will you free us?" said a second voice, also childlike.

"I can promise nothing without knowing more. Free you from what? What is your peril? Show yourselves."

"We cannot cross the circle."

"Human, then? I shall come out to meet you."

"No, we are inside. We cannot leave."

"I see no one."

"We have been dreaming for so long," said the first voice.

"You must free us," said the second.

"Yes. How?"

"Look inside the stones."

Inside? I put my hand flat on the nearest standing stone, not to waken power, but just to feel the age-pitted surface of the menhir. I felt nothing out of the ordinary. The stone was cold, as was everything within the circle—bone chilling cold, like the iciness of the grave. I walked around the menhir; it seemed the same on all sides. I reached as high toward the lintels as possible, then crouched, running my fingertips near the base. If there were a secret door or passage, I could not discern it. I probed with my mind instead of my hand. *There!* A faint hint of something waiting, dreaming, suspended in time, locked within the stone.

"Free us," said the first voice, "or let us die. We have been waiting for so long."

"I don't know how to find you," I said. My frustration built. They sounded like children's voices, small and pitiful, pleading for release from a kind of prison I could not comprehend.

"Cast down the stones."

Each of the twelve menhirs was easily three times my height, perhaps extending half the same distance underground. An army of engineers, using ropes, levers, shovels, scaffolds, and teams of horses or oxen could, with tremendous effort, break apart the stone circle. I knew of only one other power strong enough to move the megaliths, but I dared not try to raise the Sleeper, even if I could manage it. Half the continent of Leonais was still rebuilding from the last time I had done so, nine months before.

Perhaps I needed a less direct type of action, something less physical, more subtle. Words of command had never come at my behest; they only graced me at times of great need, or in moments of inspiration. I could not summon one by premeditation. I felt neither inspired nor in personal danger, but something about standing within the ambit of the stone circle led my mind in eldritch pathways, suggesting possibilities that could not exist elsewhere. I moved to stand beside the pond, where the potentials were strongest.

I narrowed and focused my perception until only the emanations of the menhirs existed. The bone-deep cold increased. The sun disappeared, suddenly hidden by thick clouds. Snow fell on my shoulders. The pond froze solid. I felt the yearning, the age-old ache, from within the standing stones, took it inside myself, and made it my own. I recalled how, in times past, I had called people to me with only my wordless desire. I reconstructed that feeling, and stepped confidently forward onto the ice until I stood in the exact center of the circle. Simultaneously, from each of the twelve menhirs, a child stepped out of the stone.

The deep underground chime rang once for each child, and then the clouds scudded away, the sun shone strongly, and the deep cold evaporated. The pond's surface cracked and melted, leaving me standing knee-deep in icy water. The stone children came toward me, each pace a struggle, becoming more flesh and less stone with every step forward. Ghostly nacre light blazed from each, hiding their features and bodies. I couldn't even tell their ages, although I was sure they were very young. By the time they reached the pond, their motions were fluid and full of life. They circled the water, linked their hands, flared together briefly to an intolerable brilliance, and then faded from view.

One by one, the lintels cracked and fell. The menhirs toppled ponderously outward, breaking apart as they crashed. Huge clods of dirt and stones flew in all directions as the bases of the standing stones ripped themselves from the ground. A shard from one of the bluestones cut my left cheek. I covered my face with my good arm and waited it out. It took several minutes, but eventually only the sound of the streams trickling into the pond remained. A bird trilled tentatively, and then others joined in.

"You're welcome!" I called out somewhat crossly, but no reply came. The stone circle was devoid of power now, and nowhere could I sense the children. Whatever they had been, whatever the purpose of their imprisonment, they were gone.

I stood in the water for a moment, then wearily climbed over the rubble and started back up the steep slope of the dingle. I am seldom given to know the nature of the powers I either wield or contend against. The only things I knew for sure were that my feet were cold, I was exhausted, and I had loosed another mystery upon the world.

I had thought the passage down to the bottom of the dingle arduous; the climb back up gave new meaning to the term. My right leg ached, and my left arm was useless. Using my good hand, I grasped at saplings and half-climbed, half-slithered toward the top, gathering mud and forest debris as I went. Benlyn caught my arm and pulled me up the last steep slope.

"How much of that did you see?" I asked after catching my breath.

"I saw nothing, lord, but I heard the stones fall."

"Nothing else? No lights in the sky, no snowstorm?"

"No, lord. What occurred down there?"

"An unexpected task," I told him. "It has exhausted me. Go ahead and send for the carriage you promised."

Benlyn's troop waited at the juncture of the forest path and the Justian road. If they had heard or sensed anything of my detour, they didn't mention it. The riders were disciplined enough to refrain from questioning me. Benlyn gave swift orders, and two riders took off at a gallop. I settled against a tree to wait. I was more fatigued than I had known, for I fell asleep almost immediately.

I woke briefly when Benlyn pressed a wet cloth to my cheek to stanch the bleeding from my cut.

"My lord," he said, "we carry spare clothing in our packs. Would you like to change from your wet things?"

"You aren't my servant, Benlyn," I said, irritated. "And I'm no lord. Stop treating me with such deference. It diminishes us both."

"As you will," he said stiffly. "Sleep until transportation arrives."

I meant to apologize for upbraiding him, but fell asleep again before the words left my mouth. I didn't wake until the vehicle showed up. It was a wain, not a carriage, but I didn't care. As long as I didn't have to walk or ride horseback, I was content. Benlyn gave me bread, dried meats, and wine. I thanked him, and he seemed to forgive my earlier harsh words. I settled more or less comfortably on the straw in the open cart and endured the bumpy ride to Landing with little more than my own thoughts for company.

King Ashe had built a large tent city just south of where the gigantic starships stood. The canvas tents were blue and white, billowing gently in the early afternoon breeze. Each tent flew Ashe's sigil atop its center pole. I was pleased to see that it was not a military encampment. Even though plenty of the King's Guard stood at strategic posts throughout the camp, most of the people I saw were tradesfolk, scholars, courtiers, or monks.

The town of Landing itself, the first settlement of the Second Colony, had insufficient lodgings for such a vast array of visitors. I couldn't even see the town from this side of the starships, although I noticed the hilltop to the north where the monastery perched. It seemed Ashe had temporarily moved his entire court up from Jappa to camp around the starships; at least a thousand men and women were roughing it with the king. The overall mood was cheerful, and the courtiers wore their finest outfits. Smoke wafted up from a huge cooking pit on the east edge of camp, and jauntily dressed youngsters bustled back and forth continuously, taking food and wine wherever demand was loudest.

The grandest tent would be Ashe's, of course, and I spotted it long before Benlyn pointed it out. Even if it hadn't been the largest tent, I would have known it for royal lodgings by the way it stood slightly apart from all others, with courtiers clustered thickly about, and pages wearing livery similar to the King's Guard boldly thrusting through the crowd, cocksure of their importance.

Benlyn drew his troop to a halt, dismounted, and helped me from the back of the wain. "My lord," he said quietly, "your clothing—"

"Never mind it," I said. "I'm not here for a formal audience."

My tone and look of determination dissuaded him from protesting further, but he gathered several of his guards with his eye and tried to lead me in a processional to the king's tent. Two men with trumpets trailing long felt streamers raised their instruments to their lips. Before they could herald my arrival, a strong wind of my desiring arose and, with pinpoint accuracy, ripped the trumpets from their hands. I kept a tiny whirlwind in my right palm, ready for further need.

I turned to Benlyn. "You've been kind to me," I said, "so I shall do you a kindness in return by leaving you behind. This may not be a happy meeting. I don't know what the king wants. Restock your supplies, tend to your horses, and wait for me. I will inform the king of your courtesy."

Without waiting for his answer, I limped toward the main entrance to the king's tent. A dozen guards—not of Benlyn's troop—swords drawn or arrows nocked, tried to block my progress. Not wishing to harm them, but also feeling irritated and impatient, I used the winds to blow them several dozen feet to either side. While they were still recovering their feet and just beginning to roar in outrage, I strode past them and entered the tent.

Ashe sat at a long worktable in the center, surrounded by advisors and military men. His russet hair was long, tied back in a ponytail. He needed no crown to mark him as king; both his mahogany skin and regal manner identified him more surely than any pomp or jewelry.

My small whirlwind scattered the papers and maps on his makeshift desk before I could quench it. Ashe glanced up, recognized me, and curtly said, "Leave us." His advisors started to protest, but he cut them off. "Leave us," he repeated, this time with the ring of command in his voice. Angry shouts from his guards outside made him add, "Tell everyone to calm down. Post a guard, but no one is to enter."

I waited until the tent emptied out, then limped forward to the edge of the table.

"Sorry about your papers and things," I said mildly. "You're looking well."

"My god, man, you're all mud and twigs."

The stridency of the shouting outside died down as those

evicted from the tent relayed Ashe's orders. I brushed feebly at the detritus from my experience in the dingle, giving up after a moment's effort told me it was useless. "Sorry. I had an adventure on the way here. I can't stay long. Maran is due any time now, and I promised her I would be there for the birth."

"Doesn't she have servants? I can send doulas, birthing women, physicians, anything you need."

"We are well prepared, but thank you. By the way, your man Benlyn took good care of me. Don't blame him for my appearance."

Ashe stood up, poured two generous cups of wine, and came around the table. He handed me one goblet and gestured to a pair of high-backed chairs.

Grateful to take the weight off my bad leg, I seated myself, neglecting the courtesy of waiting for the king to sit first. I realized my error only by his slight hesitation and lifted eyebrow.

"Ashe," I said, "you know I'm not used to courtly ways. No disrespect intended. I should also confess to knocking over several of your guards on the way in. They're likely furious, but I don't like weapons pointed at me. I think I saw a few long guns among them. I'm surprised you allow handheld firearms."

"Flintlocks, yes."

"Aren't you worried they'll explode? Even cannons are unreliable."

"You'll notice I'm not wearing a pistol, and you'll never see me fire a rifle, either, but the infantry likes them."

"A crossbow has nearly the same range, and better accuracy. Not to mention you can reload faster, and you don't have to worry about a crossbow blowing your face off. No one used firearms in the war with your brother."

"Grey," he said impatiently, "are you really planning to spend our time discussing weaponry?"

"No, sorry. I was explaining why I tumbled your guards off their feet."

"Did you hurt anyone?" he asked.

"No, I just surprised them. Unless someone landed badly and twisted an ankle, I only wounded their pride."

"If anyone on Leonais can be excused, you can," he said. "I wouldn't have my eyes, life, or throne without you. Bards should be singing your praises in every tavern. I am mindful of your sacrifices. I should grant you lands and titles, castles and servants."

I waved my good hand in dismissal, inadvertently sloshing some wine from my overfull cup. "Please don't. I wouldn't know what to do with them. And I'd prefer to keep the manner of your ascension between us. At heart, I'm a very simple man."

"Grey, you are the most complex individual alive."

"Don't forget the muria," I said. "Beside them, I really am just mud and twigs, as are we all. But leave that. Your man said your need was urgent. I take it the hierophants finally agreed to open their sacred books?"

"Yes, although I don't know why. My royal demands went unfulfilled at first. Apparently, even a king cannot command the monks. The ordinary ones didn't even know what I wanted, and referred me to the hierophants. The hierophants told me only the abbess could make such a ruling. The abbess herself was especially rude. She refused my summons, and I had to choose between having her dragged out of the monastery, or going to her for an audience. I chose the latter out of respect, but she told me my influence was merely secular, and refused to budge until a few weeks ago."

"That's all she said?" I asked. "I know the monks are proud—even arrogant at times—but you, well, you're the *king*, not some lowly petitioner."

"She implied that that made it worse. According to her, the

crown has no authority over religious matters. She also told me that unearned knowledge is more dangerous than ignorance."

I laughed heartily and took a sip of wine. "Well, *that* part is true, at least. I've never met the abbess, but I can tell you why she gave in. I sent a letter to the monastery saying I'd knock over the starships if they continued to make excuses and deny us access."

Ashe's face drained of color. "You didn't! You wouldn't! The starships are sacrosanct."

"To me more than to them, but they don't know that. They're only human, so my threat was credible enough. I'm just surprised it took them this long to capitulate. Their first few replies were cordial refusals, but when I persisted, the tone became antagonistic, even a bit bellicose. They told me rather bluntly to mind my own business. So in my last letter, I escalated things by threatening the starships."

"How in the world did you arrange correspondence? You live in an enchanted valley. Messengers wouldn't be able to find you."

"Itinerant monks pass through the forest regularly, going back and forth from their rural posts to the monastery. I waylaid a few, figured out their schedules, and arranged to meet them every now and then. They weren't happy about acting as couriers, but they know what powers I control—even though they think my lack of physical eyesight diminishes me."

"Speaking of that—can you still see through my eyes?"

I smiled tightly, intending that to be my only reply. During the civil war, Ashe's eyes had been put out by his brother. I had donated my own to restore Ashe's vision, but kept the ability to see through them. The trick required a tremendous amount of effort unless he and I were in close proximity, but he didn't need to know that. Better, perhaps, to leave him wondering. I held the smile and said nothing.

"Can you?" he persisted.

The stricken look on his face changed my mind; he deserved

an honest answer. "I don't spy on you, if that's what you mean. I won't deny having peeked from time to time to measure the rebuilding progress, but it's been months since I've felt the urge. You seem to be kinging it without the need for my help."

"I'm glad you approve," he said dryly, letting his face relax.

"Oh, my approval is irrelevant. I don't agree with everything you've done since we overthrew Gaheris, but you have your job, and I have mine. Part of my job was convincing the monks to cooperate. I'm glad they finally conceded, but their timing couldn't be worse."

His mind darted past the scarf I wore over my eye sockets. I let him penetrate that far, but not beyond. I had almost forgotten he was a mage; it startled both of us when I reflexively slapped his mental inquiry away.

After an awkward moment, I used mind-speech to say, *Let us accord each other the respect of privacy.* I lifted my goblet, and waited until he nodded and sipped, then drained my own cup completely and stood up. "I should leave. May I borrow your man Benlyn again?"

"But the hierophants, the books—" Ashe protested.

"We've waited three thousand years. A few more weeks or months won't matter. You can do all the pompous ceremonial things while I'm away, then, when I return, we can examine the documents—together, if you'd like. I saw on my way in that you've gathered scholars and tradesfolk. We'll need them to make sense of the records, since I doubt the monks will explain."

"What pompous ceremonial things do you mean?"

"Ashe, you know priests. You can't expect them to say, 'Here's our secret cache of forbidden knowledge, please rummage freely.' They'll insist on prayers, holy oils, singing, chanting, mystical hand motions, and so forth. That's a king's duty to endure. I don't have the patience for it. But back to your man—may I borrow him?"

"Benlyn is Duke of Amrhyn."

"He told me he was from Sallas."

"He was, originally. His principal task now is cleaning up the mess you left behind in Amrhyn when you woke the Sleeper."

I hesitated. "In a very real sense, I *am* the Sleeper. I think it will either die with me, or pass into permanent dormancy. For now, I can assure you that the Sleeper is under control. And I was fairly sure I'd killed all the Amrhyn sorcerers—and their horrid religion along with them."

"Most of the ones in Amrhyn, yes. We're still searching for a handful that Gaheris brought into Jappa, just as some of his most loyal soldiers hide in cotholds or farms. Most of my brother's troops were unwilling, ensorcelled into his service. They woke from his influence when he died and are loyal to me now—or at least loyal to Leonais, which my advisors tell me is not precisely the same thing."

"It wouldn't be," I agreed. "What of the rest?"

"Sadly, a few served willingly. Those most twisted go to trial and then the gallows. A small portion remains in prison or paying restitution. I expect to eradicate the last traces of my brother's madness by winter. The rebuilding of Jappa should be finished by then, too, and I'll have a citadel to return to."

"Then what's the problem?" I asked.

"It's complicated. The Amrhyn sorcerers were also the local government. You left the people without proper leadership. Amrhyn has always been a quasi-independent region, with only a token allegiance to the throne, but we need their horses and grain. Production and delivery require a degree of governance, and Cevak is being unreasonable."

"Who is Cevak?"

"The highest-ranking sorcerer left in Amrhyn. He's causing trouble. Trade and commerce have become unreliable. You should visit there after Duke Benlyn restores order. The central grasslands stretch from horizon to horizon. It is a beautiful place, in a lonely way." His eyes lost focus for a moment; he shook his head, blinked, and continued: "The downs and moors, the chalk cliffs, the uncountable bays and beaches—they defy description. I haven't been there since I was a child, but I still remember. . . ." He trailed off, eyes unfocused again.

I didn't want a travelogue; I wanted information. I coughed to get his attention. "So you created a dukedom and gave the fief to Benlyn?"

"Just so," said Ashe, recovering from his reverie. "I needed a dependable man."

"Why the devil would you send a duke—one with important work on the other side of the continent—to fetch me?"

"Because your wife's blasted valley is invisible. Duke Benlyn is a remote relation, with a touch of Captain's Blood in him. I hoped it would help him penetrate the enchantments. It took him weeks, but he obviously succeeded."

"Only because I let him. I had planned to spend the morning gathering herbs that don't grow well inside the valley. Instead, I've spent most of the day vying with stone children and being carted around like a sack of flour in the back of a wain. Your pardon, Ashe, but I must get home immediately."

"Then Duke Benlyn is yours to command, at least for the day. But tarry a moment more. I would like to hear about these stone children."

"It would take too long," I said. "And I don't understand it myself."

He waved his hand. "That can wait for your next visit, then. Before you go, I need to ask you about Avermorn. I've tried sending ships to the northern continent, but each has been beaten back by the winds, no matter what route they try."

"That effort was probably unwise. The muria don't want humans on Avermorn. Why invite trouble?"

"Then they were not your winds that prevented my fleets?" he persisted.

"Mine? No, although I pity your sailors. Why would you want to go there?"

"Because of something the hierophants said. They told me that Vastil forbade them from sharing the records. I wanted to ask the other elves why."

I couldn't conceal my start of surprise. *Vastil!* The name dredged up unwelcome memories of the dungeon. Why would one of the muria be involved with the monks? I pondered it for a moment. Denying access to technology fit with everything I knew of Vastil's motives, but I hadn't known he had revealed himself to the hierophants. Several things clicked into place. This explained the self-importance and obnoxious display of superiority of the one hierophant I had met long ago. It also explained the old "forgotten or forbidden" saying. All technology and engineering that hadn't been forgotten on Leonais had been forbidden by Vastil in his campaign to keep humanity subservient.

"Did you tell the monks about your ships?" I asked.

"I saw no reason to refrain, since they already knew of Vastil."

"Then that explains the timing. Now they know they've been cut off." At Ashe's quizzical look, I added, "The muria do not work independently of each other. Vastil was the instrument of oppression for both humans and nina, but they strive amongst themselves. We will probably never understand the intricate power games they play. Leave the muria alone, Ashe, and pray they leave us alone."

"I'm not a religious man. I don't expect prayer to help."

"Then hope instead. You don't want to come under muria scrutiny."

"But you killed Vastil," Ashe said. "I thought perhaps that was why the monks had finally agreed to open their records."

"I killed *one* of him. Remember that 'muria' means 'many-bodied.' There are only five muria persons: Tamil, Bastion, Vastil, Ulat, and Qol. Each person exists as a single consciousness spanning thousands, perhaps millions, of bodies. Yes, I killed one of Vastil's avatars, but that's like getting a haircut for you or me. If the hierophants dealt with Vastil behind our backs, they almost certainly knew that much—and it wasn't until your missions failed that they realized Vastil would not return. It also means that Ulat has been keeping her promise, which is good news. However, Ashe, I beg you—my leg is aching, and it's a long journey back to Maran. May I leave now?"

"Of course," he said, standing up. "I'll order a proper carriage, and an entire entourage to escort you. You may not want to be treated like a prince—"

"Gods, no! I went nameless for most of my life, and would prefer to maintain my anonymity."

"Legends abound already. After what you did in Jappa, you can never really be anonymous. Too many people saw you on the citadel steps."

"I'd hoped that after nine months, people would forget," I said.

"Forget someone who held a flaming sword while riding a unicorn across Justian Bridge? Forget the man who shook half the planet with earthquakes? Forget the man who defeated my mad brother, toppled the citadel, and then refused the crown? I don't think so. The stories have only grown, not diminished. And your looks are against you, too. You are . . . memorable, Grey." His tone was gently chiding, even compassionate, but his eyes held an odd intensity.

"The sword didn't flame," I protested weakly. "I only swung it once, and nearly decapitated myself."

"Does that really matter? Legends always exaggerate. You are a prince of the realm, whether you hide in Maran's valley or not. I insist on this. In fact, I want you to bear a token of the royal house, so that at need you may command any of my people. It's indecent for you to travel like a pauper, at the mercy of any bandit or roadside misfortune." He pulled a heavy gold ring from his forefinger and offered it to me.

I regarded the signet ring with distaste for a long moment, then acquiesced. I had no intention of ever using it, but it would be ungracious to refuse. He clearly wanted to honor me. "Thanks," I said, taking the ring. I didn't think it would fit any of my fingers, so I put it on my thumb. "It may prove useful someday."

"I sincerely hope you never need it, but better to be prepared, eh?"

"I suppose," I said. "Listen, Ashe, I understand why you'd move court during the rebuilding in Jappa, but why tents? Wouldn't temporary shelters be more comfortable?"

"This area has recently suffered from ground tremors. My engineers thought tents would be safer, and the whole thing is only meant to last until winter anyway."

"Earthquakes?" I asked darkly. "Do you mean like—"

"No, nothing like the big ones; just a bit of shaking. Relax. Convey my best wishes to Lady Maran, and hurry back."

"I shall. I'm as eager to see those records as you are."

Ashe lifted his voice in a stentorian bellow. "Ben! Stop eavesdropping and come inside."

A moment later, Benlyn pushed aside the tent flaps and entered. He bowed to Ashe, then, after a moment's study, repeated the gesture toward me.

"Yes," said Ashe meaningfully, his eyes flicking rapidly back and forth between Benlyn and me. "Let it be known, but quietly. Lord Grey doesn't like attention."

I had no idea what he was talking about, but Benlyn nodded curtly. "It shall be made known, sire," he replied.

"Ben, I want you to escort Lord Grey home."

"My troop is already saddled and waiting, sire. We have a carriage ready."

"No," I interposed quickly. "Just you."

Ashe said, "A command from him is a command from me. But show him your arm first."

Benlyn cocked his head, then shrugged and removed his outer cloak. He pushed up the sleeve of his right arm. The marking I saw there made my blood run cold. "The Archon's sigil," I whispered. "You served Gaheris."

"Unwillingly," he said, without any hint of discomfort or embarrassment. "I was ensorcelled, as were most of his soldiers." He casually covered up the brand and replaced his outer cloak.

I turned to Ashe. "Why show me this?"

"I wanted you to understand how much has changed in the past nine months. The duke served my brother under enchantment. You liberated far more than you knew when you relieved my brother of his mortal burdens."

"Killed him, you mean. Why euphemize? And that was Maran's doing, not mine. Gaheris died under a pile of burning golems."

"Nevertheless. I was there in the dungeon, part of your gestalt, however briefly. I know your mind. Now I want you to know mine. Duke Benlyn is my most trusted ally. I place your life in his hands with full confidence."

Ashe strode back to the table and began reorganizing the papers and maps I'd scattered at my entrance. I started to say something, but Benlyn gently nudged my elbow. "That's our cue, lord," he whispered. "We've been dismissed."

I shrugged and left the tent without another word.

Outside, we found Benlyn's troop guarding the tent flap. Others —from fancy courtiers to armed soldiers and nervous pages— waited a decent distance farther. Benlyn took several troops and advisors aside and held a short murmured discussion with them. They all looked at me oddly afterward, but said nothing. I waited as patiently as I could until Benlyn was back with me.

I asked, "If you ride double behind me, can we make it back by dark?" Then I remembered his station, and added, "My Lord Duke—or is it Your Grace? I know nothing of styles or titles."

He smiled slightly, dismissing the matter of titles. "It would be my pleasure to take you, lord, and you evidently have the king's permission to call me whatever you want. But to return on your schedule, we will have to canter or alternate walking and galloping."

"Can you keep me in the saddle without jouncing me to death, or worse, tossing me off entirely?"

"No, you don't know how to relax and move with the mount. There's a trick to it, but not something you can learn without practice."

"So, what, then?"

"The same way we started today. You sit the horse, and I'll walk in front."

"How long will that take?"

Benlyn looked at the sky, stroking his beard, apparently judging how much daylight remained. Then he lifted his shoulders. "There are shorter paths than the roads. I can get you back perhaps two hours after sunset. There are no clouds, so starlight should be enough for secure footing, as long as we don't rush."

I sighed. "The sooner we start, the sooner we'll arrive."

"Aye, lord. Let me help you up." He held his horse's bit with his left hand, and boosted me up with his right. "Easy, Snuffles," he said as the horse pranced sideways.

I looked down at Benlyn. "You named a warhorse Snuffles?"

"It's from the sound he makes when he smells oats. Does it matter, lord?"

"I guess not. In fact, it makes me like him more. It's just a funny name for a stallion."

"He's a gelding, lord, but that doesn't make him any less fierce in a fight. I wouldn't dare put you on a stallion; the king would have my head." Benlyn clucked his tongue at the horse, turned its head, and we started off.

Snuffles walked placidly enough, but as the hours passed, my tailbone and thighs began to ache. By the time we reached the boulder where he had found me that morning, even my back and shoulders suffered from the strain. We didn't speak along the way, save for times when Benlyn warned me to hold the saddle horn during steep inclines. He had to help me down and steady me until my legs bore my weight again.

"Thank you, Your Grace," I said, extending my good hand, trying to express my gratitude by being courtly. After all, he had brought me safely home and treated me kindly, which seemed well beyond a duke's normal duties.

He took my hand, but instead of shaking it, he bent over to kiss the ring on my thumb. "You had only to ask, Prince Grey," he said.

I pulled my hand away in annoyance. "I'm not even a lord, let alone a prince. Can't you bring yourself to call me Grey? Pretend we're friends."

His eyes glittered in the gloom. I thought I detected some warmth in his face, but it was so admixed with pity and duty that I couldn't decipher his precise emotion. "Perhaps we can be friends, lord, but I must call you a prince as long as that ring belongs to you."

"Why? It was nice of Ashe, but I didn't really want it."

"It's not the ring, but what it represents."

"And what's that? Benlyn—Ben—Your Grace—do me the courtesy of speaking plainly."

"Do you really not understand?" He paused, peering closely at me, seeming to assess my mood. Then he straightened his shoulders. "You aren't dissembling. You honestly don't know. To put it simply, lord, until the king marries and produces an heir, you are he."

I stood with my mouth open for several long breaths. "Heir to the throne? You're mad." I twisted the signet from my thumb and thrust it at him. "Take it back to Ashe, or wear it yourself, or throw it in a river. I don't want to be king."

"Perhaps, lord," said Benlyn, folding my hand gently over the ring, "that is why he chose you. At any rate, I shall not gainsay him. If you are uneasy with your sudden elevation in rank, take comfort in its brevity. The king will marry soon, and we all pray for an heir quickly thereafter."

"So my burden is likely short-lived?"

"Most would consider it an honor, lord."

"Not I."

"Strangely, I believe you. Have I your leave to go, lord? I must get back to court yet tonight, and then gather my troops and set out immediately for Amrhyn."

I shoved the ring into a pocket irritably. "By all means. I've kept you from your duties too long as it is. Travel safely."

Benlyn saluted, and swiftly mounted Snuffles. He took a moment to adjust the reins, then with a final glance over his shoulder, trotted off. In a few moments, I heard the horse pick up speed. It was quiet enough that I could follow his progress by ear. He trotted through the woods until he gained the road, and then came the unmistakable sounds of a gallop, dwindling away until even that faded, leaving me alone in the forest.

By starlight, I gathered the lemon balm and rosemary I'd wanted, and started down into the mists. As valleys go, the slope was gentle enough—certainly easier going down than up—but between the faint stars and the heavy mists, the path was nearly invisible. I slipped once, jarring my knee, but by then I was out of the mists and could see the warm yellow lights in the windows of the manor house.

Hasq greeted me at the door, tsk-tsked at the state of my clothing, but said only, "The lady's labor has begun, sir. Your son will arrive tonight."

I thrust the bundle of herbs at him. "I'll go straightaway."

A minute later, I was sitting beside my wife at the birthing bed, holding her hand. Her contractions were still far apart, and she seemed at ease. "What took you so long?" she asked. "I've missed you."

I rubbed absently at the crust that had formed over the cut on my cheek. I would have to get Hasq to treat it before infection set in. However, as with my ruined clothing, now was not the time to worry about superficial problems.

"The king wanted words, and I destroyed a dolmen," I said.

"Why?"

"He's at Landing, waiting for the hierophants—"

"No, the dolmen."

"Oh, that. I'm not entirely sure. It seemed the right thing to do."

Hasq interrupted us. The normally unflappable majordomo had a very surprised expression on his face. "I beg your pardon, but an entire herd of nina has surrounded the house. They just stand there, staring."

"Unicorns? Did you call them?" Maran asked me.

"They no longer listen to me—you know that."

"Go talk to them anyway. I'm not going anywhere."

I limped to the doorway and peered out. Clouds had blown in to obscure the stars, and even my percipience had trouble making out details when most objects were utterly black. Yet I had no trouble finding the unicorns; their spiraled horns shone brightly in the gloom. A double ring of them regarded me gravely. With a pang for my own lost Nina, I greeted them. As always, at least since Ulat had pronounced their doom, the faerie creatures did not change form or communicate. These were the first I'd seen since the fateful night we overthrew Gaheris, the night I had lost my beloved Nina forever. I had no idea why five score unicorns would show up at our doorstep—let alone how they had passed Maran's wards to gain entrance to the valley.

They stood patiently, with only an occasional swish of tail or quiver of flank muscle to mark them as living beasts instead of statues.

"I can't stay with you," I said softly. "Maran needs me. But you are welcome here, tonight or any night."

As expected, they did not respond. I could have stayed watching them all night, just to witness their unearthly beauty, but Maran called, and I hurried back to her bedside just as a new contraction was occurring. The birthing women—all golems created explicitly for this purpose—knew what to do, but still the process was an ordeal for Maran. She had wide, generous hips, and the baby's position was correct, but the pain was considerable, especially near the end. I comforted Maran as best I could, but was at a loss. Despite all the powers at my command, great or small, this travail belonged to Maran alone; in the end, I think the only real services I provided were holding her hand, mopping her brow, and assuring her of my love. Her sandy brown hair was dark with sweat, and her normally smooth complexion was blotchy from exertion. At regular intervals, I had to remind her to breathe deeply.

During the times between contractions, I kept Maran distracted by telling her about the stone children, my meeting with the king, and my embarrassingly poor horsemanship. I didn't mention the ring. She chuckled when I mentioned the straw bed of the wain, but otherwise didn't offer many responses. I suspected she listened to my tone of voice more than to my words.

At length, the birthing women said it was time for the final push. Maran clenched her teeth, fixed her eyes on my face, and bore down with all her strength. Aiden slid into the world and gave his first cry. I counted our son's fingers and toes while the women cleaned him up, cut the cord, wrapped him in a soft blanket, and gave him to Maran to hold.

The moment Aiden touched Maran's breast, a paean of shrill neighs filled the air, echoing off the surrounding hills. The sound continued uninterrupted, only growing louder as the minutes passed. I did not want to leave Maran's side, but she asked me to go to the open window to see what was happening.

Outside, every unicorn was rearing, pawing the air, whinnying and neighing, paying homage to Aiden's birth. A sense of fierce exultation filled the valley, and tears sprang unbidden to my eyes.

"Thank you," I whispered.

They reared one last time in unison, gave a tremendous neigh, then wheeled and thundered away into the predawn darkness. I didn't understand how they had known when to come, why they had held silent vigil all night, or what message they meant to convey by such an unprecedented honor.

As with most things in my life so far, I had no idea what it all meant.

Chapter Two

In addition to the birthing women, Maran had constructed a small coterie of nursemaids and helpers, so my only tasks were to keep Maran company, admire our newborn with her, and go upland from time to time to fetch herbs.

"Can't you make a golem to gather plants?" I asked peevishly after a week of daily climbs. "That damned hill is hard on my leg."

Maran shifted Aiden to her other arm and smiled gently. "I could, but I know you too well. You need time alone to think, and it frets you to have your percipience limited to the valley. Plus, every time you go away, it reminds you why you need to come back."

She reached out with her free hand to trace the cut on my cheek. "You should have one of the servants put a salve on that wound. It keeps bleeding and forming a crust."

"They've slathered me with half a dozen potions. It only slows the bleeding to a trickle, which is why the scab keeps coming back."

"It feels rough to the touch. Maybe it's best to leave the scab and let it heal naturally."

"It's not inflamed," I said. "Why waste time on it? May I hold the baby?"

"He needs to nurse just now. Go upland and find some wild mint. I fancy some tea."

"We have plenty of mint down here."

"Just go, dear, but don't be long. Maybe that dashing young man will be waiting, and you can send a message to the king."

"You mean Benlyn? He's hardly dashing or young, and Ashe sent him to Amrhyn. Anyway, he's a duke, not a courier. He has better things to do than wait around in the forest in case I go upland."

"Then just the mint leaves will do," she said placidly. "I know you're eager to go back to Landing to spar with the hierophants, but it's too soon."

"Speaking of which, shouldn't you be up and walking by now? We could stroll the gardens together, get Aiden some sunshine."

She regarded me gravely. "The birth was harder than you know. I move around the house well enough, but the women say I should rest for another few days."

"They're just golems; what do they really know?"

"Everything necessary. And call them homunculi, not golems. Hasq, and probably the others, find 'golem' demeaning."

"Your majordomo can be a prig. He's always so very courteous and deferential, but he still doesn't accept that I belong here."

"Well, he's *my* prig. You can hardly blame him for feeling protective."

I sighed and gathered myself to my feet. "Mint, is it?"

"Please."

"Very well."

I leaned over to kiss her and touch the incredible softness of Aiden's scalp and cheeks. The few hairs he had were dark and wispy, but I knew that eventually they would turn to a full head of golden-white curls. "He doesn't cry much," I said as I straightened up. "Is that normal?"

"He's a happy baby. That's normal enough, considering his parents."

I had no reply to that, so I went to find a change of clothes. Despite my bad leg and withered arm—or perhaps because of them—I preferred to dress myself. Yet this didn't keep Hasq, ever observant, from sending a maid into my quarters to lay out clothing, braid my hair, and straighten my collar.

"What's your name?" I asked the maid. I didn't recall having seen her before. Maran had made so many golems in preparation for the birth and its aftermath that I could hardly turn around without stumbling over a new one.

"Lady Maran calls me 'maid,' sir. I have no other designation."

"That seems harsh. Would you like a name?"

"If it pleases you, sir. I have no need myself. I was only constructed to last a brief time; the regular household staff will take over my duties when I am gone."

"Well, I think it's wrong. I shall call you 'Mint,' after today's errand. Will that do?"

She curtsied, but seemed indifferent. "I shall inform Hasq of your decision," she said. "Would you like your scarf?"

"Yes, please." I took it from her and wound it firmly around my head. "You're very kind, Mint. Thank you for your help."

She curtsied again, this time a faint blush of rose coloring her cheeks. I considered asking her to join me on my outing, but then realized that Maran had been right: I treasured my time alone. It gave me the opportunity to reflect on events, time to analyze my actions and their motivations. Without sufficient introspection, I felt frustrated by life, as though I were just an object to which things happened, rather than a living creature able to make reasoned decisions.

I slipped Ashe's signet ring into a pocket, wishing I had

thought to ask Hasq to find me a chain for it. It was too large and heavy for me to wear comfortably. Although I stood taller than most Sunderlings, I was thin to the point of gauntness. What fit snugly on the king's forefinger simply fell off any of my own. I had tried wearing it on my thumb, but it felt awkward. I didn't even think about taking it to a goldsmith for resizing, because it was clearly an heirloom, intricately wrought with symbols from the royal house of Leonais, and inset with a beautifully beveled ruby. It was a much more princely gift than I had first realized; I suspected it would command a price equal to half the kingdom. And as to its significance in the outside world . . . I preferred not to dwell on that.

I set off to the east, knowing that the damnably obsequious majordomo would have me followed—at a discreet distance—for my own protection, even though I'd insisted a dozen times it wasn't necessary. The direction I chose was arbitrary, because there was no true path upland. Compass points didn't matter at all; intention was everything.

Maran's valley was all sizes and none. The pastures and gardens surrounding the manor house always stayed pretty much the same, maintained by Maran's presence. She imbued the valley with its characteristics simply by living there. No preset boundaries limited its scope. Should I choose, I could walk forever amongst the gentle hills and fields without ever reaching the outside world. It required a certain turn of thought to either enter or leave the valley, and only Maran could implant the necessary mental state. To the best of my knowledge, the valley was proof against sorcery and percipience, as well as to normal human sight. Amrhyn sorcerers had kidnapped Maran once, but she had been upland then, above the mists, at the very borders of her realm. I don't think they could have found her otherwise. I suspected it had been incaution on her part—or great luck on the Amrhyns' part—that had led to her capture.

My own access was simpler. Maran had led me the first time, implanting the necessary knowledge. I doubted I could teach another, even if I wanted to. The magic was Maran's, not mine, and it was solely by her grace that I could find my way.

The path I chose, perhaps creating it as I went, led along a stream, gently winding up from the valley floor into the mists. It was a pleasant enough walk at first, but the last hill—no matter what route I took—was always steep. I was out of breath and cursing my game leg by the time I reached the crest, stepped from the mists, and regained the outside world.

⸻

I didn't recognize this part of the woods. It was entirely possible that I had never emerged at this point before. The trees were tall and stately, widely spaced, but met overhead in a lush canopy that only allowed dappled green-gold light to reach the forest floor. The earth beneath my boots, carpeted with soft humus from age-long cycles of falling leaves, gave me the irrational desire to run barefoot. I saw no trails that might indicate deer or other wildlife. Very few plants grew beneath the arching canopy; even deadfall was rare. I wandered through the trees, seeking a glade or meadow that might support the wild mint Maran had requested. Except for my footfalls, the forest was utterly silent.

After several minutes of searching, I concluded the fault was mine. One needs to concentrate on the destination during ascent, and I hadn't been paying attention at all. I had therefore exited somewhere random, far from my usual spot on Colonial Plain.

In one sense, this part of the world was utterly unlike anything I had experienced before. At the same time, it also seemed very familiar. Lost in the beauty and majesty of the forest, it took me several minutes to recognize the flavor of my feelings. Qol had led me through such a forest nearly a year ago. It had only been a vision, but it had been a vision of Avermorn. I touched the mighty boles of the trees, letting my fingers trail over the bark, feeling the slow movement of sap within. If this was another vision, it lacked the dreamlike quality of the first. I felt solid and mortal; at the same time, I felt I was intruding where I had no right to be.

I doubted that even Maran's boundless valley extended across the seas to the northern continent, but the feeling of not belonging grew stronger with each breath. I had just decided to turn around and retrace my steps when I heard gentle laughter ahead of me, accompanied by the soft splashing of water.

I moved forward, emerging at length into a small clearing covered in short, vibrantly green grass. Two children stood barefoot, hand in hand, facing a marble fountain, watching the play of light on the water. They seemed oblivious to my presence. They had long, snowy white hair, unbraided, hanging straight as curtains to the middle of their backs. I judged them to be no more than eight or nine years old, though it was hard to tell from behind.

I cleared my throat, and asked, "Qol?" My voice sounded rough, mortal, out of place.

The children turned, and I saw they wore only sheer gauzy singlets, so thin I could see their limbs through the cloth. Each sported blue and yellow flowers behind their ears. Their features and sizes were so alike they might have been identical twins, although one was male and the other female. I felt none of the instinctive awe that muria normally provoke in mortals. They had the same indefinable beauty, with faces I knew I would not be able to recall later, but none of the overpowering eldritch quality that inspires humans to kneel. Their blue eyes glittered like sapphires, accentuated by the alabaster white of their skin. Even their eyebrows and lashes lacked color.

"Not Qol," said the girl. Her voice held none of the harmonic overtones or complexity I had come to expect from their kind.

They were clearly muria, but unlike any I had met. Save for their unearthly beauty and lack of pigmentation, they could have been human children.

"If you are not Qol, then—who?" I asked. "Which of the five?"

"Ketlan," said the boy, "none and all. We have not yet chosen our affiliation. We veil ourselves so that you are not beguiled."

The name brought back memories from partial explanations given by both Qol and my lost Nina. The muria cherished their children beyond all else, and the name meant "beloved." Ketlan was what the muria called them before they grew up and joined one of the five muria group minds. These children were not avatars of Tamil, Bastion, Vastil, Ulat, or Qol, but individuals.

"We lean toward Ulat," said the girl, "but have many years to decide. Other outcomes tempt us strongly."

"How did I get here?"

"You did not," said the boy. "We came to you in our dreams."

"But surely this is Avermorn, not Leonais."

"Avermorn is more than a place," continued the boy, "it is a state of mind. Observe the fountain."

"How old are you? You look like children, but speak like adults."

"Age is a process," said the boy, "but Ketlan do not suffer the pangs of human childhood. While yet in the womb, our minds have access to the accumulated wisdom of the five. Physically, we grow more slowly than humans, but puberty already threatens. With it looms the necessity of choice. We therefore opt to delay. Intellectually, we are already older than you can conceive."

Very little of his speech was comprehensible. I gathered they were older than their appearance suggested, and they had a measure of control over their physical development, but neither thing affected their mentation. They were already adults in every way that counted. I didn't think further questioning would bring better answers, so I changed tack.

"Don't you have individual names? If I call you both 'Ketlan,' how do you know to whom I speak?"

"We will know," said the girl. "Your mind is open to us. We have private names, but they are not for your use."

"Observe the fountain," said the boy again.

I drew nearer, and they stepped aside to grant me access. It was unlike the fountain Qol had shown me, but just as beautifully made. The marble, lightly veined and immaculately worked so that I saw no joints, contained a small pool of pure water. Five jets sprayed the water skyward, from where it fell back with hardly a sound into the pool. I felt a sudden strong desire to drink, but I dared not—not without permission.

"Do you see it?" asked the girl.

"I see beauty beyond bearing."

"Look deeper," said the boy.

I knelt, and reached forth my good hand, but stopped. They had told me to look, not touch. I stared into the water, studied the five spouts, and examined the marble. "I see nothing but purity," I said at last.

"He is blind," said the girl. She sounded disappointed.

"Yet he has been marked," replied the boy. "There is yet hope."

I stood up and looked at them. They were holding hands again, their eyes sorrowful. "Tell me what I should see," I begged.

They ignored me, and spoke only to each other. "Aiden will see it," said the girl. "This man's mark may only be a herald."

"Qol could tell us," said the boy. "This man is Qol's child."

"I do not wish to involve the five," said the girl. "Individuality yet beckons."

"As does nihilism," countered the boy.

"We must bide," insisted the girl, "and remain Ketlan."

In unison, they concluded, "We are too young," and turned

back to me as if they had explained something or answered my question.

"What are you talking about?" I asked. "How am I marked? How do you know my son's name?"

"Unbind your scarf and kneel," the boy instructed. As I complied, the girl filled her hands with water from the fountain and spread it over my empty eye sockets. The touch of the water was shockingly cold; the kind of cold that feels like burning. Together, the children murmured something in another language.

"Your blindness is condign," said the boy, "but it will hinder a future need. Do not mistake our action today for kindness."

My percipience—the second sight that allowed me to see in the dark, peer around corners, and navigate the world without assistance—didn't lessen, but my physical sight changed. I felt my eyeballs growing, filling the empty sockets, reattaching to muscles. Soon, acuity returned. As it did, the vision of the Ketlan, the fountain, and Avermorn itself gradually faded.

The majestic forest, with its gracious avenues and arching canopy, became ordinary woods. Squirrels scampered overhead, and a rabbit hopped out of the underbrush. I regained my feet beside a large boulder on Colonial Plain, the useless scarf dangling from my right hand, the evanescent sensation of fountain water on my face already gone.

What kind of man would I be if I complained about getting my eyesight back? Most men would weep with joy. However, I knew muria gifts always came with a price, and this one might be higher than I could afford to pay.

Humbly, I turned to the task that had brought me upland today. Within a few minutes, I found some wild mint, stripped the leaves, and folded them inside my scarf. The scarf itself went into my back pocket, and I turned to the boulder, thinking it was high time I got back to Maran. Perhaps she could help me make sense of what had happened.

I entered the mists and started the long walk into the valley. After the first steep hill, I concentrated on the manor house, seeking the shortest path. In moments, I found a rivulet and followed it until it joined the main river that provided water to the rich pastures. From there, it was only a mile, perhaps less, of easy walking. Two golems, no doubt set to watch for my return, hurried ahead of me.

Hasq greeted me at the front door. "Welcome back, sir," he said, bowing slightly. "You seem to have lost your scarf and gained a pair of eyes."

"Things happen," I replied. I didn't intend to be cryptic; I just didn't care to relate my story. I pulled the scarf from my pocket and handed it to him. "There are fresh mint leaves in here. Lady Maran wants tea."

"I shall have boiling water prepared immediately. Should I have the scarf cleaned and returned to you?"

"I don't think I'll wear the scarf again. What color are my eyes?"

"Blue, sir. May I ask—?"

"No," I said shortly. It was irrational, but I didn't feel like explaining anything to a golem right then. Then a sudden thought struck me. "Can you or the other servants leave the valley?"

"Only if the lady of the house allows it, sir. She has not seen fit to give that ability to any of us."

"Where is she?"

"In the back parlor, sir."

"Thank you, Hasq. That will be all."

The majordomo nodded his head and turned toward the kitchens, holding my folded scarf with two fingers. I went the other direction, and found Maran resting on an overstuffed couch in the back parlor. She didn't look up at my arrival; her eyes were closed. The gentle rise and fall of her chest told me she was likely asleep. I dragged up a chair to sit beside her, but even that small noise was enough to disturb her rest. She stirred, blinked, and sat up.

It took her a moment to focus, but then her face tightened, and her green eyes locked onto my blue ones.

"How—?"

"I am plagued by children of late," I said. "First by a group of twelve locked in stone, more recently a pair of Ketlan."

"Muria children? Here in Leonais?"

"They reached me somehow. The boy said Avermorn was a state of mind as much as a physical place. They showed me a fountain, and because I couldn't see what they wanted, they did this." I gestured toward my face. "I can see normally now."

"Why?"

I shrugged, letting my frustration show. "They only said, 'Do not mistake our action for kindness,' which is typically uninformative. They also mentioned a 'future need,' but failed to explain *that* either. My second sight seems unaffected, so I have to conclude normal eyesight is a god-gift of some sort, with the cost yet to be revealed."

"Tell me everything," she insisted.

I started the story at the beginning, but was interrupted almost immediately by the arrival of a maid carrying a tray with two steaming cups of tea. "The baby is still sleeping soundly, ma'am. The nursemaids said you would ask. Here is the tea you requested."

"Thank you, Mint," I said, recognizing the maid. She blushed a tiny bit and managed to curtsey without spilling anything.

"My pleasure, sir," she said. "Hasq has approved your choice of name."

I gave one cup to Maran, and took the other for myself. The maid curtsied again, and left us alone. Maran leaned back on the couch, cradling her teacup and eyeing me strangely.

"Did I hear that right?" asked Maran. "Did you name one of the homunculi?"

"It seems inappropriate, somehow, that only Hasq has a name. You implied earlier that they had feelings. Speaking of golems—"

"Homunculi."

"Yes, well, your servants. Can you make a man to act as a courier? I mean with the ability to leave and reenter the valley, ride horses, and find his way around upland? It might be useful to have some way to communicate with Ashe that doesn't require my climbing that damned hill."

She considered it. "I think so, but does it have to be a man?"

"It doesn't matter to me, but upland women with rank or authority almost always travel with entourages, whereas a male courier, journeying alone with suitable attire, wouldn't draw attention."

"Then I'll need a butterfly. Yellow would be best."

A wind of my desiring arose and quested through the gardens. In moments, an orange and black butterfly, easily the size of my palm, fluttered through the open window and rested on her arm. "Will that do, or should I keep looking for a yellow one?"

"It's fine," she said, gently lofting the butterfly. It flew up to the mantel and perched there, wings folded vertically, awaiting Maran's will. "It will take me some time. I need to gather the materials first. A homunculus such as you require is more complex than a house servant."

"Could he also teach me to ride a horse without killing myself?"

"*I* can teach you that."

I gestured at her semi-reclined posture. "I know you're an expert horse person, but you said you needed more rest."

"Equestrian, dear, not 'horse person.' Do you need to learn right *now*? What's the hurry?"

"The courier can take messages, but he can't examine the

monks' books, or substitute for my interactions with Ashe. If I'm to travel back and forth to Landing, I'd prefer not to walk."

She seemed taken aback. "But there's a monument in the valley, and another near Landing. You needn't walk very far."

"Monument?" I echoed.

"Henge," she clarified. "A ring of standing stones. The megalithic uprights are menhirs, and the capstones are lintels."

"Oh, you mean dolmens."

"*You* always say 'dolmen' or 'faerie mound,' but what we have on Leonais are monuments, most in henge shape. Some of them are dolmens, others aren't."

"What's the difference?"

"Prehistoric Terran dolmens were mostly tombs, and very few were full rings. All of ours are henges or simple standing stones. The proper term is monument. But honestly, everyone will know what you mean no matter which word you use. I'm not always consistent myself."

"Okay, I'll keep that in mind. I knew there was one in the valley, but how does that help? Your enchantments prevent all forms of unsanctioned travel. If the dolmens are exempt, that's a gaping security hole."

"The key word is 'unsanctioned.' With my permission, you will be able to use the monument. You could get out now, but not back in. I'll need some of your blood to grant you inbound access. Or wait—perhaps a hair with do. Bend forward."

Mystified, I obeyed, and she plucked out a single long strand. She inspected it critically, looking closely at the root. She nodded to herself, tucking the hair carefully into a pocket of her gown.

"That will do," she said. "Now, start your story again. I want to understand what happened to you."

"Wait," I said. "I don't understand. How can you control a dolmen?"

"Where do you think the valley's power comes from? A very

long time ago, I chose this location, unlinked the monument from the network, and have been siphoning its energy ever since. I will now reconnect it, but only for you. That's why I needed a live hair root. Your genetic material will form the key."

"And you learned to do this how?"

"Long study and perseverance. I grew curious about the dolmens when I was young; they are the greatest source of power in Leonais. By trial and error, I explored my abilities into existence."

I leaned back, eying her with interest. No matter how accustomed I was to Maran's magics, she could still surprise me. "So," I said after a long pause, "could you open doorways between places, as I do? Step from one location to another without crossing the distance between?"

"As far as I know, only sorcerers can do that."

"I'm not a sorcerer."

"Grey," she said patiently, "after Aiden was conceived, you broke my enchantments. You may not have studied sorcery, but you can't deny what you are."

I found her assessment disquieting. It implied I was somehow akin to the Amrhyn sorcerers, and while my conscious mind vigorously denied the relationship, my subconscious said I was an idiot for needing someone else to point it out. "Okay," I said after a moment. "I can quibble with the word, but not the conclusion."

"So tell me your story again. Start from the beginning."

I told her of the majestic forest, with its high canopy and its uncanny quietude. "It *felt* like the Avermorn Qol showed me," I said, "and it felt like I was really there. But the boy implied it was just another vision."

"What, exactly, did he say?"

I recited the strange conversation, only half of which had been directed at me, and I told her of the fountain with five spouts. I tried to describe the unearthly beauty of the Ketlan, and their queer duality of childlike adulthood, but foundered quickly. As always with the muria, mortals can only truly see them while they stand before us; the memory fades as soon as we look away, leaving only a sense of mystery and loss behind. I tried to describe *why* they were beautiful, but all I could remember clearly was how the piercing blue of their eyes contrasted with the pale whiteness of their skin and hair.

"Grey," she said, seeming to choose her words carefully. "How many muria have you actually met?"

"Three. Qol, Vastil, and Ulat."

"I saw Vastil in the dungeon and Ulat outside the citadel. Your own skin is white as bone, but the muria I saw with you, although fair compared to most humans, had the same honey-gold hue as my own skin. You're describing something different—muria who look more like you than like me."

"It may have been sheer chance that the Ketlan I met were so pale," I said. "They were very much like one another, perhaps brother and sister—or even twins."

"I wonder. You met Qol more than once. Was it the same Qol both times?"

"Yes. At least I think so. Wait—haven't you met Qol, too?"

She looked away from me. "Why do you ask?"

"When we first met, you told me that you and I were the same, both made by Qol. I believe you mentioned recognizing his 'tool marks' on my soul. How could you know that unless you knew Qol?"

"It was a very long time ago; so long that we can't compare. The body Qol wore back then has likely turned to dust by now."

"How long ago? How old are you?" I asked.

"Old enough to evade that question. You saw Qol twice, and Vastil and Ulat only once, right?"

"Yes." I was beginning to see where she was going. Our experience with muria was very limited. Each of the five muria persons was many-bodied, and I had no reason to expect that any particular one I met would resemble the rest. The mind would be the same, but not the physical form. "Do you think they deliberately choose which bodies to show us, in order to hide something?"

"It seems as reasonable as any other guess. We'd have to see more of them to know. It may be important. We know the muria were originally human, and have suffered many mutations. The same mutations that give them their mental powers may weaken their bodies."

"Weaken? The muria I've seen all seemed quite healthy—at least until I dropped a ton of masonry on Vastil. The Ketlan weren't frail."

"They shouldn't have been so white, either. You said they wore only gauzy singlets, and were barefoot in a forest glade. That implies they are accustomed to spending time outdoors. Why weren't they tanned?"

"I can't tan," I said. "But I don't burn, either."

"Perhaps you can't tan because Qol didn't know how to give you the ability. I don't tan, either. I'm always the same color no matter how much time I spend in the sun."

I hated being reminded that I was a made thing, like one of Maran's golems, or for that matter, like Maran herself. Qol had made us both, but not using the same pattern. Qol had obviously known how to embed pigment in her skin, even if it was a constant amount rather than a dynamic reaction to sunlight.

"What difference does it make?" I asked.

"Except for Vastil, who was in a dark dungeon, haven't all the muria you've seen worn cloaks covering their faces and bodies, regardless of the weather?"

That was certainly true, but it proved nothing. I pointed out that one may wear a hooded cloak for many reasons, anonymity chief among them. "What are you suggesting?" I asked. "I still fail to see the point. The sample size we have to work with is too small to draw any conclusions. We've never seen them eat or drink, either. And Vastil had a cloak with him in the dungeon. He just wasn't wearing it."

"Doesn't that point to an unusual sensitivity to sunlight? This may be a weakness we can exploit."

"What evidence do you have for that?" I asked.

"None. I'm only thinking aloud. Perhaps when you meet the hierophants, you can find out if they knew the same Vastil we met, or if he looked different."

"You say 'he,' but they might have met a female Vastil."

"True, but tell me—is Qol male?"

I honestly didn't know. The one I had met wore a male form, but by definition, Qol was many-bodied. Certainly some of him must be female. But I could no more think of Qol as female than I could conceive of Ulat as male. One was a he, the other a she. They were qualities that had nothing to do with their bodies.

As if reading my mind, Maran continued: "I suspect that each of the five is either masculine or feminine, without necessarily being male or female."

"We only have the three examples. Qol and Vastil were male and masculine. Ulat was female and feminine. Bastion and Tamil might be neuter or some gender for which we have no name. We just don't know."

"What of the children, the Ketlan?"

"Definitely a boy and a girl."

"Could you see beneath their raiments?"

"No, but I didn't try, either."

"Then how do you know? By your own account, they were too young to show sexual differences. And remember, muria don't have facial hair beyond eyebrows or lashes, even as adults."

How could I forget? Qol had made me in their image. I had never shaved, and never would, despite being a grown man. "We are made things," I said. "There's no point comparing us to muria, or even to normal humans. When I first met you, I thought you must be hauflin."

"Hauflin—you mean half-elf? Why would you think that?"

"In a world where almost everyone has dark brown skin and hair, you stand out as much as I do. You're halfway between normal and me. Qol chose our coloration for reasons he'll probably never reveal."

"'He'?" she chided gently.

"Until I meet a female Qol, I'll continue to think of him as male." My patience with the conversation was waning rapidly.

"What if you meet one of each at the same time?" she asked. "The same mind, but one body female, the other male?"

"I have no idea. I'll have to ask them, I guess."

Maran said nothing for a minute, cradling her teacup, but not sipping from it. Her eyes had a far-off look, as if she glimpsed something in the future that only she could see.

"If their seed is failing," Maran said at length, "perhaps they are vulnerable."

Her comment brought me up short. What part of our discussion would make her think the muria had any trouble reproducing? "Do you know something I don't?" I asked.

She pursed her lips and shrugged. "I'm just wondering if they are hiding a weakness, something we could exploit against them."

"We're not at war with Avermorn."

"Not presently, but I like to plan rather than be surprised. That the Ketlan contacted you gives me pause. What else are they considering? I want to know their vulnerabilities ahead of time."

I couldn't imagine any muria being vulnerable, except if caught by surprise, the way I had killed that one body of Vastil's. It hadn't diminished him a bit. I said as much, and Maran laughed very gently.

"I didn't mean they need to fear humans, even manufactured

ones like us. I meant they might be facing extinction. Isn't *that* worth considering?"

I found her line of speculation inutile, since our pool of information was so miniscule. Maybe most of the muria were melanin-deficient, and they had only chosen to show us avatars that weren't. If so, what difference did it make? I saw no point continuing. Instead of answering her question, I said, "Our tea is cold. I wasted the trip upland."

"Maybe not. You *did* get your eyes back. Have you thought that the 'future need' the boy mentioned might be something desirable?"

"Do you believe that?"

"I don't know," said Maran, "but the elves always have their reasons, and their plans span centuries or millennia. It would be unreasonable for us to hope to understand their actions. It's like watching a chess game played with one move every human lifetime. Who could grasp an elf's strategy?"

"I'll call your golems 'homunculi' if you remember to call the elves 'muria,'" I replied. "But all this talk—what do you expect me to do? I can't go to Avermorn and perform a survey."

"No," she agreed, "at least not yet. But in the meantime, please ask the nursemaid to bring in Aiden. It's time to feed him."

"I thought he was sleeping."

"That may be, but I was thinking of myself. My breasts hurt."

"All right. You know best."

"Usually."

"I do love you, you know." I said after a moment.

"Yes, dear," she said, patting my good arm. "And I love you, too. Now take these teacups away and send for our child. I'll work on your courier tonight, so he'll be ready for your trip tomorrow."

"What trip?"

"To test the monument and tell Ashe about the baby."

"I doubt the king cares much about newborns. He has more important things to worry about."

"More important than Aiden?" She sounded skeptical.

"Not to me," I said hastily, "but to Ashe, yes. Kings are strange creatures. They always seem busy holding court, rendering judgments, worrying about crops and trade. To him, a baby is just a baby."

"Yes, kings are consumed by duty. Have you considered that, of all people on Leonais, you might be his only real friend? He can discuss things with you freely, which must be an absolute luxury for him."

"He has courtiers," I said.

"Each of whom wants something from him."

I hadn't thought of it that way before. Although I wanted things from Ashe, too, my relationship to him wasn't that of a petitioner. Could Ashe actually think of me as an equal, a friend? I resolved to spend more time listening, less time talking. I kissed Maran thoroughly, and prepared to take my leave.

Just as I reached the door, she said, "On your way back from Ashe, you should stop by Tessa's. We haven't visited her in months, and she'll want to hear all about the baby, too."

"Tessa? Yes, a visit is overdue, but why would she care about the baby?"

"Grey, don't be thick. After our experiences in the dungeon together, Tessa and Torrey are *family*. Of course Tessa will be interested."

"What do I say? Aiden can't even focus his eyes yet."

"Just tell her that he's healthy and happy, and that he can recognize your voice."

"He can?"

"I think so. His mood changes when you talk to him. He's the right age."

"I can't sense anything from him other than when he's

hungry, upset, needs to be changed, or sleeping. I can't wait until he starts talking."

"In two years or so, when he begins to talk, he'll only tell you the same things you sense now. It will be years and years before you can engage with him intellectually. Enjoy the stages as they happen—each phase of development only happens once."

"I won't tell the nursemaid, then. I'll bring him to you myself."

She smiled at me and said, "There's hope for you yet."

CHAPTER THREE

THE FOLLOWING MORNING, I asked Mint to bring me warm
clothing. Although Maran's valley knew only endless summer, I
intended to visit the dolmen, which was always bone-freezingly
cold, even without daring the tomb beneath the ring of standing
stones.

She brought me my normal clothes, rich silk and linen, but
also brought a heavy woolen cloak with a hood. It was a good
compromise. The servants—probably acting on Maran's orders—
insisted on dressing me in finery unless I demanded something
plain. I had to admit that I had become accustomed to princely
attire, even though I was acutely aware that I didn't deserve it. As I
finished dressing, I tucked Ashe's signet ring into my vest.

Mint served me breakfast in my rooms, apologizing for
Maran's absence; the lady and the child were still asleep. I let my
mind inspect Mint as she went about her chores of opening the
drapes, changing the bed linen, dusting, and seeing to my needs.
From the outside, she appeared to be a normal housemaid; from
within, she was all sawdust, cobwebs, mold, old rags, and utter

concentration on her duties. I felt a shadow over her heart, although she seemed content in her role.

On impulse, I asked, "Do you want to come with me today?"

"If you wish, sir."

"No, I'm asking if you *want* to go. An outing. An adventure. Get some fresh air; see things outside the manor house; maybe even meet the king if I can get the dolmen to work."

"The lady would miss me, sir."

"That's not an answer. I doubt she'd miss you. She has far too many servants as it is. Answer for yourself, Mint."

She curtsied reflexively. "If I may be so bold, sir, I would like it very much."

"Then you must stop calling me 'sir,' at least while we're out. Just call me Grey. And no more curtseying. Dress for a walk and meet me by the front door."

She half-curtsied, stopped herself, smiled shyly, and left.

I limped from my rooms to the front door, where I found a man garbed for travel. He wore a blue uniform resembling that worn by the King's Guard, high leather boots, and carried a heavy cloak over his shoulder.

"Good morning, lord," he said.

"Who the devil are you?" I asked.

Hasq appeared from around the corner, as if he'd been waiting for me. "Sir, this is Brand, your new courier. As you can see, he is ready to accompany you. He is schooled in courtly speech; and he can enter or leave the valley without a guide. He is also an expert horseman and will give you lessons when you ask. Further, he can act as your bodyguard and guide on your walks."

"Brand, eh?" I shook the courier's hand, but sensed little more than his firm grip. I had to strain to detect the homunculus underneath. Brand inclined his head a fraction and said nothing. I turned to Hasq and said, "I'm taking Mint with me today, too. We're headed for the dolmen."

"Brand is your companion, sir. It is not seemly—"

"Nevertheless, Mint is coming," I said, using a brusque tone that brooked no contradiction.

Hasq yielded. "I shall have a late supper ready upon your return, sir."

"Late?"

"The lady indicated you would likely be gone all day, sir."

I'd envisioned a quick test of the dolmen network, with only a few brief stops. By telling Hasq I'd be gone all day, Maran gave me oblique permission to linger during my visits with Ashe and Tessa; perhaps even enough time for extended conversations with each.

"Make it cold meats, cheese, that sort of thing," I told him. "Something you can cover and hold ready. We may return early, or we may not return until tomorrow."

"Very good, sir."

It didn't bother me to have the majordomo use honorifics. Perhaps it even pleased me. In all things where Maran or I failed to overrule him, his word was absolute law within the manor house. It may have been a measure of my insecurity, or just a reflection of his intransigent insistence on formality, but it brought a tight smile to my face when he called me "sir" as if I were a properly titled lordling.

I clapped him on the shoulder, and said, "Good man." I found it reassuring that he still felt like a golem to my touch. I could sense the components from which he had been constructed, unlike with Brand.

"Brand isn't like you," I observed.

"No, sir. He is of a different order. Because he must be able to enter or leave the valley on his own, he must be sturdier. Brand is very nearly human. He needs to eat, drink, and sleep."

"I didn't know Maran could do that."

"Neither did I, sir. She has surpassed herself to please you."

A moment later, Mint joined us, wearing a sweeping green

gown instead of her maid's uniform. She looked for all the world like a highborn lady-in-waiting, white lace gloves and all. She had unbound her hair from its normal tight bun, and I realized for the first time that her face was beautiful. "You forgot a cloak," I told her. "The dolmen will be freezing."

"I am not able to feel heat or cold . . . Grey."

"But you, Brand? I see you have a cloak."

"Yes, lord. Lady Maran has graced me with most human frailties."

With a nod of his head and a nearly imperceptible gesture, Hasq sent both Mint and Brand outside to wait. "A moment, sir?" he said to me.

"Yes?"

"You do Mint no favors by treating her above her station, sir. Although it may entertain you to pretend she is a lady, she is a homunculus, and not one made to last long."

"Then why shouldn't she enjoy herself in the time she has left? I am aware of her nature, but I don't believe that lessens her."

"A name may define, diminish, or elevate a person, according to its use," Hasq insisted. "As you, sir, should know better than most. You were innominate, going by an appellation of convenience. Then you took upon yourself the mantle of a mighty name, and nearly tore the world in two. You finally relinquished it for an unassuming sobriquet given to you by a long dead little boy whom you loved. Names have power, sir; you should not treat them lightly."

I considered the majordomo carefully. It was by far the longest speech I had ever heard him make, and I wondered at the impulse that had driven him to make it. Until just now, I had not thought him capable of subtlety, or subject to philosophical musings. Nor had I ever believed he would dare correct me. What had Maran made? *I give the semblance of life,* she had told me once; but now I wondered if she gave more than she intended. Golem or not, sophisticated thoughts lurked behind Hasq's carefully subservient mien.

"Hasq, are you are actually chastising me?"

"Yes, sir. It seemed needful, for your sake as much as for hers. Recall that I am the second of my name."

"I remember, although I'm surprised to learn that you do."

"I have no memory of my former life, sir, but the lady has told me much."

"Does the name 'Hasq' have some meaning of which I'm unaware?"

"Only to me, sir. Is that not enough?"

His reply felt like a punch to the stomach. How long had I spent searching for a name, only to discover that qualia came not from a bestowed moniker, but from intentionality, the representational stance one took when faced with moral choices?

"Yes, that is enough," I said after a pause. "I shall consider your words carefully. I suspect that you are much more than a majordomo. I regret my former assumptions."

"Such was my intent, sir. You need to act with more forethought now, given the ring you hide in your pocket."

Of course he knew about the ring. Nothing in the manor house escaped him. But his words disturbed me. "What ideas are you trying to wake in me?" I demanded.

He smiled slightly, gesturing toward the door. "Useful ones, I hope. Have a pleasant day, sir."

I could have insisted that he explain. I could have commanded him to walk into the fire. In both cases, he would comply without demurral. However, I accorded him the respect he deserved, and let the matter drop. *Restraint is a kind of power, too*, Maran had once told me. I practiced restraint assiduously in that moment, saying only, "You have soot on your jacket, Hasq." He didn't, but would spend the next several hours looking for it.

Outside, the sun had long since evaporated the dew. The sweet scents of honeysuckle and roses from the gardens suffused the morning air. I gathered Mint and Brand with a wave, and limped off toward the horse pastures. Brand took up a position slightly ahead of me, leaving Mint to walk beside me. Still stinging a little from Hasq's rebuke, I didn't offer Mint my arm. Instead, I enjoyed watching her discover huge branching oaks, rolling green hills, the river and all its tributaries, the wildflowers, and the clever stonework of the fencing, outbuildings, and pathways. As we drew near the water, robins, blue jays, cardinals, hummingbirds, honey bees, and butterflies flew, droned, or flitted through the valley. Rabbits cropped weeds, grasses, and clover, freezing at our approach, then, perceiving no threat, resumed foraging.

After we passed the base of the first hill, Brand stopped, pointing to a deer trail that climbed gently from the water's edge toward a thicket of trees nestled between two hills. "This way, lord," he said.

"The standing stones are much farther south."

"The lady has created a shorter path to ease your journey. The dolmen no longer requires a full day's walk. The stones haven't moved, but the hills surrounding them have. This deer trail is now the quickest route."

"Well, lead on, then," I said brightly. There were advantages to being Maran's husband. I did not know what magics she employed to alter the landscape, but the overall organization of the valley had never been a constant. Once sufficiently far from the manor house, the countryside changed according to her whims.

As the deer trail narrowed and steepened, I finally did extend my arm to Mint. She had chosen heels to match her dress, and found the uneven ground difficult to manage. More than once, her ankle turned, and she would have fallen without my support.

We entered the trees finally, finding the ring of standing stones only a short way inside. I felt the towering menhirs long before seeing them. As if in an act of insubordination to all I knew of science, they radiated cold rather than absorbing heat. No lintels graced this circle; the standing stones had raggedly rounded edges and displayed many different sizes and shapes. The king stone at the center overtopped them all, dark basalt, menacing.

"Do you feel it?" I asked Mint.

"What should I feel?"

"Latent power. Overbearing cold. A network of invisible bands connecting this dolmen to all others on Leonais."

"No, Grey, I feel no chill, but I observe that no grass grows within the circle, and the surrounding trees look as if they're leaning away, trying to escape."

I smiled at her use of my name, but turned to Brand. "And you?"

"Stones and dirt, lord. A sense of great age. Naught else."

"Try again," I said, rapping my knuckles on the nearest menhir. To my eyes, the bands of power sprang to life, multicolored, crossing and arching like bright ribbons at a festival, but stretching far out of sight to connect with other dolmens. Were I to touch the king stone itself, I could rouse even more energy, making the bands of light visible to everyone on the continent. Such was not my intent today; the gentler power was all I needed.

"A faint rainbow, lord," said Brand, "nearly invisible."

"I think I see a glimmer, like when I hold a dish under soapy water," said Mint.

I unslung my cloak from my shoulder and donned it properly, pulling the hood over my head for protection from the cold. Brand did likewise.

"Come into the circle with me. I want to try something." I limped forward past the menhirs, until I stood beside the king stone, the nexus at which the bands of light were strongest. I beckoned with my good hand for Mint, and after a moment's hesitation, she joined me. Brand strode boldly into the circle, seeming unconcerned. "Each of you put a hand on my shoulders," I said, "and grip tightly. When I say so, take one step forward with me."

I plucked on various strands as if they were lute strings, searching for a particular feeling, an emanation I could recognize. I had learned long ago that I need not travel dolmen-to-dolmen, although that was the easiest path. Instead, I sought a person. *Ashe*, I thought. *Show me Ashe.*

My words, spoken aloud or not, were only for my benefit. I could not command the dolmen network, but concentrating on my target helped me sort the strands. A thick orange band, throbbing with energy, caught my attention. It led off to the northeast. I followed it with my mind, and felt a reciprocating tendril of thought speed back in my direction. I twined my fingers in the orange band, tugging very gently.

"Now," I told my companions.

As we stepped forward, a doorway seemed to open in the sky, and with the single step, we left the dolmen behind. Our feet landed on the canvas floor of Ashe's tent in his makeshift camp near the starships. The doorway snapped shut behind us, and I realized with sudden rue that I had not planned for a return journey. I would have to find another dolmen, or make the long trek back overland.

I had also neglected to consider that Ashe might not be alone.

At our sudden appearance in the king's tent, a dozen swords sprang from their sheaths, accompanied by an uproar of outraged shouts, not only from the King's Guard, but also from five white-robed monks, three pages, and six or seven aged scholars. A servant let a flagon of wine drop. Another, balancing a tray of meats and cheeses, tossed the plate into the air and ran for the exit. A group of finely dressed ladies behind the king lifted their skirts and prepared to follow. The King's Guard crouched low, advancing toward us without hesitation. I quickly flipped back the hood of my cloak, allowing my shock of white hair to show.

"Hold!" Ashe bellowed. "Everyone hold!"

The King's Guard froze in place, but the monks, ladies, pages, scholars, and servants milled in confusion, some loudly demanding an explanation, others whispering to each other nervously.

"Grey," complained Ashe, "*must* you?"

"Sorry," I said. "I keep forgetting. Allow me to introduce my companions. This is Brand, a courier, and Mint, one of Maran's ladies."

"Your Majesty," said Brand, removing his cloak and bowing to the precise degree that etiquette required.

"Your Majesty," whispered Mint, somehow managing a deep curtsey while looking utterly flustered.

"Swords away," said Ashe to the Guard. "And the rest of you relax, too. What my old friend lacks in protocol, he makes up for in theatrics. His tricks can surprise the unwary, but there is no need for fear." He waved to the servant who had dropped the flagon of wine. She was about sixteen years old and had regained her composure. "Bring more wine, and find the idiot who dropped our lunch before he brings an entire company of soldiers."

She nodded and said, "Sire," before slipping out of the tent.

Ashe turned wearily back to me. "*Really?*" he asked. "Your last misadventure was only two weeks ago."

"More like eight or nine days," I said. "I'm finding it hard to keep track. Maran is keeping me busy, and I've had another adventure. At least this time, I didn't bring a whirlwind into the tent with me."

"Why aren't you wearing your head scarf?"

I said nothing, just waited. It took him several moments; then he suddenly strode forward, gripping my shoulders and staring closely at my face. "Your eyes," he whispered in wonder. Then his expression changed to one of alarm. "Does this mean *my* eyes. . . ?"

"It's a long story, but I don't think you have need for concern."

"I still have nightmares from when Gaheris—"

"We all have nightmares from those days," I said gently. *And*, I added, using mind-speech, *we are not alone.*

Good point, he replied the same way.

Ashe shook his head to clear it. Then he gave brisk commands to his Guard to take up station outside the tent. To the others, he said, "Ariel, please stay. The rest of you, give us a minute."

In the general shuffle that followed, one of the monks passed close to me, and I noticed his robe wasn't plain white, but elaborately embroidered. He also wore fine gold filigree chains of office around his neck. A hierophant, then, but one who tried to slip out meekly with the rest of the monks. I caught at his sleeve, causing him to look up. I recognized his face, mostly from the gold flecks in his eyes and his jutting grey beard, but also from his haughty expression. "Hello, again," I said cheerfully. "I never did learn your name, but I have learned quite a bit about truth and duplicity, thanks to you."

He lifted his eyebrows. "Oh?"

"When we first met in the muddy fields of Wyland valley, you told me I was not muria. I wondered at the time how you could be so sure. Since then, I've found out that everyone who ever greeted me that way had met the elves. Petty of you not to tell me at the time."

"Prudence, Grey, not pettiness. And I was under vows."

"Do you two know each other?" asked Ashe.

"No," I said shortly. "Not really. He threatened to kill me once."

"Holy One, is this true?" asked Ashe, looking back and forth between us with active interest. "Did you have any idea what you were doing?"

"My assigned task," said the hierophant stiffly. "He has since justified my distrust."

"Lord Grey is my honored guest, and you will treat him accordingly."

The hierophant and I both snorted at the title, which only intrigued Ashe more. "Perhaps the Holy One should stay. We do have things to talk about together, and I suspect the conversation will be lively. Threats and insults on both sides, no doubt. And we must discuss the records. Nothing but promises and delays have been forthcoming."

"Let him wait with the others," I said. "I don't have time to bicker. I can stay awhile today, and I plan to come regularly after this. We'll have plenty of leisure to banter."

The hierophant did not move until Ashe waved him away. Then he inclined his head—to Ashe, not to me—and withdrew.

"Now then," I said. "I've introduced my companions. My intent is for Brand to go back and forth, carrying letters so we may keep in better touch. Maran reports that the birth was harder than expected and wants me to stay in the valley most of the time, though there will be days, like today, when I'm free to linger."

"You'll take orders from her, but not from me, is that it?"

I chuckled. "You can't expect me to answer that."

"Rightly so," agreed Ashe. "Is Lady Maran doing well? And the babe?"

"Yes, both are fine. Maran is merely tired. The boy's name is Aiden. He doesn't do much yet, but I have great hopes. But we are being impolite. Mint, as you have gathered, this is the king. He's a very pleasant fellow when not surprised by unexpected guests. Brand, this is the man to whom you are to bring messages—only to him, unless Maran or I address the letters elsewhere. I have in mind for you to bide here for now, since the king will probably have news long before I do." I turned to Ashe. "May Brand quarter with your soldiers?"

Ashe nodded absently. "Find the staff sergeant and tell him to assign you a tent," he said to Brand. "I'll send for you when needed. You can eat in the general mess along with everyone else." He held out his hand, not as king to subject, but as one soldier to another.

Brand nodded curtly, shook Ashe's hand, bowed, and excused himself.

Ashe cocked his head. "And you, Grey? You say Maran and the boy are fine, but you look hollowed out."

"I think that's my normal look now," I said. "At least my clothes are clean this visit."

"You still have that cut on your cheek. I'd have thought it would stop bleeding by now. Do you need one of the court physicians?"

I felt my cheek gingerly. The pebbly texture seemed more pronounced than before, and the scab itself seemed a bit larger. It began near my hairline, above where my left ear used to be, and curved down toward my nose in a gentle arc. When I pulled my hand away, I saw faint streaks of blood and clear fluid on my fingers. The cut was weeping from beneath the scab. I wiped my hand on my cloak and shrugged. "Maran says to leave it alone."

"As you will." He beckoned to the woman he had asked to remain. She glided to his side and regarded us gravely. "This is Lady Ariel of Draycott," Ashe announced. "A very distant cousin. We are betrothed. Ariel, this is Lord Grey. You've heard me speak of him."

Ariel inclined her head graciously. "Lord Grey, Lady Mint, I am pleased to meet you." Her voice was rich with overtones, polished and yet velvety. She was nearly Ashe's height, with creamy brown skin and dark, wide-set eyes. I guessed her to be in her late thirties, about the same age as Ashe. Her curly brown hair fell in a loose mass over one shoulder. I liked her instinctively and made an effort to smile.

"Begging your pardon, ma'am," said Mint nervously. "I am no lady."

"Today you are," I said briskly. "Stand up straight and look them in the eye. They may be royalty, but you are my guest."

Mint lifted her shoulders. "I am pleased to meet you, too," she said, her tone stronger.

"Ariel," said Ashe, "would you entertain Lady Mint while I speak with Grey? That girl will be back with wine soon, and if she's as quick-witted as she seems, she'll also bring food for our guests."

As Ariel took Mint under her wing, Ashe and I withdrew to a small table in the corner of the tent. I relieved myself of the cloak. Although it was autumn in Leonais, the tent shielded us from the wind, and it was stuffy inside. Ashe and I took chairs at the table. This time, I remembered to let him sit first.

"Tell me about your eyes," Ashe said.

"There isn't much to tell. Some muria children interfered for their own obscure reasons. I'm glad to have normal eyes again, but even happier that they left my second sight alone."

"Muria children?" he asked. "That's curious."

"As far as I know, the adults abandoned the continent after Ulat doomed the nina to unicorn shape. Ulat promised that the adults would no longer interfere, but didn't say anything about the Ketlan."

"I don't know that word," said Ashe.

"Ketlan is a generic term for muria children before they affiliate with one of the five adults. It means 'beloved.' Ketlan aren't many-bodied yet; each child is a singleton, an individual. Their bodies look young, but their minds are fully adult from before birth."

Ashe frowned, slumped forward, and rubbed at his brow. "And Ulat lets these Ketlan wander Leonais without supervision?"

I shrugged. "It's complicated. The children weren't really here. They reached out to me mentally from Avermorn. Distance seems to have little meaning for them. Even operating remotely, they were able to restore my eyes."

Ashe's frown deepened. "I find that disturbing."

"It bothers me a little, too," I admitted. "But they seem harmless. Whatever they're planning, I don't think it has anything to do with you or your kingdom. Like all muria, they're playing a long game of their own devising. I doubt we'll ever know their true purpose."

Ashe straightened. "I'll be guided by you in this matter. You're the expert."

"Hardly," I protested, shifting uncomfortably on my chair. "I know a few things, and guess more, but I don't understand the muria. I do, however, trust Ulat's promise."

Ashe studied me for a few moments, then abruptly changed the subject. "Your companions today are golems," he said. "Mint is obvious, but I wouldn't have known about Brand if we hadn't shaken hands. It took most of my willpower not to jump out of my boots. He looks human enough. I doubt anyone else at court will give him a second glance."

"I had to ask about Brand, too," I said. "He's apparently one of a kind, something Maran crafted at my request. I'm surprised you could tell. But, Ashe—I've never understood your magery. Is it inherent, like mine?"

"No, it comes from years of careful training. Royal blood appears to be a prerequisite. We have tried teaching the arts to others, with no success. Even among us, the gift varies. My brother

Gaheris was able to master the lightning, while my powers are limited to heightened perception. For example, I can tell if someone is lying."

"Did you feel my touch through the dolmen before we appeared today?"

"I felt *something* familiar, but had no time to worry out the details. Just an odd tingling, then you materialized. The court will be talking about it for months, and the monks will be displeased."

I said, "The monks have never liked me, so one more bit of magic won't make things worse. The displeasure will be mutual. But about recognizing lies—the hierophants claim to detect falsehood, too."

Ashe laughed long and hard. "They lie. They are intelligent and alert, and have made a science of observing minutiae, but they are not soothsayers. Not only have I caught them lying to me, but they have failed to notice when I misled them on several occasions."

"Why would you do that?" I asked.

"To test, of course. They are devious, and I don't trust them, even though they've promised to open their secret records— something, by the way, they still insist on having you present for." He broke off, looking around suddenly. "Ah, the wine! With, as predicted, food. Will you stay for an early lunch?"

"Just the wine, please. Mint will appreciate it, although she'll only pretend to sip." I gestured over my shoulder, where the two ladies stood talking and laughing gaily with each other. "I think she's having the time of her life. Congratulations on your betrothal, by the way. Ariel seems nice."

"She is. I've known her since we were children. The nobles have decided the king must marry and produce heirs." He didn't sound bitter, but his words carried a faint touch of asperity.

Mindful of his tone, and of Maran's suggestion that Ashe

might consider me a confidant, I asked carefully, "And how does the king himself feel about that?"

"Resigned, but not unhappy. We can't have the throne contested again. Ariel is a very good choice. Her family is well connected, her breeding is impeccable, and she is a very gentle person. Don't let her beauty fool you; she's twice as clever as I am. We were childhood sweethearts, so I imagine we'll come to love each other again eventually."

"That reminds me," I said, digging in my vest pocket for his ring. "I want you to take this back. Benlyn explained its meaning."

"You shall hold it until I have another heir."

"Ashe . . . I can't be what you want."

"I speak now as king. The ring is only a token of the reality." His tone softened. "Although I command this, I also ask it. The kingdom requires stability. You are an important temporary placeholder. You needn't take the throne; just guide the succession. Your reputation and power will secure the next in line. If I die, the throne swings to my mother's family. I am the last direct lineal descendant of Captain Leonais—for now."

I sighed and put the ring back in my pocket. "May you have many children, and soon. When is the wedding?"

"Midwinter, after we return to Jappa. You are invited of course—although I'd prefer you to show up the way normal people do. You didn't come to my coronation."

"We didn't travel much the first several months, and you know we had no visitors. But I watched part of the ceremony through your eyes."

"Yes, eyes," he said slowly. "Your new ones still bother me. I don't know what such a gift means, and all my dealings with muria have led me to believe they never give with one hand unless the other hand takes something away. Are you sure you still control the winds? Are we safe from the Sleeper?"

"Not to worry, Ashe. Nothing has changed. Vastil said I

couldn't wake the Sleeper without help from the nina. He was probably telling the truth. However, neither primary sight nor second sight keeps me from being a fool. This outing was to test my control over the dolmen and to visit you. It will be several more weeks, I think, until Maran will let me spend significant time wrestling the monks with you."

He blinked a few times. "How does that make you a fool? You arranged for Brand to carry messages, and you dote on your wife. What else could you do?"

"I could have thought about how to get back home today. I let the doorway close behind us. I can only open a new one from within a dolmen. The nearest one I know is way up by Luvar." I accepted a goblet of wine from the servant, thanked her, and turned back to Ashe. "Neither Mint nor I know how to ride."

"That's awkward," he said. "But there's a dolmen on the far side of Landing. A carriage could get you very close in less than an hour."

"Maran said that, too, but I didn't feel it in the network. It may be dormant, or protected somehow. I also worry that transferring *out* of Maran's valley might be significantly easier than transferring *in*. I don't know if it's possible."

Ashe swirled his wine thoughtfully. "The only way to know is to try, I suppose. How many people on Leonais can work the dolmens the way you do? I don't know the extent of Maran's enchantments. I can only sense the use of power, not take advantage of it unless someone like you wakes the lights for me. The Amrhyn sorcerers may still pose a threat, but there are few of them left."

"Even one is too many where the safety of my family is concerned," I said. "Yet Maran mentioned something about sanctioning my own use of the dolmen in her valley. It certainly worked to bring me here. She said she'd unlocked it for me alone."

"What *is* the extent of her power? She is not a mage, with

learned magics like my own. She is not much like you, either. I thought she could only make golems and shield her valley."

"'Only?' That's quite a bit. I can do neither." I toyed briefly with the idea of explaining that Maran and I were made things, manufactured by the muria to serve distinct purposes. Then I discarded the notion. It wasn't something Ashe—or other humans—needed to know. I drank more wine while considering my words. "I think she hasn't discovered her limits. Or rather, I should say that her inclinations govern what she attempts. The desire for privacy dominates her, and she wants to raise our child in peace. Beyond that, she seems pleased to indulge me. I don't know that she has limits that aren't self-imposed."

"Are you saying she's a potential threat to the realm?" asked Ashe, his tone suddenly that of a king.

"Not at all," I said quickly. "Relax. She is no more threat than I am, and probably considerably less, since she is disinclined to meddle in affairs of state or blunder about wielding powers she doesn't understand. You'll have to trust her, just as you trust me. My fondness is for unraveling mysteries. Hers tends toward maintaining peace and isolation."

"To Lady Maran, then," said Ashe, raising his goblet.

"To Maran," I agreed. We both drank, and he signaled the servant girl to refill our goblets.

A new fit of giggling and hushed whispers came from Ariel and Mint. The two of them still stood near the center of the tent, but now Ariel's hand firmly clasped Mint's, and they held their heads close together.

"The ladies seem to be getting on well," I observed. "I've never heard Mint laugh before. Lady Ariel must be very kind to entertain her so."

"She's probably telling dirty stories."

I had to look at Ashe twice before I realized he was joking.

I took a few moments to chuckle with him, and then got

down to business. "The carriage you offered would be welcome," I said. "We can try the Landing dolmen first. If that doesn't work, we can use the carriage for transportation back toward Maran's valley, at least as far as the roads will take us. We can walk thereafter."

He caught the servant girl's eye. She immediately approached.

"A coach and four, quick as you like. Our guests have an errand, and I've a mind to make it a royal outing. Oh, and tell Kiril his attendance is required."

"Sire," she said, and quickly ducked outside the tent.

"Who is Kiril?" I asked.

"The hierophant standing with his ear to the tent flap this whole time. I want to see his face when you wake the dolmen," said Ashe. "And the ride together may prove instructive. I intend to wring some answers from him."

"I may not be able to rouse the dolmen to power," I reminded him. "If I fail, it might be best to hide that from the monks."

"You won't fail. Even if you don't wake the lights, you can do something else dramatic. Since he won't know what to expect, any trick of yours will do."

"Dramatic? I? Are you making fun of me?"

"Never, my friend, never, although you *do* have a flair for outrageous acts of sheer effrontery. Even if you don't impress him, you can insult him. Kiril is a stuffy old crow, so full of wounded dignity that I'm constantly surprised he doesn't burst. As king, I must call him 'Holy One' and show deference, just as he must pretend to honor my rank and title. You are under no such obligation."

"I don't hate the hierophants," I said slowly. "I just don't respect them. They have taken too much upon themselves, even if Vastil gave them orders. I won't know whether to praise or curse the monks until I see what they've preserved of the ancient knowledge. That day is coming—very soon, I hope—

but it may not be today. I have another stop to make on the way home."

"Oh?"

"You remember Tessa and her grandson Torrey?"

"Of course. I've been sending them money, and, although they don't know it, a nearby garrison constantly watches over them. We're still looking for Lane, Tessa's son. He served as a foot soldier, but had no military experience. Most such did not do well in the war, but we haven't given up hope."

"Decent of you," I said.

"What kind of king would I be if I failed to honor their sacrifice?" He meant the question to be rhetorical and didn't wait for me to answer. "Why are you going there today?"

"Maran wants me to tell them about Aiden. She thinks Tessa will be interested."

"Of course she will be. Convey my regards while you're there, and if you discover they want for anything, let me know."

"I will—assuming I can get the dolmen to work. If not, I won't have time to see them today."

"Well, even if your experiments with the dolmen fail, you can at least poke at Kiril a bit. Find out why he insists on opening their books only in your presence. I have the best minds on Leonais assembled in this camp—architects, engineers, tradesfolk, scholars —all waiting, growing more impatient by the day. I am impatient, too, although I understand your situation at home."

Ashe stood and straightened his jacket. "Ladies," he called across the tent. "We are to have an adventure. Please make yourselves ready for travel."

Lady Ariel looked startled for a moment, then smoothed her face and pointed to the table, where the platter of meats and cheeses lay untouched. "Your Majesty, we have not yet offered repast to our guests."

"Mint doesn't eat," I murmured softly enough that only Ashe could hear me. "Please don't embarrass her."

"Lord Grey informs me that his schedule is stringent," said Ashe. "Perhaps our guests will join us in a meal another time. For now, please find suitable outdoor clothing. We shall take the carriage, but may need to walk, too."

"Warm clothes and umbrellas, my lady," I said. "It may rain later."

Ashe looked surprised. "Really? The last time I looked, the sky was clear."

Again pitching my voice only for him, I said, "You said I should have some theatrics prepared."

He acknowledged my whisper by nodding. Aloud, he said, "Lord Grey suggests a storm may be coming. I've found it wise to take his weather sense seriously."

"Of course, sire," said Ariel. She escorted Mint from the tent, and I started to follow, but Ashe held me back until they were out of earshot.

"Aren't we leaving?" I asked.

"It will take them at least thirty minutes to choose cloaks and shoes," he said, eyes twinkling. "In the meantime, I'm famished."

Chapter Four

I found out what a king means by "coach and four" when the carriage showed up. I had expected a cart or wain with a weary dray horse. Instead, four huge horses, harnessed in pairs and hitched to a gilded four-wheeled cage, stood patiently waiting, liverymen and grooms by their sides.

The cage, complete with roof, doors, and cleverly designed folding steps, had two upholstered bench seats facing each other, with plenty of room for five. Kiril stood beside the carriage, a scowl on his face that disappeared whenever Ashe glanced in his direction, only to re-form as soon as the king looked away. Since the grimace seemed directed at me, I wore my most winsome smile, and otherwise ignored him.

While we waited for the ladies to join us, pages kept bringing notes to Ashe from his advisors and staff. Today's outing was not on the royal schedule, and, with an apologetic glance at me, he finally surrendered to his duties.

"I'll be back soon," he said. "Some matters of state demand my attention. Perhaps you and the Holy One can renew your acquaintance. Feel free to explore the camp—the pages will find you. Or you may wait in the comfort of the carriage."

"Majesty," acknowledged Kiril, climbing into the coach and claiming one entire bench by dint of sitting exactly in the middle, with his arms spread wide.

I gazed at Ashe's retreating back, then shrugged and took the remaining bench.

"Kiril," I said breezily. "It's good to learn your name at last."

"You remain irreverent and arrogant," he replied.

"I'm unlikely to become devout, if that's what you mean. You know what I hold sacred—knowledge. Your pointless withholding of the ancient records irritates me more than a little. The last time I asked you for knowledge, you told me that even the questions were forbidden. The hierophants have much to answer for. Humanity deserves its heritage."

"What do you know of humanity?" he asked, thrusting his chin forward.

How much had Vastil told him? I wondered. I decided that, as in our first meeting, I would make him work for anything he got from me.

"I know that humanity once commanded forces that would seem like magic today. Power to travel the stars. Power to terraform the planet so that Sundering could support Terran life. Power to heal intractable diseases. Power to create materials like the ship's metal. Power to produce artificial light, defeating the cycle of the sun. Power to create machines that fly through the air. Power to speak instantly to anyone across the entire planet. And a thousand other abilities, not to mention their incredible tools."

"You dare speak to me of magic?"

"I said 'would seem like,' but yes, why not?"

"Magic is an abomination; espousing it is heresy."

I shrugged. "Power is power. The kind I seek should be everyone's to wield, lowborn or noble, devout or apostate. I would gladly trade the small magics I possess for the knowledge you have kept hidden for three thousand years. It is not arrogance that drives me, Kiril. It is thirst."

"We have our reasons," he said stiffly.

"Perhaps, but until you explain them, why should anyone trust you? You have let the muria dictate the rules. What reason did Vastil provide?"

"As the abbess told the king, unearned knowledge is more dangerous than ignorance."

"Trivially true, and essentially meaningless. At the time you first started hiding things, the knowledge had been earned. The Second Colonists were engineers and scientists, men and women who devoted their lives to learning, who came here in good faith, bringing their tools, their machines, and their vast store of hard-won knowledge with them."

"Did the tragedy of the First Colony teach you nothing?" he demanded angrily. "They lost their humanity, trading it for unholy powers. They loosed horrors upon the world, not the least of which were the muria themselves. Captain Leonais struck a bargain that kept muria and humans apart."

"Then why would you do Vastil's bidding? I know how the First Colonists became muria. The induced mutations weren't their fault."

"They allowed themselves to be seduced. Isn't that crime enough? We did what Vastil commanded because we were unable to refuse."

"Unable? You mean unwilling."

He abruptly leaned forward, his fists clenched in his lap. "I should have had you killed when I had the chance."

"Your loss, humanity's gain. If you find me so abhorrent, tell me why you insist on my presence when opening your books."

"The abbess suggested it, and the council of hierophants agreed unanimously."

"I don't understand, but I would like to. I don't know anything about your abbess or council. Your entire hierarchy is a mystery to me."

He sat back, eying me speculatively. "So your arrogance does have limits. I had begun to wonder."

I found that my own body had tensed. I forced myself to relax, muscle by unwilling muscle. "Kiril, we need not be enemies," I said after a minute. "You have been preserving the ancient knowledge against the day when it would be safe to reveal it again. I have removed the muria from the equation. Vastil no longer forbids, and both the king and I feel the time is right. Why do you still resist? I'm not trying to be difficult."

His eyes narrowed. "Threatening to knock over the starships isn't an act of belligerence and extortion?"

"I meant only to get your attention."

"You have it. Where is the king taking us today?"

"I thought you were listening at the tent flap," I said, perhaps a bit too flippantly. The muscles in his face tightened, and I could tell he was biting back reply after reply. In the end, he said nothing but, "I couldn't hear anything clearly."

"We're going to the dolmen just northeast of Landing," I said.

Kiril suddenly smiled and widened his eyes. Instead of disarming me, his expression raised my hackles. "How interesting," he said. "How interesting, indeed."

I was about to ask him what he meant, but Ashe returned, interrupting the conversation. He stuck his head into the carriage and said, "The ladies are on their way. How are you two getting along?"

"Kiril threatened my life again," I said. "Otherwise, it's been a pleasant conversation."

Kiril scowled at me, but turned a bland face to Ashe. "Your Majesty, I am pleased to report that the first of the records will be revealed today."

Ashe seemed delighted. "Oh? Should I bring scribes? Do we need to stop at the monastery?"

"Neither scribes nor scholars will be required today, sire. After I have unlocked the reliquary, your people may have free access going forward. The hierophants will bring them copies of whatever they require. The original records must remain within the reliquary. As to the monastery, nothing of importance is stored there, save copies for our own study."

"Then where are the originals?" Ashe and I asked at the same moment.

Kiril chose to ignore me and give his answer to the king. "The monument, sire. The one here at Landing was the very first, made by Justian himself. It is unlike the rest."

"You mean it's not a tomb or a faerie mound?" I asked.

Kiril continued speaking only to Ashe. "Grey is misinformed, sire, which happens among the ignorant and superstitious. A few monuments have been repurposed as tombs, but only long after their original function was lost to memory. None is a 'faerie mound' in the common meaning. The monument at Landing is a reliquary, designed to preserve sacred objects and records against the ravages of time."

I recalled my first visit to Landing, nearly a year ago. The docent assigned to me had only echoed set pieces, and had no real understanding of history. "'Everything of value was removed' from the starships," I recited aloud. "Was it moved to this reliquary?"

Kiril finally deigned to look at me. "That is our belief," he said. "Handed down generation after generation. The art of opening the starships passed with Justian and his engineers."

"You mean you don't know," summarized Ashe, his disappointment plain. "Holy One, I thought the job of the hierophants was to safeguard such arts."

"Sire, we have done our best, but we could not preserve secrets that were never entrusted to us."

Ashe persisted. "You said, 'The first of the records.' Why not all?"

Kiril stiffened, but looked away from the king. He seemed to study his sandals for a long moment. In a low tone, he finally said, "Sire, words fail me. It will be easier to show you than to explain."

"Why must Grey be there?"

"Again, sire, demonstration is better than words," said Kiril.

A sudden bustle amongst the liverymen and grooms interrupted the discussion. Ariel and Mint dawdled toward us, their arms linked, chatting merrily with each other. An honor guard of twenty soldiers followed. Kiril and I exited the carriage to greet them. The grooms checked the horses' tack and harnesses. Two of the liverymen climbed atop the carriage to the driver's seat; a third stood ready to help the women mount the steps.

The ladies had not only found fur cloaks and outdoor footwear; they had changed gowns. Mint seemed completely absorbed in her finery, and didn't look up; Ariel, while continuing to talk to Mint, cast a sharp glance at us, gauging the mood. Her eyes danced rapidly between Kiril and me, measuring the tension, and then locked on the king, mutely appealing for guidance.

Ashe gave no outward sign, but responded. "My Ladies," he said, "your beauty graces us. We are ready to depart."

Mint blushed at the compliment, but Ariel only inclined her head and gestured for Mint to precede her. They took opposite benches, and the king followed them up the steps to sit beside Ariel. Kiril shouldered me aside and sat next to Ashe, leaving me the open position beside Mint.

I didn't mind going last; not only was I the only commoner present—not including Mint's ambiguous rank—but it let me study both Ashe and Kiril simultaneously. The remaining liveryman folded the steps and closed the carriage door, then stepped up to ride on the sideboard, his head studiously facing forward.

———

We set off through the camp, the honor guard following on foot in two columns behind us. The dirt lane through the camp itself was bumpy, but once we gained the main road toward Landing, things smoothed out and we picked up speed. In the town of Landing itself, the road was cobbled, and we slowed again, winding through the narrow streets. Somehow, word had got ahead of us that the king was coming through, and crowds lined up to cheer our passage. Both Ashe and Ariel made a show of waving through the carriage windows, but the hierophant sat stonily, his eyes never looking outside.

I took Mint's gloved hand in mine and asked if she was enjoying herself.

"I could never have imagined," she answered breathlessly, her head constantly swiveling to see as much as she could of the shops, markets, and crowds.

I was happy for her, but could have done without the crowds and luxury. Since the alternatives were walking on a crippled leg or suffering the indignity of riding horseback, I didn't complain. I resolved, however, to start riding lessons with Brand as soon as possible. The slowness of our progress felt too much like a processional, and our route through a thickly inhabited town made me claustrophobic. I imagined galloping at ease across the low hills, following no foreordained track, the king by my side, riding swiftly and easily to our destination. The pleasant daydream occupied my mind as we traveled.

Before long, the cobbled streets lay behind us, and the cheering throng thinned to nothing. The road veered northeast from here, heading toward the port city of Halmar-by-the-Sea.

Beneath the hard pack of dirt lay a Justian road of ship's metal; our carriage seemed to fly freely. The guards behind switched from marching to jogging, their formation undisturbed by the change in pace.

After about a mile, though, the road forked into three. The largest branch turned sharply southward to avoid the hills and continue toward the coast. The middle way led backward from here, winding up to where the monastery lay nestled in the hilltops. The third, much too narrow for the carriage, led directly north. The drivers drew the team to a halt, and the liveryman on the sideboard stepped down to open the carriage door and unfold the steps.

"This is our stop," said Ashe. "I'm afraid we must walk from here, although it isn't far. Shall we? Holy One, I believe you should lead."

The lane was only wide enough for us to walk single file, and the king waved half the guards to precede us. He signed the remainder to await our return. We lined up, Kiril first, then Ashe, followed by Ariel and Mint, leaving me to limp behind them as best I could.

I felt the emanations from the dolmen before it came into view. The path wound along the side of a gentle hill, and water ran through the vale at the bottom. We turned a corner, and the dolmen lay exposed before us, crowning the top of the next hill north. A wooden bridge, braced with thick timbers, let us cross from the crest of one hill to the other without having to follow the winding path down through the vale and up the far side. It also let us avoid having to ford the river at the bottom of the gorge separating the hills.

Ashe told his guards, "Take up station here at the foot of the bridge. We'll go on alone." He then gestured for Kiril to proceed. The hierophant nodded and led the way.

As with the dolmen where I had freed the stone children, this one showed no sign of desuetude. All the bluestone menhirs were intact and upright, with lintels of a lighter color, likely sandstone, capping the circle. Unlike any other dolmens, though, it had no declivity in the center, no king stone. The circle's diameter was large enough to let two hundred people stand inside without crowding. Within the circle itself, and extending perhaps twenty feet beyond the boundary, granite and marble paving covered the earth. At the very center stood a rectangular building, half temple and half citadel, with a flat roof made from the same material as the lintels, held up by fluted columns. Figures cleverly carved into the columns gave the impression of caryatids, but only as suggestions of faces and robes, not as full bodies. I wondered whom the figures were meant to represent. I saw no carvings with names, nor indeed any type of lettering. Neither tree nor shrub grew on the hilltop, but a dozen white-robed monks tranquilly tended to flowers and decorative plants growing in wooden boxes surrounding the temple doorway.

I extended my percipience into the stonework and discovered inner supports of ship's metal. Even the paving lay atop a metal plate. This dolmen was actually a metal structure, from top to bottom, dressed in stone. I couldn't imagine the tools Justian had used to warp what seemed like solid stone to wrap the framework so seamlessly. I was far more interested, however, in what lay beneath. Under the temple's floor lay a honeycomb of passages and chambers, all of ship's metal without the stone dressing.

Kiril paused at the apex of the bridge, so we could see the pristine magnificence of the structure. He gestured, acting as docent for us. "Above us to the left, the monastery overlooks this point. You can see the dome and spires from here. Before us, at the foot of the bridge, rests the first—and largest—of the monuments. We believe Justian built it before sealing the starships, although the exact sequence of events is lost to history. As you know, the officers of the Second Colony became the first monks. We have preserved this place unchanged ever since. The only doors to the temple are the ones you see from this vantage. The complete Book of the Ship rests inside. Only initiates of the deepest secrets have crossed the threshold, or read the entire Book—until today."

The women gazed speechlessly, but Ashe put everyone's feelings into words: "It's beautiful," he said. "I didn't know such things existed. The dolmens I've seen have all had fallen or broken stones. I should have visited here long ago. It's a pilgrimage point, isn't it?"

Kiril nodded. "One of the holiest, although we only allow pilgrims to view it from the monastery's overlook."

"There are no guards," Ashe pointed out.

"None is needed," said Kiril. "The temple protects itself."

"It's metal," I burst out, unable to hold my tongue any longer. "I can see where you have patched the stone cladding to preserve the illusion. Your artisans have skillfully hidden millennia of weathering. What lies beneath the temple floor?"

Kiril turned to face me. "I have said that the first records would be revealed today. The Book of the Ship must content you."

"Grey?" Ashe asked wonderingly. "What do you see that I don't?"

"The complex is huge," I answered, "much larger underground than above. The chambers beneath are guarded somehow. I can't perceive the contents, but the tunnels extend for miles to the north and east, buried under the hills. It's all ship's metal down there, and I can't see through it."

"As should be," said Kiril stiffly. "You do not understand the grace granted to you today. It is not wholly earned." He turned to the king. "Begging your pardon, sire, but our devoir is strict, as are our vows. Not even kings can pass the doors without the cooperation of the hierophants."

Ashe gazed at Kiril with something approaching distaste,

although his tone, when he spoke, remained respectful. "Holy One, I am glad the day has finally arrived, and I thank you for your cooperation."

"Thank Grey, not me, sire. It is his bold irreverence that grants you admission."

"Never mind that," said Ashe curtly. "Carry on."

Kiril folded his arms into his robes, nodded, and led us across the remainder of the wooden bridge and down to the paving. As we passed the megaliths—I couldn't really call them menhirs, since they were artificial—I surreptitiously flicked the nearest with my thumbnail. No lights sprang up in response, even though their emanations heightened. I wondered if I would be able to use this dolmen for travel. I had not sensed it as part of the continent-wide network, even though it was clearly the blueprint from which all the others had taken their pattern. As we entered the circle and approached the temple, a deep coldness enveloped us, and static electricity filled the air, making our flesh tingle.

Mint, impervious to the cold, nevertheless felt *something*, for she left Ariel's side and came to clutch at my arm. "Don't worry," I told her. "It's just a building."

I had misread her completely. Her face, when she looked up at me, evinced no fear, but only awe. "This is our way home," she said, "but I want to see inside first. It's so peaceful and beautiful here."

I hoped it was our way home, but I didn't share my doubts with her. Kiril halted before the doors and waited for everyone to gather around him. Now that we were closer, I could see that the entrance consisted of two massive doors, made of ship's metal, hinged so they opened inward. No stone cladding disguised them, and no decoration or handle adorned them. Even three thousand years after their creation, they hung so perfectly that I could barely distinguish the seam where they joined at the center.

Kiril placed his palms flat on the mighty doors and then stood back, his arms outstretched to either side. To normal eyes, he might be praying, or casting a silent spell of invocation. I, however, saw multicolored bands of light stretching from his fingertips to the four corners of the doorway. The doors gleamed, as if struck by a sudden ray of sunshine. They parted at the seam and swung noiselessly inward.

I cast a quick glance at Ashe, who gave me a knowing look in return. If the king could see the lights, I reasoned, the invocation that opened the doors was a form of magery—something that could be learned by adepts like Ashe. And *that* meant that Kiril's talk of needing a hierophant for access was sheer bluff. It also meant that Kiril himself was a hypocrite: He used the very magic he claimed was heresy.

Kiril strode boldly into the temple and stepped to the side, one arm open in invitation for us to follow. Ashe took Ariel's arm and I kept hold of Mint's as we crossed the threshold. I shot a question in mind-speech to Ashe: *Don't you find it odd that Kiril resorted to magic to open the doors?*

I've noticed that priests often arrogate privileges to themselves that they deny to others, Ashe thought back, his mental tone wry.

No, not that. Why would a technological stronghold built by Justian require magic? Wouldn't you expect a lock and key, or some other mechanical mechanism?

For all my magery, I don't know what magic is. I can't perform miracles. I'm not like you, Maran, or the muria. I only have heightened perception and mind-speech. Perhaps the ancients could build doors that respond to a specific sequence of thoughts. A non-mechanical kind of key.

Possibly, I replied. *Do you think Kiril will tell us?*

Ashe snorted aloud, causing Ariel to look at him quizzically and making Kiril scowl. Ashe quickly turned the snort into a kind of cough and kept his face impassive. *Let us see,* he thought to me.

But please keep the mind-speech to a minimum; it gives me a headache.

Now that we were inside the temple, my eyes revealed what had eluded my percipience. No building whose bones were made of ship's metal required interior columns for support, regardless of the high vaulted roof; the entire windowless interior was one gigantic room. The flooring of highly polished rose-hued marble lay atop the ship's metal underneath. Yellow-white light emanated directly from the walls and ceiling, casting a strong but directionless luster throughout the room, illuminating everything without glare. It was very cold inside the chamber.

A small altar, encased in glass, occupied the center; the remainder of the internal space was nothing but row after row of tall bookcases. The shelves were of ship's metal, and the books themselves were very strange—only flat, apparently solid rectangular plates, with markings where a book's spine would be. I picked one up, turning it this way and that, and almost dropped it in surprise. The plate, less than half-inch thick while on the shelf, quickly expanded into a full-sized book, replete with hundreds of leaf-thin metallic pages inside. I suspected my body heat had activated it. I marveled yet again at the technology of the ancients, and then started to estimate the size of the library. Each bookcase had ten shelves, and reached from the floor to well over my head. At ten thousand books per case, times the hundreds of cases, this was certainly the largest repository of writing on Sundering. I set the book down on the cold marble floor and squatted, observing it curiously until it resumed its former size. Then I put it back where I had found it. Ashe watched my experiment with interest, but didn't touch any of the books himself.

Kiril let us wander for a moment, and then called us to the altar. "Here rests the Book of the Ship," he said reverently. "As I believe you already know, the original was lost, some say purposefully destroyed, but the first monks reconstructed much from the fragments that remained. A vacuum protects the fragile paper and binding. We do not open the casing. Inerrant copies are available for the hierophants' study—and, as of today, for your perusal."

I gestured at the hundreds of thousands of books on the shelves surrounding us. "Why aren't these volumes protected, too?"

"The other books are originals, not copies. They came with the starships, likely official manuals or remnants of the crew's private libraries. As far as we can determine, they are indestructible. We have lost the art of their making. Fire, water, insects, and age do not affect them. They expand when handled, then resume their compact shape a few minutes after being put down. They are not ship's metal, but rather some kind of flexible material that behaves much like paper, save for being imperishable. Thus, no protection is required."

Ashe reached out a hand toward a book, but then paused. "May I examine one?" he asked.

"By all means," said Kiril. I didn't like the way he said it, or the expression on his face. He seemed far too haughty, too self-satisfied for a man who had just yielded the monks' most valuable secrets.

Ashe took down the book, warmed it between his palms, and then opened it. We all crowded around to look at it with him. Only the hierophant did not move.

After several moments of tense silence, Ashe said, "I don't understand. Grey, what do you make of it?"

"It is another language," I said, "one I have never encountered."

"Lady Ariel?" asked Ashe.

"I cannot read the markings, sire," she replied.

"Holy One," said Ashe sharply. "Are all the books like this one?"

"Yes, sire."

"Do you know the language?"

"No, sire. The art of reading the books has been lost."

I felt a sinking sensation. "What of the Book of the Ship?"

"We have oral tradition, and Vastil translated several ancient portions of the copies kept at the monastery. No elf has ever set foot in this building, or even expressed interest. Of the translated parts, some comprise the stories memorized by the acolytes. Docents and itinerant monks teach simplified versions of those stories to the public. The restricted sections, such as Captain Leonais's own words, and the logs from his officers, along with additions and commentary by abbots and abbesses, remain reserved for the hierophants. Translations accompany the copies we use for study. The majority of the Book remains indecipherable. This is why I said that only the first of the records would be revealed today."

"Are you saying these books are in some unknown muria language?" asked Ashe. "I thought they were the records from the Second Colony."

"Sire, the language is our own, but the nature of language itself is to change over time," said Kiril, tucking his hands into his robes again. "Over a very *long* period, the changes add up. If you look closely, you will undoubtedly see some lettering that resembles modern writing, but even the sounds associated with those letters have changed."

I tried to keep my anger under control. "You should have been copying and translating continuously," I said, "notating the changing meanings as they occurred. Now, after three thousand years, it's too late."

"Perhaps that would have been wise," said Kiril, his expression still intolerably complacent. "Had we been so commanded, we would have done that very thing. The first monks saw no need, and the orders handed down to their successors were simply to preserve things unchanged. You cannot blame us for lack of foresight by those three thousand years dead."

"The devil I can't!" I snarled. "All along, you claimed to preserve the ancient knowledge, but you're nothing but frauds. You barely know more than illiterate peasants do. You're the custodians of nothing."

"Grey," said Kiril patiently, as if explaining to a child. "Long ago, you asked if we had the knowledge you seek. I never said we did. I only told you that the questions were forbidden."

May I kill him now? I shot in mind-speech to Ashe. *The insult to you is outrageous. They have lied to uncounted generations.*

Wait, Ashe thought back. *I still have questions.*

"But the muria could provide translations?" he asked Kiril.

"They are effectively immortal," I reminded him. "No doubt they *remember* the older forms of speech. Translation would be a trivial task."

Kiril said, "We only have Vastil's work, not explanations. Likely, Grey is correct, but we do not know for sure."

"If they remember," said Lady Ariel softly, "then they could translate the rest. How may they be persuaded to help us?"

"They cannot, my lady," said Kiril. "*Lord* Grey," he continued, nearly choking on the honorific, "has sent the muria from Leonais, and the muria do not permit the king to visit Avermorn. Grey asked no permission before driving his unholy bargain to change the balance of power on Sundering. In his highly limited wisdom, *he* chose to hide the contents of this reliquary from all humans. Ask of him, not us. We no longer have access to Vastil or his memories."

"What the devil are you playing at?" I demanded. "Why did you need me present for this farce?" The god-winds stirred fretfully, swirling through the massive doors. I released Mint's arm and gathered a handful of wind, enraged, ready to eviscerate the hierophant.

"Yes, Holy One," agreed Ashe, his tone dangerously sharp. "Why insist on his presence? Indeed, why bother bringing us here today at all? You could have just told us the records were inaccessible."

Kiril remained calm. If he could perceive the rising godwinds, he gave no sign. If the king's anger—or mine—bothered him, he concealed that, also. "Sire," he said to Ashe, "we are here by your own command. You said we were to visit the monument, not I. As to Grey's presence, we thought it best to have the proper object for your anger at hand. You are disappointed and unhappy, as we knew you would be. His punishment, like his crime, should be secular, not ecclesiastical. Or would you prefer that he make good on his threat to topple the starships?"

"You're a smug bastard, aren't you?" I asked. "I can't believe I ever felt sympathy for you, or believed you understood holiness. Have you always been such an ass?"

"Hold, both of you," said Ashe. "I thought I would enjoy hearing you quarrel, but only because I believed there would be a reward at the end of all the bickering. Instead, I am bitterly disappointed. Holy One, I am taking this book with me—"

"Sire, it is forbidden!"

"—regardless of your rules. Perhaps my scholars can decipher it. I will also take the translated version of the Book of the Ship you proffered. I am minded to read Captain Leonais's own words, and those of his officers. Perhaps they will shed some light on this 'devoir' you have so righteously observed."

Kiril started to object, but Ashe held up one hand to forestall him. Although Ashe was not wearing his crown, he suddenly stood straighter, all king, regnant and undeniable. "As of this moment," he said coldly, "I dissolve your order and revoke your authority. The docents and itinerants may give lectures at Landing, tend to the ill, and continue your humanitarian efforts.

But all initiates, from acolyte to hierophant, must remove their chains of office and go barefoot, on pain of death. I have spoken."

Kiril stiffened and then relaxed. Otherwise, he did not react at all. A very long silence followed the king's speech, and then Ariel said meekly, "Sire, consider the commoners. They revere the monks, and won't understand the reasons for your commands. Can you not offer some mercy? I ask not for myself, or for the Holy Ones, but for your subjects."

Ashe smiled fondly at her. "Very well. The priests may go shod. But they must be banished from this place, and prevented from wielding either spiritual or secular influence. The King's Guard will take over their duties."

Kiril eyed the king carefully, his hands still tucked into his robes. "King Ashe," he said thoughtfully, "you have true Captain's Blood, and your authority is unquestioned. The line of kings is as ancient and honorable as the lineage of the monks themselves. But you cannot even open the doors to this temple. How will you enforce your edict?"

Grey? asked Ashe in mind-speech. *Time for something dramatic?*

My hands were already full of the god-winds, and I was so angry at Kiril that I could barely think, let alone speak. Without moving or even changing expression, I let the god-winds rage. With a flick of thought, I brought the entire dolmen to life. Multicolored bands of light filled the air outside, arching high into the sky to connect with every other dolmen on Leonais. Only Kiril, Ashe, and I could perceive them, but no one else needed to know what I had done. At the same time, for the less percipient, a storm of my desiring formed over the temple itself, dumping torrents of rain. Lightning struck the roof a score of times, and the thunder made the ship's metal of the building screech in protest. Using winds from my hand, I slammed the mighty temple doors shut. Then, reaching out to the bands of light I had awakened outside, I forced them open again. Three times, the doors clanged closed and reopened. Rainwater from outside the temple flooded across the threshold. The thunder deafened us all.

The lightning broke small pieces of the temple's stone cladding to rubble, but I reined in my power so the building itself remained undamaged.

Enough? I asked Ashe in mind-speech.

Was that the Sleeper? he asked in alarm.

No, just me. I'm angry.

Turn it off, please. I think we're done here for today.

I released the winds, but I could not as easily dismiss the storm itself. Through the open doors, we saw the tremendous downpour dwindle from a raging thunderstorm to a normal autumnal torrent. Even that slacked off after a few minutes, although the precipitation did not stop completely. Enough rain had sloshed across the doorway that we stood ankle-deep in cold water.

For the first time since I'd met him, Kiril lost his composure. The blood drained from his face, and his self-righteous expression changed to fear. With the last handful of god-winds, I tore the chains of office from around his neck and flung them out the doors.

Nice touch, said Ashe in mind-speech. I could feel his anger still boiling internally. I breached protocol a bit to see what other actions he was contemplating, but he was still so full of unbridled rage that nothing coherent emerged.

Be cautious, I thought back. *He may be goading you to act rashly. Kiril is petty, but he isn't stupid. He had to have known how you would react. He played us both for fools today.*

I'm still the king, thought Ashe hotly.

Not if the commoners rise up on the side of the monks. Please be careful.

"Grey," said Ashe aloud. "I'll deal with the situation here. You have other errands. It's best you be about your business."

I could recognize a dismissal when it was that blatant. I turned to Mint, who had drawn back from me, and gestured for her to take my arm. "Shall we go?" I asked, finding my voice surprisingly normal. I couldn't tell for sure, because my right ear still rang with the echoes of thunder.

She picked a book off a shelf at random before clasping my arm. "May I have this?" she asked.

Ashe nodded, and I shrugged, starting to pick through the ribbons of light for one that would lead us to Maran's valley. "A souvenir?" I asked. "You certainly deserve one. But wait one second."

I found the same thick orange band we'd used this morning. I wrapped the end around my fingers and tugged gently. The doorway opened, and I stuck my head through to verify that the other side showed the grassless circle of the dolmen in Maran's valley. Satisfied, I pulled my head back and let the doorway close, but kept hold of the orange ribbon. We would need it later.

"Grey—" began Mint.

"Just another second, please. This is difficult." I pawed through the thousands of strands, trying to identify one that would take us to Tessa. Eventually, I found a purple streamer, spiraled and thin. It felt right, but there was only one way to know.

"Grey—" said Mint again, but the concentration required to hold two strands simultaneously didn't give me time to listen. At length, I had control of both ribbons, and I transferred them to my withered left arm, mentally tying a knot to hold them in place. I felt like a balloon tethered to two strings pulling in opposite directions. The sensation was vaguely disturbing.

"Almost done," I said to Mint. To the others, I said, "Good-bye for now!" and moved Mint's hand to my shoulder. With the forefinger of my good hand, I twanged the purple streamer. With a single step forward, Mint and I left the temple and appeared by the broken-down shed in Tessa's backyard. I thought for a moment that I felt another mind watching me, but the sensation passed. Who but Ashe could have ridden in thought beside me to witness our passage?

Mint pulled at my sleeve to get my attention. Except for the two bands of light I needed to hold, I quelled my awareness of the dolmen network to see what she wanted. "Sorry," I said. "I was distracted."

"Grey," said Mint, undisturbed by our sudden translocation. "I don't want the book as a souvenir. I want it because I can read the ancient writing. I thought Lady Maran would like to read it, too."

"If you can read that," I said wonderingly, "why didn't you say something at the temple?"

"No one asked me."

Chapter Five

"That's a hell of a thing to keep to yourself," I said. "How can you possibly read a language that's been dead for three thousand years?"

"The lady made me so," said Mint humbly. "I don't pretend to understand how it works. I'm only a homunculus, after all. I believe, however, that when Lady Maran makes us, she gives us language the same way she imparts the skills and knowledge needed for our duties."

I led Mint through the yard toward the house. "Do all the golems—pardon, homunculi—have the same language abilities?"

"I wouldn't know, sir."

"None of that. Keep calling me Grey. This is your day for wonders. Enjoy it. But tell me this—how could Maran know an ancient language?"

"I don't know," she said, "but perhaps the language isn't ancient for her."

"What do you mean?"

"You should ask her. Hasq says we are not to answer questions about the lady's past."

We pushed through the weeds at the back of the house, rounded the corner, and reached the front porch. I knocked on the door and waited. I didn't like Mint's answer or its implications, because Maran herself had been evasive about her age. Could Qol have possibly made her so long ago that the book's language was still fresh for her? Maran appeared to be middle-aged, perhaps a bit younger. I myself looked to be in my thirties, although I had walked the world fewer than two years since waking up in the high desert. Had Qol made her immortal, a fixed age forever? What kind of woman had I married?

I knew better than to query Mint for more details; it had obviously discomfited her to say as much as she had. Instead, while waiting for Tessa to respond to my knock, I asked, "What's the name of the book?"

"*The Principia*, by someone named Newton. At least that's what's on the spine."

"Who the devil is Newton? What's the book about?"

Mint flipped through several pages. "I can't tell you, Grey. I can read the words, but they don't make any sense to me, and there are many drawings and equations. It has something to do with mathematics."

"A starship manual?" I asked.

"It has the feel of something older, because it's written in one language on the left hand pages, and another on the right. It seems like a keepsake from someone's private library."

I was about to ask her more, but the door creaked open, and a small head poked out. Torrey, nearing ten years old, looked mostly unchanged to my eyes. He was perhaps a bit taller than on my last visit, but not by much. He had let his hair grow out, and now wore it braided like mine, although since his hair was much thicker and curlier than my own, his braids were more like thick strings than fine tresses.

"Grey!" he exclaimed happily, leaping onto the porch and

throwing his arms around me. "Grandma will be so happy. Did the baby get born? Where's Maran? Who's this lady? Are you hungry? Do you want to see Zoxo? Did you bring a unicorn? How long can you stay? Why do both of you have wet feet?"

"Whoa," I said, hugging him hard, then pushing him gently back. "We can stay for tea, and my limit for questions is one at a time. This is Lady Mint. Perhaps we should go inside and greet your grandmother."

"She's resting. She sleeps a lot. Come in, come in. I'll go wake her up."

Mint and I sat at the small wooden table just outside the kitchen while Torrey disappeared into the back of the house to rouse Tessa. Mint eyed me speculatively. "Is that the boy with your ear?" she asked.

I fingered the nubbin where my left ear had been. Most days, I forgot about it, since I could hear perfectly well with my right. "Yes, Torrey has my left ear. He's quite proud of it. But don't mention Owen. Tessa is still grieving."

"Owen is the boy who died in the dungeon," said Mint. "I've heard the lady mention him."

"He was one of the bravest boys I've ever known," I said. "He tried to fight an Amrhyn sorcerer using only his bare hands."

"So did I!" said Torrey, popping back into the room with the kind of happy, boundless energy only youngsters enjoy. "Grandma is on her way. I'll start boiling the water."

He busied himself in the kitchen, making far more noise than stoking a fire and putting a kettle on the stove should decently cause. Crockery rattled, pots clanged, cutlery jangled. "Where's Zoxo?" I called over the racket.

"Sulking," he called back, "but she'll show up. She got out of her cage again."

"Grey?" came a familiar and beloved voice. "It's been over four months."

I immediately stood up, and Mint followed my lead. "I'm sorry, Tessa, but Maran didn't want to travel during the last half of her pregnancy. This is one of Maran's people, Lady Mint."

Tessa emerged from a back room, her gait unsteady, but her smile of greeting undimmed. She looked older than I remembered, until I realized she had stopped dyeing her hair. The grey strands, as thick as Torrey's, were tied up in a bun, and she wore a simple house dress and slippers.

"I'm pleased to meet you, ma'am," said Mint.

"Likewise," said Tessa. I moved to help her into a chair, dismayed to find her wobbly on her feet. During my previous visits, she had seemed invincible. I quickly surveyed her legs from the inside out, but perceived no disease or infirmity other than old age and arthritis in her hips.

"Thank you," she said as I got her settled. Her voice had lost none of its power, for she raised it over Torrey's clatter and called, "Bring our guests tea and the rest of that lemon cake."

"Grandma!" Torrey protested.

"I know it's your favorite, but guests come first. I can always make more another day."

Torrey sighed, a long, drawn-out affair meant for effect. I couldn't help but grin, and I saw Tessa's eyes twinkle.

"First, the messages," I said. "The king sends his regards, and asks if you need anything."

"My youth, perhaps," said Tessa, "but I doubt the king can provide that. We're grateful enough for the money he sends. It's sufficient for our immediate needs, with plenty left over to pay Torrey's tuition at school in town. I reckon the king has a hand there, too, because our tiny village suddenly has five new teachers, all with fancy titles."

"Torrey attends school now?" I asked curiously. For most of my life, I hadn't known anyone but the poor folk of cot and hold, whose highest conception of education was a good apprenticeship.

The thought of the bouncy, irrepressible youngster with his head bent over books in formal study seemed somehow incongruous. "Does he enjoy it?"

"He endures it," said Tessa, with a gleam of satisfaction in her eyes. "Someday, he'll appreciate it, too. But surely you have other messages?"

I nodded. "Aiden was born nearly two weeks ago. Maran found the delivery difficult, but both mother and child are doing well. She promises to visit herself when the child is old enough to travel."

"How much did he weigh? How long was he at birth? Tell me everything."

I blinked. Did women stretch babies to determine length? I had no idea. "Um, Maran says to tell you he's healthy and happy, and that he can recognize our voices already. He sleeps a lot."

"That's good. Was he born with hair? What color are his eyes?"

"Hair, yes; a few black strands. Maran says it will turn blond eventually. His eyes were a kind of muddy blue at birth. Maran says they'll turn green to match her own. I don't know how long any of that takes."

"You're the father, you should know these things."

"Well, he seems to nurse all the time. I think that's a good sign. He's starting to look fat to me."

Tessa searched my eyes for a moment, then sighed and looked to Mint. "Lady Mint, what is he leaving out?"

"Not much, ma'am," said Mint. "Aiden's color was good. Reflexes and muscle tone were normal for a full-term birth. No airway obstructions, normal heart rate. He's already lost the posturing of a newborn, and moves all his limbs appropriately for his age. He has a firm grip and a very good pair of lungs. He cries less than most babies, but Lady Maran says that's because she can anticipate his needs. He's happy and aware of his environment. It won't be long before he can focus his eyes better."

"Thank you, Lady Mint."

"Just Mint, ma'am. I'm not much of a lady."

"Then you must call me Tessa. You're a fetching young thing. I'd like to think I had half your beauty at your age. Where in the world did Maran find someone so competent to help out?"

"Mint has been with us for a couple of months," I put in. "She was owed a day off, so Maran sent her with me today." Tessa didn't need to know that Mint was a golem. Her only experience with homunculi was during the battle in the dungeon where she had lost Owen. I saw no reason to bring up those memories.

Tessa swung her gaze back and forth between us for several moments. I could tell she was on the verge of asking for more information. Then she took a deep breath and moved on. "Tell me the rest of the messages, Grey."

"That's it, I think. The king and I visited with a hierophant today. I think I'm developing a proper friendship with Ashe—at least, that's what Maran says. I don't have enough experience to judge."

"My hips may be going, but my brain is still sharp, young man," she said tartly.

"Pardon?"

"Your eyes, Grey, your *eyes*. How did you get them back?"

Torrey popped his face around the divider separating us from the kitchen and stared at me, his mouth wide open. "You got your eyes back? How did I miss *that?* Can you see now?"

"Oh." I had honestly forgotten. "It's a long story, most of which I don't understand yet. A pair of muria children decided I needed them. And," I added for Torrey's benefit, "I could see without them, you know. Just as I can still hear through your ear."

"You don't listen, do you?" He looked simultaneously worried and embarrassed.

"Of course not," I assured him. "Now get back to the kitchen and let your elders talk."

He mumbled something to himself as he disappeared, and I laughed harder than I had for a very long time, gales of clean mirth that blew through me like fresh air immediately after a spring rain.

"Proof!" he called from the other room, and I had to laugh again.

Tessa cocked her head sideways, a slight wrinkle in her brow. "What did he say?" she asked.

I just shook my head, still chuckling. "Nothing important," I said at last. "He's a very clever boy, and he deserves his privacy. But to answer your earlier question more fully—yes, I can see like others now. It hasn't diminished my ability to see at a distance, or perceive things normally hidden. Think of it as a restoration, not a diminution."

"As you will," said Tessa, "but I think congratulations are in order nonetheless." She raised her voice. "Torrey, how long does it take to boil water?"

"I'm trying to find clean cups. Be there in a second, Grandma."

We three adults shared a brief smile. The concept of youth, I realized, was completely different for each of us. For Tessa, it was a period of her life sixty years gone. For Mint, it was just a concept, not a set of memories. I shared far more in common with Mint than with Tessa, although I thought of my youth as the time before power woke in me, when I lived innocently with Brawley's family in the gentle folds of Wyland valley. Brawley's son Drust, in so many ways reminiscent of Torrey, had given me the name Grey.

Tessa interrupted my reverie by asking, "And the last message?"

I knew what she meant, but had been avoiding the subject. "The king's men are still searching for Lane, but with no luck so far."

"My son was not a willing soldier, you know. He was a merchant before the press gangs drafted him. If he ever had to swing a sword against the enemy . . . well, I don't think he would have fared well. He sold fruits and vegetables at the town market. He was fat and jolly, and never wished harm on anyone."

I hadn't known exactly what Torrey's father had done for a living, but Tessa was almost certainly correct about the outcome. Unskilled foot soldiers, especially those drafted unwillingly, were likely to fall in their first battle. "There's still hope, Tessa," I said kindly. "So many fighters are still missing, many of them simply displaced. Lane may yet return to you. If it is within the king's power, you will be reunited with your son."

Torrey emerged from behind the divider, carefully balancing a tray overburdened with four teacups, four small plates, a steaming pot, and a large plate stacked with square-cut lemon cakes. "Are you talking about my father?" he asked.

"Yes," I said, "but there's no news yet. The king himself has commanded his Guard to search. He could be anywhere on the eastern seaboard. The companies formed and re-formed, and some went as far north as Halmar-by-the-Sea, while others went down to Jappa. The king hasn't given up hope, so neither should you."

"Is this the same King's Guard that watches over our house?" asked Tessa. "They failed to keep a dog from mauling one of our chickens. How good can they be?"

"You weren't supposed to know your house is guarded," I said. "The king felt better knowing someone was watching. And no, not the same ones. His officers are the ones searching for Lane. The ones here are concerned with thieves or brigands, not dogs or chickens."

"I'm old, not blind. They sit on horses at the tops of hills, and gallop away if they catch me watching them. They might as well be waving flags to announce themselves."

"I suspect," I said slowly, "that they are deliberately visible. It tells undesirables to keep moving. They want to be seen—but by others, not by you."

Tessa huffed. "Silly plan."

"Before you put down that tray," said Mint suddenly, "may we move to the porch? I'm finding it very hot in here."

"You heard the lady," said Tessa. "Set things up outside."

Torrey, with the tray already halfway to the table top, shrugged, nearly upsetting the tray and all its contents. He quickly recovered with skills that would do an acrobat credit, and backed out the front door to arrange things.

I looked at Mint curiously. She couldn't possibly feel overheated; Maran had made her without the ability to sense temperature. I had expected her to decline the tea and cakes with some polite excuse, just as she had refrained from eating or drinking with the king. She still clutched the book she had liberated from Kiril's reliquary, but pulled off her white lace gloves and loosened the ties in the front of her bodice. I had no way to communicate with her privately, and I didn't want to embarrass her in front of Tessa, so I stood, offering my good arm to help her rise. Once she was on her feet, I did the same for Tessa.

We reseated ourselves outside on the porch bench, and Torrey started distributing plates and cups. Mint thanked Torrey, but declined, saying she wasn't hungry. Tessa asked if she preferred something different, and I decided it was time for a distraction.

"I almost forgot," I said. "There's more news. The king has become engaged to Lady Ariel of Draycott. They plan the wedding for midwinter, at Jappa. You and Torrey are invited as honored guests." I made a mental note to remind Ashe I was making promises on his behalf. "Also, a man called Brand may stop by from time to time. He's a courier, a little shorter than I am, with curly brown hair. He'll be wearing livery. Maran thought he could substitute for our lack of regular visits by taking letters back and forth."

Torrey sat on the porch railing, legs dangling, somehow managing to balance his plate on one thigh while sipping tea and munching the lemon cake simultaneously. Tessa and I took the more dignified approach of setting our teacups on the bench and concentrating only on our plates. My left arm, normally numb, was starting to ache from having the two invisible strands pulling at it. I did my best to ignore it, and used my good hand to nibble at Tessa's lemon cake.

Tessa said, "I don't travel well these days, and midwinter seems especially hard. Will the king mind if we don't attend?"

"I think he'll understand," I said.

Torrey burst out, "Even if Grandma stays home, I could go with you and Maran. I'd like to see a royal wedding. And it would be nice to see Owen laid out in the Tomb of Kings. We haven't been to Jappa since—" He stopped abruptly, looking guiltily at his grandmother. "I'm sorry," he whispered miserably.

"Don't mind me," said Tessa, brushing a tear away. She very deliberately set her plate on the bench. She hadn't touched her tea, and I didn't think she would. Her face crumbled into a map of creases for a moment, and then she forced herself to relax her features. One by one, the wrinkles smoothed out, and she attempted a wan smile. "First Lane, then Owen. It catches up with me sometimes. Please don't stare."

Mint reached out and took Tessa's hand. "I'm very sorry for your loss," she said, with genuine sympathy in her voice. "It must be very hard for you. How may I help?"

"You're very kind," said Tessa, "but there's nothing to be done. If one lives long enough, loss is inevitable. Accepting it is hard, though, especially when I'm overtired."

"We shouldn't have woken you from your nap," I said. "We didn't think."

"Don't be ridiculous. What else do I wake for, save Torrey's needs and your visits? Mint, would you care to take a walk with my grandson? He can find his lizard and tell you all about it."

"I'm tired myself," Mint answered. "I'm happy to sit here with you."

Again, I looked sharply at Mint. Fatigue was not something Maran had built into her repertoire of behaviors. Perhaps she was just being kind. But no, it was more than that. It *had* been a long day, full of new things, new people. She was, underneath her fine gown, just a golem housemaid. I realized it was entirely possible I had worn her out by taking her through the dolmens, making her witness my altercation with Kiril, letting her observe the king's wrath. I had ignored Hasq's warning and treated Mint as a human woman. She wasn't built for the kind of stress I had imposed.

"Are you ill? Do we need to go home?" I asked, giving her an excuse to retreat to the safety and familiarity of Maran's valley if she wanted.

"No, I'm fine," she said. "I'm enjoying meeting all of your friends."

Tessa said, "Everyone except Torrey is probably tired. Mint, I would like a few minutes alone with Grey."

"Of course," said Mint immediately. She stood up and reached out a hand to Torrey. "Shall we find your pet?"

"Zoxo is probably hiding in the grass behind the house. She likes the insects there." He hopped off the railing, casually catching his falling plate before it hit the floor, and took Mint's proffered hand. "Come on, I'll show you. She doesn't do tricks, but she blinks a lot. You'll like her, but she bites sometimes, so you have to handle her carefully."

Tessa and I waited in silence until the other two disappeared around the corner of the house. "Mint *is* tired," I said, "and we should probably go soon. What can I do for you?"

"I want you to take Torrey."

"I don't know if Maran will be up for traveling with a newborn at midwinter, but if we go to the wedding, the king will provide a carriage. I'm sure there will be room for Torrey, too. Maran and I both love him."

"I know, but that isn't what I meant."

I didn't like her tone. Her voice had a kind of finality to it, a resignation that was unlike the Tessa I knew and loved.

"When I'm gone," she went on relentlessly, "I need to know he'll have a good home. With luck, he'll be grown by then and can take care of himself. But just in case. . . ."

"Don't talk like that, Tessa. You aren't *that* old."

"I'm seventy-five, and moving slower every day. It's not just my hips that pain me." She paused, examining my face. "Don't look at me like that. I'm not planning to die tomorrow. But simple prudence dictates that I make arrangements in advance. I want to know you'll take Torrey in, treat him as your own son, in case something happens to me. Promise me."

"The king has healers," I said. "They can help with your hips. I've examined you myself, and the only problem I see is arthritis. Your heart is strong."

"My heart is broken," she said simply.

I sat in silence for a minute, respecting her grief. Then I said, "I cannot change the past, and I don't know how to heal your grief. But I think it's something one learns to live with. Nothing will ever be the same, but you have survived other griefs, and you will survive this one. Please, no more talk of dying."

"Nevertheless, promise me."

"Of course Maran and I will take care of Torrey. You didn't need to ask. For that matter, if you want to move to our valley, you and Torrey—even Zoxo—are welcome to live with us. It would be good for Aiden to have a grandmother, and for Torrey to have a little brother."

Tessa sighed, picked up her cold teacup, rotated it a few times between her palms, and put it back down without drinking. Her eyes wandered across the porch, out into the fields where her son had once raised produce for the market. She sighed again, and looked back at me. "It's not that simple, Grey. I've lived most of my life in this house. I don't want to move. When I finally die— someday—I want it to happen in my own bed."

"Then I promise to visit more often. You have many years left to make lemon cakes for us. You want to hold Aiden. You want to watch Torrey become a man. There are a thousand things left to do."

"Yes, of course, and I plan to do them. I can live more easily now that I have your promise."

"You have it. Unconditionally."

She patted my good hand. "I think your friend is tired of hunting for Zoxo. No one but Torrey would put up with that lizard. And I can see you're in pain today, too. Your left arm, yes?"

I couldn't think of any way to explain it to her, and there wasn't a need. I just said, "You amaze me. In the midst of your own grief, you can tell that my arm hurts. Yes, it aches sometimes, and today is one of those days. It rained up north when we were with the king."

"Then you should take your friend and go home. She's one of Maran's golems, isn't she?"

"How could you tell?"

"She can't dissemble. She didn't eat because she couldn't, not because she wasn't hungry. It's why I didn't mind asking her to walk with Torrey. But, Grey, she *is* tired out."

"I know," I said. "I overdid our activity today."

"You like her—as a person."

"She is a person. Just a different sort. I'm learning that all the homunculi are people. They have feelings and desires, even fears. I suspect some of them are wiser than I am. Maran has always said that she gives the semblance of life, not life itself, but spending time with the golems has made me reevaluate my own experiences."

"Tell me."

I had told her and Torrey my life story on the way back from the war, so she was one of the few humans with whom I could speak freely. "Well," I said, "you remember that Qol fashioned both Maran and me with different gifts, different mindsets, and different purposes. Qol once drilled me, with my life in the balance, about what it means to be human. I'm wondering now if I would have answered differently had I understood how little I differ from Maran's homunculi. We are all manufactured beings, in one way or another. Your parents made you; you made Lane; Qol made us; Vastil made Gaheris; and Maran makes golems. Why are you and I human while the homunculi are not? What spark do they lack? The courier I mentioned, Brand, is so humanlike that no one without special abilities can tell he's a golem. Maran is really a miracle."

Tessa nodded. "Treasure her, then, and your son, too. Now go. We've talked too long as it is, and I know you too well. If I encourage you, you'll still be debating, doubting, and second-guessing yourself until midnight, even if I say nothing. You think too much, Grey, especially about questions you can't resolve. Trust in your humanity; I have no doubt of it. You're fully human, no matter what else you may be."

"Tessa—" I broke off, unsure of what to say. "I'm glad you're in our lives. Thank you for making Mint feel welcome." I leaned over and kissed her cheek gently.

"Good-bye," she said.

"For now," I replied. I pulled myself to my feet, and limped around the back of the house to find Torrey and Mint. They were knee-deep in weeds beside the old shed, poking around with sticks.

―――――

"We haven't found the lizard," Mint told me, "but not for want of trying."

"Zoxo is still sulking," said Torrey. "What did Grandma say about going to the wedding?"

"If Maran and I go, you may go with us."

"That's good," he said seriously. "Did Grandma talk about Owen?"

"Only a little. Don't worry about it. Grief takes time."

"I miss him, too."

"I know. So do I. But we have to leave now."

Torrey's face fell. "I thought you would stay for dinner, and tell me about your unicorn and that cut on your cheek and your time with the king."

"I can tell you one thing. The night Aiden was born, a hundred unicorns came to the valley and reared."

"That's amazing!"

"Exactly what I thought. Mint, do you have the book? Are you ready to go?"

"More than ready, Grey. This has been the most astonishing day of my life. I can't believe all the things I've seen and done."

"Put your hand on my shoulder," I said to her. To Torrey, I said, "Watch this! You may see something even more amazing."

"Wait—I found Zoxo. She's on your cloak. She must like you."

He transferred the lizard to his own shoulder, and insisted that Mint take time to admire it. Then he looked back at my cloak, and said, "Eww, gross. She got skoda on you." He brushed the lizard feces away and said, "Good as new. What kind of amazing thing are you going to show me?"

"Watch," I told him. I untied the knot holding the two strands of light together on my left arm and wound them around separate fingers of my right hand. The sudden release of pressure felt wonderful. "This will be fast," I warned Mint. "I'm going to try something new. Don't let go of my shoulder, and remember to step when I do."

"I'm ready."

I tugged gently at the spiraled purple ribbon, then immediately plucked the thick orange one. "Now!" Mint and I took one step, and we flew down the track of the purple ribbon, instantly transferring to the orange. We didn't even have a chance to glimpse the dolmen at Landing. In the space of one heartbeat, we were back in Maran's valley. I let the doorways close, and released the ribbons with a sigh of relief. Holding them under tension the entire time we were with Tessa had exhausted me, but at the same time, I was jubilant. It worked! I could travel two strands in sequence. This opened possibilities I had never dreamed of. Could I do the same with several strands? A dozen?

Mint suddenly swayed against me and would have fallen if I hadn't caught her. "Mint?" I said, easing her gently to the barren ground. "Was that too much for you?"

"No," she said weakly. "It wasn't enough. I could never have imagined a day like today. Thank you for sharing it with me."

"Can you walk back to the manor? I can carry you."

"Just let me rest a minute. I need to know something."

"Anything."

"What did Torrey say that made you laugh so hard? I wanted to join in, but that wasn't something you shared."

It couldn't hurt to tell Mint. "I told him to let his elders talk, and he muttered under his breath that he was at least seven years my senior."

"How can that be?"

"I've only been alive for two years. He's nine, going on ten."

"I've only been alive for two months," she said, her voice fading. "But now that I think about it, I wasn't really alive until today."

"There will be other days," I said. I stooped beside her, ignoring the pain in my bad leg, and cradled her head with my good arm. "I'll be more careful in the future. I didn't know all the excitement and traveling would tire you like this."

Mint let the book slide from her grasp. "No more days. Grey, hold me."

"I am holding you."

"I can't feel you," she whispered. "I can't feel anything now. Thank you for today. It was splendid. *I* was splendid."

"You were indeed. Just rest. I'll carry you to the manor house." I tried to gather her up, but she was already gone. Twigs, moss, wet leaves, and rags fell through my fingers. A blue moth fluttered up, and I watched until it had flown out of sight. Mint's empty gown lay on the ground beside the book.

I picked both up, and limped back to the manor. Hasq was waiting inside the door, as usual. I handed him the gown. "It's probably ruined," I said, "but she won't need it again anyway."

"I did try to warn you, sir," said the majordomo.

"Good for you. Show some sympathy." I grabbed him by the collar and shook him. "She was a *person*, damn you!" I shouted. When he didn't react, I let go of him, suddenly so weary I could hardly stand.

"She was, sir. And now she is not. Brevity does not imply lack of quality. Will you see the lady tonight, or shall I send supper to your rooms?"

"Just leave me alone. Give this book to Maran. Tell her Mint got it for her. And the next time you feel inclined to lecture me on philosophy, keep your damned mouth shut."

"Good night, sir," he said very softly.

Chapter Six

Aiden awakened predawn, and I, who had not slept all night, responded to his cries almost as quickly as the nursemaids did. All he needed was changing and some attention, so I dismissed the nursemaids and told them to let Maran sleep in.

A wooden rocking chair in a quiet corner of the front parlor had become my favorite place to spend time alone with Aiden. Propping my left elbow on the arm of the chair gave me sufficient stability to use my withered arm to hold him, leaving my good arm free to play with him.

Although he couldn't focus his eyes at things more than ten or twelve inches away, he seemed to enjoy looking at me, especially if I unbound my hair and let it fall freely within reach of his hands. This forced me to keep my head bent so that, even when distracted, I could maintain eye contact within his focal distance. He was just old enough to start smiling spontaneously, and he smiled with wide unblinking eyes while I rocked him and told him stories.

It didn't matter what I said as long as I kept my tone bright; hearing language was important for his development. Being relatively unimaginative, I couldn't make up stories on the spot, and I disliked making random baby noises, so I told him about myself, my friends, and our adventures. He clutched my hair, seeming delighted just to hear my voice. This position, with my head bent over his, gave me an excellent opportunity to study his face and look for changes, although disentangling my hair was usually a painful process. For a child who could barely hold his own head up for two seconds, he had an immoderately strong grip.

This particular morning, I told him about Mint. Not wanting dark memories to overwhelm my storytelling, I related only how she had spent her last day, describing all the things she had seen and done, how her experiences had introduced her to joy and laughter for the first time. I told Aiden how much she had enjoyed talking with Lady Ariel, meeting King Ashe, sharing Tessa's home, and seeing the wildlife and trees in the valley. I described her gown and her white lace gloves, and I tried to explain how radiant her smile had been.

"The muria have the same problem you do," said Maran softly.

I prised my hair free from Aiden's clutches, and looked up.

"How long have you been listening?" I asked.

"Only a few minutes. I just woke up. The servants are starting breakfast. I feel well enough to go riding today. I need to get my abdominal muscles back in shape."

I considered her appearance. She wore riding leathers, but with a pale peach button-down blouse—presumably to make it easy to feed Aiden without having to change clothes. Her thick shock of sandy brown hair had been brushed back and tied with a ribbon that matched her blouse. She seemed as strong as the day we'd met, with nothing to indicate she'd given birth only a couple of weeks ago. "You look marvelous," I said, "all things considered."

She sat on an overstuffed armchair near my rocker. "Give me Aiden," she said.

I glanced down. "He's still smiling at me. I don't want to give him up."

"One never tires of that," she agreed. "He'll cry soon enough. He's not smiling at you; he has gas. What do you mean by 'all things considered?'"

"Well, to start, are you really three thousand years old?"

She laughed and shook her head, making the tiny bells in her earrings jingle. "What in the world gave you *that* idea?"

"Mint said you could read the ancients' writing. Did Hasq deliver the book?"

"*The Principia* by Newton? Yes, and I can read it, even if I don't understand much of it. I've never seen an odder object. It seems to change shape without any moving parts. Where did you get it, and what does that have to do with my age?"

I briefly related all that had transpired at the reliquary, dwelling chiefly on Kiril's duplicity and how bitterly disappointed Ashe and I were. It took several minutes to cover everything, but Maran paid rapt attention. I concluded by saying, "The hierophant told us that language changes over time, and has now changed enough that no human left alive can read it."

Understanding bloomed in Maran's eyes, making them sparkle. Then she sobered, and looked thoughtful for a few moments, as if trying to puzzle out the proper way to explain something difficult.

"Grey, did you go to school?" She didn't wait for my answer. "Of course you didn't. Qol created you with certain knowledge— maybe not the subjects you would have chosen to study, had you been graced with a childhood and normal education—but knowledge nonetheless. You never had to learn to read and write. He did the same for me, but our gifts are different. You can't ride a horse or swing a sword. I'm expert at both. You can control the winds, heal injuries, and perceive things at a distance; I can do none of those. I presume," she said, musing aloud, "that Qol cannot give a gift the muria do not possess themselves. It's evident that, from among all the abilities he could have granted, he chose to give us each different things. Qol chose to make you a warrior— however unwilling—while I was made for other tasks."

"So you were born able to read ancient writings?"

"I wasn't born any more than you were. My entry into the world was gentler than yours, but no less confusing at first. And yes, languages are among my gifts. In addition, I have spent many years studying in order to learn more. I enjoy languages."

"Languages, plural?"

"Did you really think there was only one? You know the muria have invented one of their own, and you told me you heard the Amrhyn sorcerers chanting in another tongue. Those are only two, plus the language we speak now. The First and Second Colonists brought many languages with them, and not just the many tongues they spoke amongst themselves."

"And you can read or speak them all?"

"I haven't encountered all of them, so I don't know. Everyone on Leonais, save for odd corners of the continent, speaks the same language now. It was different at the beginning, and even today, there are dialects that are hard to understand until you've trained your ear to them. I traveled widely in my youth, before settling down here. Haven't you browsed my library? I've been collecting books for a long time. Many of them are modern, but just as many are ancient—copies of copies of copies of books written so long ago the tongues were already considered 'dead' languages even when the *First* Colony landed. Newton wrote his *Principia Mathematica* in a language called Latin. My own copy is in French. The one you brought from Landing has Latin and Portuguese side by side. It's what scholars call an heirloom book, treasured by collectors, but not useful for its content. It was foundational at the time of its publication, but superseded by later works. I don't understand advanced mathematics, so I can't tell you much more, except that the royal library in Jappa has thousands of books written in ancient tongues. Dead languages don't suffer the ravages of change over time. Scholars have to learn them to study the classics."

"So you're *not* three thousand years old?" I asked.

"A lady does not discuss her age. But think about it, Grey. The muria have been bearing children and losing bodies to age or accident throughout their history. Their immortality is mental, not physical, because their group minds allow them to remember everything that any one of them learns. If they cannot give a gift they do not possess, they couldn't have made me to last forever. Like you, I had a beginning. And again like you, I will eventually die."

"You didn't actually answer my question," I pointed out. Just then, Aiden opened his mouth wide and began squalling. "He's hungry, I think," I said, passing him to Maran.

"Yes, he's hungry." She unbuttoned her blouse and positioned Aiden so he could suckle. "If you absolutely must know, I am significantly older than I look. My appearance doesn't seem to change as the years go by, except for more worry lines and wrinkles. Most would think I'm in my mid-forties, perhaps early fifties. Don't you *dare* say I've aged well."

I bit back my reply, for I was about to say that very thing. I didn't see any wrinkles. Her heart-shaped face showed only maturity and confidence. Instead of pressing her about her age, I asked, "Why did you say the muria have the same problem I do? What problem?"

"Think how it must be for them. You know how they come across as detached and dispassionate; sometimes so remote they don't seem to have emotions at all? I think it's a psychological protection mechanism. How could they bear to become attached to ephemerals like us? They watch as generation after generation of humans go by. We must seem like mayflies to them. It's a wonder they can abide dealing with us at all."

"I thought they were just snobs."

"You know better. I overheard you telling Aiden about Mint. You suffer the same difficulty as do the muria. It's very hard to let an ephemeral go after you've become attached."

I stood up and stretched my back, implicitly refusing her bait. "I'll have to tell Ashe that you can translate the books," I said. "I imagine he'll be overjoyed, and want to send an armload each day."

"I won't translate anything unimportant," she said placidly. "Let him command me all he wants; I'm not his subject. I'm not a scribe, either, and—if the other books are anything like this one— it wouldn't do him any good."

"Why not? All the knowledge of the ancients lies waiting."

"Brand or another homunculus can translate as needed, and Ashe can call on his scholars for additional help—but you don't understand what you're asking for. *The Principia* would take a lifetime of study, plus mastery of a dozen other sciences, to make sense of it. You and Ashe want instant answers, but there aren't any. It will take generations of scholars, each building on each other's work, to regain the kind of interlocking knowledge you seek. It's all of a piece. Say you wanted to relearn the ancients' healing techniques. Medicine and physiology require biology. There is no biology without chemistry. Chemistry depends on physics. Physics requires advanced mathematics. The list goes on. You might learn a few superficial items, but each discipline is interdependent with all the others. To get underneath any one thing and truly *understand* it requires studying everything else, too. Did you think you could just read a single book and learn to fly the starships?"

"No," I said, while resentfully acknowledging to myself the

more truthful answer would be *yes*. "I suppose," I said at last, "that I didn't realize how complicated the ancients' technology would be. Gaining it has been my goal for as long as I can remember. Now you're telling me it's all wasted effort."

She levered herself out of the overstuffed armchair without disturbing Aiden. "Not wasted, Grey. Not a bit. But it won't do you or Ashe much good personally. If the scholars begin now, our great-great-great grandchildren will benefit."

"Is that supposed to comfort me?"

"No, dear, it's supposed to make you start thinking long-term. It will be interesting, and perhaps instructive, to read the complete Book of the Ship. But these other books are for future generations to study. Let's go eat breakfast. By the time we finish, Aiden will be ready for a nap, and I'll have a precious hour or two to ride before he wants me again."

"By all means," I said, gesturing for her to precede me to the dining room. She had given me sufficient grist for my mental mill to occupy me for hours, perhaps weeks. I thought of Tessa: *You think too much, Grey, especially about questions you can't resolve.* So true. I limped silently through the manor at Maran's back, resolving to spend more time thinking about problems that I had at least a chance of solving.

The house servants, quiet and efficient as always under Hasq's watchful eye, had a sumptuous breakfast waiting. The food wasn't fancy—just ham, eggs, mushrooms, sausages, beans, toast, jam, juice, and tea—but they served us on crockery that might rival the king's, and the linen tablecloth and napkins were freshly ironed.

Between mouthfuls, I told Maran the remaining parts of my story from yesterday, being especially careful to relay Tessa's words as exactly as I could. I fretted aloud that I had been insufficiently encouraging and consoling, but Maran assured me I'd done as well as any man could. I took it as a compliment, even though it didn't sound like one.

"We'll have to visit more often," said Maran, "or at least send letters regularly. I wish I could let her hold the baby, but it's far too soon for him to travel, either by road or by dolmen. Tessa sounds lonely, and Torrey can be exhausting. He's a good boy, but he's at that age."

"He seems to be caring for her more than she takes care of him," I replied. "He struck me as being remarkably mature for his age. He can't help his inexhaustible supply of energy, or his sass, but he isn't scatterbrained. He seemed very solicitous."

"They're clinging to each other, as is proper in shared grief," said Maran. "He hasn't even had his tenth birthday yet. At that age, boys need oversight. Perhaps I could fashion a servant to send them, one like Brand who can operate beyond the confines of my valley. It's exhausting work for me, but a general purpose servant who can cook, clean, and keep Torrey out of trouble might be a good gift."

I glanced uneasily at the two house servants standing quietly with their backs to the dining room walls, ready to see to our needs. I didn't like talking about making more golems while they listened. It seemed somehow unfeeling, perhaps even indecent.

"The king sends Tessa money regularly," I said. "And he will send more if I ask him to. We can hire people from Tessa's village to help out." I waved my good hand to encompass our luxurious dining room, and by extension the entire manor house. "Her home is pretty plain compared to what we have. I think she only has four rooms in total. She doesn't have space for a live-in servant, and somehow, knowing her, I don't think she'd feel comfortable being waited on."

"Do you still feel guilty about the riches of our valley and our lifestyle?"

"Sometimes," I admitted, then added, "yes, actually, most of the time. I haven't earned any of this—the fine clothing, the innumerable servants, the rich appointments, our herd of horses, a private and pristine water supply—I'm not used to it. It's not the way commoners live."

"I decided not to be a commoner a long time ago," said Maran dryly. "I granted myself my titles. Who on this continent could deny me?"

"But that's the thing. You decided. How many people get to choose?"

"Probably very few," she said quietly. "Does that make it wrong? We could leave the valley together and live as paupers. Would that ease your conscience?"

"Of course not."

"Then finish your tea and take Aiden. I'm tired of eating one-handed."

I snorted and waggled my good hand at her. "Try doing everything that way."

"No, thank you. I have my own burdens, Aiden being chief among them at the moment."

I hastily took a last sip of tea and wiped my hands and face. I noticed more blood and clear liquids from my cheek on the linen. How long would it take that blasted cut to heal? I felt the skin gingerly. There was no pain at all, just a rough texture under my fingertips. I dabbed at it with the napkin until it was mostly dry, and then got up to relieve Maran of the baby. Aiden, full to the brim with milk, would undoubtedly sleep until he needed changing again.

Hasq arrived as I was reseating myself. "Pardon the interruption, ma'am, but Brand just rode in. I've asked him to wait in the back parlor. I've assigned a groom to take care of his horse, and have arranged breakfast for him."

"Why make him wait or eat by himself?" I asked. "We have more than enough food here."

"Yes," said Maran. "Ask him to join us immediately. He can

deliver his messages while I finish breakfast. Please arrange for more hot tea. This pot has gone cold."

"Very well, ma'am," said Hasq, making a slight bow.

Brand came in a few minutes later, smelling of horse sweat and leather. His fingernails were dirty, but his uniform looked to have been recently brushed. I suspected the majordomo had hastily tried to make Brand more presentable. If Maran hadn't said "immediately," Hasq would probably have made him bathe, too.

"Lord Grey, Lady Maran," said Brand. "The king asked me to ride here quickly. I left before dawn and did not stop, save to spare the horse."

"Sit," I said, waving to an empty chair. "Eat first, talk later. You must be exhausted. Did the king send letters, or give you verbal messages?" I mentally revisited the journey he had made based on my own experiences, first in a wain, second riding on Snuffles with Benlyn. Brand must have spent two or three full hours at a gallop. I felt sorry for the horse, but knew that Maran's grooms would not only rub it down and curry it, but also check for injuries.

Brand unslung a heavy leather pouch from his shoulder, and gratefully seated himself. One of the servants brought him a plate, napkin, utensils, glass of water, and a cup for the tea that would eventually arrive. He looked to Maran for permission to serve himself. She nodded, and he spoke while piling his plate high. "His Majesty sent a book and a letter, along with a number of other things of lesser importance."

"Give me the letter," I said. "I can read it while you and Maran eat."

He dug in the pouch at his feet and withdrew an envelope sealed with the king's sigil. I shifted Aiden to my left arm, wishing for the support of the rocking chair, and started to take the letter from Brand. Aiden chose that moment to wriggle inside his blanket, and I realized it wasn't safe for me to hold him using just my withered arm. I hesitated, and Maran noticed immediately.

"Hasq!" she called.

"Yes, ma'am?" said the majordomo, appearing, as usual, as if he had nothing to do but wait just out of sight for Maran's call.

"Take Aiden to the nursery. He's ready for his nap."

"Of course, ma'am. At once."

"Thank you, Hasq. Tell the nursemaids to let him sleep as long as he can. I'm hoping to go for a ride after breakfast."

I kissed Aiden's head, and then carefully transferred him to Hasq's waiting arms. I took the letter from Brand, broke the seal, unfolded it, and began reading silently.

Maran and Brand made small talk while I read. Maran only toyed with her food, but Brand ate heartily. I wondered idly if the king had sent him without victuals for the trip, or if Brand always ate so much. I read the letter through several times. Maran caught my eye after I refolded the parchment, and I shook my head ever so slightly. This was not something to discuss in front of Brand.

Maran lifted a hand, and two servants instantly came forward to pull out our chairs. Brand started to rise, but Maran waved him back. "Finish your meal. Lord Grey and I will take our tea in the front parlor. If you lack anything, ask for Hasq. You can leave the book with him, too. We'll rejoin you after my ride. Then you may sleep until we've written a letter for you to take back."

As we left, Brand was already refilling his plate. I tucked the letter under my left arm, and offered my good one to Maran. She accepted gracefully, and we walked down the hall to the front parlor. One of the servants followed, but Maran said, "Bring the tea when it's ready, but otherwise leave us alone. Close the door behind you."

We settled side by side on the upholstered seat built into the bay window's enclosure. The sun gently warmed our backs as we sat facing the interior. "Well," Maran said after a moment, "how bad is the news?"

"It could be worse," I answered. "Ashe read the entire Book of the Ship—the translated parts, that is—and is eager to discuss it. It's mostly log entries, kind of a cross between a diary and a duty roster. Most of it appears written by the Second Colony's officers and senior staff. Ashe thinks very little came from Captain Leonais himself, but those entries may be the untranslated parts. He sent a copy for us; that would be the book still in Brand's pouch. You, of course, can read the entire thing, although Ashe doesn't know that. Should we tell him?"

"Eventually, I suppose. I'm in no hurry. He'll find out that his scholars can decipher it as well as I. But none of this sounds like bad news."

"Ah, yes. The hierophants are the main problem. They're refusing his command to remove their chains and give up their positions. Instead, they spent yesterday afternoon fomenting trouble about it, claiming that the crown has no authority to meddle with religious affairs. Kiril, it turns out, is an excellent orator, even a demagogue. He and his fellow hierophants are preaching rebellion. The commoners are furious with Ashe."

"His command was needlessly cruel," Maran observed, "and probably pointless in the first place. Didn't you say Lady Ariel warned him?"

"Yes, and so did I, but he was extraordinarily angry, with good reason. Those old frauds deserve to be turned out. He means to enforce his order, at sword point if need be."

"It doesn't matter if they're frauds. The people venerate the monks the same way they revere the starships themselves. We must find a way for Ashe to back down without losing respect."

"He won't grovel and beg forgiveness, if that's what you mean."

"No, that would be demeaning for him personally, and

diminish the crown's authority overall. A compromise must be found."

The servant knocked politely, and entered the room bearing our tea. He served us, and then left again without a word, closing the door behind him.

Maran cradled her teacup in her palms and breathed in the steam. I set my cup on a side table and turned on the seat so that my left cheek was exposed to the sunlight streaming through the bay window. The warmth felt good. I fingered the scab gently and examined my hand afterward. More blood and colorless fluid had come away at my touch. "It's not healing properly," I said irritably. "I don't understand why not."

"Have Hasq put a plaster over the top to seal it. If that doesn't work, we'll have to cut away the scab and see if there's an infection lingering underneath."

"I'm not a little boy who's skinned his knee sliding on gravel," I said.

"No, but the cut acts like the same kind of injury."

"Don't worry about it now. There's more from Ashe."

"Oh? Starting a religious war wasn't enough?"

I let my exasperation show in my voice. "Leave off. He's doing his best in a bitterly disappointing situation. Do you remember Benlyn, the duke who was supposed to bring order to Amrhyn?"

"I only know what you've told me about him. Didn't he bring you back from Landing a couple of weeks ago?"

"That's the man. He's running into trouble down south. The grain is growing heavy on the stalk, but no one will work the fields. Apparently, there were more sorcerers than we knew of, and they're trying to take back control of the region. Their leader Cevak has forbidden anyone to take the duke's orders. The entire harvest is at risk, and Benlyn's soldiers can't cope with sorcerers."

"Are the Amrhyns using magic to fight?"

"So far, it's just threats and posturing, but Benlyn's report suggests it will be open warfare before winter. Ashe asked me to go to Amrhyn and put the sorcerers in their place. I think he wants them all dead."

"Is that something you can do? It took all your power to fight the sorcerer in the dungeon, and that was only one man."

"Two. I threw the first one down the garderobe."

"You know what I mean, Grey," said Maran very seriously. "You cannot wake the Sleeper to fight them. They have lightning and fireballs at their fingertips, and likely other powers just as terrible. You can't defeat them by calling up thunderstorms or tornadoes. You can't swing a sword or ride a horse. You can't even *get* there without using the monuments, and you know the sorcerers can monitor them."

I rested my forehead in my good hand, thinking of my trip from the reliquary to Tessa's yard. I *had* felt another mind in the network at the time, and assumed it was Ashe; but what if it had been an Amrhyn sorcerer instead?

I was suddenly very aware that yesterday had been a long, tiring day, and that I hadn't slept all night. I felt unutterably weary, nearly unable to think straight.

"What can I do?" I asked.

"Decline Ashe's request. You've done more for him than anyone else."

"He didn't ask. In his letter, I mean. He phrased it as a command. I don't know what to do."

"You can go to bed," said Maran firmly. "Hasq told me you didn't sleep, and you're still grieving for Mint. You're worried about Tessa. You're heartsick with disappointment about the monks' records. You've done enough for one day. While you're sleeping, I'll take my ride. Maybe the fresh air and exercise will give me some ideas. Grey, listen to me. You don't have to do anything *now*. The monks and sorcerers will wait, and so can the damned king."

She stood up, found a coverlet, and brought it to me. "You're too tired to walk to your rooms. I can have the servants carry you, or you can sleep here. Choose. Either way, you must stop worrying and sleep. We'll talk this afternoon, and compose a letter to the king together."

I was too fatigued to argue. I accepted the coverlet and was fast asleep before she left the room. Her good-bye kiss lingered on my lips and followed me into my dreams.

CHAPTER SEVEN

I DIDN'T WAKE until near nightfall and might have slept longer, save that the servant going through the manor to light the candles and lamps accidentally banged the fireplace grate with a poker. The clang of metal on metal was enough to disturb my dreams and eventually rouse me.

I lay for a few minutes with my eyes closed, listening to the quiet bustle of activity throughout the manor; then I yawned widely, pivoted my legs off the cushion, and sat up with my back against the bay window.

Someone had removed my boots while I slept, and my feet were cold. The perpetual summer of Maran's valley did not preclude occasional rainfall, nor prevent chilly evenings. Tonight, I sensed by sniffing the air, would feature both. I extended my percipience throughout the valley. Clouds covered the sky, pregnant with moisture, obscuring the stars. Two grooms led horses into the stables. A gardener brought tools into a shed. A shepherd roamed the hills, rounding up the last of the strayed sheep. Four miners toiled underground, indifferent to the sun. Two house servants laid out dinner in the dining room under

Hasq's supervision. Another built up fires, one by one, in the manor's innumerable hearths. A cook busied himself in the kitchen; a scullion looked on, polishing silver while waiting for something to clean. A single nursemaid cared for Aiden, who was currently sleeping. My own valet lurked in my rooms, apparently doing nothing but waiting in case I should wander that way and want something. Maran's personal maid did much the same in her chambers, save that she occupied herself with dusting. The barber and the seamstress, having no current duties, helped the house servants with the fires and candles. Both the smith and the carpenter labored in their separate workshops. If I hadn't missed anyone, only twenty homunculi remained in the valley.

I pulled on my boots and stood. Maran waited for me on a divan in the drawing room, languidly sipping wine. She had changed from her riding leathers into a sweeping evening gown of emerald green, and her heart-shaped face lit up with pleasure to see me.

"Brand is gone," I said. "I can't sense him anywhere in the valley."

"He left early this afternoon, carrying your letter to the king. The situation was volatile, so I sent him as soon as you finished your letter."

I lifted my eyebrows. "*My* letter?"

"Well, Ashe's note was addressed to you, so I thought it best if you were the one to reply."

"Thoughtful of you," I said, pouring myself a glass of wine. "What did I say?"

"You solved all of his problems and told him to leave you alone for now."

"Ah, well, then I should nap more often. Exactly how did I solve the realm's troubles while sleeping?"

"Grey, close the door and come sit beside me. We need to talk."

I limped over to the divan, seated myself, and leaned back against the cushions. The hearth roared merrily, too recently lit to have settled into gentle flames and embers. The scent of cedar filled the room, mingling pleasantly with Maran's perfume. I wondered if she—or her maids—chose fragrances to match the ambiance of the drawing room and fireplace. I wouldn't put it past her.

"So," said Maran once I was comfortable, "I read the king's letter several times. I found one thing you neglected to report. He had yet to post his orders disbanding the hierophants. Everything happened very quickly, and it was just word of mouth, most of it coming from the monks. Ashe hadn't even had a council meeting yet—that was set for late afternoon today—so nothing was official. Hence the need for Brand to hurry back. 'You' told Ashe that when he did post orders, that the punishment would only apply to Kiril, for a period of ten days, for the crime of lying to the king. He should reaffirm his support for the monks, and be saddened by the necessity of this minor penalty. By the time *that* circulates, the hierophants won't be able to whip up mobs. The king will have dispensed justice with mercy, and the crown will still honor the monks. It will also have the effect of making the hierophants seem like scaremongers after they spent yesterday afternoon frightening the commoners over what turns out to be an ordinary civil punishment for an ordinary civil crime."

"Aren't I the clever one? Will my advice work?

She shrugged. "You sounded very sure of yourself in the letter."

"I wonder," I mused, working through the possibilities. "Kiril will know the king backed down, even if everyone else accepts the official story. It may embolden him to further irreverence toward the crown. The one thing that man doesn't need is more self-aggrandizement. What if he flouts the modified punishment and continues preaching sedition?"

"In that case, the gods may see fit to strike him down with a lightning bolt," she said with an impish smile.

"Meaning me. Just the threat would be enough, I think. The only time I've seen him lose his composure was at the temple, when I raised a storm. He was scared out of his mind."

"Just so," she said, raising her glass. "Find a quiet way to let him know you're watching."

We toasted Maran's solution in silence, and then I asked, "How did I respond to the Amrhyn situation?"

"That part is more complicated." She rose and poured more wine for each of us, then began pacing and talking. "I read the entire Book of the Ship, and not just the parts that had already been translated. We can go over it in detail later. Ashe was correct in surmising it consisted mostly of log entries—ordinary things, for the most part, documenting all the steps involved in bringing the starships down from the heavens, the early days of creating the Second Colony, the disturbing hallucinations everyone suffered. You and I know that the nina were responsible, but the Second Colonists had no clue."

Maran went on to describe how the scientists had tried to isolate the phenomena, using all the tools at their disposal. They had built things called "Faraday Cages"—whatever those were—and used powerful sedatives and anti-psychotic drugs. They studied the atmosphere, water, plant life, fungi, soil bacteria, even pollen from trees. Nothing explained the hallucinations, but they discovered many puzzling things about them. Most people were helpless against the onslaught. But their best scientists and engineers seemed to have a degree of control—they couldn't stop the hallucinations, but everyone near them saw whatever they saw. Justian, for example, always saw tiny winged horses he called "pegasi," and anyone within a mile or two of him saw the same creatures—until he left the area. Captain Leonais only saw pillars of fire, like lava erupting from an active volcano. When near him, others saw the same thing. From this, the scientists concluded that, despite their inability to detect or control it, something called "telepathy" was at work; I'm guessing that means something like mind-speech. Somehow, the imaginings of a few could determine the form of the illusions for others. When those with powerful minds were away, chaos reigned among the others.

"I only know half those words," I objected. "How does this help? We understand the nina now. Ulat explained them."

"It helps because knowing how the Second Colonists looked at the world lets us understand their decisions. A few months after the Second Colony was established, they decided to leave."

"But they didn't leave. Everyone on Leonais is a descendant of theirs."

"They never got the chance. One day, after Captain Leonais had reportedly gone mad, a stranger appeared to him. With a wave of his hand, the stranger made the pillars of fire disappear. And—I think this part is more important than we knew—the lava the captain saw was *not* just an illusion. It burned everything it touched. The captain had crawled to a high peak to escape it, but all around him, flames raged. Half of the original settlement burned to the ground before the stranger appeared. Justian was the only officer strong enough to stand beside the captain, and his tiny pegasi were consumed by the jets of fire."

From that point, Maran told me, all the reports came from Justian, who, along with other officers, took command, although they pretended to act only at the captain's orders. They very quickly came to understand that the stranger was not human, although he looked human at first glance. And the stranger wasn't alone. All across the newly settled lands and at the great docks where the starships were still being unloaded, similar strangers appeared. Everywhere the strangers went, they restored peace and sanity. The hallucinations, if that was the proper term, faded away.

"Of course," Maran said, "you and I know the strangers were

muria, but it took Justian a long time to understand they were actually descendants of the First Colony, mutated by their long exposure to the nina into something decidedly nonhuman. They never came to understand that the muria were many-bodied, even though all the evidence they needed was right there. Each stranger identified as 'Bastion,' a name the officers mistook for a very old word meaning 'fortress' or 'place of refuge.' The colonists believed the muria came to help. They described Bastion, in all his bodies, as gentle and patient."

Maran finished her wine before continuing. "In a sense, this was true. Bastion promised the horrors would not come back as long as the colonists did not travel to the northern continent. Justian wrote, 'The peoples of Avermorn are insular and unsociable. They desire, above all, to be left alone. Center is secure for now.' The captain's last entry was given verbally, and Justian notes it may be apocryphal. 'They are devils, and they have infected us. We can never leave Sundering, nor let any other ships land.' He appears to have worried 'the contagion' could spread off-planet."

Maran paused to let me absorb the tale. It didn't differ significantly from oral legend, or even what the docent monks taught. Then I caught the glaring omission. "Why the destruction of technology? If Bastion removed the nina, and the two colonies agreed to keep apart, we should be living in an advanced scientific society now, not scrounging for sustenance like prehistoric Terrans."

"That remains unclear; it's not recorded in the Book of the Ship. There are some hints from other officers. It seems that Justian followed the captain's last order, and placed a star in the sky to warn off anyone else. They called Sundering 'quarantined,' and 'slagged the engines' before sealing the starships permanently. But Justian preserved all of their tools and machines, including devices called 'flitters' or 'jumpers,' which flew through the sky.

They used these flitters to map the entire planet. Most of the tools used something called a 'neural interface' for control. And many of the world-building machines were converted to weapons, able to hurl destruction at targets all the way around the globe."

"*That's* not in the legends!" I said.

"No, not at all. Not even a hint. I believe, from what I've read, that the gentle, helpful Bastion never returned from Avermorn. Instead, Justian was foolish enough to land on Avermorn, and Vastil came to destroy the threat."

I thought for a moment, trying to recall what Nina—my own Nina, that is, not the indigenous race—had told me. *Ulat commanded it, and Vastil did it, and Qol did not stop them. Tamil and Bastion stood aside and let it happen.* "I suppose that fits," I said slowly. "I don't know why the Second Colonists would feel the need for such weapons, or why Justian would invade Avermorn, but from what I know of the muria, they would find such things intolerable."

"We don't know he invaded, or even that humans went there. I'm just guessing, dear. Perhaps merely flying overhead to determine Sundering's geography was somehow a threat."

"I don't suppose they saved the maps?" I asked, imagining what it might be like to see all of Avermorn laid out for inspection. Leonais itself had been well mapped by sailors, merchants, and various kings who had sent explorers to every part of the southern continent, but we knew almost nothing about Avermorn.

"No," said Maran. "Or at least, not as part of the Book of the Ship."

"Did I tell you that Ashe tried to send ships to Avermorn? They were all driven back by insurmountable winds."

"When was this?" she asked.

"Just before the hierophants decided to open their records. I told him it was a bad idea."

A soft knock on the door distracted us. "Yes?" called Maran.

"Dinner is ready, ma'am," came Hasq's voice.

"We're on our way," she replied. She refilled our wine glasses, and we headed toward the dining room. To me, she said, "You told Ashe the right thing. We don't know why the muria want secrecy."

"It might just be privacy," I suggested. "They've shown me little fragments of Avermorn in visions, but never any of their cities, their industry, or even their homes. Only forests and fountains. I've been thinking about how it was wind that defeated Ashe's ships. I have some small expertise there, and I've always wanted to go to Avermorn."

We seated ourselves at the dining table, and Maran waited for the staff to finish serving us before replying. "That may be the worst thing you could do. We know they have no compunctions about human life. What if you did breach their borders, and they sent Vastil again in retaliation? Punishment might not be subtle this time. They didn't have to work indirectly last time, by subterfuge and misdirection, letting us think we were fighting amongst ourselves. It could be more like the first time, an invasion in force. Do *you* know their limits? I don't. The most powerful weapon we have is the cannon, and our metallurgy isn't even good enough to keep the cannons from occasionally exploding during use."

"They dress simply, seem to live simply, and get around by foot or horseback," I pointed out.

"Grey, that's what they choose to show us. You know better than most that they are masters of deception. They never lie directly, but they have no problem speaking in half-truths or letting us draw the wrong conclusions. This is the same question we dithered over a couple of weeks ago. We don't even know that the bodies they show are representative of their race."

I concentrated on eating to give myself time to think. In the end, I had no choice but to agree with her. "We just don't know enough to guess," I said.

"Good. Leave the elves alone. We have enough problems."

"Speaking of which, you never told me what 'I' said about the Amrhyns in 'my' letter to the king."

"Oh, that," she said deprecatingly. "You said you begged and pleaded with me to make an army of homunculi that you could lead against the sorcerers. You warned him it would take some time."

"How much time?"

"My work will take weeks. Then they become your problem."

"And I'm supposed to become an army general and defeat people who can throw fireballs? Golems burn, you know."

"Homunculi, please. And it *will* take me weeks. But that's not the real reason for the delay. You need time to investigate what's underneath the reliquary at the Landing dolmen."

"Oh?" I said, lifting my eyebrows. "Is that all? I know nothing about military tactics, I've never held command, and I'm crippled. I'm utterly unprepared to be a water boy, let alone a general. What were you thinking?"

"That you're *you*," she said calmly. "You specialize in the impossible. You may not have studied war, but I have. My homunculi won't need a real general; I'll supply sergeants, warrant officers, lieutenants, and captains. You'll have Benlyn to command the human armies and plot overall strategy. All you need to do is neutralize the sorcerers so Benlyn can conquer using conventional means."

She paused, and I looked at her in frank horror for a moment. Finally, my voice more than a little strangled, I asked, "That's all, is it?"

"Of course not," she replied in a soothing tone. "Relax. There are wheels within wheels here. I have reason to believe Justian hid some of his weapons under the reliquary. If not weapons, at least artifacts—tools—you can use for the battle. Just hints from the log entries. If those tools exist, and you can learn to operate them, you'll have a tremendous advantage."

"Is any of this in the already translated portions?"

"None of it." She grinned happily. "So now you know more than the king and the hierophants put together—at least for now."

"Those vaults are of ship's metal. I can't even see inside with percipience, let alone break them open."

"So you'll have to find the key. I don't have *all* the answers."

I remembered how Kiril had been able to open the reliquary, seeming to use magic. Maybe it wasn't magic after all. *Perhaps,* Ashe had said, *the ancients could build doors that respond to a specific sequence of thoughts.* If that were true, the keys I needed would be mental, not physical.

"What else was in the untranslated parts? Anything that explains what a 'neural interface' is, or how it works?" I asked.

"No, nothing like that. The entries assume the reader knows the vocabulary. We don't. The actual phrase was 'afferent-efferent neuronic control system.' I know the individual words, but not their combined meaning. I cobbled together 'neural interface' because it seemed to imply some sort of connection between minds and machines. I don't think very much of the information will be useful. Reading the entire Book of the Ship provides more details about the early days of settlement, but little else of immediate value."

Minds and machines, I thought. It fit with Ashe's intuition, but gave me no handle on how to access such a mechanism.

We ate the remainder of the meal in silence, each occupied by our own thoughts. The rain started while we ate, but so gently at first that I wasn't sure if I heard drizzle from outside, or merely the fire crackling as it settled. I swiveled my head a few times, using my right ear to determine whether the noise came from the window or from the hearth, but still couldn't tell. Before long, however, the distant rumble of thunder provided the answer. Our servers left their spots by the wall to close the dining room windows. I used my percipience to look quickly throughout the manor, and found house servants closing windows or drawing shutters everywhere.

When Maran had finished eating and called for more wine, she caught my eye, gauging whether or not I needed more time for introspection. I wasn't ready to talk yet, but it was unfair to ask her to provide a silent vigil while I brooded. I forced a smile.

"Do you want to talk about it?" she asked. "I can't tell."

"I'm still thinking about the Book of the Ship," I said. "Ashe won't be happy. And your plan for me to lead an army terrifies me—"

"No, the other thing."

"Oh." She knew me too well. "You mean the staff. Yes, I noticed."

"And?"

I signaled the house servants to leave, and waited for the door to close behind them. "Except for a nursemaid, we're back to the normal complement. You didn't make the extras to last very long, did you?"

"I only needed them in the weeks leading up to the birth, and for a little while afterward. Tomorrow, Aiden will be two weeks old. While it will take several months for me to recover fully, I no longer need extra help. Do you think me cruel? I know you became very attached to Mint."

I thought a long time before answering. Finally, I offered an observation instead of a reply. "Your homunculi are *people*, dear. I didn't understand how human they were underneath, not until Hasq lectured me; even then, I missed some of the subtleties. Did you know Hasq has philosophical aspirations? He's a deep one, although he seldom reveals it. And Mint was *alive*, in a way I'm having trouble distinguishing from ourselves. Before her, I had thought of them all as things, like garden shovels or window curtains, tools or paraphernalia to serve a limited purpose. I didn't really understand they were living beings."

"Yes, they are people, but not like us—and not like normal humans. They have only the life and personality I give them; all of it comes from me, my own mind, my own personality, my own memories, my own energy. Each one I make is like tearing out a bit of my soul. When they expire—'die' is the wrong word, because they're not truly alive—those bits return, like water droplets merging back into a still, secret lake in my mind. I told you a long time ago that I only knew how to give the semblance of life, not the real thing."

"With Hasq, Brand, and even Mint, I can't tell the difference."

"They're ghosts, Grey. Echoes of me. When you interact with them, you're engaging with me, or an echo of me. If their personalities are multifaceted, it's because I'm a complex person. If they have feelings or desires, it's because I chose to share those parts of myself. Each homunculus is unique, because, like all humans, I have different moods and different ideas from day to day, even from moment to moment."

"So, you're like the muria? Existing in many bodies at once?"

She shook her head emphatically. "No, once a shout ricochets, the echoes are not the original sound. I have no mental or physical connection to them."

"So are they copies, or offspring?"

"Both and neither. They issue from me and partake of my essence, but each is an individual. I must choose, during their making, the gifts and abilities each receives; I make those choices based on the use I intend for each one. You might be better off thinking of them as garden shovels. The better the tool, the more time and effort it takes to make; and the longer it lasts. I put a lot of effort into Hasq, because his job is multifaceted and demanding, and I don't intend for him to expire any time soon. I put even more of myself into Brand, because of his unique requirements. But in the end, they are just tools, not really alive except as ghostly aspects of me. I don't feel guilty when one of them expires. You shouldn't either. What you loved in Mint was the echo of me. What you respect—or dislike—in Hasq comes from me, too."

I pushed back from the table, and limped over to the window. The steady rain streaked the glass, and I watched lightning flicker over distant hills. I couldn't shake the feeling that Maran was omitting something, either deliberately or because she didn't understand the extent of her talents. "I wonder how Qol feels," I said. "His handiwork seems much like yours."

Maran remained at her seat, and spoke to my back. "He started us, the way a man and woman start a baby, just later in our lifecycle and with much more control. But we are not ghosts or echoes. He allows—actually insists—that we develop our own personalities, our own volition, and our own intentionality. When we die, no part of us flows back into him."

"Are you sure of that?"

She chuckled very gently; nevertheless, her rich, deep voice seemed to fill the room until the next clap of thunder drowned it out. "One's mind is such a pervasive and necessary illusion that I cannot imagine being without a soul," she said. "And, no, before you ask, I cannot define 'soul' for you, no more than I could haul mine out and spread it on the table for inspection. Do you doubt you have a soul?"

"No, but I think phenomenology is complicated. Mint was self-aware and reflective. She took intentional stances, and showed both sympathy and empathy. She possessed *agency*. I'm not sure her soul, or whatever you want to call it, was any less real than my own."

"You wouldn't be the man I love if you didn't have such thoughts. Qol knew what he was doing when he made you as an existentialist philosopher king who is nevertheless a warrior and compassionate lover. You not only love me, you love the entire human race. What other combination of qualities could have achieved your victory in the war?"

"Pragmatism and a desire for self-immolation would have sufficed," I said somewhat stiffly. "Come stand at the window with me."

"Shall I bring your wine glass?"

"No, thank you. I've had enough."

We watched the distant lightning together, I with my good arm around her shoulders. "I remember the day we met," I said quietly. "You enchanted me, mostly with words, but also with the magic of your valley's influence. You didn't love me. You used me."

"I didn't know you then," she said.

"You only wanted my seed, so you could make Aiden."

Maran made a small sound of protest, but I continued anyway. "Think back," I insisted. "Remember how it really happened. The following morning, I knew you had conceived a child because I sensed his potential. I saw visions of him from the future, but I wasn't in most of them. I was angry. It's taken me this long to understand why."

"Tell me," she whispered. "I know I treated you poorly."

"That part was just the surface. I got over it quickly, and I forgave you just as quickly. My real anger sprang from grief—grief that such a beautiful child, created by us, barely recognized me. I took it as a presentiment of early death for me, for why else would I be absent? I decided then, and still decide every day, to be part of his life as long as I can. I never expected to live through that terrible time in the dungeon, but I did, and I renew my vow daily."

When I fell silent, Maran turned away from the thunderstorm and studied my face instead. "You're crying, sweetheart."

I still stood silently, looking out the window, unwilling to meet her scrutiny. I felt the sobs shaking my body, but I didn't move or try to dash the tears away.

"Tell me," she urged softly.

"Something is going to happen," I managed to say at last. "Not something good. Something that will separate me from you and Aiden."

"Is this a prophecy? Are you seeing the future now?"

"It's not a vision, it's a feeling. Something terrible will happen."

"All this talk about the homunculi has confused you. You are not an ephemeral, at least not in human terms. Nothing inimical can enter this valley, not while my will dominates. You are safe here with me. And I do love you, you know, no matter how our relationship began. I have never loved anyone more. Sleep in my room tonight."

I turned away from the storm to kiss her. She was crying now, too.

"I love you too, but what kind of relationship do we have that makes us both weep?"

"Damp," she said. "It doesn't bother me. Please stay with me tonight. We haven't made love in months."

"Aiden was in the way, and then you were recovering. Isn't it too soon?"

"It's early, but not too early," she said, smiling through her tears. "Most women would need longer, but I am not most women."

"You certainly aren't," I said. I managed to stop crying, but I couldn't quite bring myself to match her smile. Instead, I took her hand and led her through the corridors until we reached her rooms. The maid who normally brushed her hair and helped her disrobe glanced at our faces and quickly dismissed herself. Maran and I undressed each other quickly, but made love very slowly, finally falling asleep together, listening to the incessant pounding of rain on the roof.

I woke up sometime after the rain stopped, but long before dawn. I lay quietly in bed beside Maran, and tried to reconcile my emotions. I had deliberately lied to her for the first time. My "feeling" had indeed carried the aura of prophecy, and I knew the day was coming when she would have to choose between my life and Aiden's. I had no doubts about whom she would choose. In her place, I would do the same.

I still didn't know how long we had, or what event would precipitate her need to choose, but I was uncomfortably aware of my mortality. Maran stirred restlessly, not quite awake, but no longer fully asleep. "Again," she murmured, reaching for me.

What better way to refute death than the attempt to create new life? I cooperated energetically, for the moment putting aside my dread of the future and concentrating on the eternal now. Philosophy be damned; there are experiences that transcend time and subjective awareness.

Afterward, I was able to sleep soundly.

I woke to bright sunlight streaming through the open window. The smell of ozone still lingered, making the entire valley seem newly born. I levered myself up on my good elbow and yawned. Maran sat in a chair by the remains of the fire, nursing Aiden. She wore a light muslin morning dress and a pair of slippers. Maran's maid glanced at me, but continued brushing Maran's long, sandy brown hair, with only a hinted curtsey in my direction.

"Good morning," Maran said, without looking up from the baby. "Your valet has a hot bath and fresh clothing waiting for you. Today will be warm. By noon, the ground will be dry enough for me to go riding again. I can give you a riding lesson, if you want."

I looked in the corner where I had last seen my trousers, shirt, doublet, and boots, along with Maran's evening gown, underclothes, and heels. The corner was bare. I slid my legs from under the sheets and sat on the edge of the bed, waiting for my head to clear.

"Good morning," I said. "I don't really want a bath."

"Dear, you need one."

"That doesn't mean I *want* one."

Maran looked up, smiling. "You're back to being petulant. That's good. It means your dark mood passed with the storm. Go get cleaned up. I asked the cook to make something special for breakfast."

I sighed, stood, and padded naked through the hallways until I reached my own set of rooms. Someone had thrown open my windows, too, and drawn back the curtains and drapes. The bedroom glared with sunlight, despite the dark paneling. My boots, cleaned and polished, rested beside the door. Ashe's signet ring, which had been in my pocket, lay atop the dresser. I suspected a servant had polished it, too. A fresh set of clothing lay neatly arrayed on the bed. My valet emerged from the bathroom, accompanied by a billow of steam.

"Your bath awaits, sir," he said brightly. "If I may suggest—" He stopped speaking suddenly, seeing the glowering look on my face.

"Suggest away," I muttered.

"Your braids are quite tangled. To get your hair clean, I should unbraid everything, wash and dry you thoroughly, and then redo the braids."

Thinking of Mint, the last person to braid my hair for me, I said, "You mean curry me like a horse. Can't we just get this over with quickly?"

The omnipresent Hasq appeared at the doorway. "Is there a problem, sir?" The look he gave my valet was withering.

"No," I muttered. "I only suffer from an excess of service and a lack of personal rectitude."

"Would you prefer to bathe and dress yourself, sir? Or be attended by a different servant?"

I faced him squarely. "Hasq, what's my valet's name? How long will he last?"

"I see," he said, his face blank. "Your angst persists." He made a subtle hand gesture to the valet, and the poor man fled. "If I may say so, sir, your words do you no credit. Is it proper to ameliorate your mordancy about one staff member by abusing another? For shame, sir."

I almost asked him where he got his vocabulary, but then remembered Maran's explanation from last night. Not only his wording, but also his attitude, was an articulated echo of Maran herself. I swallowed my anger and accepted his rebuke in the same light.

"I'm sorry," I said.

He nodded. "That's quite all right, sir. You owe no apology to me. Before I recall your valet, allow me an observation, if you will. Your tone, and the lady's tone, set the mood for the entire manor. We may not show it, sir, but we feel it. You are still not accustomed to having personal servants, and your discomfort shows. May I recommend a few courtesies?"

I felt awkward, standing there naked while the impeccably dressed and groomed majordomo lectured me. Nevertheless, I nodded for him to continue.

"Address us by name or by role only if you require a reply. Do not thank us for performing our normal duties. Say 'please' only if making a request, or if intending to answer 'yes' to a question; never when giving an order. If we are in a room, and you require privacy, tell us to leave; otherwise ignore us as if we were furniture. We do not listen to your conversations. If we are serving you, and you no longer need our services, say simply, 'That will be all.' A quiet 'thank you' in the same situation is an alternate form of dismissal. Otherwise, express thanks only if you ask us to do something unusual, or a task normally assigned to another. Does that help, sir?"

"*You* don't act like furniture."

"It is a function of my role, sir. A majordomo is required to be both observant and solicitous."

"And you offer advice, even admonitions."

"That, sir, is also one of my functions. I am required to run the household smoothly, which sometimes requires a degree of intervention. If I displease you, sir, then—"

"You don't displease me, Hasq. Just don't be so insufferably correct all the time."

"I shall endeavor to err upon occasion, sir."

I looked at him sharply, sure he was making fun of me. His face remained utterly bland, free of any hint of humor. Then I shrugged. He was both unperturbed and imperturbable, qualities I sometimes envied.

"That will be all, Hasq. Send in the valet. I'll apologize to him."

"Very good, sir, but if you would allow me to manage the staff, it may be less awkward for both of you."

"You know best. Do as you will."

I hadn't used his name or asked a question, so he did not reply. Instead, he bowed slightly, turned, and left the room.

I followed the billowing steam to the bathroom, and eased into the tub. A few moments later, my valet entered and quietly began unbraiding my hair. I let him wash it without saying a word, but I took the sponge from him when it came to cleaning the rest of my body.

I let him dry me thoroughly and dress me, then sat patiently while he rebraided my hair. I didn't want to admit that Maran had been right about the bath, or that the valet had been right about my hair, but I felt refreshed and relaxed afterward.

"Are these clothes appropriate for a riding lesson?" I asked, fingering the fine linen of my doublet with uncertainty.

"Oh, no, sir," said the valet. "You will want riding leathers for that. This clothing is your morning outfit."

"How many times a day does a gentleman change his clothes?"

"That depends on the gentleman's activities, sir. Typically, one dons comfortable but seemly attire for breakfast, without a jacket except when entertaining company. At luncheon, the jacket is required. Evening wear is much more formal."

"I've always worn just one outfit a day, sometimes for more than a day, unless I get things dirty."

The valet made no reply.

"Have I been in error?" I asked.

"You are the lord of the manor, sir. Whatever choice you make is correct."

"Meaning I haven't been acting as a gentleman, I suppose." Before he could reply, I waved him to silence. "I should like you to perform two favors. First, prompt me privately if I make a mistake in protocol. I am *not* a lord, but I'm trying to learn. Second, ask Hasq if you may have a name. If he agrees, and if you want one, choose it for yourself. That will be all for now."

I put Ashe's ring in the pocket of my doublet, and then followed my nose to the dining room, leaving the valet to suffer his own moral quandaries, if such was possible.

Maran sat at the dining table, awaiting me. The house servants had exchanged last night's elegant lace tablecloth for a plain white covering. The candelabra had been replaced by two vases of fresh-cut roses. No place settings had been laid yet. Maran held a mug, from which a pungent but somehow pleasing odor arose.

While the servants busied themselves with setting the table

and bringing food, I seated myself. "What are you drinking?" I asked. "It smells nothing like tea."

"It's coffee," she said. "A gift from the king. Brand brought it yesterday, one of the 'other things' he mentioned. Apparently, it's very popular at court. It's the treat I promised you for breakfast."

"I've heard of it. Made from a Terran bean, yes? Only grows on the southern slopes of the Abuttal Mountains. Isn't it terribly expensive?"

"Well, it *is* a gift from the king. Try some."

Before I could think to ask, one of the servants brought me my own steaming mug. I sipped gingerly, letting the taste linger on my tongue before swallowing.

"It's bitter," I said, "but only at first. It's also very hot."

"It's supposed to be hot. Do you like it?"

"I don't know yet." I was the kind of person who preferred to let my tea cool to room temperature before gulping it down. It would take me a while to get used to sipping. I decided to treat it like wine, taking only tiny samples and paying attention to the way the flavor changed as it went down. I took several more small sips, and then set down the mug.

"I don't think it agrees with me," I said.

"It's an acquired taste. I didn't like my first cup, but am quite enjoying this one. Let's see how the flavor mingles with breakfast."

Unlike yesterday's, today's morning meal was light; just eggs, toast, and jam. "Where's the ham?" I asked.

"The cook will make you a full breakfast if you want, but I discovered yesterday that riding on a full stomach made me uncomfortable. I'm in terrible shape."

"So you still mean to torture me by giving me riding lessons?"

"Like the coffee, it takes some time. Horses can be joyful, once you learn how to communicate with them and how to flow with their motions."

"I'd been thinking about visiting Ashe again," I said.

"He's not expecting you for weeks. Remember 'your' letter? I was planning to start building your army after your riding lesson."

"I'd still like to go," I said. "It's not just Ashe. I want to examine that reliquary and the tunnels underneath."

"You mean you'd like to avoid being taught by your wife how to ride a horse." She took a bite of toast, and washed it down with coffee. "Oh, my, that works well together. Try it."

I obligingly spread jam on my toast, and experimented. "It's still bitter," I said after a few moments.

"Do you mean the coffee, or needing lessons from your wife?"

"Hah," I replied. "Wordplay in the morning, horseplay in the afternoon."

She smiled at the ambiguity of my answer, but just said, "Brand will be back with the king. You can take your lesson from him if you insist. But there are far fewer witnesses here."

"Meaning you expect me to fail?" I asked.

"You can manage a walk without worry, but everyone fails with the more complicated gaits, at least until taught. Your problem, dear, is that you keep thinking of horses as if they were Nina."

I heard the capital letter and knew she was referring to my own lost Nina, not the race of nina in general. "I still miss her," I said.

"How did you manage to stay on her back?"

"That was mostly her job. At first, I was scared to death and rode lying down with my arms around her neck. Then I learned to relax and trust her to keep me safe."

"Horses—at least good, intelligent ones like mine—are the same. As long as you and your mount respect each other, your horse won't dump you to the ground. I won't try to teach you to ride a destrier. My horses are all gentled to the saddle, accustomed to being ridden for pleasure."

"It won't be the same."

"Of course not!" she said, sounding offended. "I'm not asking you to betray Nina's memory or to accept a substitute. But unless you enjoy jolting along in a cart or wagon pulled by a dray, you need to become an equestrian."

"One short lesson, then," I agreed. "Then you can work on my army while I go back to Landing."

I used the remainder of my toast to clean the eggs from my plate, but didn't try the coffee again.

"How long do you expect to be gone this time?" asked Maran.

"That depends entirely on what kind of success I have. Anywhere from half a day if I fail to a week if I succeed."

"If you're going to be gone more than a day, send Brand back with news, so I don't lie awake worrying about you."

"You never worry," I objected, "because you have faith in me."

"I have more faith in you than in most. But that doesn't mean I don't worry. Faith is a wonderful thing, but it's no substitute for having your arms around me."

"Arm," I said.

"Are you really trying to provoke me? I hoped yesterday's dark mood had stopped looming. If not, you should stay here."

"I was attempting humor."

"Let's see if you can laugh after falling off a horse a few times. Go change, and meet me by the stables."

Recalling my valet's advice, I nodded. "Give me a few minutes." I signaled to the servants that we were finished, then pushed back my chair and went in search of riding leathers.

Chapter Eight

THE RIDING lesson wasn't half as bad as I'd feared. Maran chose a gentle mare for me, taught me how to approach it, how to let it get to know me, where to put my foot, and how to swing my leg over without grabbing at the horse's mane or neck for stability.

"Hold the reins loosely," she said. "You won't be using them much today, but you need to learn what to do. Just sit back in the saddle today, with your spine straight and your head up. Don't try to stand in the stirrups, and keep your knees away from her sides. You'll learn more in later lessons."

She led me around the pasture at a walk a few times, and then got on her own steed, a magnificent gelding nearly twice the size of my mare, to ride beside me. "This is Aster," she said, settling comfortably into the gelding's saddle. "Your mare should follow his lead, but if she strays, nudge her with one knee. Horses move away from pressure, so if you want her to go right, press with your left leg. Understand? Don't kick with your heels, or press with both legs at the same time, not until you understand what those signals mean. If she doesn't respond to your knee pressure, slap her neck *very* gently with the reins to get her attention."

"What if she starts running?"

"She won't, but if she becomes willful or playful, she may test to see if you're serious. In that case, shift your weight forward so your heels press down more on the stirrups, then apply soft, but equal pressure with both knees. She'll stop immediately."

"If you say so," I replied doubtfully.

"Let's walk around the pasture together. She should follow me, but if she just stands there, tap gently with your heels. *Never* kick. And don't try to get down by yourself just yet. You have to learn how to dismount safely."

We went around the pasture a few times, and my mare placidly followed Maran's gelding, although every time we stopped, she wanted to crop the grass and was unwilling to move on unless I tapped her sides. Maran's horse, in contrast, was anything but placid. He wanted to run. Somehow, Maran kept him in check with only clucking noises and subtle shifting of her weight; she never used the reins. Both horses could amble, a pace somewhat faster than a walk, but slower than a trot; it was a trained gait. After I was comfortable with the walk, Maran took us ambling along the river. My mare wanted to break into a trot, but Maran said I wasn't ready to "post" yet, and then had to explain what that meant and how to keep the mare ambling.

Back at the stables, the groom used a stepstool and had me practice mounting and dismounting several times. After I'd mastered the trick, he had me do everything again without the stool. He showed me how to check the girth and straps, but told me not to worry about them for now, since he would always be present to make adjustments until I learned a lot more.

Overall, it was a very pleasant experience, not terrifying at all, and my tailbone didn't ache afterward, although my thighs did. My respect for Benlyn's handling of his warhorse went up several degrees.

I went back to my rooms to let my valet help me out of my

riding leathers. I told him I wanted something suitable for an informal lunch, stressing the informal part.

He raised his eyebrows. "Sir, you asked me—"

"Yes, but today is different. I'll be leaving the valley immediately after lunch. I want my normal trousers, shirt, and doublet, plus a cloak. I may have to wear the same outfit for several days, so it has to be comfortable."

"Very good, sir," he said, finding black trousers with a matching vest. Both had yellow piping along the seams. I sent back the white shirt with ruffled sleeves, asking for something plain, dark, and durable. When he finished, I still looked too princely for my comfort, but I tucked Ashe's signet into my right trouser pocket and remembered not to complain. The valet offered me a handkerchief of soft cotton.

"What's this for?" I asked.

"For dabbing your cheek, sir. The wound still weeps."

I folded the handkerchief and stuck it under my vest. "Did you talk to Hasq about obtaining a name?"

"Yes, sir. He said it was my choice."

"Good. Did you pick one?"

"I'm fond of the name Virgil, sir. I searched the lady's library while you were riding. I found a book called *The Aeneid*, which includes, 'Do the gods light this fire in our hearts, or do our mad desires become our gods?' I found the question both evocative and inspiring, although my translation may be faulty. The old Earth languages don't fit modern speech well."

"Well, then, Virgil, you've made a good choice, and I hope one day you can answer the question. When you do, let me know. In the meantime, I'll leave you to your reading. I intend to be gone for quite a while."

"Very good, sir."

Lunch was an abbreviated affair; just cheese, cold meats, bread, and wine, consumed while standing. I told Maran I wanted to take my mare to the dolmen, to spare me from limping so far on my own legs. She agreed, provided I only walked the horse, and that the groom accompanied me to lead it.

"My valet has chosen the name 'Virgil' for himself. Never heard of the chap, but he apparently wrote some interesting things. Will you teach me to read the prehistoric books from Earth?"

"Yes, but we should start with something easier than Latin. The primary language used in the Book of the Ship will have words and lettering you can recognize. You'll only need to learn the changes between then and now." She was feeding Aiden as we spoke, and her tone was confident, even breezy. I bent to kiss them both, and discovered a curly golden-white wisp of hair on Aiden's head. It was just a single strand, but it made me look more closely. He still had the long dark hairs with which he'd been born, but I perceived faint white fuzz on his cheeks and on the top of his head.

"Isn't it awfully early for him to start growing hair?" I asked.

"Each baby is different," said Maran. "And I think Aiden will be even more different than most. He's growing very fast. But these hairs aren't new; you can see them because we're standing in the sunlight."

"Don't let him start walking while I'm away," I said.

She just smiled and shifted Aiden to her other breast. I kissed them one last time, and limped around to the stables.

I collected the groom and my mare, got up on her back with only a little bit of help, and we set off for the dolmen. At the deer trail, the groom made me dismount. "Going up a steep hill on a horse without training is not a good idea, sir," he told me. "You need to balance differently. We can practice upon your return. Shall I wait for you here?"

I recalled how Benlyn had instructed me to shift my weight and clench the saddle horn on inclines. I hadn't fallen then, and didn't think I would now. I said as much to the groom, but he shook his head. "The lady gave strict instructions, sir. No risks until you've had further lessons. Shall I wait for you?"

I sighed, silently cursing Maran's over-protectiveness. "No. I don't know how long I'll be gone. I'll find my own way back to the manor."

"Very good, sir."

I trudged up the deer trail, pulled on my cloak, and slapped a standing stone to bring forth the lights as I entered the circle. The deep underground chime began to toll, but I ignored it for now. I sorted through the multicolored ribbons and streamers, looking for one that led to the temple north of Landing. I found over a dozen leading to Amrhyn, a score leading to scattered spots around Jappa, a few leading to the valleys on the shoulders of the Abuttals, and many isolated singletons on Colonial Plain. I even found the dolmen near Luvar, where I had once spent an entire winter tormented by fever visions, and where I had listened to the most beautiful music in the world. The temple at Landing, however, was not among the strands.

I mentally brushed all the streamers to one side, puzzled. Each dolmen on Leonais connected to every other, so why couldn't I find the first, the primary, the most important dolmen of them all? I knew that, by concentrating hard enough, I could find—or perhaps create; I wasn't sure of the mechanism—a ribbon to lead me to a specific person, regardless of location. To test, I hunted for Tessa. Nearly immediately, one of the smaller ribbons caught my attention. I dismissed it, and concentrated on Torrey. The same small ribbon glimmered at me, indicating Tessa and Torrey were likely together. I did the same test for Ashe and Ariel. Their ribbons led different directions. Ashe's went northeast, toward the tent city by the starships. Ariel was back in Draycott, far to the south.

Of them all, only Ashe was aware of my touch. I sent a mental call down his ribbon: *Just experimenting. Sorry to bother you.*

His reply was only a sense of worry without words, and then the contact was gone.

On impulse, I looked for Maran. A thick viridian band came instantly to my questing fingers; I gave it a loving stroke and was gifted by a fleeting vision of her suddenly raising her head with a smile of recognition. If nothing else, I had proved I didn't need to walk home, at least not from this particular spot. I mentally tied Maran's ribbon to my belt. It faded to invisibility, but I could feel a slight tension at my waist.

I searched repeatedly for the master dolmen at Landing, but had no success.

I supposed I could have gone to Ashe, or even Kiril or Brand, and arrived reasonably close to my destination, but it bothered me that I couldn't locate the temple directly. Of the thousands of strands, not one would serve my need.

I could touch the king stone and wake all of the bands to visibility for everyone on the southern continent—that would certainly give me additional power, but it would also alert any lurking sorcerers to my precise location, and perhaps break the wards Maran had placed to secure this dolmen.

Yet even as I stood there trying to puzzle out the mystery, the underground tolling trebled in volume, and I felt a questing mind arrow out of the southwest, soon joined by another. I immediately disengaged from all the ribbons except Maran's and stood stock-still. The strands thrummed like giant harp strings. I sensed the other minds, like vast groping tendrils, flying past overhead, touching every arching ribbon of light; but they could not find me, or even the strands that led here from every other dolmen. The enchantments that hid Maran's valley from the outside world also, apparently, concealed this dolmen itself from the rest of the network—at least as long as I wasn't actively manipulating the lights. I waited, holding my breath, until the searching minds gave up. They could obviously detect my use of the dolmen, but not my location.

That gave me an idea. I could locate this dolmen from elsewhere, but only because Maran had specifically granted me permission. She had needed a hair root to do so, although I had no idea why or how that worked. Could the dolmens have some kind of genetic lock? If so, perhaps the master dolmen at Landing had a similar kind of protection. I had encountered one other henge unconnected to the dolmen network—the ring where I had freed the stone children. *That* dolmen had died, lost all its power, when I broke the lintels and cast down its standing stones.

I hurried out of the circle and sat on a rock, my chin in my good hand. I waited until the chiming stopped and the lights dimmed and finally winked out, considering all I knew about the dolmen network. The sum of my knowledge was paltry. I knew that I could stand in the middle, touching nothing, and sense others using the network. I knew I could select a ribbon and use it to open a doorway between places. I could send messages across the miles, too, as long as the recipient could hear mind-speech in the first place. And at one time—perhaps never again—I could rouse the Sleeper by exerting my will on the king stone. Some dolmens required keys, while others could become completely disconnected from the network.

The list of things I didn't know was much longer. I had no idea what the ribbons of energy actually represented. I didn't understand my personal relationship with the Sleeper, or, for that matter, whether the Sleeper was a force of nature, a living being, or just an aspect of myself. I didn't know why Justian had disguised Landing's temple as a prehistoric Terran monument, or why it was the blueprint for all other dolmens. What was so special about a henge of standing stones? Why was it so insufferably cold inside the circles? Why did ordinary humans feel such a sense of dread and forbidding near the dolmens? For that matter, why didn't I?

I began to doubt the wisdom of using the dolmens at all. I knew they had all been raised at places where power concentrated; but I didn't know if they were lenses or sources. Perhaps they were connected to the nina species, their own unique and indecipherable energies. My own Nina had snorted indignantly when I had asked her if the muria built the dolmens. *Elves never touched this place,* she had said. Perhaps because they could not?

I recalled that Justian had tried to hide the Second Colony's technology from the muria and that he had been acquainted with the nature of the nina. Had he somehow married the two? If so, the mechanism of operation would be technological rather than magical. Anyone should be able to use the dolmens, but very few could. None of it made sense; everything was baseless conjecture, self-contradictory and unaligned with my own experiences. If the dolmens *didn't* operate by magic, how could there be sorcerers, or people like Ashe, or indeed someone like me?

Maran's supposition was that the muria could not imbue gifts they themselves did not possess. Since Qol had made me, he should be just as able to operate the dolmen network as I. But I had never sensed the touch of the muria within the web. I wanted very badly to reenter the circle, wake the lights, and see if I could reach Qol, or travel to Avermorn on one of the faerie ribbons.

I dared not. If my guess was correct, and Justian—or his fellow engineers—had created the dolmen network to outflank the muria, I might inadvertently be handing the muria the key to unrestricted travel.

Key? I wondered, remembering Ashe's comment again: *Perhaps the ancients could build doors that respond to a specific sequence of thoughts. A non-mechanical kind of key.* I also recalled how I often spoke names, either aloud or just to myself, to help me sort through the strands of light.

I touched the nearest menhir to wake the lights, and reentered the circle. I stood beside the king stone, my mind open to whatever possibilities the dolmen offered. "Landing," I said loudly. When nothing happened, I tried with "primary," "temple," and "reliquary." Still nothing. I nudged the king stone with the toe of my boot. "Landing!" I repeated. Nothing happened. I thought back to what Maran had reported from the Book of the Ship. Justian had written, *Center is secure for now.* Perhaps "Landing" was a newer name for the same place. I shrugged and tried it. "Center!" I shouted.

A silver ribbon, nearly as broad across as my shoulders, flat and sturdy as it were made of ship's metal, immediately sprang to life, and the underground chime tolled exactly once, far more loudly than usual. I touched the ribbon with my forefinger, trying to feel where it led. Instantly, the questing minds from the southwest reappeared, no longer flying far above, but heading directly toward me. I sensed triumph in those remote minds, and a moment later, two blue-cowled Amrhyn sorcerers materialized within the circle, one to either side of me. They were already chanting in their strange language, and they crooked their hands in that curious gesture I recalled from the dungeon, ready to raise lightning or throw fireballs. They were ancient men, withered and bent, but their faces under the cowls held nothing but deadly competence.

I didn't hesitate. Disconnecting myself from the lights wouldn't help, nor would fleeing to Maran—the sorcerers were already *here*. Instead, I did the opposite: I slapped the king stone with my good hand, drawing forth as much power as I could. The Sleeper rumbled far below, stirring but not waking, and the underground chime belled like cannon fire. The sky lit up in an explosion of rainbow colors. I wrapped band after band of energy around myself to form a shield.

The sorcerers hesitated, fear showing in their eyes.

I twined several ribbons around my good hand, having no idea how I could use them—but power was power, and the more I controlled, the better.

The sorcerers backed several paces, watching me closely, their arms falling to their sides. The cold inside the circle grew so bitter that I felt frost forming on my face.

I stood there, my hand full of energy, my body wrapped in living spangles of light, wishing I knew how to bring forth the green lightning I had once wielded back in the dungeon. The Sleeper's power was inaccessible to me, just as Vastil had predicted. I didn't know how to fight the sorcerers, and I didn't dare transport myself elsewhere, leaving them inside the valley to ravage at will.

The sorcerers watched with dread on their faces. When I did nothing with my amassed energies, their expressions turned from fear to wonder, from wonder to astonishment, from astonishment to eager aggression. They raised their hands again, and static electricity filled the air. I was only a breath away from becoming a smoking corpse where I stood. I used the god-winds to buy me a few precious moments. Sudden cyclones of my desiring arose, one over each of them, tearing their blue cowls away. They staggered under the onslaught, but kept their feet, raising energy shields of their own to block the winds.

In that one moment before they recovered enough to kill me, a word of command, birthed by desperation, came unbidden to my lips, and my chin dribbled pure fire as I spoke the word aloud. In response, twelve flames shot across the sky, burning more fiercely than all the ribbons of power put together. They landed in a tight circle around me, incandescence made flesh, seeming to face outward, interposing themselves between me and danger.

The sorcerers fled through the dolmen network. I mentally tracked them as they transported to a dolmen near the coast of the West Ocean, far to the south in Amrhyn. I marked which ribbon they had used, both so that I could be sure to avoid unintentionally touching it, and so that, when the time came, I could visit ruin upon them.

I let my grip on power fade, taking with it the awareness of the wide silver ribbon leading to Landing. In moments, all the dolmen's lights, both visible and invisible, winked out, and some warmth returned to the air. Fully mortal again, I regarded the twelve flames that still burned so brightly I couldn't see the beings behind them.

"Who are you?" I asked.

They dropped their hands and turned to face me. I strove, using both percipience and normal sight, to pierce the veil of brilliance surrounding them. I could only see vague outlines of limbs, small and slender. With a shock—the kind that comes not from surprise, but from acknowledging something already known —I realized they were children. The formerly stone children I had freed.

"Thank you for coming," I breathed.

"A favor for a favor," said one of them. "You are now repaid. But we cannot be commanded twice."

Another added, "Do not link any dolmen directly with Center. Doing so opens doorways you cannot control. You are fortunate that we responded instead of more sorcerers."

I shielded my eyes with the flat of my good hand, trying to make out a face or two, but it did no good. Their light masked them as effectively as a shield. "Will you tell me your story now?" I asked. "How you became locked in stone, who did it to you, why you couldn't escape by yourselves, how you came here, who you are?"

"Ask the wind," said several voices in unison. Nina had once said the same thing to me when unable to answer a question. They linked hands again, still facing me, and seemed to rush forward, but without actually moving. I flung up my cloak for protection, but I felt nothing but a small hand on my shoulder, followed by no sensation at all. I fancied that the one who touched me had whispered, "Patience," before moving on. When I dropped my cloak, I was alone, standing beside the dormant king stone in an otherwise empty dolmen. I didn't see anything I could do with my new information, other than heed the warning, so I shrugged and resumed my earlier plans.

I checked that Maran's ribbon was still connected to my belt, then woke the lights briefly, selected Ashe's strand, knotted it to my belt beside Maran's, twanged it impatiently, and took one step forward.

Ashe was just dismounting from his horse at a hitching post beside a rose-hued marble edifice with monks lining the steps. I glanced around and recognized the view, if not the building itself. Below, seeming tiny in the distance, the temple stood within its immaculate stone-clad circle of menhirs. That meant the building beside us had to be the monastery. "I never really wanted to come here," I said.

The king and his two grooms whipped their heads around. "How on Sundering do you manage to materialize silently?" demanded Ashe. "What happens to the atmosphere you displace?"

I lifted my shoulders. "It probably swaps places with the spot I occupied before coming here," I answered. "I don't know, but I'm disappointed to learn there isn't even a whoosh or pop to announce me."

"Did you come to see the abbess with me?"

"Not at all. I came to talk to you, and to visit the reliquary."

"Why are you suddenly tanned?" Ashe asked.

I felt my face carefully. "Burned, not tanned," I said when my fingers encountered tenderness. The scab on my cheek felt like rock that had melted into my skin. Maybe it was finally healing.

"All right, burned, then. How? Are you all right?"

"I'm fine," I said. "As to how—blame the stone children. I don't think the sorcerers got to me, but it was a near thing."

Ashe walked over, his boots crunching on the gravel. He took me by the shoulders and shook me a bit, his face filled with concern. "You're talking in riddles again."

"Occupational hazard," I replied. "I fancy a stroll around the grounds, somewhere away from listening ears. Where are your guards?"

"At the foot of the hill, waiting for me. Weapons are not allowed near the monastery." He let go of my shoulders and sighed with mild exasperation. "You'll be the death of me yet," he said. "The abbess can wait. I fancy a stroll, too." He waved at his grooms to stay behind, then took my arm in his. "They say," he remarked as we crossed the graveled area toward a patch of grass, "that on a clear day, you can see the ocean from here."

I rather doubted that. The hill wasn't very high, and the sea separating Leonais from Avermorn was at least a hundred miles north of us. If there was no mist, we would be able to see the mighty roads that led from Landing to the ports and cities on the coast. But even those roads would narrow to points and vanish from our perspective. I realized the king wasn't serious; he was making casual conversation for the benefit of the listening monks. So I played along, speaking only of inconsequential things until we rounded the corner of the monastery. Here the gravel ended, and a vast greensward presented itself, sloping gently downward in the middle distance, but flat where we walked.

At length, we came upon a stone bench nestled in a garden. I darted a question at Ashe: *Safe now?*

"Likely," he replied aloud, "as long as we speak quietly. It's time you told me the full story of these stone children, and why you mentioned sorcerers."

I settled onto the bench, glad we had found a place that didn't require more walking. I spoke while he paced back and forth in front of me, telling him of the dingle I had discovered, the dolmen I had cast down, the incandescent children, and all of today's happenings. He bit his lip to keep himself from interrupting. I don't know if I remembered every detail, but I conveyed the gist well enough—both the parts I understood and the parts that mystified me.

When I had finally finished, he paced a moment more, his face very thoughtful. Then he sighed and sat beside me. "I suspect, Grey, that you are meddling with powers that exceed you, as you did once before when you woke the Sleeper. I'm not sure the kingdom can survive another catastrophe."

"That's a strong word," I suggested.

"Can you think of a better one? First, all those people you killed on Justian Bridge with your hurricane. Then, all the buildings you ground to rubble—killing even more people— when you caused earthquakes across the continent."

"I didn't mean to kill anyone but your brother," I said. "You've shared my mind. You *know* I had no intention of—"

"Yes, I know, I know," he said impatiently, "but you're missing the point. These powers you touch, sometimes with control, sometimes without, are dangerous. *You* are dangerous. In addition to all the other reasons the monks hate you, they consider you a mass murderer. And now the sorcerers have threatened you. Can you honestly tell me the land is safe from what you will do in retribution for their attack today?"

I absorbed that in silence. The king's words mirrored my own self-recriminations, my self-doubts, and my agonizing guilt over what I had done in the past. It was all very well to live peacefully with Maran in her valley and pretend I was an ordinary man, but in the outside world . . . I was destruction incarnate, even without the Sleeper's rage to empower me.

"I cannot deny," said Ashe when it became clear I had no

answer, "that you ended our civil war abruptly and thoroughly. Just as I cannot deny I benefited from your actions, or that you freed far more people than you killed. Maybe there was a gentler way to accomplish your goals, but I suspect not. Gaheris did much to limit your options. I would have died in that dungeon without your intervention."

"Perhaps you should send me away," I said miserably, staring at the tips of my boots. "I can stay in Maran's valley forever. Or you could send me to Amrhyn to let the sorcerers finish me. Or even Avermorn, where the muria would probably unmake me."

"You misunderstand," he said gently, causing me to look up. "I said all of that to make you *think*, to make you more mindful of others, less reckless with yourself and the powers you encounter. It doesn't mean you aren't still my friend. You will spend time with Maran; doubtless, the situation in Amrhyn will require your presence, too. But between times, I want you at court, or at the reliquary, helping me understand the records."

I felt touched by his remarks, for there was genuine warmth in his voice, not just the overweening needs of a king commanding a subject for assistance. I decided to tell him that Maran and her golems could read the Book of the Ship. Before I finished explaining, he waved me to silence.

"Yes, my scholars can read the ancient writings, too. I found that out as soon as I showed the first one. But reading and understanding are very different things."

"I've been thinking about that," I said. "Why did Kiril say, 'The art of reading the books has been lost'? You and I each discovered quickly that academics across Leonais have retained the skills and knowledge; they lacked only the Book of the Ship itself. If the monks are so dedicated to preserving learning, they would know that Vastil wasn't the only one who could translate from ancient to modern."

"Kiril is a political creature," said Ashe. "Make no mistake about that, no matter how much he prattles about religion. He may have taken a stance in order to further an agenda. Or it might have been just another delaying tactic."

"But it's such a *stupid* lie," I said angrily. "Clever lies can be useful, but Kiril knew we would find out the truth almost immediately. He's like a little girl who denies stealing a peach, but with half still in her hand and juices dribbling down her chin. Stupid lies are pointless. They only demonstrate that the liar can't be trusted."

"Maybe he didn't know he was lying."

"Kiril? I don't believe it. He's too smart. He took advantage of our ignorance to gain, at most, a day's reprieve. Then you got angry and tried to dissolve the order of hierophants."

"Hmmn." Ashe considered my comments for a minute. "That may actually have been his entire goal—to provoke me into a rash action that would set the crown against the monks. He certainly lost no time turning into a demagogue and encouraging the crowds to rebel. Thank you for your letter, by the way. I took your advice, and charged only Kiril with a crime. That's actually why I'm here today. He's refused to comply with his punishment, and I'm here to get the abbess to enjoin him from preaching until the ten days are up. My guards tell me he's currently in Halmar-by-the-Sea, continuing to exaggerate the conflict."

"And the other hierophants?"

"Once they saw the published edict, they abandoned Kiril's cause and went back to their normal duties. I don't know how the public can handle it. Reality can't change from day to day, based on which sermon they've heard most recently. How can they not remember yesterday's truths?"

I muttered something to myself.

"What was that?" Ashe asked.

"There's a very old saying about priests and parishioners. It was churlish of me to repeat it."

"Hmmn," said Ashe again. "I know which one you mean. But I refuse to believe the public is inherently simpleminded, or that they expect priests to contradict themselves because it's 'holy truth' instead of everyday truth."

"Well," I said. "I don't know. Some of the wisest people I've known had no book learning at all. And some of the most clever are fools at heart. It may even be easier to mislead the smart people, because they are too confident in their own intelligence. If I had your burdens instead of my own, I'd be happy that the hierophants are no longer preaching sedition, but equal duty to the crown and church."

"Church?" he asked with a lifted eyebrow. "That's a very old word, and not one the monks encourage. Their duty, they say, is to knowledge itself, not to any gods. They even dislike it when people call them priests, although I can't see why an accurate description should offend. They offer prayers and blessings, after all."

"I'll ask Kiril, the next time I see him. My list of questions for him is already fairly long."

"You can visit him in prison, if the abbess doesn't shut him up. Speaking of her, I should probably go inside. Are you going back to the reliquary? Shall we rejoin at suppertime?"

"I had planned to go there today," I said. "But now I find I'm too tired. You've given me a lot to think about. I'll return tomorrow instead."

"As you will." Ashe stood, stretched, and eyed the monastery walls with distaste. "If you're not going to the reliquary, perhaps you'd care to meet the abbess. Listening to her gives me a headache. Maybe she'll take a different tone with you at my side."

I hauled myself to my feet. "She's all yours," I said, with a smile. "Our paths may cross someday, but I'm in no hurry. Oh, one last thing. Could you send Brand with some money to Tessa's hamlet?"

"Aren't I sending enough?"

"This is for something else. Maran thinks we should hire a lady from the village to help with cooking and cleaning. Nothing too extravagant, or Tessa would decline. Brand can make discreet inquiries and smooth things over. Maran's other idea was to make a live-in golem maid, and I know Tessa would reject that."

"I'll make the arrangements immediately," he said. "Is Torrey benefitting from the scholars I sent to teach at his school?"

"Five of them may have been too much. Torrey's bright and intuitive, but not the bookish type."

"I was hoping that someday I could give him a place at court, perhaps even a position of responsibility. For that, he'll need a proper education."

"I see."

"You disagree?" he asked.

"No, I just don't know if that's the kind of life he wants."

"Who does, at that age?"

I couldn't argue. It was a truism, no doubt, but I had no personal experience with being a child. Comments like the king's only served to remind me I was only two years old. "Well," I said after a bit, "I'll talk to you tomorrow, then. Let me know if my disappearance makes any noise."

Without waiting for a reply, I untied the two strands at my belt and twined them around my forefinger. With my middle finger, I plucked the first, then immediately the second, stepping forward. My single pace took me from the monk's garden to the front parlor of the manor house without any sense of transition. The change from autumn to summer was more profound than my journey.

"You're back early," said Maran, looking up from a book. Aiden slept in a cradle beside her.

"I've a lot to tell you," I said. "Is it too early for dinner?"

"No, I'll inform the servants. I have a lot to tell you, too. We have an unexpected visitor."

"Oh?" I was intrigued, but also tired and hungry. "Virgil will want me to change," I said. "See you in the dining room."

"Make it a half-hour or more. I need to feed the baby, do my hair, and change my own clothes. Wait!" Her tone suddenly shifted from complacency to alarm. "Are you *tanned?*"

"Slightly burned. I'll ask Virgil for ointment, and tell you about it over drinks."

She nodded, reassured by the unconcern in my voice.

A few moments later, I surprised Hasq in the corridor leading to my rooms. "I didn't know you were back, sir," he said. The glower on his face did not bode well for any servant who had failed to report my presence.

"Hah!" I cried involuntarily. I had finally caught him off guard. Then I restrained myself. "Your lookouts and spies are doing their jobs, Hasq," I said, repressing my glee. "I came a different way."

"May I ask—?"

"Not today," I said, pushing past him. A few moments later, I was safely ensconced in my quarters, Virgil tending to my burned face and dithering over the proper clothing for our meal. Was this an early dinner or a late lunch?

"The degree of formality required depends as much on your intentions as the sun's position in the sky," he explained earnestly.

Still smiling over being able to surprise the nearly omniscient majordomo, I undressed and told Virgil we wanted an early dinner. Satisfied, he began arranging my outfit.

"What of your unicorn, sir? Shall the cook prepare something for her?"

"My what?"

"The unicorn that's been waiting outside the manor since midday," he said, as if that explained anything.

"There's a unicorn outside? Right now? Here in the valley? Are you joking?"

"I thought you knew, sir."

"Forget the frippery for now," I told him sternly. "Get me anything I can put on in two seconds, or I swear I'll run outside naked."

Trembling with anxiety over my urgency, he found trousers and a shirt. I didn't bother letting him do the buttons. I was already running, barefoot, my shirt flapping behind me.

Hasq waited quietly by the front door. "'Hah' to you, too, sir," he said without any expression at all.

"Move!" I commanded curtly.

Hasq silently swung the door open, and stepped to one side. I raced past him into the early afternoon sunlight, trying to look in all directions at once.

"To your left, sir, under the trees," called Hasq.

I peered through the leaves, and my heart stopped. There she stood, tail whisking, one hoof upraised as if I had startled her mid-prance. I walked very slowly toward her, barely breathing, half-afraid it was an illusion of some kind.

"Nina," I said when I had closed the distance. "Nina?"

She knelt on her forelegs and lowered her head gracefully, her spiraled horn blazing blue-white, inviting me to ride. I closed the eyes of my body, slid easily onto her back, and clenched a handful of her silky mane.

Smoothly, as if my weight were no burden at all, she whinnied and took off at a wild gallop.

Chapter Nine

She flew across the grounds, past the lake, and up into the hills. Her motion was so smooth that I hardly noticed when she took the last hill, her great hind muscles bunching to leap up the steep path. We emerged upland, the valley mists left behind, still at a gallop.

"Where are you taking me?" I shouted.

She made no answer, even when I repeated the question in mind-speech. I got back only a feeling that suggested our destination wasn't far.

In what seemed like only moments, we had retraced my earlier path to the dingle on Colonial Plain. She leapt down into the hollow, nimble as a goat, barely slowing her pace until we reached the dolmen I'd thrown down. She skidded to a stop beside the pool of water at the center of the fallen stones, and knelt again so I could dismount.

"Nina, Nina, Nina," I found myself saying. "I thought I'd lost you forever."

She looked at me compassionately, but did not change shape

or communicate. Her horn lost its brilliance, but did not fade to invisibility. She regained all four hooves and just stared at me.

A sinking feeling twisted my stomach as I stood beside her, looking into her liquid brown eyes. She seemed so familiar, but the deep wordless bond we once shared was absent. *All nina are now, after a fashion, your own beloved Nina,* Ulat had said when pronouncing their doom. "After a fashion" is not what I wanted. I craved the companionship of the one nina I had known so well, the one who was sometimes a woman, sometimes a unicorn, sometimes just a naked flame wrapped in shadows, but always and forever my friend.

"You're not my Nina," I said at last.

She didn't respond, but her look became sorrowful.

"Why did you bring me here?" I asked.

She swung her head so that her horn pointed directly at the pool, and waited.

I limped forward. The water seemed unchanged from my last visit—only a few feet deep, so clear and still that it both reflected the clouds above and showed every pebble at the bottom. I saw nothing worth examining, and was about to say so when I felt her warm breath at my cheek. Her horn suddenly blazed silver, lighting the entire pool, erasing all reflections.

I knelt on my good leg and peered into the pool. I could no longer see the bottom. Although the surface was mirror-like from the brilliance of her horn, it showed neither my face nor the sky above. Instead, I saw visions, overlapping, all happening at once, some just misty impressions, others as clear as if I were staring into a real looking glass.

I tried to use my percipience to sort out the images, but quickly found that the eyes of my body were better suited. I concentrated on one of the vivid images. It was Aiden, perhaps eleven years old, shouting in euphoric jubilation, both arms upraised, his long golden-white curls swinging from side to side as he rode a unicorn across a green field. A moment later, the image changed. Now his hair, darkened with moisture, hung dankly around his shoulders as he splashed happily in the middle of a small lake, laughing and turning somersaults in the water. He waved gaily to someone on the shore. I suspected it was the lake in Maran's valley, but the vision didn't last long enough for me to pick out any landmarks.

"Aiden!" I called out, but the vision was gone.

Next, I focused on the image of a statue, its back to me. Pigeons rested atop the statue's head and arms. The statue seemed familiar, but without seeing the face, I was at a loss. A family of three shared a picnic at the statue's feet. They were blurred, out of focus, and I couldn't even make out their bodies, let alone their features. Only sizes and general shapes came through, along with a sense of coloration.

That vision faded, too, replaced by an army of golems, marching in formation. I saw Benlyn astride his warhorse to one side, accompanied by a phalanx of archers, pikemen, and mounted soldiers with drawn swords. On the other side, I saw myself, shading my eyes against the sun, seeming to be looking across at an army advancing toward the golems. The opposing forces were armed with swords and spears, and a group of blue-cowled sorcerers stood in their midst. As I watched, a fireball flew from the sorcerers toward the line of golems, and the first of the homunculi began to burn.

I pulled my head away sharply. "Is this prophecy?" I asked. I hadn't minded the first few visions, but the last one disturbed me deeply. It was never my plan to engage in a full battle with the Amrhyns. Benlyn's task was to unify the region, and my forces— not even created yet—were supposed to be entirely for backup, perhaps intimidation, in case everything went to hell.

The unicorn beside me gave no answer other than to gesture at the pool again. I resigned myself to not knowing if I saw possible futures or inevitable ones. These visions didn't have the same feeling as when I experienced prophecy on my own; I had no surety of their truth. Hoping to catch a glimpse of Aiden or Maran, I refocused on the surface of the water and waited for one of the vague images to resolve into clarity.

This time, the vision was of the dolmen at Landing, all its lights lit, the temple doors open, a man emerging. I didn't recognize my own face, but the limp and withered arm left no doubt. I seemed to be carrying something in my good hand. A deep but inchoate sense of danger accompanied the image of the dolmen. I bent closer over the pool to see better. But as I moved my head, the vision dissipated, darkened, and changed focus to Kiril. The hierophant's face was haggard, and his fine robes were rags, but his eyes burned like coals, undaunted. A shackle chained him by the neck to a stone wall, and I realized suddenly he was in prison. Someone sat on a stool with his back to me, apparently conversing with Kiril—or perhaps interrogating him.

The unicorn beside me dimmed her horn, and all the visions disappeared. I got unsteadily to my feet, feeling drained of energy. "Why show me these things?" I asked. "And why here, of all places? The stone children are gone, and this dolmen has no power left."

She looked searchingly into my eyes, as if trying to communicate, but in the end, just shook her head, whickered softly, and knelt for me to mount.

The ride back to Maran's valley, including the descent through the mists, was even faster than our outbound gait, as if she could not unburden herself of me fast enough. My white hair and white shirt snapped and fluttered behind me, pale oriflammes they, and I rode with my good hand upraised in a triumphant fist, having no need to hold on with anything but my thighs. If she had any trouble negotiating the valley's enchantment, it didn't show. In a very short time, she came to a halt beside the manor's front door.

When I did not dismount immediately, she shivered her flanks and reared. I slid backward over her rump and landed unceremoniously in a rose bush.

By the time I had disentangled myself from the thorns and regained my feet, she was already gone.

Hasq, imperturbable as ever, stood beside the open door. "You'll be wanting that change of clothes now, sir," he said.

"How long was I gone?"

He glanced at the sky for a moment. "Perhaps twenty minutes, sir. The lady is not yet ready for dinner. Your dismount was somewhat less graceful than expected, but if I may offer an observation, no one who can ride a unicorn bareback at a gallop really needs riding lessons."

"Horses are larger, less intelligent, and have no reason to keep me from falling off."

"Perhaps mutual trust is the requirement, sir."

"Perhaps," I agreed. My shirt, still unbuttoned and flapping freely in the breeze, had become rags from my struggle with the rose bush. Scratches covered my arms, back, and chest. I wordlessly removed the shirt, gave it to Hasq for repair or disposal as he saw fit, and went to find my valet.

Virgil was waiting in my rooms, dinner attire still laid out on the bed. Instead of dressing me immediately, he applied sticking plaster to the worst of my scrapes, added a thick woolen undershirt to the pile of clothing, and re-anointed my face with the same burn lotion he had used before my wild ride. "Please hold still, sir," he said. "This will only take a moment. You will be on time to meet the lady for your repast. The house servants are still setting up the dining room, and the cook is just finishing his preparations."

I held still for him, reassured that I wouldn't disappoint Maran by being late. In only a few minutes, he had finished stanching my cuts, applying his lotions and plasters, and got me into my dinner outfit. He straightened my collar after I'd pulled it with my forefinger to loosen it, added a jacket, and stood back to appraise me. "You look very presentable, sir. Do you require anything else?"

I wasn't sure if "very presentable" was a true compliment or just what a valet said when making the best of a bad job. I lifted the tail of my jacket so I could pat my trouser pocket. "Where's Ashe's ring?" I asked.

"On the dresser, sir. Do you want it?"

"No, I'm good for now, Virgil. I'll want to change to something more comfortable after dinner. Did you get a chance to read today?"

"Hasq assigned no other duties, so I've been reading ever since you left this morning."

"Still on *The Aeneid*, or did you finish it?"

"I did not finish it, sir, but I have moved on to other material. I found a book entitled *A Brief History of Sundering*, written some thirty years after the Second Colony's establishment. The author's name caught my eye."

"Oh? Who wrote it?"

"It is attributed to Justinian Pontifex, sir."

"I don't know the second name, but the first one sounds like Justian with an extra syllable. Could it be the same person?"

"I believe so, sir. 'Pontifex' is a very old word meaning 'bridge-builder,' and other records indicate that 'Justian' is a corrupted diminutive for the proper name 'Justinian.' I checked the Book of the Ship, and the lettering there shows the older spelling."

My interest quickened. "Does it say anything about dolmens?"

"Only in passing, sir. It calls them monuments, and mentions that the project has been completed."

Thirty years to build all the dolmens? I supposed Maran had read it and could tell me more, but I said, "As you browse the library, Virgil, please keep an eye out for anything related to

'Center' or these monuments. The history of the monks would be of interest, too."

"Very good, sir. This book mentions the monks in rather disparaging terms, as if the author and his friends had suffered a schism with them."

"Oh?"

"It doesn't give details, sir. The volume concentrates more on the building of the first cities, and the creation of the Amrhyn region as a separate entity. Justinian—or Justian, as I should say—appears to have moved there after the split amongst the monks."

"Well, *that's* important, too. Add it to your list of things to watch for."

"Yes, sir." Virgil hesitated uncomfortably.

"Out with it, man," I said. "What else?"

"As much as I enjoy our discussion, sir, it is my duty to remind you that the lady is likely waiting for you by now."

"Oh, right, dinner. Okay, I'll leave you to your research."

He bowed, and I sprinted through the hallways toward the dining room. My bad leg would pay a price for my rush, but later, after I was seated in comfort. I found Maran standing beside the hearth, sipping from one wine glass, holding another for me.

I kissed her cheek, took the glass, and downed the contents in one long gulp. I knew it was rude, but after today's events, I needed something to help me relax. I held out the empty glass for a servant to refill and then limped to the table, Maran beside me. I put down my wine, waved off the servant holding her chair, and seated her myself. I took up my own place across from her.

"So," she said, "Aiden is asleep and won't wake for hours if we're lucky. Who goes first? Hasq informs me that you already know my news."

Of *course* the majordomo had told Maran about the unicorn. He had probably also told her of my wild ride and unceremonious dismount into the rose bushes. "If your news was about the nina, then yes, I already know. We went for a ride together." My throat tightened as I spoke, and I could barely finish the sentence.

"Don't cry, dear."

I wasn't aware than I had been, but when I brushed at my cheeks with my fingertips, I found moisture. "Sorry," I said. "It was confusing and disappointing. I thought at first that she was my own Nina, you see. 'Unexpected visitor'? *Really?* You could have warned me."

"You know it couldn't have been your old friend," she said softly. "Not since Ulat's doom came upon them. I thought you'd realize that immediately. I didn't mean to cause you sorrow."

"Hindsight and hope seldom go hand in hand."

"Don't be bitter, either. Tell me about your ride."

While servants silently laid out our meal, I recounted everything I could remember about the trip to the dingle and the strange visions I'd seen in the pool. I forgot to eat, caught up in my story, until Maran asked if the roast displeased me.

"No," I said, taking my first taste and finding it both tender and delicious. The texture was perfect, too—toothsome but nevertheless seeming to dissolve in my mouth. I didn't even need a knife to carve off bites; the side of my fork was more than sufficient. After swallowing, I said, "The food's fine. Your chef is a wonder."

"Yes the cook is very good at his job, so do him the honor of paying attention to your food. You have more to tell, but it can wait until after our meal."

"Only small talk while eating, is that it?"

"Conversation needn't be mindless, but it should concentrate on each other, and pleasant, uncontroversial things. We are both dressed formally, after all, and eating off my best china. I see that your facial burns are healing well. I don't even think the skin will peel. That scab on your cheek, however, looks like granite from here, and it's larger than it used to be. Does it hurt?"

"No," I said. "It doesn't even weep fluids. I think the burning sealed it."

"I wonder if we should have a surgeon excise it. You'd have a nice scar you could tell everyone came from fencing with the épée."

I tapped the scab with the nail of my forefinger, and it gave a hollow click. "No surgery for me," I said. "What happened to pleasant conversation?"

"Sorry. I should congratulate you on your appearance. Your jacket sets off your shirt and hair nicely. The combination of colors suits you."

"Thank Virgil for that," I said. "You, as always, look splendid, dear."

She didn't blush—Maran had no room for false modesty—but she inclined her head and accepted the compliment with a smile. "You might," she said after a moment, "look even more like a prince if you wore that ring you try to keep hidden."

"Hasq?" I asked.

"Naturally. It's his task to know and to inform me. He believes it to be the royal signet ring of the House of Leonais. Is he correct?"

"I think so. Ashe gave it to me. Did Hasq tell you what it means?"

"For you to have it, you mean? No, but I can guess. The king has made you his heir. That's probably something you should have shared with me, since it affects our family directly. The ring—if it's the one I know of—is older than you might imagine. Captain Leonais himself wore it, three thousand years ago. Your pocket or dresser is probably not the best place for it."

"The heir-in-waiting thing is temporary, only until Ashe and Ariel have a child of their own. And I don't wear it because it doesn't fit me. I tried to give it back to Ashe after I found out what it means."

"Hasq can have a chain made for you. And trying to give it back was likely a blunder."

"So Ashe informed me. He was rather adamant about it. I may have offended him. I suppose he thought I knew what it meant when he first offered it to me."

Maran raised her voice slightly. "Hasq!"

"Yes, ma'am," he said, edging smoothly into the dining room.

"Have the smith make a gold neck chain for Lord Grey's ring. The smith can repurpose one of my own, or use his imagination. It needs to be sturdy enough that it doesn't break, and long enough that Lord Grey can hide the ring under his clothing. He is disinclined to wear it on his hand."

"With a clasp or a solid loop threaded through the ring, ma'am?"

"Solid," I answered for her. I don't want any chance of losing it."

"Very good, sir, ma'am," he said. "It will be ready by morning. I'll inform the smith immediately." He bowed, turned smartly on one heel, and walked rapidly away.

I took a sip of wine and eyed the entrance to the hallway speculatively. "The smithy is in a separate building," I said. "How long would it take Hasq to respond if you called for him again right now?"

Maran sighed. "Grey, I don't know why you fight with him."

"Not fighting, just wondering. He seems omnipresent. And honestly, I think we're beginning to enjoy our mutual mock antagonism. He even made a joke today."

She seemed astonished. "He did?"

"Yes, he said 'Hah!' to me when I discovered that a unicorn was waiting. He was paying me back for saying the same thing to him when I snuck into the manor without his knowing about it."

She frowned. "I'll have a word with him. A majordomo shouldn't—"

"No, please don't. Let us work out our relationship together. I'm coming to respect him in ways I never thought I would, and he's learning to treat me the way I prefer. Let it be. Let's talk about something else.

Before responding, she waved for a second serving of roast and potatoes, and a refill of both our wine glasses. She took a deep swallow, then busied herself with her plate, not looking up to speak. "We could talk about your riding lessons," she said.

"Once a day, is that what you're thinking? The first lesson was nearly painless. I think I'm ready for more challenging endeavors."

"Based on Hasq's report, I don't think you need any practice at all."

"A horse is different from a unicorn," I pointed out. "The first is trained to respond to certain behaviors from its rider; the second is sentient and can anticipate my needs."

"Your mare is so well trained that she might as well be sentient. It may not be self-reflective awareness, but it's intelligence nonetheless. She is taller than a unicorn, won't kneel for you to mount or dismount, and requires a saddle so you can hold the horn, but otherwise is much the same."

I doubted that. "By the way, what's my mare's name?"

She lifted a piece of bread and inspected it critically before deciding not to taste it. "Butter," she said.

I obligingly passed her the butter tray, and she laughed. "Thank you, but I was answering your question. That's your mare's name—Butter. I gave her that name because of how smoothly she trots."

"Fits," I agreed. "She's been very gentle with me. And Butter is a better name than Snuffles."

She laughed hard enough to make the bells in her earrings jingle. "Who," she gasped, "would name a horse Snuffles?"

"Snuffles is a warhorse," I said, somewhat defensively. "It's

Duke Benlyn's mount. Something to do with oats, if I recall correctly."

She wiped her mouth with the corner of her linen napkin to hide her mirth. "I'm done eating," she said after a few more bites. "You?"

"I'd like to finish these potatoes and carrots," I replied. "But if you—?"

"No, no, take your time. Let me tell you about Aiden's day while you eat."

Aiden's day turned out to be less exciting than the potatoes. He had slept, eaten, pooped, burped, sprayed pee all over one of Maran's blouses while being changed, eaten again, and promptly gone back to sleep. I tried to evince interest, since it so clearly mattered to Maran to describe each detail, but she could sense my boredom after a few minutes, and wound down.

When I had cleaned my plate and leaned back so the servants could clear our places, I said, "He sounds like a healthy and happy baby, like every day."

"Colic is coming," she said. "It always does in the first month or three."

"That means crying for no reason?"

"No *discernible* reason," she corrected me. "It always seems very important to them."

I gestured toward the doorway and stood. "Tea in the back drawing room," she told the servants as we walked past. At her words, I dashed back to the table, finished the wine in my glass, and hurried to rejoin her.

I offered the only wisdom I had. "Between your instincts and my percipience, we should be able to figure out why he's colic-y."

"Is that a word?" she asked, settling herself on the divan facing the fire and patting the seat beside her.

"Should be if not," I said, in an attempt at humor that fell flat. I didn't want to sit yet. Too much remained on my mind. The formal dinner was over, so I took off my jacket and loosened my collar. I felt better almost immediately, but still didn't sit. Instead, I paced back and forth in front of the hearth, trying to organize my thoughts. The sedate and secure manor house, with its stuffy rules about formality, contrasted too strongly with the dolmen, the sorcerers, the stone children, Ashe's disturbing words, and the odd visions in the reflecting pool. I couldn't calm down enough to speak.

Maran knew me well enough to hold her silence and let me pace, only looking away briefly at the interruption when a servant brought the tea. After that, she sat calmly, cradling her cup, watching me pace. Her face told me she knew I was near exploding. For some reason, that made things worse. How could she be so tranquil, when she knew I was frothing inside?

"It's all skoda!" I burst out finally, using the vulgar term for excrement I had learned from Torrey. "I don't understand any of it!" I picked up my teacup, started to sip, then changed my mind and threw it across the room, where it crashed against a wall.

Hasq appeared as if the breaking cup were synonymous with his name. He took in the spilled tea, the china fragments, and my mood all in an instant. He bowed slightly to Maran and exited without a word. A few moments later, a maid with a brush and dustpan entered, swept up the broken teacup, used a rag to absorb the spilled liquid, replaced my cup with a fresh one, curtseyed, and left, all in silence.

"Time for you to calm down," said Maran placidly, setting her own teacup on a side table as if afraid I would break it next. "I already know you're upset and frustrated," she continued. "Tell me why."

"I don't know where to start."

"Tell it like someone else's story. Start at the beginning and relate everything in sequence. We can make sense of it together after you get it all out. When you hold it bottled up inside you, neither of us knows what to do."

She made sense, as always. I took a deep breath. "Justian's real name is Justinian Pontifex," I said, my tone clipped. She waited for more, but I just stared at her until she responded.

"I knew that from the Book of the Ship and other documents," she replied comfortably. "It's not important; just one of the thousands of ways language has evolved over the generations. It's a very small change, actually, considering the length of time. Why mention it?"

"Virgil told me."

"I see," she said, clearly not making the connection at all. "Why don't you keep pacing and thinking, and talk when you're ready to make a point."

I took a deep breath. "We—not us specifically, but all of King Ashe's subjects—are descended from Captain Leonais and the original settlers. I think the Amrhyns are descended from Justian."

"And he knew more about the operation of the monuments than anyone else," she said, her eyes unfocused. "So you think the sorcerers get their power from knowledge he passed down."

"How else could they know so much?"

"Offhand, I'd suggest they've studied and experimented. They've had three thousand years, mostly in isolation, to do so. But you may be right. How does that change things?"

I ran my hand through my hair and flopped onto the divan beside her. "I have no idea. I just thought it odd. We know so little of how the Second Colony was founded, what battles they fought with each other."

"The muria would probably know," she suggested.

I snorted. "Find me one, and I'll ask. But I can guarantee they won't answer meaningfully. Before I tell you my story, tell me how and when that nina appeared in the valley."

"I don't think my wards affect them," she said. "Remember, a hundred of them showed up the night Aiden was born. But at the same time, I don't really care. The nina offer only beauty and enchantment, not any danger."

"I guess that answers how, but not when."

"Hasq reported that his scouts—"

"His spies, you mean."

"—his scouts, including your groom, saw the entire dolmen light up. I went to the door to verify, and I could see the bands of energy sparkling and throbbing, seeming to stretch from horizon to horizon, reaching far outside the valley. I thought you were experimenting. Then the lights winked out. Shortly thereafter, the nina came prancing down the hillside in full glory, not trying to be subtle. But she acted very shy after reaching the manor house. No one could approach her. She then took up station, apparently waiting for you."

I took a moment to absorb that. The nina had appeared when I had—ever so briefly—opened the valley to the entire world. It could be a coincidence, but I doubted it. I had probably summoned her, as I had summoned the stone children. Each came for different purposes, but driven by the same event.

"About the dolmen. . . ." I trailed off, staring into the distance.

Maran took my hand. "You're calm now. You've already told me about your experience with the nina, the visions you saw. Now tell me what happened at the monument."

"I was trying to reach Center—the monument at Landing— and woke more power than I expected."

"Yes?"

I sighed and began relating the events, striving to capture for her not only what had happened, but my feelings at each point. I sensed that a dry recitation would be unhelpful, since my attitudes, intentions, and reactions had been a large part of *why* things occurred as they did.

Her grip tightened when I told about the sorcerers being able to identify my location and enter the valley. "I warned you to be careful," she whispered.

"I thought I *was* being careful, but I didn't know what to be careful about. I certainly found out. I won't make that mistake again."

She closed her eyes, a look of deep concentration on her face. "I don't sense anything in the valley that doesn't belong here," she said after a minute. "Try with your percipience."

I mentally expanded my senses until I encompassed the entire manor house and surrounding countryside. Since the valley had no proper limits in size, I kept widening and widening my search until I finally gave up from sheer exhaustion. Maran waited quietly until I had finished. "Nothing," I said. "Not even the unicorn. The dolmen's lock still holds, exactly as I left it. Everything else seems perfectly normal. What time is it, anyway? The sun's going down already."

"Late afternoon," she said absently. "What does it matter to us? Tell me how you escaped the sorcerers."

I told her about the sudden, unexpected intervention of the stone children, and their warning that they would not answer a second summons. Then I told her about my conversation with Ashe, and the troubling thoughts he had awakened in me. "He's more subtle than I realized," I said. "He's always been decisive and pragmatic, but I never appreciated how well he could sum up complicated problems. I wonder if the abbess will support him against Kiril."

"Siobhan is very practical, even if stubborn and rude," Maran said.

"Shi-vaan? She-vown?" I echoed. "Who's that?"

"The abbess. Her name is Siobhan. You won't be able to pronounce it correctly. Try 'Shihv-awn' to rhyme with 'lawn' for an approximation. It's an affectation, a very obscure Terran name meaning 'the gods are gracious.' The vowel sounds no longer exist, and the spelling would drive you mad. She assumed the name upon her elevation from hierophant to abbess. It's a tradition for abbots and abbesses to take a holy name. Their former names get discarded, forbidden from use. They *become* their office, or so they claim."

I stared at her in wonder. "How on Sundering do you know that bit of trivia?"

Maran stirred uncomfortably. "I knew Siobhan from before she became abbess. She was just a hierophant I met during my youthful travels. I made the mistake of using her old name when we met. She set me straight rather brusquely, gave me a lecture in etiquette, and terminated the audience."

"So you've been to the monastery? You've seen the monument?"

"Yes, that's how I knew to tell you it existed."

"And when, exactly, did all this happen?" I asked.

She dropped my hand, picked up her teacup from the side table, and made a show of drinking. Staring into the depths of her cup, she said quietly, "You know I traveled extensively before settling down here. I occasionally journeyed upland afterward, too. This particular trip was to Halmar, to consult an old scholar about translating a book. On the way back, I did what most tourists do, and stopped at Landing to see the starships and the monastery. I asked for an audience with the abbess out of curiosity. I had no idea she might be someone I once knew."

"How long since you had seen her?"

Maran shrugged. "It's hard to say. Perhaps a dozen years. Time passes without markers in the valley. Unless I concentrate on the outside world, I tend to lose track. Why ask? It really doesn't matter."

"So how old is Siobhan?" I persisted.

"She was already in her seventies when I first met her, even older when she became abbess. I'd guess she's near ninety by now, maybe a bit older. This man Kiril you told me about—I presume he's in line, waiting for her to die. He's old, too, isn't he?"

"His beard is grey, and his face is very full of wrinkles," I said thoughtfully. "I wonder if old age is a requirement for hierophants. I've only met the one. Did I remember to tell you that Ashe planned to put him in prison if Siobhan couldn't keep him quiet?"

"Yes, and one of your visions in the pool seems to predict Ashe will make good on that promise. This suggests that the abbess can't—or won't—act to silence him. I wonder which situation obtains."

Now it was my turn to shrug. "The visions seemed very realistic, but they didn't have the heavy inevitable feel of true prophecy. I know something of that art, although I can't prophesy on demand. It's like a word of command—something that comes on its own, without my volition."

I remembered the prophecy I had suffered only recently, the one that had caused me to lie to Maran for the first and only time. I saw no reason to reveal it now. A crisis, whose nature I couldn't yet divine, would force her to choose between Aiden and me, and she would choose our child. I couldn't begrudge her a decision she had yet to make. I saw no benefit in burdening her with foreknowledge.

"Tell me again what you saw of Aiden's future," she said. I could feel her hunger for reassurance, so I complied.

"I only saw him twice. Once riding a unicorn bareback, once swimming in a lake. Both glimpses were very brief. He seemed a bit older than Torrey is now. If I had to guess, I'd say he was around eleven years old. Less of a child's thin chest than Torrey's, but nothing approaching an adolescent or adult's musculature. He could have been twelve or even fourteen, if he ends up gaining puberty late. He was happy, even shouting for joy."

I winced suddenly and pulled my knees together, making a small sound somewhere between moan and a yelp.

"What is it?" asked Maran quickly.

"Nothing important, I suppose. I just realized Aiden wasn't dressed in either vision. The lake makes sense, but riding a unicorn bareback without any cushioning or protection. . . ? Maybe he was just shirtless. That must be it. I mean, he *couldn't* do that, could he?"

"You look to be in pain yourself," Maran observed dryly.

"The very thought of riding bareback without trousers is enough to unman me, even in imagination," I said, shuddering.

"Some prehistoric Terrans rode that way," she said. "Maybe there's a trick to it, or maybe you just didn't notice his clothing. If he was shouting with joy, he couldn't have been hurting."

"True," I acknowledged. "I wish I could have seen his eyes, or talked to him across the years." I reminded her of the two times I had reached forward—or Aiden had reached back—to let us see each other. She had shared only one of those episodes. I had brought him from the future into the dungeon, hoping to elicit his help freeing Nina from Vastil's orange balloon-like entrapment.

"Yes, I remember," she said immediately. "How could I forget? The image scared my brain with wonder and joy. He was about the age you're describing, and he was soaking wet. He seemed glad to see you, and surprised to see me."

"Maybe the lake I saw today was the one from which I pulled him then." I tried to rephrase, but stopped. It was difficult to conceptualize, let alone describe, seeing an event today that hadn't happened yet, but related to an event from before he was born. Past and future threatened to crash into each other, a sequence-defying mystery that tangled my tongue as well as my mind. Perhaps all prophecy defied causation. I recalled thinking once that destiny was malleable, something subject to strength of will.

That stroke of inspiration had triggered my realization that the god-winds were not blowing me hither and yon, but were something I could consciously control. Could the prophecy of Maran's choosing Aiden over me be a similar event, something I could change by *willing* the circumstances to be different? It was an idea to ponder, but not one to share.

"You were right about his eventual hair color," I said, changing the subject slightly. "He will have golden-white curls, longer than even my hair."

"Were they frizzy tight curls like Tessa's, or loose ones like the waves in my hair?"

"Very loose, flowing in fine ringlets. But even riding at breakneck speed, the wind didn't pull it out straight behind him. It whipped in all directions, flying freely. I hope he wears braids most of the time."

"You want him to be like you."

"No," I said reflexively, then immediately added, "yes, of course I do. But I was thinking more of his valet. I pity the person trying to control that unruly mop."

"Did you sense the god-winds in him, the way you described before he was born?"

"The visions didn't show that," I said shortly, only then realizing it was something I should have looked for.

"Ah, well," she said, sighing. "Take the visions for what they were—guesses, maybes, or warnings. I don't think the nina can foretell the future, but they have ways of seeing and anticipating that are utterly unlike human or muria perceptions. Ulat forbids them speech, so maybe the reflecting pool was the only way the nina could share ideas with you." Maran paused, eyeing me critically. "You have already had a very long day. You told Ashe you'd return to him tomorrow, and I have an army to start creating. Perhaps we should go to bed."

"It's barely dark."

"We can think of something to occupy us until bedtime," she said with the impish smile I knew very well. "I want to see if you were truly unmanned by that vision."

I gave her my good hand and let her help me to my feet, then lead me, hands still linked, toward her rooms. As we walked, I wondered about the family I had seen picnicking at the foot of an unknown statue with pigeons on its head. Although the vision had been blurry, I was nearly certain the woman had been Maran, and the child a toddler Aiden. The third person, however, had not borne my shape. Even sitting as he had been, he was too short for my stature, and his skin and hair had been brown, not white.

Chapter Ten

Maran helped me forget my worries for a long time. When we finally separated, reduced to fond caresses across the pillows, I was tired enough to sleep.

She got up early to tend to Aiden, but let me rest until breakfast was nearly ready. Virgil, with many apologies, shook my shoulder until I was fully awake. "The lady will be waiting, sir. I've morning clothes ready for you."

I groaned, rolled over to swing my legs down, and peered at him blearily. Yesterday had been exhausting, more emotionally than physically, but I wasn't very hungry. "Something informal and quick, I hope."

"Yes, sir. The lady said to serve breakfast in the drawing room."

"Virgil, I'm tired of changing outfits. In fact, I don't want to talk about clothes at all. Can we do riding leathers, with a heavy cloak ready? I'll be away again today, leaving shortly after the meal." I held up my good hand to forestall his protest. "I know, and I'm sorry about it. Please go arrange things. I need to wash— not bathe—and then get moving. See to it, will you?"

"Very good, sir. I'll meet you in your rooms."

Twenty minutes later, Virgil had me clean and dressed. I wore Ashe's ring on a heavy gold chain under my chemise. For some reason that only he understood, Virgil insisted on adding a short cape to my outfit. It clasped at the collar, and hung to my middle back. It was tri-toned, brown and black on the outside to match my leathers, and a deep but vibrant red on the inside. I felt like a fool and was about to say so, but I had abused the poor valet's sensibilities too much already this morning, so I didn't argue with him. Except for the gaudy cape, I looked plain enough to suit me.

"If Hasq can spare you," I said, smoothing back my braids while inspecting the cape dubiously in the mirror, "I'd like you to continue your research today. I know you've been reading for pleasure, but you can do that while still keeping an eye out for the things I mentioned yesterday."

Virgil stood behind me to help tighten my braids and tuck in loose strands. Without pausing his work, he said, "My pleasure, sir. Hasq has relieved me of all duties save caring for you."

I peered at his reflection in the mirror. "Is that normal?"

"No, sir, but I sense many changes coming to the manor house. The lady had the servants work through the night, some gathering materials, others building a workshop and temporary quarters. The tasks are not fully completed, but Hasq sent me to wake you, with instructions that I must do whatever you suggest. Apparently, he—and the lady—think my reading is important. I'm glad of the confirmation from you, sir. I enjoy the task."

I remembered suddenly that the homunculi, saving only Brand, neither slept nor ate. I turned to face Virgil, suddenly full of questions. Maran's golems probably *always* worked through the night, which went a long way toward explaining how the seamstress managed to produce an endless supply of new or mended clothing and why the manor never lacked for essential supplies like firewood, candles, food, and other household items.

It also explained why each of the horses in Maran's herd was always freshly groomed, and how a servant could always be standing ready to see to our whims.

"Where do you get the kerosene for the lanterns and lamps?"

Virgil blinked. "We don't use kerosene, sir. We use olive oil, pressed from the grove on the other side of the lake. Can't you smell the difference?"

"I never paid attention. What about butter? We don't have cattle."

"Hasq says we did, sir, but long ago. The lady couldn't find a place for them where the odors didn't eventually waft into the manor. We have goats, as you've seen in the fields and hills. They provide milk, cream, and butter. We also have sheep, chickens, ducks, pigs, an ox, wheat, flax, barley, oats, and—"

I waved him to silence. "I get it. The valley is self-sufficient, like Maran herself. But where does the seamstress get silk and fine linen?"

"Silk comes from the cocoon of a kind of worm that feeds on our mulberry trees, and linen is woven from flax. Flax has many other uses, too, including lamp oil and wicks. It is also an ingredient of our soap." He hesitated, and then said diffidently, "This isn't arcane knowledge, sir. Are you testing me?"

"No, just asking questions I should have asked ages ago. When I go for walks in the valley, I tend to stay in the groves of birch, maple, and oak, or stroll beside the river. I haven't looked at all the crops and livestock. What you're confirming for me is that Maran knows what to grow, how to grow it, and how to use the products thereof. She implants this knowledge in you."

"Just so, sir. She has studied the farming arts extensively, as well as minor industries like stonemasonry, bricklaying, and ironmongery."

"Do our hills contain veins of ore? Where do we get our

copper, iron, gold, silver, tin, or zinc for making brass? I know Maran has miners, but I don't know what they do."

"Sir, the hills are rich with many minerals and precious stones."

"And now she has you making temporary quarters. For whom?"

"Barracks might be a better term, sir. The lady needs a place to house the warriors she intends to make. We have the first building finished, as well as six new smithies. We'll build more barracks as they become needful. Each unit can house two hundred soldiers."

"Virgil, you're a wonder. You've eased my concerns tremendously. I now know that Maran wasn't joking, or speaking from arrogance, when she said she could make an army of golems."

"Homunculi, if you please, sir. Or just men and women, if your courtesy extends that far. We are works of art, expertly crafted. Although we are all, in a fashion, an image of the lady herself, we are each individuals."

"Yes," I said quickly, "yes, of course. Forgive my hasty and indelicate speech. You know how much I value you."

"No offense taken, sir, but if that will be all, breakfast is waiting."

I nodded cordially and shook his hand as I left my rooms. In the hallway, I stopped to sniff one of the sconces on the wall. It was indeed burning olive oil. I went to the back drawing room, but found it empty. Reversing course, I followed the dark-paneled corridors to the front of the house.

Maran stood in the front parlor, holding Aiden and nibbling at a slice of cheese. The bright yellow sunshine streaming through the window created a prismatic halo effect around her head. I squinted against the sudden glare, and crossed the room to kiss her and the baby.

"Good morning, love," she said. "Nightmares gone now?"

"Nightmares?" I repeated, still blinking in the strong sunlight. "I don't recall any."

"You tossed in your sleep, calling out various names. I almost woke you on several occasions, but each time I reached out my hand, you quieted on your own."

"What names?" I asked curiously.

"Mine, Aiden's, and Nina's—mostly."

"Mostly?"

"You also seemed to be begging Qol for something. I couldn't make out what you wanted from him."

"I never dream of the muria," I protested. "Sometimes I relive the battle in the dungeon, but that's not really the same thing."

"Last night, you did. Or seemed to. I can't enter your mind to see your dreams."

"You reached me once," I reminded her. "When the sorcerers captured you and transported you to the dungeon. You called out for help. How did they get into the valley, anyway?"

We moved to the window seat, our backs to the overpowering sunlight. Facing away from the glare allowed me to spot the trays laden with food. My stomach suddenly growled, loudly enough that we both giggled.

"Get something to eat, then sit beside me," she said. "I've already finished my breakfast."

I filled a plate with cold meats, cheeses, and grapes, took it back to the window seat, and settled beside her. Aiden chose that moment to begin crying. Maran unbuttoned her blouse to let him suckle.

"The sorcerers," I prompted, popping a grape into my mouth.

"I'm sure I told you this on our way back from Jappa," she said. "But I don't mind repeating myself. I was upland, expecting to meet some traders. I needed leather, proper cowhide, one of the very few things the valley lacks. The sorcerers stepped from thin air—the same way you do—and killed the traders before I had time to blink. They took the silver I'd brought to pay the traders, then took me, too. I had my épée, but no chance to use it. They enclosed me in a kind of cage, with bars made of light. That's when I screamed your name. The next thing I knew, I was chained to the dungeon wall."

So, I reasoned, *the sorcerers knew the multiple-strand trick.* Now that I knew it myself, I understood how they could have captured Ashe, Tad, Maran, Tessa, Owen, and Torrey, stepping from place to place without traversing the miles between. It might have taken them only a few minutes to gather all six of the hostages designed to force my hand. I hadn't acted from nobility when saving them, as Nina had suggested; sheer terror and anger had driven me. Perhaps that act, more than any other, proved my humanity.

"You did tell me the story," I said, "but I had forgotten the details. It makes more sense now that I understand the dolmens better."

I concentrated on eating then, while Maran explained her plans for the army. She would make the officers first, while her energy reserves were fullest. The foot soldiers involved much less effort, so she would save them for last. She planned to finish within three weeks, and hoped for sooner.

"How many?" I asked around a mouthful of ham.

"I was thinking a total of five thousand."

I nearly choked, and went to find some water. "Five *thousand?* Against a ragtag band of untrained farmers and a handful of sorcerers?"

"I could manage six, if you think it's needed," she said calmly. "Amrhyn is a large territory. I wanted a mounted brigade, but my herd is too small, and not trained for fighting."

"I can always ask Ashe for horses. But you realize, don't you, that Ashe's entire army in the civil war numbered fewer than three thousand. The Archon's complement wasn't much larger, at least not at first. You could have turned the tide of battle all on your own."

"I didn't have a general to lead them, and, frankly, I didn't want to become involved. I knew the muria were directing things, and the war we observed was only the outward sign of their machinations. A single muria could, if bothered, dissolve all my warriors to dust just by unbinding them from their bodies. I did not perceive Vastil's hand—I didn't even know he was in Leonais—but I sensed Qol from time to time when I went upland."

She picked at a loose thread in her blouse, and shifted Aiden to her other breast. His happy, wet, gurgling sounds seemed undisturbed by the transfer.

"Could the muria," I said, thinking through the consequences carefully, "breach the enchantment of your valley the way the nina can?"

"For all I know, they've infiltrated a dozen times. If so, they haven't shown themselves. I'm not easy to hoodwink, especially here in the valley, but I'm far from omniscient. If one of them chooses to walk my hills in secrecy, I wouldn't know. But they're gone now, aren't they, all back in Avermorn?"

"Ulat implied that Vastil and Qol would withdraw, but her exact promise was that they would no longer interfere in human affairs. She offered no assurances about herself or the others. Remember how clever they are with half-truths and misdirection. Those Ketlan found me somehow."

"You were upland then," she pointed out, "and it was a vision. They neither came here, nor took you there."

"I wonder," I said, my breakfast forgotten. I stared at the walls of the drawing room, lost in thought.

"Grey?" she asked, rising worry in her tone. "What do you see that I cannot?"

I stirred. "Maybe nothing. But I keep coming back to what the Ketlan boy said about Avermorn being a state of mind, not just a place. Could Qol and Vastil have withdrawn into Avermorn without physically leaving Leonais?"

"You worry too much. I haven't been upland in months, but you have. Many, many times. Have you felt Qol's presence?"

"No, but I haven't exactly been searching. I've been too busy with other things. Speaking of which, I should get going."

"To Ashe, as you promised?"

"Yes, and to the reliquary if possible. I also want to check on Tessa."

"You mean Brand's work on her behalf."

I smiled. "A bit of both. I only asked Ashe to send Brand yesterday, so he may not even be there yet."

"Give them all my regards. Tell Tessa I'll bring her the baby when he's old enough to travel, either by coach or by monument."

I stood up, brushed off my clothing, and bent to kiss her and Aiden. Then a sudden thought struck me. "How will I get *five thousand* soldiers to Amrhyn in time to do any good? It's probably four hundred miles away, maybe more."

"The monuments, of course. The southernmost tip of Amrhyn is almost six hundred miles from here in a straight line, assuming you can ignore the rivers, valleys, and mountains. I've studied the maps. But a monument makes distance irrelevant."

"Yes, but there goes your notion about a mounted brigade. Animals shy from such places. Even the trees lean away, as if they want to escape proximity."

"A trained horse goes where its rider directs."

"You *say* that."

"I do," she asserted confidently. "Test it today by riding Butter through the doorway in the sky. She likes you and trusts you. She may be uneasy, but she'll obey as long as you make your intentions clear."

"Hmmn. Okay, I'll test it. My guess is that she'll bolt, dragging me back to the stables by one leg. With luck, it will be my good leg stuck in a stirrup, not my bad one. Give me a nice funeral, please."

She made a tsk-tsking sound and waved me away. Before I reached the hallway, Hasq appeared, holding my cloak for me. "I've alerted the groom to expect you, sir," he said.

"I just this second decided to ride. How could you—?

"The lady anticipated your decision, sir. She informed me this morning you would require your mare."

"So," I said slowly, drawing out the syllable and glaring across the room at Maran, "you would have goaded me if I hadn't thought of it myself, is that it?"

"'Goad' is an ugly word. I would have suggested it, no more."

"And you still think I don't need any more riding lessons?"

"Nina taught you more than I ever could. Trust the horse, slip her a lump of sugar, and be about your business. Aiden has just burped all over my blouse. I need to change." She paused briefly, head bent, sniffing. "So does he."

"Skoda," I muttered under my breath. There never was any arguing with Maran. I let Hasq help me wrestle the cloak over my useless left arm, then stopped before he settled it onto my shoulders. "Do I need the cape *and* the cloak?"

"Yes, dear," said Maran, rising from the window seat and reaching for a cloth, all without disturbing Aiden, who appeared to have gone to sleep. "Don't be petulant. It's unseemly."

Still muttering under my breath, I stalked out the back door and made my way to the stables. The groom had Butter saddled and ready, complete with a stepstool to help me mount. "Good morning, sir," the groom said brightly. "It looks to be a lovely day, although I fear rain tonight."

I briefly considered giving him rain right then, but realized it was unfair to take my disgruntlement out on him—or anyone else. I was mostly angry with myself, for the way I'd let Maran skillfully outthink and outmaneuver me.

I took a few moments to fondle Butter's head and pat her flanks. "Hello, sweetheart," I said, crooning a bit. "Today will be an adventure."

Looking over my shoulder, I asked the groom to fetch a lump of sugar or an apple that I could take with me. While he was doing that, I kicked the stepstool aside, put the toe of my left boot in the stirrup, grasped the saddle horn with my right hand, and hoisted myself up. My bad leg, not needing to bear my weight, swung easily over the mare's back to find the other stirrup. Mounting would be easier if I could use my left arm, but I had sufficient strength to manage with my right. I gathered the reins in my good hand, holding them very loosely. By that time, the groom was back, with both sugar and an apple.

"Put them in my right-hand pocket," I said.

The groom didn't say anything. He went around to the other side of the horse, fumbled at my cloak until he found the pocket, and deposited the treats.

"Let's go, Butter," I said, slapping the reins gently against her neck and pressing ever so lightly with my heels.

Butter started out at a sedate walk, responding instantly to knee pressure for guidance. She knew the path beside the river well, and once she figured out where I wanted to go, didn't need any steering at all. I kept the reins slack, and enjoyed the ride. I could tell she wanted to run, but a horse—even a small one—is *much* taller than a unicorn. I wasn't scared of heights, not exactly; my fear pertained to the prospect of falling off. Nevertheless, once we'd cleared the grounds surrounding the manor, I gave Butter her head, and let her break into a trot.

Benlyn had been right to warn me that trotting required a trick, but he hadn't known that I had long since learned it. Riding a horse and riding a unicorn were completely different experiences, but the gaits were similar enough that Butter and I moved together easily. A true equestrian would doubtless jeer at my posture and technique, but I couldn't care less. When only a mile remained before the sharp turn up toward the dolmen, I tapped my heels to her flanks and urged her into a gallop.

She took off with a will, and we flew down the path. I began to understand why riders formed such intimate bonds with their steeds. It was a mutual friendship. She loved carrying me as much as I loved riding her.

She was unhappy when I reined her to a halt at the turning—I think she wanted to run all the way around the lake—but at a nudge from my left thigh, she willingly climbed the deer path leading toward the dolmen. I leaned forward, holding the saddle horn, as she lurched forward, her hindquarters doing most of the work.

When the deer trail verged left, I steered her through the underbrush toward the dolmen, still needing only thigh pressure. I dismounted at the first menhir. Butter rolled her eyes and tossed her head, flanks shivering, clearly not wanting to go further. I made soothing noises, clucked my tongue, and fed her the lump of sugar. After that, she let me lead her into the circle. Her flanks still quivered, but she stood by me, even after I dropped the reins. "Good girl," I said. "The hard part's over. You won't see what comes next."

I raised the lights, selected the strand for Tessa, as well as a ribbon for Ashe and one that led back to the stables. If I could master two strands at once, why not three?

On impulse, I tried mentally tying them to the saddle horn. Butter didn't seem to mind, and my mental knots held well enough that I felt confident releasing the strands from my hand.

I remounted, plucked the strand for Tessa to open the doorway, and urged Butter to walk forward. It was disconcerting to see her head and forelegs disappear before I crossed myself, but Butter had no reaction at all. To her, it was just a few paces, no matter that the ground changed from bare stone to lush grass. In fact, she dipped her neck to graze. Reluctantly, I told her to wait. When she resisted, I tried mind-speech. It didn't exactly work, but neither did it fail. As good horses are wont, she obeyed as soon as she sensed my determination.

Her hooves made practically no sound in the grass of Tessa's back yard, but thudded loudly on the hard-packed dirt at the front of the house. Torrey must have heard the clopping sound, for he burst from the door and ran to meet me. He was shirtless and barefoot, despite the autumnal chill in the air. His expression radiated joy.

He stopped suddenly, his face falling. "That's a horse," he said, disappointment evident in his tone. "I thought it would be a unicorn."

"The surprising thing, young man, is not that she's a horse, but that I'm riding her."

"Let me take the reins," he said. "Did you ride all the way from Maran's?"

I dismounted and surrendered Butter to his care. "Sort of. It's hard to explain. Is your grandmother up? Why aren't you at school? And why are you limping?"

He led Butter with the easy confidence of someone who understood horses. Over his shoulder, he answered, "Yes, she's with our new housekeeper, probably yelling about the way dishes should be stacked. School doesn't start until noon, so I'm home, reading today's lesson. And I hurt my leg jumping from a tree."

I extended my percipience to examine his leg from the inside out.

I quickened my pace to catch up, and pulled both the boy and the horse to a stop. "You're lying," I said flatly.

He turned quickly. "Okay, I wasn't studying."

"I meant about your leg. There's nothing wrong with it."

"*You* limp," he said stoutly. His earnest brown face was defiant and boldly unashamed, but he avoided meeting my eyes.

Suddenly I understood. A complex welter of emotions flooded me, so mixed that I couldn't put names to any of them. He had tried to emulate my braids—although he could never accomplish it with his coarse, bristly hair—and now he had adopted my limp. What next? Would he stop using his left arm?

I crouched, ignoring the shriek of protest from my bad leg, so that my face was level with his. "Look at me," I said softly. He glanced up, then hung his head. "Look at me," I said again. When he complied, I continued, using the same soft but unrelenting tone: "Torrey, you are like a son to me, but I'm not Lane; I can never replace your father. You don't have to look like me, act like me, dress like me, or pretend to have my injuries. I love you because you're *you*. The boy I know is healthy and happy, well fed and on his way to becoming well educated. The boy I know loves his grandmother more than anything on the planet. The boy I know—the boy I love—is whole in body and heart. Rejoice in your health and youth. Leap from trees, stare at the stars at night, enjoy your friendships, have daring adventures, take care of your grandmother, pay attention to your lessons, and be a *boy*. Stand tall, son, stand tall! Be yourself, first and always. Love me back if you want, or spit in my eye and tell me to go to hell. It won't change how I feel about you."

I paused, giving him a chance to respond. When he just kept staring hungrily into my eyes, I said, "Now is when you either hug me or punch me."

He chose the hug. Tessa's voice ringing across the yard spared him from having to reply to my lecture. "Grey, is that you? I need you! *Now!*"

I got up from the squat, using one of the mare's straps for help. "Yes, Tessa," I called back, "be right there."

I spared a glance at Torrey, half-expecting to see his lip tremble, or a tear leak from his eye. Instead, I got a glare.

"Are you okay?" I asked.

"Why *can't* you be my father?" he demanded hotly.

Flummoxed, I hesitated, then said, "Lane may still be alive."

"He died in the war. Everyone knows it, but no one will say it in front of me."

He was old enough to make the statement; he was old enough to hear the truth. "You're probably right," I said gently. "I know it's hard. And I know it's been a long time. You lost your brother and your father, but you still have your grandmother, and she loves you more dearly than you can ever know."

Now tears came, but it wasn't the weeping of a child longing for his parent. These were adult-like tears, welling up from within, driven by emotions he couldn't put into words. "Grandma's wonderful," he said, "but it's not the same. You told me to be a boy, to enjoy my youth. How can I do that without a father?"

"Grey!" bellowed Tessa from the porch. "I'm not getting any younger."

My lips quirked, and, after a moment, so did Torrey's. "She certainly hasn't lost any volume," I observed. "Take the horse around back. Her name is Butter. Let her graze. Don't worry about tying her up. I'll brave your grandmother's wrath. I promise to think about what you said."

Torrey wiped his cheeks with the back of one hand and led Butter away. It felt very odd to have the invisible strands of dolmen energy disappear around the corner of the house, but I sensed they were still firmly attached to Butter's saddle.

I crossed the remainder of the front yard, limped up the porch steps, and gave Tessa a hug. "What took you so long?" she snapped. I supposed it was a form of greeting. I just smiled at her, and together we entered the small house.

The interior differed subtly from my memory. It took me a moment to spot the changes. The floor, freshly scrubbed, practically gleamed. The tabletop, normally piled high with used plates, cups, and utensils, shone as if polished, and not a single dirty dish marred its spotless surface. The disorderly pile of gloves, scarves, coats, and mittens beside the doorway had transformed to a neatly folded and sorted array, set on a rack. I had little doubt the rest of the tiny domicile had benefited from the same treatment. "Everything looks very nice," I said.

"Humph," said Tessa. "Nothing is where it belongs."

"This is all from one cleaning this morning? You must adore your new housekeeper." I tried to set a tone telling her how she *should* react to what amounted to a benevolent home invasion.

Tessa would have none of it. "That dratted woman is out back, planting flowers. Flowers! In *my* garden."

"I can see how you might prefer weeds," I said, unable to keep from grinning. Then I sobered. "Tessa, if you prefer, I can make her go away. I was the one who sent her. I thought you needed help."

"You? You? It was that Brand character, bursting in, taking charge, making me sit sipping tea while that woman destroyed my home."

"Yes. If you recall, Brand is the courier I told you about. He was in Landing yesterday. I asked the king to send him to arrange a housekeeper. He must have ridden all night to get here so quickly. If you must blame someone, blame me—or Maran; it was her idea, too."

Tessa's mien softened a bit. "How is the baby?"

"Pooping and throwing up when I left. So, essentially, the same as always."

"His eyes should be starting to change color, and he should be able to recognize faces by now."

"I think it's still too early for that."

"Men! What do you know?"

"Well, for one thing, I know you're angry. I promise to check Aiden's eyes the next time I see him. In the meantime, do you want me to dismiss the housekeeper?"

I steered her to the table, pulled out a chair for her, and then seated myself on the opposite side. I could see she wasn't nearly as upset as she pretended. She wiped imaginary dust from the tabletop, but didn't answer my question about the housekeeper. Instead, she put her elbows on the table, rested her chin in her hands, and asked, "What were you and Torrey talking about?"

"He misses his father," I said simply, and let it rest with that.

"He worships you, you know. He needs a man in his life."

I shifted uncomfortably on my chair, but didn't reply. I couldn't say more without betraying Torrey's trust.

"Where did you get the horse?" Tessa asked.

"It's one of Maran's. I guess she belongs to me, now."

"So you'll visit more often?"

I smiled again. "As often as I can. Between the king and Maran, I don't have much control over my schedule. Maran says she'll come as soon as the baby's old enough to travel."

"The sooner the better!" Tessa said passionately. "I want to see him while I still can."

"We've been through this before, Tessa," I said, still smiling fondly. "Aside from arthritis, you're in good health."

"Do it again, that doctor thing you do. Look at everything this time, not just my hips."

To humor her, I extended my percipience, and scanned her from head to toe. My smile faded, and I focused my senses carefully on her brain, not liking what I found.

She must have seen my expression, for she just nodded. "Thanks for the second opinion."

"You knew about the tumor." It wasn't a question.

"Since before your last visit. I spent some of the king's money on fancy city doctors. They complained about not having machines that could take pictures inside, the way the ancients could, but they said the signs were unmistakable."

"It extends from your hindbrain all the way to the frontal

cortex. It's pressing on your optic nerves," I said. "Is that why you want to see the baby soon?"

"Well, why else?" she asked tartly. "How fast is it growing?" She meant the tumor, and also, *How long do I have?*

"I can't tell. I wish I had thought to examine you thoroughly on my last visit. Because I didn't, I have no baseline for comparison. You'll have to tell me. Your sight was fine last time, but now you have trouble?"

"Yes."

"That suggests it's progressing rapidly. I'm sorry, Tessa. I don't know how to fix something like that."

"No one does," she said without bitterness. "I went to the doctors when I started losing my balance. Now I'm losing my sight."

"You and Torrey should come live with us. Right away. Maran knows more than I do about medicine. Maybe she can—"

"Please!" Tessa interrupted. "I told you before that I wanted to die in my own bed, and nothing's changed—except the bedclothes. I want my old messy bed, with my comfortable musty pile of quilts and stained sheets. Tell me you understand that much."

I stared at her for a few moments, trying to gauge both her intent and her resolve. At length, I sighed. "Yes, I understand. I'll dismiss the housekeeper immediately. You may have your beloved clutter back. You've earned it."

"And Torrey? Will you take him with you?"

"Not today. But I'll post Brand here. He can stay with the King's Guard, but visit you daily. If needs be, you can send him to fetch me. You'd be surprised by how quickly I can get here."

Tessa lifted her chin from her cupped hands and nodded to herself. "I don't have as long as I hoped, but it won't be tomorrow or next week. I'm thinking of taking Torrey out of school for a while, so we can spend more time together."

"You'd have to tell him why," I pointed out carefully.

"He already knows, in his own way, that something's wrong. I've messed the bed more than once, and the poor child has had to clean it up. I doubt he knows what it means."

"Still, you'd have to explain keeping him home. Why burden him ahead of time?"

"You think it's better for him to come to wake me some morning, and find he can't?"

"No, no," I said hastily. "I wasn't thinking. Perhaps instead of a housekeeper, a nurse would be better. A nurse could take care of you without telling Torrey any details."

"Brand is enough," she said. "Discussion over. Torrey can keep going to school. I'll tell him I'm dying, but won't mention how soon. If you think about it, that's true of everyone, everywhere, all the time, starting at birth. I just need to find the right words. I don't know how to begin."

"Do you want me to—?"

She chopped one hand sharply through the air. "Absolutely not."

"You know best," I said, hoping that was true.

She seemed disinclined to talk about anything else. She just sat at the table, staring off into some inner distance that only she could perceive. I wanted very badly to enter her mind, share my love and compassion, perhaps alleviate some of her distress; but Tessa was a proud woman, and deserved privacy in her grief.

After a few minutes, I cleared my throat. "I'll go discharge your helper, collect my horse, visit with Brand, and be on my way. What time of day do you want Brand to visit?"

"He can check for a heartbeat any time he wants, but I'm at my best mid-mornings. Afternoons, I usually nap. In the evenings, I sometimes lose track of myself. I've wandered off a few times. It disturbs me that once, when Torrey found me, I didn't recognize him. I thought he was Lane."

"I'll take care of it," I promised. "Is there anything else I can do for you? The best physicians on the continent will be on your doorstep tomorrow morning, maybe sooner, if you only give the word."

She gazed at me blearily. "Could they help?"

I looked inside her head again, visualizing the tumor's size and position. "No," I said. "I don't think so."

"Then be sure to say good-bye to Torrey, and come back soon. Bring the baby, if you can."

I went around the table, kissed her on both cheeks, and pressed her hand in mine so she could feel warm, honest, human contact.

My heart was heavy as I limped out of the house and around back. I found the housekeeper—a very pleasant woman in her mid-forties—weeding and planting winter flowers. I explained that we had no criticism of her service, but that Tessa, very set in her ways, preferred to keep house herself. I told her to seek out Brand tomorrow and collect two weeks' wages. She argued a bit, saying Tessa clearly needed help, but I remained firm. Eventually, she collected her things and left.

Torrey, who was inexpertly trying to groom Butter only a few feet away, heard everything. He didn't interrupt, but he whistled his relief when the woman had gone. "I thought I was the one who had to fire her," he said.

"Where did you get a currying brush?" I asked.

"Stole it," he said cheerfully. "From a stable down the road. This is a beautiful horse. What did you call her again?"

"Butter, from her smooth ride," I said. "You shouldn't steal things."

"Oh, I'll return it," he replied airily. "I only needed it for a bit." His tone changed to one of studied nonchalance. "What did you and Grandma talk about?"

"I didn't tell her what you said, so I won't tell you what she said. Fair's fair."

"I guess," he admitted. "But some conversations are more important than others. Don't different rules apply?"

"Take the brush back, and then go to school. Come right back afterward, okay?"

"I know *that* much," he said scornfully. "Grandma needs me most in the evenings. She'll sleep while I'm at school."

"Make sure she eats, and gets plenty of water."

"Will that make her die any slower?"

I bit my lip and refused his gambit. "Good-bye, Torrey. Mind your manners. Maybe on my next visit, I'll take you for a ride on Butter."

He cocked his head, pondering both my lack of denial and my promised treat. "Whatever you say, Grey."

I took the reins from him, let Butter sniff my hand, mounted, and rode off to find Brand. My day had just begun, and I already felt worn out.

I finally tracked down Brand in the hamlet's tavern. He was drinking ale and slurping stew, chatting noisily with several men of the King's Guard who shared his table. Only a few other customers occupied the common room. I limped to Brand's table, took off my cloak, and seated myself. The tavern's interior was hot from its cook fires, and the stew smelled delicious.

Brand didn't notice me at first, but then one of the King's Guard stiffened and sprang to his feet at rigid attention, holding a salute. Brand and the other guards joined him immediately.

"Oh, stop that and sit down," I said irritably.

"But, lord!" one of the guards started to protest.

Brand waved him to silence and resumed his chair. The others followed more slowly. In a low voice that wouldn't carry to the other customers, Brand said, "Prince Grey does not enjoy attention."

"He does, however, enjoy stew," I said. "Would you fellows be good enough to order some, and give us the table? I need to speak to Brand alone."

Unsuccessfully suppressing their instinct to salute again, the guardsmen excused themselves. A few minutes later, the innkeeper's wife brought a tankard of ale and bowl of stew, bowing as she served me and thanking me for visiting their humble establishment. At my wave, she hurried away.

"How can everyone in this blasted tiny town know me?" I asked Brand.

"Your clothing marks you as nobility, and your visage is well known. Of course, all members of the King's Guard also know your new station."

"Tell them to keep it to themselves," I muttered. "It's temporary. And I tried to dress like an ordinary person today."

"Saving the cape, lord, your clothing is quite plain. However, it is also of fine fabrics, cut to fit, expertly tailored, and without any sign of wear or tear. They are a rich man's clothes. You might as well be wearing a coronet."

I grunted in acknowledgement. The stew was still too hot to eat, so I stirred it aimlessly, trying to figure out the ingredients. Maran's chef would certainly find the meal substandard, not fit to serve, but it smelled hearty and wholesome to me. "What is this?" I asked, digging out a piece of meat and holding it up for inspection.

"Lamb from local flocks, my lord."

"Stop calling me that. No one else can hear us now. You know what I am, and I know what you are. Can't we share a meal as equals?"

"No, sir, we cannot, for many reasons. First, I am superior to you in many ways. I am younger and stronger, with all of my limbs intact. I am an expert fencer, rider, swordsman, bowman, and rifleman—all skills you lack. I can cook, camp, scout, fight, or plan an entire campaign with equal ease. Further, I am better educated. All Lady Maran's amassed study of military history and strategy echoes in my head. Where I lead, soldiers follow without question. The lady made me to be more than a courier."

"Your humility astonishes me," I said, looking at him askance.

"I haven't finished, sir. You outrank me. You outrank everyone except the king. You wield magics and possess second sight. You can control the dolmens and speak words of command. You prophesy. You have a special relationship with the nina shared by no other human. Last, you have triumphed in battle against muria and sorcerers. I possess none of these talents. We are not equals, sir, and never can be. I would lay down my life for you; I was made so, and I am true to my purpose."

I paused before answering. As always, the sophistication of a golem's mind could catch me off guard, especially at odd moments when Maran's own personality shone through. His speech sounded rehearsed and polished, but I knew it wasn't. He spoke spontaneously, directly from his heart, sparing neither of us. He could weave words to strike with the deadly accuracy of an arrow. I decided it was worth trying to explain things to him, maybe even unburden myself.

"Prophecy only brings grief ahead of its time," I said, keeping my voice low, but letting my intensity ring. "My rank has meaning only if the king dies, something no one wants. The nina no longer speak. I'm useless in a fight; prior successes were sheer happenstance. I'm lonely and frightened most of the time. One of my friends is dying a meaningless death. Second sight lets me see her suffering, not how to heal her. I cannot read the hierophants' books; I don't even know what to look for. I cannot utter words of command at will. I don't understand how the dolmens actually work." *And my wife will forsake me one day*, I added silently. "So tell me, Brand, what good am I, and what should I do?"

"First, lord, you should eat your stew and drink your ale. Both will alleviate your feelings of inadequacy. I assure you, they are false feelings, a dark mood you must escape. The greater the man, the greater the trials—but also the greater the achievements. Second, you make Lady Maran happy, and have a son to nurture. Speak less of doing, more of being."

"You are just echoing Maran's beliefs. Have you considered that she may be wrong about me?"

"No, lord. I have heard the king speak of you. He is your true friend, and that is not a prize easily won. He trusts you above all others. You misjudge yourself."

"So we can't be equals, but we can be friends. Benlyn said much the same, although he was more succinct."

"The duke? My lord, he is the only man I know who can best me at wrestling, swordplay, and chess. He is formidable, to put it mildly. Take his advice if you eschew mine. Measure yourself by the quality of those who honor you."

I finally took a bite of the stew, finding it just as savory and satisfying as its aroma had promised. "Self-doubt is my greatest gift," I said after swallowing. "It never fails, and never leaves. Get yourself more ale, and sit with me while I eat. I need to tell you about Tessa. She's going to need your help, perhaps quite a bit of it."

Brand rocked back in his chair, studying me. "Now I understand your dark mood and bitter words, lord. You grieve for Tessa before her time. But the darkness is a liar; you must not heed the lure of despair. How long does she have?"

"Charitably, with luck, a month. More likely weeks, maybe only days. It depends on which direction the tumor grows, and how quickly. Once it affects her breathing or heartbeat. . . . You're to visit her every morning, and contrive to send me a message should the end become evident. You may not have much time after perceiving a change. I will figure out some way to come more often myself. Some of the guards should watch for her wandering at night. She's at the point where confusion reigns in the evenings."

"Understood, lord. It shall be done as you command. May I do aught else to ease your heart or ease her situation?"

"No. I dismissed the housekeeper. She'll be coming to you for wages—be generous. She didn't deserve dismissal, but Tessa won't stand for a stranger in the house, and she won't leave home herself."

"And the boy, lord? Should you not take him to Lady Maran?"

"Tessa won't have it."

I concentrated on finishing my stew, and Brand let me devour it without interruption. He excused himself briefly to fetch more ale, and, after I finished eating, we drank in contemplative silence, until we had drained our flagons.

I wiped my mouth. Brand had been correct to predict that supping would make me feel better. But duty called. "I must go talk to Ashe, visit the temple, and then return to Maran with the sad news," I said. "Thank you for talking to me."

"My duty and my pleasure, lord." He sat waiting, and I realized it was my place to stand first. I did so, only then realizing I carried no purse.

"I have no coin to pay for the meal," I said as Brand arose from the table. I felt very awkward. "I'm not accustomed to carrying money."

"The innkeeper would not take your coin, lord. He will hang a sign after you leave, proclaiming the tavern is patronized by royalty."

"Well, I'll be damned!"

Brand smiled, but only with his eyes. "Likely all of us will be, lord. It is the fate of most men. If you meet a saint, let me know."

I had no response to that, so I turned on my heel, scooped up my cloak, and limped back outside. Butter stood waiting patiently at the tavern's hitching post. She lifted her head and whuffled a happy greeting at my approach. A strong easterly wind brought hints of an oncoming rainstorm from the coast. Autumn was in full force, and my weather sense suggested the rain, when it finally arrived, would be bitterly cold and blatting, perhaps mixed with the first snowfall of the season.

I worked Butter's reins free from the post and mounted. I hadn't tried the two-strand trick from horseback before, but I saw no reason it wouldn't work. I plucked Tessa's strand to open the doorway back to the dolmen, then immediately twanged Ashe's to take us on from there. While the doorway held, I urged Butter to a trot. We took the passage into elsewhere, leaving Tessa and Torrey far behind, but still very present in my thoughts.

CHAPTER ELEVEN

We emerged onto the cobblestones in the midst of Landing's crowded high street. As usual, I hadn't perceived the passage through Maran's dolmen; but chaos erupted immediately. Before I could rein Butter to a halt, we knocked down a fruit stand, startled an old woman wearing hoop skirts and a scarf, and nearly trampled a small child who had been examining the fruit.

The woman snatched the child to safety, retreating against the stone walls of the shops lining the streets. Fortunately, all eyes were elsewhere, and I had not injured anyone. I recalled that I could look through a doorway before traversing it and resolved to make that my practice henceforth. It might also be better to walk the horse instead of trotting.

Butter, jittery from the clatter of the falling fruit stand, and surprised to find herself in a constricted space surrounded by noise and obstacles, took a minute to settle down. I patted her neck and reassured her it wasn't her fault. She calmed and stood still, but we were still in the middle of the street. Lateral movement, as I had seen Maran demonstrate during exercises called "dressage," was not something I knew how to ask the mare to do for me. With

Nina, a thought would have sufficed; with a horse, equestrian skills exceeding my own were required. So I swung down, and led Butter into a nook between shops, getting us away from the center of the high street. I remembered the apple in my pocket and gave it to her. I finally had the luxury of looking around.

A small procession from the east wound its way through the town. Mixed jeers and shouts of outrage from the crowd followed it. Two fancy horses held the lead, ridden by liveried guards with plumes on their helmets, followed by a dray pulling what looked like an upright cage. Behind them, a full company of the King's Guard followed single file. High street didn't have enough width for them to ride abreast of each other. I and the other onlookers flattened ourselves against the storefronts to let them pass. When the cage came alongside me, I saw an old man, standing up and clinging to the bars for support against the swaying and jolting, scowling at everyone.

Those beside me, finally able to see the prisoner, took up the mixed cheering and squawks of anger. I tried to gauge the overall emotional mood. The crowd seemed split very unevenly. The majority approved of events, while only a few voices shouted loudly in protest. The King's Guard kept their eyes focused strictly forward, neither encouraging nor dispersing the crowd.

I had expected to materialize somewhere near Ashe, but he was not among the guards or in the crowd. I realized suddenly that I had chosen the ribbon for his location early this morning, and it was now afternoon. He must have moved in the meantime. That was something worth remembering, a likelihood I had never considered. I had no opportunity to select a new ribbon for Ashe now, so I watched the prisoner, wondering what was going on. Surreptitiously, I raised the hood of my cloak up and pulled it tightly around my face. I had a fleeting thought that I must look like an old woman with a shawl, but dismissed it. I didn't care what others thought of me; I just wanted to avoid recognition.

The old man in the cage tried to emulate noble suffering, but his anger was too evident, and he couldn't keep from swiveling his head back and forth to survey the crowd. His head was recently—and badly—shaved, including his beard. He wore a dirty old robe, more like a beggar's tatters than proper clothing. It wasn't until I caught his eye for a second and saw the gold flecks that I recognized him.

Evidently, the king's audience with the abbess hadn't gone well. Ashe must have sent guards to Halmar-by-the-Sea to drag Kiril back for punishment. I rather thought the disgrace of shaving him and dressing him in rags were unnecessary and ignominious, but it hadn't been my decision. Still, I felt a bit sorry for him.

When the procession had finally passed, I mounted Butter and joined the rear of the line. We cleared the high street and left the town behind. Here, the road opened up, and the group broke into a trot, taking up a formation surrounding the cage on all sides. The ride must have been dreadful for Kiril, forced as he was to stand in the cage with only the bars to keep from falling. I felt even more sympathy for him, then remembered who he was and what he had done. Perhaps he deserved this humiliation.

I didn't know our destination, so I let them pull ahead and followed at a judicious distance. The monastery and the dolmen lay behind us, on the other side of Landing. Our current course lay due west. As far as I knew, this road only led to the starships and Ashe's tent city.

One of the guards finally noticed me and wheeled his horse to race my direction, his sword out. I loosened my hood and threw it back to show my face, hair, and eyes. I slowed Butter to a walk, my good hand upraised to show I held no weapon. The guard hauled his huge gelding to a skidding stop before he reached me, and looked me over carefully. Then he sheathed his sword and saluted smartly.

"Your pardon, lord," he said, evidently recognizing me. "Sergeant Nix at your service."

"Will you ride with me, sir?" I asked. "I'm short on news and want to see the king."

"You mayn't call me 'sir.' I'm only a sergeant. But I'll ask the captain's permission to detach. Bide just a moment." His voice had an odd singsong lilt, rising in the middle and end of each phrase, and his vowels were subtly wrong, but I had no trouble understanding him.

He kicked his horse to a fast gallop and rode to the head of the procession to speak with one of the guards wearing a plumed helmet. I let Butter walk sedately, following the road without any need for guidance, until he galloped back, wheeled again, and took up a walk beside me.

His horsemanship didn't have the grace or style of Benlyn's or Maran's, but he seemed firmly in control. He pulled off his helmet and held it under one arm. A frizzy shock of wild orange hair sprang out, and I noticed his face and hands were heavily freckled.

"You're from Halmar?" I guessed.

"The hair, you mean. No, farther south along the coast, a tiny fishing village called Lesser Niggleton. We have many towheads and redheads, even occasional blue-eyed folk—but nothing like your eye color. It's our only claim to fame."

"Where is Greater Niggleton?"

"No idea. If there ever was another town with the same name, everyone's forgotten it."

I gave up, not for lack of interest, but because more pressing matters were at hand. I liked Nix; his lilting voice and breezy manner made him approachable, and his accent was unlike any I'd encountered before. In addition, he forgot to call me 'lord' with every other breath. I would have enjoyed chatting with him, but I needed information just now, not a companion.

"Sergeant, where are they taking Kiril?"

"The Holy One, you mean? Never knew he had a name. There's a fort, long since in ruins, not far from the starships. I wouldn't blame you for overlooking it, since it's half-buried in a hillside. The king had it repaired months ago for grain storage, but we cleared everything out to make a prison."

"And where is the king? Will he meet us at the fort?"

"Doubtful," said Nix, running his free hand through his hair, and then leaning over to spit on the ground. I took it to be something he did regularly, not a comment about the king. After clearing his throat, Nix continued: "He's likely holed up with his advisors. We had a report come in from Amrhyn this morning. The important folks aren't happy."

"What was the report?"

He rolled his eyes and made a rude gesture before remembering his manners and my rank. "They'd never tell me, lord."

"I'll ask the king, then," I said thoughtfully. "Were you assigned to me for the day, or just for this ride?"

He grinned. "I reckon that's up to you. I'd not mind shirking camp duty. The captain just said to guard you."

"Then let's go to the fort first. Afterward, we can find the king. If there's time left, you can escort me to the monastery, or rather the dolmen below it."

"Can you trot that beast? It's known you don't ride well."

"I can even gallop now. I had an excellent teacher."

"Let's see if you can keep up, then," he said. He put his helmet back on, slapped the reins and gave his gelding a solid kick with both heels. The poor beast leaped forward, transitioning from walk to gallop nearly instantaneously. I had no mind to kick Butter, and I had no need. The moment Nix's horse took off and I tapped the mare's sides, she raced to follow. We drew abreast of Nix, and then pulled ahead. I again felt the fierce joy of riding as if I were part of the animal. I craned my neck, watching Nix fall farther and farther behind. He crouched nearly flat, his rump lifted off the saddle with his heels carrying his weight, and he whipped the reins back and forth shouting encouragement. The distance began to narrow slightly, but it was obvious his large, spirited gelding was already going near its top speed. Butter, on the other hand, had not yet reached her limit and wanted to go faster.

I took pity on Nix's horse, and slowed Butter to a trot. We had only galloped for perhaps a quarter-mile, so neither horse was sweating hard or breathing heavily. The cold air might have helped. Galloping at that speed in the blazing heat of summer would be much more arduous.

"Is that a racehorse?" Nix asked when he caught up to me. He was out of breath, even though his horse was not. "I've never seen a mare move like that."

I wondered briefly if Maran's training regimen had included racing. I rather thought it was just good breeding, a willing heart, and a good road. I patted Butter's neck fondly, and said, "No, she just likes to run. She comes from the best stock on the continent."

"Well, she's a beauty, and moves like magic—" He broke off, eyeing me strangely. "Unless you're the magician, lord. Were you cheating?"

"I?" I laughed. "That kind of magic isn't in my bag of tricks, Sergeant."

"Do you want to arrive ahead of the others, or after? It seems you have the choice. They're only trotting, and it's not far now."

"I want Kiril settled into his cell before I see him," I said. "Let's continue at our current pace."

Perhaps fifteen minutes later, we caught up with the rear of the procession, and followed them to the fort-*cum*-prison. At the fort itself, amidst the general melee of so many riders jostling for position, I dismounted, gave the reins to Nix, and asked him to see to Butter's needs. Nix led his horse and mine off to find water and provender. "I'll want you later," I called after him. "Don't wander off."

"Aye," he called back.

I paced back and forth, trying to keep out of Kiril's sight, until they had taken him from the cage and carried him into the building. Then I waited more, so they would have a chance to settle him in place. Eventually, most of the guards had emerged. I pushed my way forward, introduced myself to the captain, and said I'd like to go inside.

"Lord Grey," the captain protested, blocking the entrance. "The king said no visitors."

I just stared at him, letting the hardness I felt inside surface in my eyes. He rocked back on his heels, but held, determined to follow his orders.

"Do I look like a visitor?" I asked softly.

"No, lord."

"Then stand aside, good fellow. I won't be long. Are there torches within?"

"Yes, lord," he said, finally moving away from the doorway. "Torches and two guards. If you require anything, ask of them. I'll see your orders followed."

"Thank you, Captain."

I strode past him, into the dank dimness of the fort. The first torch, in a stand alongside the wall, told me which way to turn. Around a bend, I found two guards, a second torch, and Kiril's cell.

With a shock, I recognized the stone walls and general look of the place. He wore the same shackle I'd seen in the reflecting pool, but attached to his waist, not his neck. No stool waited in the foreground, and all his hair was gone, but otherwise the match was nearly perfect. His eyes really did seem to burn like coals in the torchlight. *Not exact,* I thought, humming in the back of my throat, my mind racing. *Anticipatory, then, but not truly prophetic.*

What else in the visions shown by the nina might be subtly wrong?

There were no bars; his cell was merely a deep embrasure off the main passage with a narrow cruciform balistraria through which defenders would have shot arrows back when this building was an active fort. Kiril's chain guaranteed his captivity; it seemed securely fastened to a large iron ring embedded in the wall. I measured its length by eye, deciding it was long enough for him to sit or lie down, but not reach me.

"Hello again, Kiril," I said cordially.

"Come to gloat, have you?"

"To check, rather. I didn't know of your arrest until they were already bringing you here. These stones are cold, and will only get colder at nightfall. Would you like my cloak?"

He spat. Unlike Nix's gesture, this was aimed at me. He crossed his arms and glowered.

Whether he wanted charity or not, I shrugged off my cloak and tossed it at his feet. "Have they given you food or water yet?" I asked.

One of the guards behind me stirred. "Lord, we have not. The captain—"

"See to it, then. He may be the king's prisoner, but we do not treat civil crimes with torture or deprivation. Also bring a bale of hay, so that he need not stand or lie on bare stone. And a stool, so that I may sit while talking." When the guard didn't move, I turned my head and barked, "Now!"

The guard scrambled to obey.

"You seem very comfortable giving orders," Kiril said. "Your arrogance has increased. I had thought it already unbounded."

"I'm discomfited by your treatment. I would not have chosen this for you. At the same time, I wonder why you allowed it. All you had to do was obey the king. Didn't the abbess tell you to keep quiet and suffer your mild punishment with grace?"

He shrugged. "The king has no ecclesiastical authority, and the abbess cannot command me. I've earned autocephaly after all my years of service."

I tried to puzzle out the word he'd used. "Big-headed?" I guessed.

"No, self-directed, head of my own congregation. The abbess is not my superior, and I do not answer to her. Anander is the only other autocephalous hierophant. It means we are next in line for her chair."

"Why not wait your turn with decorum and patience? Siobhan is very old. It won't be long. Preaching sedition in the meantime won't further your cause. If you want to become abbot, you must lead rational people as well as mobs. Does your ambition blind you to reality? The other hierophants have deserted you, and the king's jurisdiction is clear. Incitement to treason is a secular act. When you foment unrest and encourage the public to disobey their lawful ruler, you are not acting from religious authority. Your clout derives from demagoguery, not spirituality."

"I told you when we first met that religion is not our devoir," he said.

"Then stop using religious words and trappings. 'Ecclesiastical' means you consider yourselves clergy or priests. I'm told you disdain such designations, but you can't have things both ways. Either your authority comes from the gods, or it is exactly as secular as the king's. We both know which is true. Why the ceremonial robes, the claim to religious authority, and the pious blathering? Your devoir is knowledge, like mine."

"So my crimes are hypocrisy and pretension?"

"The only *crime* I know of is lying to the king. Specifically, you told him that the art of reading the Book of the Ship was lost. It took us less than a day to uncover your falsehood. Also, the other books in the reliquary can be read by scholars. The 'dead' languages are actually easier for the academics. You know all this, yet you lied. Your real mistake, Kiril, is being a pompous ass."

The guard came back, followed by two others. They lofted a bale of hay in Kiril's general direction, making him step aside smartly to avoid being struck. Then, while one guard stood ready with a spear hoisted, the other laid a bundle of food and a flask on the hay. They departed hastily, and the original guard set down a stool for my use before resuming his posture alongside his fellow against the opposite wall. They stood at ease, swords sheathed, and studiously ignored us. I understood their training well enough to know they would neither listen nor speak, unless addressed directly.

I seated myself, glad to take the weight from my bad leg.

Kiril just glared at me, unwilling to reply, so I gestured at the supplies and said, "You needn't starve yourself to prove a point," I said. "Eat, drink, sit on the hay and relax. I'm tired of trading barbs anyway."

Kiril considered the wisdom of obstinacy for a long moment, eventually deciding pragmatism was a better philosophy. He sat down and unbundled the food packet. Inside he found ham, bread, cheese, and a few apples. He set the apples to one side, probably saving them for later, and made a sandwich from the rest. After he'd finished half the sandwich, he unstoppered the flask and took a long draught from it.

"Better?" I asked.

He nodded, but did not reply.

"You needn't thank me, but you could answer a question."

His eyes narrowed. "What question? Does your arrogance permit you to acknowledge ignorance?"

"I said I didn't want to spar. Stop it. I want to know how you opened the reliquary doors."

"You would call it prayer, or dismiss it as pious blathering."

"Skoda," I said calmly, deliberately choosing a crude word, not to shock or offend, but to cut quickly through his bluff. "You honor no gods, and, I suspect, don't believe in any. But prove me wrong. Pray your way out of this prison. Go ahead. I can wait."

"Again, you speak blithely and disparagingly of things you have never studied, Grey."

"I believe the usual excuse at this point," I said with an edge in my tone, "is that one should not test the gods, nor ask for demonstrations that would eliminate the need for faith."

"I'm not interested in sophistry," he snarled.

"Oh? I thought it was your chief pastime. Me, I prefer actual answers to real questions. To my eyes, you used magic to open the doors. What would you call it?"

"Impertinent. I really should have killed you when we first met. At the time, I sensed only unknown potentials. I didn't know you would become perverse, wicked, and irreverent."

"More wordplay. You insult instead of answering. I decline the distraction. How did you learn to use magic?"

"You are a simpleton, a fool. I will not explain holy things to a heretic."

"An actual refusal? I'm delighted. We're making progress, Holy One. I'll ignore the continued rudeness and presume you know the answer." I leaned forward on the stool, bringing my face dangerously close to being within his reach. "If it wasn't magic, then it can't hurt to explain. If it was, then you really are a hypocrite. You strike me as a very clever man, bound strictly by ethical rules that make you uncomfortable at times. This is one of those times. You do not allow self-deception or deliberate hypocrisy. Therefore, you evade and misdirect. The time for games is over, though. Yes or no, did you use magic?"

He resumed eating his sandwich, eyeing me warily, as if I were a newly discovered species with odd physical traits that he found both fascinating and repulsive. I resumed my upright posture on the stool to wait. At length, he finished his food, took another long pull from the flask, and asked, "Are you hauflin, half-elf, as Brawley claimed? I know you are not muria."

"We'll save the muria discussion for another day. I have many questions for you about them. In the meantime, I have good reason to be confident in my humanity. As you told me yourself long ago, if there are hauflin in the world, no one knows of them." I paused for several deep breaths, and then continued: "Holy One, you still have not answered my question. Are you stalling to come up with a better lie?"

"I do not lie."

"That's demonstrably false, and it's why you're in shackles."

"I misspoke. Within the strictures of my vows, I do not lie. To one such as you, my words can have no meaning, so a lie is the same as truth. You lack the ability to distinguish one from the other. If the antecedent is false, then the rules of implication require my statement to be true, regardless of the consequent's truth-value. Since you cannot perceive my premises, my overall implication is true, although you mistake it for a lie. I shall try to put in plainly. When *you* opened the doors, you used magic. *I* used prayer."

"Explain the difference, Holy One. I understand logic, but not its application here. You continue to prevaricate and dissemble. I see the same mechanisms at work, and the same effects. Are there meaningful differences between magic, technology, and miracles? Tell me how I err. Couldn't you see the dolmen's lights?"

"Lights?" he asked, honest surprise filling his face. "There are no lights."

"Streamers and ribbons and bands of energy, springing from the standing stones. They are normally invisible, but you invoked them to open the doors."

"How can light be invisible? That's a contradiction in terms."

"Light may be invisible if you insist on shutting your eyes," I said dryly. "I thought you were the master here, and I the student.

The lights are invisible until brought forth by an initiate. For me, it is a simple matter of wanting them. You say you did something different. Tell me about *prayer*. Pretend, if it helps, that I'm a sincere seeker of truth. Otherwise, consider that I could compel your answer. I have that power."

He settled himself on the hay, drawing up his feet to sit cross-legged. "Your threats," he said after a moment, "do not concern me as much as your ignorance. You lurch through the world, dragging earthquakes and storms behind you, substituting raw— and heretical—power for understanding. Your mistake, Grey, is confusing ontology with teleology. You mix up being with purpose. Prayer isn't *doing* anything; it's the opposite."

"I think I know those words, but I don't understand what you mean. A miracle is a miracle to me. You once espoused a scientific outlook toward gathering and interpreting data. You can't maintain that position while simultaneously claiming ecclesiastical privilege and pretending that prayer is the answer."

"I've never claimed to work miracles. I spoke only of holiness, something you fail to appreciate or even acknowledge. You are too self-absorbed to accept my spiritual authority. I cannot absolve you of sins for which you won't repent."

"I didn't ask for absolution, and the state of my soul is my own affair." *More misdirection?* I wondered. "Tell me about prayer," I said, trying to hold my anger in check.

"I've already told you. You did not listen."

"You touched the doors with your palms, and then stood back with your arms stretched wide. Those of us with second sight perceived the lights spring forth. The doors opened in response. You did *something*."

"Again, you mistake actions with outcomes. I didn't need to touch the doors or raise my arms. Those are outward signs of respect, rituals our order has maintained since the beginning. What I did was become a conduit for the holy powers, and that's a matter of being, not doing. I let all striving and desire drain from me, becoming an empty vessel."

"So, theoretically, I could do the same thing?" I asked.

He snorted. "You lack humility of any sort. You could never achieve the proper mental state. I did not *do* anything. I *became* something."

"The more I learn, Holy One, the more humble I become. Logic suggests that pride in one's humility becomes a contradiction, a kind of hubris worse than mere deceit. The *reason* you emptied your mind was to open the doors. Thus, purpose reintroduces itself. Which one of us is confused about teleology?"

"Do you think these children's word games can confuse me?"

"No, of course not. You say you wanted nothing, that your goal was humility and abandonment of both strife and desire. I merely point out that you *did*, in fact, desire something; namely, opening the doors. Can you be sure your mind was empty?"

"I recited my private mantra to clear my mind. In that state, there is no room for conscious thought. You mistake the effects of the holy powers for command or desire on my part."

Ah! "Now, perhaps, we're getting somewhere. Could a novice monk recite a mantra and open the doors?" I asked.

"No, it takes decades of mental discipline to learn to clear the mind from all distractions. The mantra is just a tool; the words themselves don't matter, only the inward-looking attitude. We call the resultant state, if successful, ego-free mindfulness."

"What if two hierophants stood before the doors, each with deep humility, reciting their mantras, but wanting different things? Suppose one of you tried to open the doors while another attempted to keep them closed."

"Such an experiment has never been tried. You are again suggesting we employ commands, or that the doors respond to our desires. It doesn't work that way."

"Have you ever tried performing all your ritual actions and meditations *without* wanting the doors to open?"

"Why would I?"

"Exactly," I said. "I think we're back to agency and intentionality. You are either unwilling or unable to perform tests that might reveal the 'holy powers' are nothing more than disguised technology. The ancients had devices called 'neural interfaces.' Have you heard the term?"

"Naturally, but I find your insinuation insulting. You mock the understanding that a lifetime of study has revealed to me, and belittle our faith. You are, to put it crudely, unenlightened."

"Then teach me. You've already explained prayer, so now tell me what lies hidden in the chambers beneath the temple."

"Ancient things," he said stiffly. "You would do well to stay away. You have no right to touch holy artifacts, or remove them from the reliquary."

I finally let my anger take control. "It's a damned *library*, not a reliquary," I shouted. "Where's the workshop that goes with it? You mention 'holy artifacts' as if they were finger bones of ancient saints. I'm guessing your precious artifacts are really just tools you've forgotten how to operate."

He didn't reply.

"Am I wrong?" I asked, my voice dangerously soft.

"Even you wouldn't dare explore the tunnels and chambers under the reliquary. If you try to move the altar to gain access, every monk on the continent will take up arms. Your thunderstorms are not proof against crossbows. A single bolt could end your insufferable insolence."

Thank you for telling me where to look, I thought. *That was a major slip*. His anger had driven him to a mistake and kept him from realizing he had yielded precious information. To keep him off balance, I just smiled and said, "We'll see. I plan to visit today."

Kiril stiffened suddenly, and bloody spittle foamed at his

mouth. I hadn't thought such a rage was possible. Then he leaned sideways, fell from the haystack, and began jerking about on the stones.

I scrambled inside his brain, found the misfiring neurons, and urged them to quiescence. His seizure subsided quickly, but he remained unconscious. I suspected his sleep would be long.

I stood up, stretched, and told the guards, "The Holy One suffers from epilepsy." At their blank looks, I added, "Seizures. Fits. Ask a passing monk if he has medication for it. If his condition is unknown to them, have a physician examine him. Do you understand? It's not a holy affliction, just a rather common physical problem. It's treatable. Don't give him wine, beer, or ale. Water is best for him."

"Yes, lord," they said in unison. Then the one I presumed to be senior, said carefully, "You were very . . . involved in your discussion. Sergeant Nix came asking for you twice."

I shook my head. "I was, as you say, involved. What did Nix want?"

"He said the king had sent for you."

"Then I suppose I must go. Have a courier bring me news of the Holy One's recovery, and forget anything you overheard."

I followed the passageways back out to daylight. I looked around, surprised that the sudden light didn't hurt my eyes. The three starships loomed impossibly high to my left, their tops hidden by the overcast sky. The wind had picked up while I argued with Kiril, and it felt damp and oppressive, but there were no individual clouds, just an unrelieved canopy of grey. It must be a mother of a storm coming, I realized. I had first felt its fingers when leaving Brand, and that was a good way south. This storm would slam the entire northeastern seaboard, reaching at least fifty miles inland. I tried extending my percipience to the East Ocean, to see if it was a hurricane or just a squall, but my second sight couldn't reach that far. Once, my mind had sailed like a hawk over the entire continent, but I had been somewhat insane at the time, so I didn't know how much of that perception had been imaginary. Kiril's shackles formed a bruising reminder of my own captivity in Henna's attic at the Luvar Inn. Henna had had the queer notion that imprisoning and torturing me would bring her luck. I had escaped the agony by fleeing into madness; perhaps Kiril would find a kinder solution.

Nix led up our horses, and I noted with pleasure that Butter had been curried. She looked sleek and eager. "Did you adjust the saddle and straps, Sergeant?" I asked. "I can't do it one-handed."

"Yes, lord. I took everything off while grooming her and letting her graze, but carefully replaced everything. I thought you'd want to ride immediately."

"How long was I in there? It's too overcast for me to see the sun."

"Nearly two full hours," he said cheerfully. "It's mid-afternoon, a good four hours left until dark. The king is waiting."

"Good man," I said absently, hauling myself into the saddle. "Lead on."

Only mid-afternoon? It felt like weeks since I'd left home, and I still had much to do. First Ashe, then the temple, then Maran, I recited silently, repeating it endlessly, matching it to the pounding of our hooves. *You can do this. Ashe, temple, Maran. Ashe, temple, Maran.* After those things, maybe sleep.

Nix whistled nearly tunelessly as we crossed the three miles to the tent city. He seemed indecently jolly, as if imprisoning a hierophant and escorting a prince were better jobs than his usual lot. I grudgingly acknowledged this was probably exciting for him, but I could not share his enjoyment. Instead, I hated him just a little, while simultaneously wishing the two of us could find a tavern, put up our feet, tell stupid jokes, and drink beer until we were thoroughly sloshed and best friends. I had never done such a thing in my life, but I was willing to try it.

Chapter Twelve

I LET the heralds with their stupid trumpets announce me outside the king's tent. A nervous young page, no older than eight, bowed and ushered me within, announcing me all over again. I was too tired to protest the formalities. Thus, for the first time, I came into Ashe's presence without startling anyone or causing panic. It felt strange.

Ashe dismissed the pages, courtiers, and most of his advisors. The two he let stay were an old military man and a middle-aged female scholar. Their clothing proclaimed their occupations, and Ashe shared their names: "Lord Grey, this is General Yarval, commander of the royal army. He's Baron Draycott in civilian life, and also Lady Ariel's father. And this is Chief Archivist Selene, of the royal library in Jappa. She's coordinating the scholars working on the Book of the Ship."

"Lord Grey," they both echoed politely.

"Pleased to meet you both," I said. To Selene, I added, "You have a melodious name. *Sell-uh-nee.* I don't think I've heard it before."

"It's Terran, from an old word for the moon."

"Moon?"

"A smaller body orbiting a planet. Sundering doesn't have any."

"We have a satellite," I said. "It's mentioned in the Book of the Ship. If I recall, it's artificial." I ransacked my memory. "Justian placed 'a star in the sky' soon after the landing, right? Would that be a moon?"

"The oldest records mention a bright star whose motions made no sense. No one in living memory has spotted it, and many astronomers study the heavens extensively, charting the course of stars and other planets," she said. "An artificial satellite would be *like* a moon, sort of, but not a permanent fixture. It would eventually fall unless maintained."

"Other planets?" I asked, my eyebrows lifting. "Other Sunderings?"

"No, just big rocks or giant balls of gas going around the sun as we do."

"The sun orbits Sundering," I protested. "You can see it happen."

"An easy mistake, my lord. One needs to study all the motions to understand them. We are still trying to grasp the details ourselves, but we're confident that the sun is the center of everything. You see—"

General Yarval cleared his throat. "All very interesting, I'm sure, but academic discussions can wait. We have more pressing business."

Selene looked mildly offended, but snapped her mouth shut without protest.

Ashe stepped into the awkward silence. "I have to agree with the general," he said. To soften his words, he added to Selene, "I would like to hear about moons and planets, but at another time." To the group, he said, "Duke Benlyn's messengers tell me the situation in Amrhyn is getting more tense all the time. It hasn't come to battle yet, but Cevak and the other sorcerers have now mustered an army of their own, making their intentions clear. It takes damnably long for couriers to ride back and forth. We've had to set up relays of them, so each may pass off messages and let the next one gallop on. I learn things weeks late. My replies take the same amount of time getting back to him."

"Wouldn't one of the tall ships be faster?" I asked. "No mountains."

"The nearest deep port is Halmar," said Ashe. "A ship would have to go all the way around the continent to reach Ben's position. The northern route has those insufferable winds, and the southern passage has treacherous currents. Ships take longer, and are less reliable than riders. A ship can founder, or spend days either becalmed or battling storms."

"Speaking of that, you should send riders to Halmar right away. There's a very big storm coming. It's too large for me to see the entirety, but I think it may be a hurricane. It won't just bring rain. If the temperature drops, we'll have snow and ice. I can't guess how much."

"Already sent," said Ashe. "You aren't the only one with weather sense. The tall ships will be far out at sea by now, waiting to ride it out. The smaller ones are in sheltered coves or bays, or hauled up on shore and lashed down. Meanwhile, the communication problems remain. I was thinking of, well, *you* as a solution."

I absorbed his intent with discomfort. The last thing I wanted was another large responsibility. "You want to use me as a daily courier?"

"No, just a scouting mission or two, to ascertain the current situation. I've told Ben to use his own judgment, but it rankles to get news so slowly. I can't advise him properly from this distance."

"I would enjoy meeting the duke again," I said. "What of our, ah, other projects?"

"You may speak freely. My chief advisors know of the special army you're preparing. How is Lady Maran doing?"

"She's busy at work already. She hopes to have five thousand, both foot soldiers and officers, within two to three weeks. I can transport them directly to the duke, or anywhere else in Amrhyn."

General Yarval blinked and coughed. "Did you say five thousand?"

I lifted my shoulders. "She's quite efficient, and they're mostly straw to start with, so materials aren't a problem. The only limitations are her energy, and the time it takes to bring them to life." Then I paused, struck by a sudden inspiration born from my conversation with Brand at the tavern. "Ashe," I said, "the plan was for me to be in charge of the, uh, special forces, but I'm not the best choice. I would just be a figurehead, with you, Yarval, and Benlyn making all the decisions. Why not free me of that mostly ceremonial duty, and let me concentrate on the sorcerers?"

Yarval bristled at my failure to use titles, but Selene smothered a laugh behind her hand. Ashe tried to ignore both of them, but as Yarval puffed out his beribboned chest and started growling, he addressed the problem. "Grey is free to violate politesse. He didn't serve at court or hold rank himself until recently. He doesn't intend rudeness; he just forgets."

Selene said, "As the only commoner present, I find it refreshing."

Yarval unruffled his feathers. "As you wish, sire."

Ashe turned his attention back to me. "If you don't command the special army, who can? Ben—" He grimaced and backtracked. "—Duke Benlyn, I mean, won't know what to do with five thousand golems."

"So it's okay to use the word?" I asked.

Ashe nodded. "Everyone here is aware of your army's true nature."

"That makes conversation easier. You remember Brand. He's

far more capable of commanding the army than I. Of course, I can still be there to observe and report back, but Brand would free me to do my real work. Assuming he's available in time," I added after a slight hesitation. "He's on an extended mission for me at the moment. I don't know how long it will last."

"Where did you send him?" asked Ashe.

"Nowhere. Or rather, I told him to stay where he was."

"I sent him to arrange for a housekeeper. He should be back already."

"Tessa's not well. I needed someone I could trust to watch her. I don't suppose you've had any luck finding Lane yet?"

"*Five thousand. . . ?*" interrupted Yarval. His voice made it seem he was still processing the improbable number and finding the concept overwhelming. Both Ashe and I stopped to wait for him. "I don't know about golems, but quantity is no substitute for quality. How will these fighters perform? They have no battle experience. Most new soldiers either run away or freeze in place when facing opponents the first time. It takes years of training to get a column to hold formation."

"Relax," I said. "They don't experience fear, or any emotion other than loyalty. They don't even feel arrows or sword thrusts. They don't need to sleep, eat, or drink. For all practical purposes, you can ignore logistics for them. Only strategy and tactics will matter. Brand can handle both easily."

"I'm minded to agree," said Ashe slowly, clearly turning things over in his mind. "Brand has proven himself among my troops already, and the duke likes him."

"The respect is mutual. Brand spoke highly of the duke this morning."

"That's settled, then," said Ashe in the tone he used to give commands. "I'll have to give him a proper army rank. He's not technically an officer, although I've brevetted him to lieutenant in the King's Guard for convenience. General, considering his duties, what's most appropriate?"

"If you intend him to join the normal chain of command, sire, he cannot remain in the King's Guard, nor exceed the rank of army colonel," said Yarval. "You should assign him to me as a lieutenant, the same rank he has now. I'll brevet him to colonel, and detach him for special duty to Duke Benlyn. He can rejoin the King's Guard afterward. This lets him command in the field without offending all your other officers, and leaves the duke with final authority."

"See to it," said Ashe.

"Very good, sire. I'll send the papers and insignia to him, and let the general staff know of his promotion."

Ashe turned back to me, looking thoughtful. "I'm sorry to say we have no news of Lane," he said at length. "Pity—not only for him, but also for Tessa and the boy. If Lane were home, he could take care of them. However, Grey, if your proposal is to work, we need Brand with us, not playing nursemaid. This 'extended mission' is likely unwise. I should send another man, or better yet a nurse, and have the general recall Brand immediately. How long will Tessa need someone? Is she on the mend?"

"Ashe, may we please sit? My bad leg is killing me."

I could have stood longer, but I didn't want to answer him right away. Moving to a set of chairs around a circular table gave me time to arrange my emotions and compose my face. "Rather the opposite, I'm afraid. She's dying. I had previously invited her to your wedding, but she won't be able to attend."

"I'm sorry to hear that. Should I send physicians?"

"No, it's too late for doctors. She doesn't have long."

Selene said, "I'm a surgeon by training. I don't know Tessa, but perhaps I could help."

"She has a rapid-onset brain tumor. It's already covering her premotor cortex and her optic chiasma. The hypothalamus is still functional, but infiltrated. She's losing control of her bowels, her balance, and her sight. She seems to suffer mild dementia, mostly at night."

"Sundown syndrome," she said. "We see it with many ailments. It means the tumor spread to her frontal lobes, too. I'm very sorry. Is she in pain?"

"She only mentions her hips, but if you send analgesics, they'd be better than anything available locally. I'm worried about her autonomic systems more than anything else. If she loses control of her breathing, blood pressure, or heart rate—"

"Yes, of course," said Selene quickly. "Your concerns are warranted. Sedatives are too dangerous, but we have some pain relievers that might help, and there are some herbs that may buy her more time by reducing intracranial pressure." She turned to the king. "Sire, if I may—?"

He waved at her. "By all means, go make arrangements. The staff sergeant will know Tessa's location. Send anyone or anything you think best. But don't go yourself. I need your expertise here."

When she was gone, Ashe eyed me curiously. "When did you become a physician? I barely knew half the words you two used, and I've trained as a field medic."

I stared into his eyes, blinking slowly, until he got the message.

He stirred and sat up straighter. "Yes, of course. I forgot about that. You must understand physiology intimately to do what you do."

"What are you two talking about, sire?" asked the general.

"Just remembering shared experiences," said Ashe. "I've seen Grey perform surgery before."

"Oh, that reminds me," I said. "Did you know Kiril has epilepsy?"

"Seizures? No, I had no idea. You didn't cause one, did you?"

"I think it's a preexisting condition. I stopped the one he had today, and told your men to ask the monks if he normally takes medication. I also forbade alcohol, and arranged for bedding. If this was his first seizure, then yes, I'm afraid it could be my fault. I pressed him pretty hard during our conversation."

"Just by *talking* to the man? What on Sundering did you discuss?"

"Philosophy and its practical applications," I said, grinning.

"That would give *me* apoplexy," said Ashe with a mock shudder.

"I assume you speak metaphorically. It wasn't a stroke; I checked for blockages and hemorrhaging. It was a regular seizure —neurons firing out of sequence. I was able to put it right, but I should avoid phenomenology and existentialism the next time we talk." Thoughtfully, I added, "Logic, ontology, epistemology, and teleology are likely triggers, too. I'll stick to practical everyday matters from now on. Maybe we can practice ego-free mindfulness together. That'll be calming."

"I only know one of those disciplines," said Ashe, "although I vaguely remember my tutors having mentioned the others."

"Epistemology is the most fascinating, in my opinion. If you—"

"Sire!" burst out General Yarval loudly, "should we really be spending time on science, medicine, and philosophy?"

"At the heart, General, everything is philosophy," I put in helpfully.

Yarval glared at me a moment, then said, "Sire, if our campaign in Amrhyn is to take place in the next several weeks, I must make preparations. The main burden will fall on Duke Benlyn and Colonel Brand, so I must resupply and reinforce them starting *now*. A month ago would be better."

"We didn't know there was a crisis a month ago," said Ashe reasonably. "But yes, you're dismissed. You have much to arrange."

"Thank you, sire," said Yarval stiffly. He pushed himself upright and stalked out of the tent angrily.

"I think I upset him," I said.

Ashe shrugged. "He's a professional. He'll get over it. I think the most disturbing thing he heard was the proposed size of Maran's army. It changes the equations of war significantly."

"So it's to be war? Are you sure? I thought the goal was reestablishing normal relations, and harvesting the crops before they spoil."

"If you can accomplish those goals without fighting, your reach exceeds mine. I have little hope, myself. This year's yield may already be lost, and Cevak seems unwilling to compromise."

"What of the commoners—the shepherds, farmers, ranchers, merchants, tradesfolk, and reapers? They won't want armed conflict. There must be leaders among them who can replace the sorcerers. In fact, if the sorcerers prove so recalcitrant and pugnacious as to insist on a war, it can only end with all of them dead. They get replaced either way. Perhaps Benlyn can organize a vote."

"Vote?"

"Each person having a say in how government works, electing leaders to speak for them. Amrhyn has always been a self-governing region—I believe you said it had only a token allegiance to the crown. Why not go all the way, and let the people rule themselves?"

"I know what voting means, Grey," said Ashe, wrinkling his brow. "I just think it's madness. They have nobles, an aristocracy, chiefly the landowners and petty lords. They are the ones to replace the sorcerers. Instead of organizing a vote, we should encourage the nobility to rebel. They hesitate now because the sorcerers are too powerful, but with your army. . . ."

"You want to send Kiril to preach at them? He does sedition well."

"Don't be facetious. I'm talking about real people suffering and dying. They need their crops as much as we do. Even without a war, they'll starve if they don't start harvesting soon. The people there are terrified. The sorcerers forbid reaping or trade, holding the land hostage against me."

"What's their true goal?" I asked. "What do they *want?*"

"Chiefly, I believe they want to cut off all contact with the rest of the continent. They repudiate the crown specifically, even the loose ties we've always shared. They are primarily exporters, not importers, so the cessation of trade won't hurt them as badly as it hurts us, and they know that gives them the upper hand."

I did him the courtesy of listening quietly, then asked with some trepidation, "Ashe, was it a mistake to create a fiefdom and make Ben the duke?"

He stood up suddenly, frustration evident in his mannerisms. He stalked angrily around the tent for a minute, then came back and undid his ponytail, letting his russet hair fall around his shoulders. He sat down and buried his hands in his hair, eyes focused on the tabletop. "What choice did I have? They started it by withholding agricultural products, cattle, and horses. I had to do something, and I hoped they would negotiate if I sent a personal representative. He had to be elevated to a peerage, to give him respectability and gravitas. The idea was to show I took their concerns seriously, and that Ben had plenipotentiary power to make binding agreements on my behalf."

"Weren't there other lands you could have given him? Making him a duke was sensible, but did you have to give him Amrhyn itself?"

"You don't understand," he said miserably. I risked reaching out my good hand in a consoling gesture, but he slapped it away without looking up. "If we have any chance of the nobles giving allegiance, or even signing a treaty, it must be through fealty to a local who outranks them. So I had to elevate Ben above the barons, viscounts, earls, and petty lords, and I had to put him *there*. The dukedom is not hereditary, so the locals needn't worry about perpetual subservience. It's a complicated compromise."

"You're right," I said after I was sure he had finished. "I don't understand the nobility at all. I thought myself only ignorant of styles and titles, but it appears there's an entire mindset and set of precedents governing them. Do the locals accept Ben's position? Will they defy the sorcerers?"

Ashe finally lifted his head. "Yes, they accept the duke. No, they won't rebel against the sorcerers. They're too frightened of being bent backward over a stone altar, or having their buildings burned. There are few sorcerers left, but they are powerful. You buried most of them alive with your earthquakes. The remainder was attacked by the nina you freed. Benlyn says the locals tell amazing tales of giants and dragons roaming the moors, searching out and killing the surviving sorcerers. Strangely, the nina did not go after anyone else. The carnage continued until Ulat bound all the nina into unicorn shape, and they went into hiding. No one knows why the nina were so fierce, but that threat passed, and the few surviving sorcerers have reestablished control of the region. Through Cevak, they claim to be the legitimate rulers of Amrhyn."

"The sorcerers perform blood rites to augment their powers. Perhaps the nina abhor the practice as much as we do. I didn't direct the nina to attack, but they were all mentally linked with me when I broke open their prison. I was busy fighting a sorcerer at the time, and he had just killed a friend. The nina probably read my intent. I wanted all the sorcerers to die, and for their horrid religion to perish with them."

"Enough of them remain to terrorize ordinary Amrhyns into submission. And they hate us—particularly you—with unbridled passion."

I said, "They likely believe I sent the nina to ravage them."

"So where does that leave things?" Ashe asked.

I sighed, not wanting to answer, but knowing now why I had seen the vision of my golem army fighting the Amrhyns. "War. Like you, I don't see a diplomatic solution. They would have killed me yesterday if the stone children hadn't come to my rescue. But Ashe," I added earnestly, "we must spare the ordinary folk as much as possible. Between Benlyn's leadership and the overwhelming force of Maran's army, they may fight on our side. If so, then when the last sorcerer is dead, they can claim the victory as their own."

"Do you know how to defeat the sorcerers, then?" asked Ashe, hope gleaming in his eyes.

"Not yet, but I'll figure something out. If nothing else, I can throw tornadoes at them. But Maran has the wild notion that Justian buried weapons or other kinds of tools beneath the temple. That's my next stop. Kiril unwittingly gave me an idea where to look."

Ashe stood up suddenly, and I followed suit. "Why are you waiting?" he asked. "Do you need me to accompany you?"

"No, just a handful of your strongest men. I've already appropriated Sergeant Nix for my personal service, but he won't be enough."

"Nix?"

"Red-haired fellow from Lesser Niggleton."

"Ah, on the coast. I know the place, but not the man. Tell the staff sergeant to assign you a squad, and take Selene with you. She can translate any instruction manuals you may discover. And find time to visit Ben soon. He needs to know our plans, and I want a report on his situation."

"Okay," I said, glancing around the tent and just then realizing Selene hadn't returned. "Where is Selene?" I asked. "Her errand shouldn't have taken long."

"She did not have clearance to reenter the tent during a private meeting. She's likely standing right outside, waiting."

"Seems like poor treatment. She was already in the meeting."

Ashe laughed gently. "My guards knew only that I was talking to you. I've left standing orders that you and I are not to be disturbed."

"So how do I explain that to Selene?"

"You don't," he said. "She already understands how the world works. Just ask her to go with you. She'll be excited by the prospect."

I started to limp toward the tent flap, then remembered my manners. "How is Lady Ariel?"

"Well, thank you. She's in Draycott, planning the wedding. It has to be a fancy affair, and most of Jappa is still in ruins. She has a thousand details to manage. Her last letter was brief, but touching. I may not get to see her again until I move the court south, so we've been writing regularly."

"Give her my regards, then," I said.

"She will be flattered by your attention."

I harrumphed and muttered, "Liar," under my breath.

Ashe's laughter followed me out of the tent. He sounded quite pleased with himself. I found Selene immediately, but I couldn't locate Nix or the staff sergeant. In the end, I had to ask one of the pages for help. The girl dashed through the crowds like a wisp, returning shortly with the staff sergeant in tow. She disappeared again before I could thank her.

I explained to the staff sergeant what I needed.

"Will a squad of ten suffice, lord?" he asked.

"Oh, not that many. Three or four will do, as long as they're muscular. If that's not enough, the entire King's Guard won't suffice. We're to ride up past the monastery on an errand for the king. Selene here will need a horse. Sergeant Nix has my own with him . . . somewhere." I looked at the milling throng helplessly.

The page came back, this time dragging Nix with her. She grinned when I thanked her, and bounced jauntily away.

Nix saluted me lazily at first, then, catching the staff sergeant's glare, stiffened and gave a proper salute.

The staff sergeant organized everything quickly and efficiently. In only ten minutes, we set off, all mounted. He had assigned a corporal and three other guardsmen, all strong, healthy young men. Nix, holding the highest rank among the guards, took charge of our troop. Once clear of the tent city, he arranged the guards so that Selene and I rode together in their midst, with himself leading the way. He had brought a heavy cloak to replace the one I'd given Kiril, and I was grateful for his forethought.

The rain started as we reached the town of Landing, and drummed steadily on the cobbles and slate roofs as we rode through high street. Before we reached the three-way fork in the road, we were all thoroughly soaked and miserable. The storm began in earnest, accompanied by nearly continuous thunder, and it became hard to see our way.

Nix started up the fork that led back toward the monastery. I had to urge Butter up beside him and shout to get his attention. I pointed at the muddy path leading to the monument. He nodded, and whirled his arm to instruct the others. We trotted single file, as quickly as the weather permitted, until we'd crossed the wooden bridge and reached the ring of standing stones.

The corporal and another guard unrolled canvas sheets from their packs, and tried tying them to the megaliths to provide some shelter from the sheeting torrents of rain. The wind grabbed at the canvas, tore the ropes from their hands, and blew everything away.

Enough was enough. I brought the god-winds to bear, going counter to the world's winds, and punched a hole in the sky. Immediately above us, slanted sunlight shone strongly. On all sides, ratty clouds, low to the ground and full of rain, continued to swirl and roar. Inside the dolmen's circle, however, a sudden silence fell, and we gathered under the patch of sunlight.

"It won't hold long," I told the others. "If you have more canvas, try rigging a shelter. Selene and I will go inside first."

Nix looked up, measuring the angle of the sun's rays. "Two hours until sunset, lord."

"Acknowledged. Do what you can for the horses—blankets or rubdowns or whatever. It's always chilly inside the circle, and they're soaked through already. When my temporary ward fails, the sun will go back behind the clouds, and you'll all get wet again."

"Mayn't we come with you, lord, horses and all?"

I had never considered it. Had anyone in history been brazen enough to take a horse inside the monks' most hallowed temple? Did I care? "Okay, yes," I said after thinking it through. "There's room, but it's even colder inside. Rig the canvas, and then follow us in."

I faced the temple, went forward to touch the doors, and then stood back a pace, my good arm raised. *Ego-free mindfulness*, I thought, trying to empty my brain of all thoughts. When nothing happened, I thought the command "Open!" in a mental shout. No lights appeared, and the doors stubbornly refused to budge. I tried several more times, using different commands, before limping to a megalith, slapping it with my hand, and waking the lights. The doors swung silently inward. Selene watched my performance with lively curiosity. I held out my good arm for her. "Shall we go?"

"Goodness, yes. I haven't been inside yet."

"But you're in charge of the scholars. Why haven't you come daily?"

"No one could open the doors," she said. "I thought you knew."

I scowled, crossing the threshold and pulling my cloak tight against the intense cold. "You mean no one *would*," I said angrily. "Any hierophant could have done it for you."

"There aren't any in town. They've all gone to remote parishes, except the Holy One called Kiril, and I believe he fled to Halmar before being imprisoned."

"Well, that can't be helped now. I'll leave the doors open this time, so you and the other scholars can have free access. The temple has flooded before, but I worry about mud and debris flung by the storm. Feel free to look around. The books are tricky; try warming them between your palms."

She wandered off among the shelves, and I concentrated on the room. The altar stood where I remembered it, marble under its glass casing, ship's metal beneath that. The same directionless light as before provided glare-free illumination. I bent over to examine the seams where the altar met the floor. I saw no sign of a hidden lever or hinge. No scuff marks marred the mirror-like marble flooring. My percipience couldn't pierce the ceiling, walls, floor, or altar, not with any clarity. I heard Selene giving small, surprised cries of delight as she found books that interested her. I mentally mapped out the chambers beneath the temple, discernible mainly by being impenetrable. I could see the outlines, no more. Selene started carrying armloads of books past me. I assumed she was stacking them by the door for the trip home. I nodded absently the first time, when she stopped to ask permission, but didn't take my attention from my explorations.

I was still studying the altar when Nix led the guard and our horses inside. The sudden clatter of shod hooves of marble set up odd echoes. Without taking my eyes from the altar, I called over my shoulder, "Tether them to something near the doorway. A bookcase will do if you can't find a ring or a post." If he answered, I didn't hear him; I immersed myself deeply in memories. At other dolmens, while standing in the exact center with the lights lit, I had often perceived eldritch abilities that would not be possible elsewhere. One such suggestion came to me now. I stepped forward, placed my palm flat on the glass case surrounding the altar, and slowly lifted my arm. The entire altar followed my upward motion to stay in contact with my palm. I didn't know if a specific sequence of thoughts had unlocked the altar, or if only the motion was required. Understanding seldom graced me in such situations.

When I had raised the altar two feet, as high as my arm could reach without breaking contact with the top, I tried swinging the bulk to the side. Instantly, weight returned, and the altar crashed back down.

I raised it again and held it hovering in the air, wondering what to do next. Finally, I recalled the inspiration that had led me to request a handful of brawny young men for this trip. "Sergeant," I called out. "Move this stone to one side."

I left the logistics to them, save only a warning to keep their fingers free from the bottom edge. If the altar fell, I didn't want amputated body parts crushed beneath it. They tried pushing and pulling from all sides, hoping, I suppose, to wiggle it free like getting a wagon wheel out of the mud. When they had no success, Nix spat disgustedly and said, "It's too heavy."

"It's weightless," I said, "floating!" Then I recalled that mass and weight were different things. Although I could temporarily remove the weight, inertia would still be in full force. The altar seemed to be solid marble under the glass, and probably weighed several thousand pounds when resting on the floor. Even five strong men would have trouble pushing it aside, especially when their only purchase was slick marble flooring.

A small voice timidly said, "We have horses."

"Thank you, Selene," I said. "Excellent suggestion. Sergeant?"

"Aye, very clever idea. We'll make a rig."

They quickly lashed ropes around the altar, and hitched a team. "We'll have to pull toward the door—there isn't room elsewhere," said Nix. "That means you'll have to walk backward at our pace. Are you ready, lord?"

"What's the pace to be?"

"Step by step, only half a dozen feet. Just enough to uncover what's hidden."

"Then count it aloud. I'll move with you."

"On three, I guess. One . . . two . . . *step!*" He called out five more steps, and then halted the team. The altar rocked a bit, but glided backward to keep contact with my palm. I gently lowered it down.

"Well, that's good rope we'll never get back," said Nix.

I saw what he meant. The ends of the rigging beneath the altar neatly chopped off at the altar's bottom edge, with no hope of recovery. The remainder of the improvised harness slithered free and fell to the floor. "Rig around the lateral edges next time," I suggested, but I really didn't care about rope just then. I hurried around the other side of the altar to see what we'd uncovered.

A steep stairwell replete with handrails, all made of ship's metal, led downward. The same indirect lighting, seeming to come from the ship's metal itself, sprang up when my foot touched the top step, revealing a closed door at the foot of the stairs. I highly doubted that the hierophants used a team of horses to move the altar, but then I guessed these stairs had lain hidden for centuries, perhaps millennia.

I hesitated at the top, thinking I might be the first person since Justian himself to explore beneath the temple. Selene came to my side while I was still debating the wisdom of going down. "Are you sure it's safe?" she asked.

"I'm sure of nothing in this place," I replied softly. "I feel uneasy. But it's likely safer for me than anyone else. Tell the sergeant that all of you should wait with the horses beside the doorway. I'll go down and come back to tell you what I find."

"I wanted to collect more books," she said. "You wouldn't believe the treasures I've already—"

"Obey me in this," I said curtly. "I want you out of the way."

She murmured her disappointment, but agreed.

I limped slowly down the steps, using the right handrail for support. The stairway was quite steep, and I wished I could use both hands. It felt more like shimmying down a ladder than descending a set of steps. I noted with interest that no screws or bolts held the railings secure. The entire stairway was one piece, designed to last forever.

The doorway at the bottom had neither knob nor latch. It was actually a pair of doors, with push-plates at waist height. I had seen such an arrangement before, mainly at taverns, where servers, their hands full, could shoulder their way through without fiddling for a latch. Those doors, of course, had been made of wood, not ship's metal. I bent over to look closely. The plates had lettering incised on them. I couldn't read the language, and wished, just for a moment, that I had let Selene accompany me. But I guessed the lettering merely said something like, "Push here," or "Watch for people on the far side."

I laid my palm on the right-hand door and pushed gently. When it didn't move, I tried leaning into it, using both shoulders. Still no good. I stopped and stood in thought. Justian or his engineers might have locked these doors, but their presence meant access to the chambers beyond was possible. I searched for a keyhole, unsurprised to find nothing. Justian didn't use mechanical locks. These doors were a miniature version of the great doors guarding the temple itself. I reached back up the stairs and out into the storm with my percipience, to contact the monument's lights. The moment I touched the streamers and bangles with my questing mental fingers, the doors before me swung silently inward, and indirect lighting filled the corridor beyond. The deep underground chime tolled exactly once, but this time, instead of sounding like a giant clangorous bell, it sounded like a voice. I couldn't make out the word it spoke, but it reminded me disturbingly of the Sleeper asking, "Who?" when I touched a dolmen's king stone.

I limped past the doorway into the corridor. As I did, distant lights jumped to life, revealing doors and chambers to all sides. These weren't faerie lights, but the soft indirect illumination of the temple and stairwell, seeming to come from the floor, ceiling, and walls. I explored several rooms, but they were empty, save for cabinets rising from the floor. Like the stairwell, the desk-like cabinets had no bolts or fastenings, also no doors or openings, not even shelves. They were shapely lumps of metal, slightly less than waist height, rounded on the corners but flat on top, likely extruded directly from the floor.

I laid my right palm on the surface of one. Multicolored lights, seeming embedded within the surface, glimmered softly in circles, curves, and straight lines. I traced one of the curves with my forefinger. A soft and melodious voice rewarded me, but I couldn't understand it.

"Hello?" I said tentatively. "Who's there?"

The voice responded, but was still unintelligible. I closed the eyes of my body, relying on percipience for a better look. The embedded lights disappeared. I lifted my lids, and everything was still in place. I tested several more times, getting consistent results. I recalled how my percipience had never been able to penetrate ship's metal. Second sight was useless here. Only physical eyes would work. Could this be the 'future need' the muria children had mentioned? It seemed unlikely to me, since history suggested the muria craved our ongoing ignorance of technology. Maybe the Ketlan disagreed with their elders. Like most things muria, it defied easy answers and remained a mystery, requiring more information before I could unravel purposes or plots. The missing clues wouldn't be found here.

I stepped back, and the surface faded to featureless grey. There didn't seem to be any danger, so I retraced my steps, and bellowed up the stairwell, "I need a scholar down here!"

A head peeked around the top of the stairs. "Coming," said Selene.

I waited patiently until she had descended, then said, "You disobeyed. You weren't waiting with the others."

"Sorry. I was too curious."

"Well, there's plenty here to sate your need for novelty," I said dryly. "Follow me."

I led her back to the cabinet that had spoken. Probably all of them could do so, but there would be time to experiment later. I placed my palm on the cabinet's top to wake it up, traced out the same curve as before, and the same melodious voice greeted us.

"What did it say?" I asked Selene.

She wrinkled her brow and chewed at a strand of hair. "I'm not sure. Can you make it happen again?"

I traced the curve again, and said, "Who's in there? Speak up!"

The voice from within the cabinet spoke at length. It kept going, until Selene clapped her hands and said, *"Ja, Malmö. Engelska tack."*

The voice immediately switched to another language. Although the change didn't help me, it seemed to delight Selene.

"I asked for English," she explained. "It's an old Terran language. The first was Swedish—I think. If not, then a related tongue. I don't know that family of languages, but English is omnipresent in the library books. We know the words, but the pronunciation has been lost. I may have a chance now, or at least a better chance."

"Who's inside the cabinet?" I asked.

"It's not a person, it's a machine. It calls itself Malmö. There isn't a modern term corresponding to its function, but I think 'control surface' will do."

"Machines that can talk? Are they alive?"

"These can talk. I don't know if 'alive' is the right word."

I frowned. "What does it control?"

She shrugged. "I have no idea. Let me try asking." She spoke to the surface, and they went back and forth for a longish time. Several other surfaces came to life while they spoke. Selene looked at me several times during her discussion with the machine, but didn't translate. Finally, after many questions and answers, a new line appeared on the surface. This one had lettering.

"Much better!" exclaimed Selene, rubbing her hands. "I got it to display the words. Now I don't have to struggle with its accent. Malmö is remarkably good at picking out my meaning, but I haven't grasped half of its replies."

"So? Ask it what it controls."

She babbled at the machine for a minute. The response came both audibly and in writing. She scanned the lettering quickly. "'Ancillary ballistics' is the best I can render its answer. But it says the 'main systems are offline' – I think that means inoperable."

"What the blazes does all *that* mean? Even when you translate, it makes no sense."

"Malmö referred me to a book upstairs in the library. I'll have to read the entire thing to understand what it's trying to tell me. But if the book is a technical manual. . . ." She shrugged helplessly. "It may be beyond us."

"What about the other surfaces?"

"Try taking your hand away."

Mystified, I obeyed. Nothing changed until I backed away to the chamber door. All the surfaces went dark instantly. Selene reached out her own hand to touch Malmö, but nothing happened. It seemed the surfaces only responded to me. Selene nodded to herself. "I thought so. It used a name for you," she said.

I thought back over my lifelong search for a proper name. "Grey" was just what people called me, a name of convenience.

This machine thing couldn't know that name. "What did it call me?"

"Controller," she said. "There was more to it, but that's all I could pick out. I think it's a title, rather than a proper name. I'd like to stay here tonight, to read that book and explore others. You can leave a couple of guards, but I don't think anyone will threaten me in this storm. I don't want to go out in it myself."

"It would be safer if you came back tomorrow," I objected.

"Nevertheless, lord. I prefer to stay. The intellectual riches here are beyond imagination."

I shrugged. "All of you may stay," I said. "If the rain is as thick and steady as I fear, the wooden bridge may be underwater or even washed away. I, however, must get home. I'll return tomorrow, but the king has given me other errands."

"Will the doors stay open?"

"I don't know about down here, but the big outer doors upstairs won't move unless commanded. I could close them to provide shelter, but then you'd be trapped inside until I return. Better to build a fire—assuming the sergeant can find dry wood."

I left her studying the machines, and hauled myself painfully up the steep staircase. Outside the temple, the storm raged unchecked. "Nix, I'll need Butter now. You're to stay the night. Do whatever Selene asks, as long as it presents no danger. She's still downstairs. Collect as much wood as you can find. The temple doesn't seem to have any venting, so build your fire in the doorway. Don't worry about making a mess; these are special circumstances. Watch for flooding, too. I'm worried about that bridge—don't even explore it until the storm passes and you have proper light."

"Aye, lord," he said, leading Butter to me. "Your mare is cold, and she's unhappy with the marble floor, but ready to ride. Are you sure you want to go outside in this weather?"

"For us, it'll just be a few steps." I swung up onto Butter, patted her neck, and checked that the saddle horn still securely held the strands I'd chosen that morning. Everything seemed intact, so I plucked the strands in the proper sequence to end up at Maran's stable. I urged Butter to walk, and we disappeared from that place.

Chapter Thirteen

The rain was continuous, but much subdued, in Maran's valley. In those few steps, Butter had carried me quite a distance inland. True night had fallen, although the difference between that and the heavily overcast sky was minimal. Not a single star shone through the heavy clouds, and all the exterior torches had long since blown out. I couldn't see to guide Butter, but she could smell her own home and knew this ground intimately. She picked her way in the dark without help from me.

I had to dismount and bang on the stable doors for attention. The groom hurried out, clucking in sympathy over Butter's condition. Warm torchlight flooded out from the stable.

"I said it would rain tonight, sir," said the groom. "I should have sent you with blankets for the mare."

"I'd hoped to have her in the king's stables overnight," I said. "That plan didn't work out. Please rub her down and give her whatever food is best. She's had a long day."

"No problems with the ride, sir?"

"None at all. She's earned her name three times over. I even managed to gallop without difficulty."

"Excellent news, sir. The lady was right."

"She always is," I said, leaving Butter in his care. I limped my way through the courtyard to reach the manor house.

Virgil, not Hasq, met me at the door. "Sir! We weren't expecting you back tonight, given your stated itinerary. Come to your quarters. Let me take your wet things, and you can dry by the fire while I find new clothing."

"Where's Hasq?" I asked.

"With the lady, sir. She's tired from her day's work, and he won't leave her side."

"Is she all right?" I asked in sudden alarm.

"Worn out and sleeping soundly, but otherwise unharmed. The baby is with the nursemaid for the night."

"She's working too hard. It doesn't sound normal that Hasq is tending to her personally. I should go see her right away."

"Ah, sir, she left orders to remain undisturbed. Hasq says he's seen this particular kind of weariness before. It comes from making too many homunculi at once. The only cure she needs is rest."

"What if I insist? She's my wife."

"Any of us will yield to a direct command, sir. If I may make a suggestion, though, I'd recommend following her instructions. Hasq is there to watch her and alert the staff to any needs. You may discuss it with her at breakfast."

I thought it over and decided he was likely giving good advice. Only minutes before I'd told the groom that Maran was always right. I should trust her—and Hasq—to know best. I lifted my good arm, gesturing for Virgil to precede me. "Okay, lead on."

We moved through the corridors, and I gratefully removed my wet cloak the moment we reached my rooms. The clothing underneath wasn't much drier. I stood in front of the hearth for a while, turning around frequently. Poor Virgil had to turn with me, trying to undo the buttons and fasteners. Finally, he made me sit, so he could remove my boots and leather trousers. He busied himself arranging a new outfit while I lounged in a chair and warmed my feet at the fire.

"Did I miss dinner?" I asked. "I haven't eaten since noon."

"I'm afraid so, sir, but the cook can make something. Do you have a preference?"

I wanted something plain, hearty, and filling. "Sausages, potatoes, and onion gravy. Mashed green peas, too, if he has any handy. Don't make him go out to the garden for them."

"I'm sure the cook has everything on hand in the kitchens, sir. Let's get you dressed. I suggest house slippers for your feet. It will take hours for your boots to dry."

I let him fuss over me for several minutes, moving only when he required it. A benign but overpowering lassitude came upon me now that I was safe and warm. It had been a *very* long day. I felt my eyelids drifting shut and struggled to stay awake. Virgil noticed and suggested I rest while he went to the kitchens to fetch my supper.

I fell asleep the moment he left the room. He woke me a half-hour later. I sat at the room's writing table to eat, then yawned widely, and dismissed him for the night.

The rain was a constant drum on the manor's roof. The day's events consumed my dreams—full of Tessa, Brand, Ashe, and the temple at Landing. The voice from the control surface narrated my fears and hopes. When it started telling Torrey how to complete his homework, I woke briefly, disoriented. I recognized my own bedding and hearth, turned over, and went back to sleep. The control surface's voice resumed, but it was all gibberish now. I felt that if I only listened long enough and carefully enough, I could make out the words. But no matter how hard I tried, the language eluded me. I woke at dawn, the rain still pounding. The devilishly indecipherable syllables of the machine's voice still echoed in my head. All told, it had not been a restful night.

I sat on the edge of my bed for a long time, trying to piece my fuzzy thoughts into something resembling coherence. I desperately wanted to talk everything over with Maran. Seeing things through her eyes normally brought clarity, or at least suggested avenues to explore.

Even through the rain, I could hear the relentless clanging coming from the smithies. The original smithy had room for only one smith, which was fine, because we had only had one smith when I left yesterday morning. The six new smithies appeared to be in full operation now; Maran must have made new smiths—along with helpers—before working on the army. I wondered if even seven blacksmiths could turn out weapons for five thousand warriors in a couple of weeks. It seemed doubtful, until I remembered the smiths would never tire, nor take breaks for food or sleep. Supplies and the sheer time it took to heat, pound, and quench were the real limitations. As far as I knew, we had no foundry to make proper steel. The swords, shields, spears, and knives would therefore be of pig iron hardened with carbon in the furnaces. Helpers would have to feed the furnaces and work the bellows continuously to keep things hot enough. I was glad it wasn't my job. The iron produced would be more brittle than steel, but good enough against pitchforks and other homemade weapons.

The racket from the smithies was enough to drive me mad, especially since I suspected it would continue unabated until Maran had finished the army. I extended my percipience to inspect their progress. Yes, it would take the seven smiths weeks to finish; from what I saw, it would be a race. There would be no peace in the valley anytime soon.

Virgil backed into the room, balancing a large tray carefully. "Good morning, sir," he said brightly. "I hope you slept well."

"I could use another night's sleep right now," I said.

"Well, then, sir, perhaps eggs, bacon, toast, jam, and tea will help. I've brought you a double portion."

I stood up and stretched. "I thought I would have breakfast with Maran this morning."

"Hasq says she is still sleeping."

"Are you *sure* she's okay?" I asked. "She usually rises before I do."

"Sir, you woke very early. I'm certain she's fine. Otherwise, Hasq would have said something. It's normal to sleep deeply after a full day's work. Didn't you yourself just say you wanted more sleep?"

"I suppose you're right," I said, trying unsuccessfully to keep grumpiness from my tone. I had really been looking forward to talking to Maran right away. Even if she couldn't help me understand the new discoveries at the monument, she had to learn about Tessa.

"I'll need riding leathers again today. I've several quick excursions to make. Please let Maran know I'll want to see her as soon as I get back."

"Very good, sir. Where shall I put the tray?"

"The writing table again, I suppose. I don't use it for writing these days."

While I filled my stomach, he laid out clothing—including another cape. I considered rejecting it, but the doleful look in his eyes told me to relax and suffer the inevitable with whatever grace I could muster. This cape, at least, wasn't purely decorative. It had a waterproof hood attached, which would come in handy today. At length, he pronounced me ready to greet the world. I thanked him for his service and went to find Butter, the cape's hood covering my braids and most of my face. Even so, I was soaked again by the time I reached the stables.

The groom had taken impeccable care of her. She seemed fresh and eager to let me ride. She nuzzled at my hand when I reached for the reins, and I realized she now associated me with treats. I asked the groom for sugar, let Butter nibble the lump from my palm, and then pulled myself into the saddle.

"Is it all right for her to have sugar every morning?" I asked the groom.

"Every now and then would be much better, sir. Too much, or too often, can lead to tooth problems and gastric distress. I very carefully balance her diet. She gets molasses mixed into her grain from time to time, as well as carrots and apples for treats. Ordinarily, she eats mainly oats, grass, or hay."

"Good to know," I said. "I shouldn't be gone long this time."

Butter didn't seem to mind the downpour. A gentle nudge sent her out of the stable and trotting down the path. She seemed to know our destination, for I didn't have to touch the reins until we were very near the dolmen. As I had done yesterday, I dismounted and led her within the faerie circle. She seemed more at ease this time, but nudged my hand for more sugar, seeming disappointed when I produced nothing. "Easy, sweetheart," I told her. She shook her neck and whinnied, spraying me with water from her mane. I wiped at my face, woke the dolmen, and selected a ribbon to open a doorway leading to Brand. I remembered at the last moment to reconnoiter first. I limped forward, holding Butter behind me, and poked my head through. Brand was ahorse, alone, plodding along a muddy trail through the rain. I mounted, and took Butter through the doorway so that we materialized beside him, paces matching. I kept the dolmen's ribbon firmly twined around my good hand.

Both he and his horse rode with heads down, so I had to call out to get his attention. "Colonel!" I said in greeting. "Congratulations on your promotion."

He looked up quickly, his hand going to his sword, then

appeared to recognize my face. He relaxed. "I'm a temporary lieutenant in the King's Guard," he said. "We don't have the rank of colonel."

"Oh, the papers haven't come through yet?" I realized while asking that it would have been nearly impossible for a courier to get here from the tent city through last night's storm. "They'll probably show up today or tomorrow. The king has reassigned you and given you a commission. You're regular army now, brevetted to colonel."

Our horses splashed through a particularly deep pocket of muddy water, and we each held up our cloaks until we reached firmer ground. "To what do I owe the honor?" he asked. His voice didn't sound as if he felt honored.

"It was my idea, based on what you said yesterday. You're a better man than I when it comes to leading soldiers. Your assignment will last until the campaign in Amrhyn concludes. Effectively, you'll be nearly equal to Duke Benlyn, each of you leading your own army. He'll make overall strategy, but you'll have full command in the field for tactics."

"I see," he said, sitting straighter on his horse. "I presume you chose me because my army will be homunculi?"

"Exactly," I said. "You're the only man for the job."

"If I may ask, lord, what are your own plans?"

"I'll be right beside you most of the time. I still need a plan for handling the sorcerers, but you can handle everyone else."

I looked around, trying to identify familiar buildings or signposts. The rain was slashing nearly horizontal now, still driven by strong winds from the east. "Where are we headed?" I asked, giving up on landmarks.

"To whatever remains of the market," he said. "I hope to take supplies to Tessa. It's not yet mid-morning."

"How can you tell in this . . . *this?*" I asked, gesturing at the wild weather as if it had personally affronted me. "And what do you mean by 'whatever remains?'"

"The winds were particularly fierce last night. I suspect most of the wooden stalls broke apart or blew away. The stone buildings should be all right, even if their roofs are leaking now."

"Well, do what you can. If things are as bad as you say, the merchants may not have any wares ready for sale. Give my regards to Tessa, and tell her I'll try to come back soon—today, if possible, otherwise tomorrow. When your papers and insignia arrive, there may be medicines for Tessa included. I still need to get to Amrhyn and Landing this morning, so this is good-bye for now."

"Prince Grey!"

"Colonel Brand?"

"Travel well, sir."

I smiled, although he had no hope of seeing it through the mist and rain. "You, too, Brand," I said warmly, "you, too."

I pulled gently on the strand, and with our next steps, Brand went nearly thigh-deep into another rut, while Butter and I transported back to the dolmen.

I released Brand's ribbon, and chose one for Benlyn. The duke was hard to locate at first. I had to speak his name aloud while sorting through thousands of streamers and ribbons. Finally, I found him and opened the doorway. Peeking through, I saw that he was still asleep. It took me a moment to figure out why. I was used to thinking of Amrhyn as south—it was, quite a long way— but I had neglected to consider it also was considerably west. The sun wasn't even up in his part of the world.

I didn't think he would take kindly to having a muddy horse appear in his bedroom, so I led Butter outside the circle of standing stones, and tied her to one of the trees that leaned away from the dolmen. "I'll be back soon, girl," I said soothingly. "You can't go on this trip."

I limped back to the center of the circle, plucked at Benlyn's strand, and took exactly one step forward, making sure I kept hold of the strand. A candle, burned down to a tiny, sputtering stub, provided the only illumination. I wondered why there was no hearth to warm the room and provide a glow throughout the night. Then I realized the room was stuffy, even hot. I went to the open window and leaned out. Even the exterior air was too warm, and no breeze disturbed the curtains.

I let Benlyn snore while I took off my cloak and unfastened the clasp for my cape. I threw both garments onto a chair. I also removed my chemise and added it to the pile. My thighs were sweating inside the leather leggings, but I'd be damned if I'd strip naked just for comfort. I searched the room for another candle, finally finding one in the drawer of a small dresser beside the bed. I was unhappy to discover a muzzle-loading pistol lying atop the dresser, along with a dish of round lead pellets and a leather bag holding what I presumed to be black powder.

I moved the stub candle as far from the firearm as the dresser's small top would permit, then lit the new candle, and held it high.

Benlyn stirred in his sleep. He had no furs or quilts on his bed, not even a cotton or muslin coverlet. Moreover, the duke himself wore only short black pants covering his groin, and the rest of his body glimmered in a sheen of light sweat. I coughed gently and said, "Your Grace?"

He rolled onto his side, but didn't wake. I repeated myself much more loudly. This time he opened his eyes, his body tense and ready to spring in any direction. He held perfectly still, though, gauging the situation. I admired his self-control.

"It's Grey," I said. "Sorry to wake you. Why is it so blasted hot in here? Do you live over a furnace or something?" I held the candle out in front of me so he could see my face more easily.

"Prince Grey," he muttered to himself. He shook his head and swung his legs out of bed. With a groan, he pushed himself to his feet and bowed formally.

"Yes, Your Grace."

"Normally," he said, "only assassins sneak into a locked room in the middle of the night. I presume your visit is less lethal?"

"Just a quick chat, if you don't mind," I replied. "But first explain why you sleep in an oven."

He chuckled. "You've not been to this part of the world before, lord. This city—Parva—lies in the middle of Amrhyn's great northern desert. It's even hotter during the day. Tonight is actually cool, by local standards. It takes time to adjust."

"I suppose it would," I said unhappily. "I thought Amrhyn was grassy plains, lonely moors, and rocky seashores."

"Most of it is, but the Parva region is just sand, rolling dunes of it, nestled in the rain shadow of the southern Abuttals. Straight north of here, you'll encounter mountains. The plains and moors are to the south and east."

"Why on Sundering would anyone choose this place for a city? Is there any water?"

"Only what people bring in. The chief utility of Parva is the crossroads. Supplies from more hospitable parts of Leonais come either down the mountains or from the northeast, by the headwaters of the Leonais River. Traders meet here, to gather goods for dispersal down south. Goods must also pass northward through here if they want to travel on the river to Jappa."

"Why not take things along the southern coast of the continent?"

"My lord, you need to see the southern coast to understand. Overland trips are nearly impossible, and the currents, especially at the tip where the East Ocean meets the West, are turbulent and deadly. But did you really come all this way for a geography lesson?"

"No, of course not. I wanted to tell you of the king's plans and take an update back to him. Sorry—the heat surprised me, and I forgot the time difference. Do you want to get dressed?"

He shuddered. "Gods, no. I can hardly wait to go back south. As to my report, it's reasonably brief. Not much has changed. I'm here to meet with tribal leaders and nobility from around Amrhyn. Parva is traditionally a neutral area. I'm still trying to get them to join forces to oppose the sorcerers. They're still refusing, mainly out of fear—although they claim it's about historical rights and privileges. All field work remains halted, and there's practically no trade outside the region."

"What size is your fighting force?" I asked.

"Three hundred on the moors, twenty here with me."

"Would five thousand extra put some spine in the locals?"

"My lord! You're joking! It would make all the difference in the world."

I rapidly explained about Colonel Brand and the golem army we were preparing. The duke need only tell me where and when to deliver them. I also discussed my—somewhat nebulous—plans to fight the sorcerers. Even if some of the local nobility decided to join the other side, our combined forces should easily defeat them. *Assuming, of course*, I added to myself, *that the sorcerers don't burn the golems to charred ruins.*

"Brand, eh?" mused Benlyn. "I remember him. He's the courier in the King's guard who's also a champion chess player. He's a good man."

"The very same," I confirmed. "He's also a homunculus, but not like any other. Few would perceive his nature. I tell you now, because you have a need to know. He speaks highly of you. I think you'll make a good team."

"I'm sure of it, even though going from the King's Guard to

the regular army—as a brevet colonel, no less—will be a difficult transition for him."

"The king is chafed by the long delivery time for messages," I said, by way of finishing up. "So I may be back soon. In the meantime, plan on three weeks until we can launch an assault. General Yarval is sending you supplies and reinforcements. Given the travel time, they may not arrive long before the new army is ready. Do you think you can persuade the nobility to join us?" I remembered the rest of what Ashe had said. "The king wants their loyalty to the crown if possible, but will accept fealty sworn to you, personally. You have full authority—plenipotentiary, if I remember—to make arrangements. Either allegiance or a treaty will do. Can you handle that, Ben?"

He shook his head in amazement. "This is wonderful news. I think today's bargaining session will prove very enlightening. Yes, I can handle it. But how in the world do you move so swiftly across the land?"

"Like this," I said, picking up my discarded clothing, plucking at the strand, and stepping back to the dolmen.

The rain nearly slapped me to the ground. If anything, it had become worse during my short jaunt to visit Benlyn. And although Maran's valley enjoyed a perpetual summer, the rain combined with the dolmen's natural chill, made me shiver and dance as I got my clothing back on. I was in such a hurry that I didn't even remember releasing the duke's ribbon. Eventually, I pulled myself together and went to fetch Butter.

The poor mare was dripping and miserable. She lifted her head at my approach, neighing a forceful reprimand at being left alone so near the dolmen's baleful emanations. "Sorry," I said, smoothing some of the water away from her nose and neck. "I can't help the rain, and I can't choose the location. Let's go elsewhere."

I led her back into the circle, and sought out a streamer for Selene. She must have still been within the monument at Landing, for nothing came to my hand. Locations were harder than people —unless I selected an unlocked dolmen—so it took me quite a while to locate a ribbon leading to the wooden bridge on the path to Center. I didn't see any need to peek ahead of time, so I mounted, pulled on the ribbon, and urged Butter forward.

We emerged at the foot of the bridge—or rather, the embankment where the bridge had been. The river had indeed overflowed its banks and climbed the sides of the gorge. The water had taken the bridge and many trees, and roared through the narrow passage unchecked, aroil with sticks, detritus, and other dross. Furthermore, the air was bitterly cold, and the ground to all sides lay under a thick blanket of snow. Even as I hauled Butter to a stop and surveyed the scene, snow and ice crystals collected on my shoulders and blew like tiny knives against my exposed cheeks.

I didn't know the signals to ask Butter to walk backward, and the trail was too narrow for me to turn her around, but her good sense came to the rescue. She backed rapidly away from the rushing water, giving us at least two dozen feet of space before stopping.

I considered the problem. I could not transport us directly to Center, and I had no way to cross the river. Nix, Selene, and the others were trapped on one side, I on the other. Rebuilding the bridge, or creating a temporary crossing, required a team of engineers, and, more importantly, time. I couldn't imagine repair crews being dispatched in this kind of weather. Reluctantly, I decided the river had defeated me.

"Trust me," I called out to Butter, hoping she would understand. I plucked the ribbon to open the doorway back to the dolmen, and then urged her forward. She planted her feet, whinnied, tossed her head, and refused to budge. I got down, finding myself ankle-deep in snow, held her reins right beside the bit, and dragged her unwillingly behind me.

She relaxed when we achieved Maran's dolmen, but both of us stood for a moment, shivering, before I selected the next ribbon and remounted. "Last trip," I told her. I opened a doorway to Ashe and rode through.

Holding onto the return strand was a habit by now, but I again forgot to check my destination ahead of time.

"Get that damned horse out of my tent!" Ashe bellowed.

"Sorry," I muttered, giving the reins to a frightened page.

"Shut the damned flap!" Ashe yelled after the page had led Butter outside. I had never heard Ashe so angry. He, Yarval, and a dozen others I didn't know stood clustered around a blazing fire pit where Ashe's worktable normally stood. I glanced upward, relieved to see a vent near the tent's peak.

"Grey," said Ashe, still nearly yelling, "you've tracked snow inside. The idea of the tent is to keep the weather *out*."

The rest of the group gave me looks ranging from outrage to disgust. Yarval scowled, but I assumed it was his habitual expression. The others? Well, I had just brought a snow-laden horse into their midst; they would forgive me or not. I hoped they would laugh about it in years to come.

"Well?" demanded Ashe.

"Your Majesty," I said, hoping a show of humility would help, "I apologize. My horse and I nearly fell into a river, and I wasn't thinking. But I came for a good reason. I've spoken with the duke."

"Well, then report."

Clearly, his irritation wouldn't dissipate soon. I brushed a significant quantity of snow from my shoulders, sidled as close to the fire as I dared, stood up straight, and tried to keep my own voice properly subservient. I related my conversation with Benlyn, leaving out the personal parts and trying to make it seem like a courier's report. When I had finished that, I added my concern about the wooden bridge and asked if he would send a rescue party.

Ashe's reply was scathing. "The entire camp is snowed in. The northern half of my kingdom is paralyzed, and we don't know how bad things are down south. No one is going anywhere, save the unlucky fools who must hunt or collect firewood. Tell me this storm is natural, not of your making. I need to hear you say the words."

"Of course it's natural," I said. "Even if I could, why—"

"You're dismissed," he snapped.

I rather thought that our friendship would cover an innocent mistake, but his tone suggested otherwise. I had played the bumbling but cheerful clown once too often—or something else was bothering him. In either case, I was no longer welcome. I bowed, turned, and left the tent without a word.

I collected Butter from the shivering page and sent the child back inside to get warm. Except for where workers had cleared paths, the snow was several feet deep. The cleared areas had already accumulated several new inches. I studied the sky before getting into the saddle. The storm was a long way from ending. Sighing, I tugged on the strand, nudged Butter with my heels, and transferred back to the dolmen.

Here it was still only rain, with no sign of ice or snow, and I trusted Maran's summer would keep the worst of the storm away. I told Butter, "Home, girl!" and let her trudge down. She skidded on the deer path and nearly lost her footing in the mud, but recovered. She found her way back to the stables without help. I gratefully turned her over to the groom and went into the manor to find dry clothing. Altogether, my adventures had only taken a few hours, although I had crisscrossed most of the continent. I had probably missed Maran's breakfast, but I wanted something hot in my stomach. Even coffee seemed like a good idea.

I was tired of being wet, tired of feeling miserable, and tired of being tired. I deserved a rest and really needed to talk to Maran about Tessa. The twice-damned smithies were still going at full speed.

Hasq greeted me in the hallway, which immediately lifted my spirits a bit. If he had left Maran's side, she must be all right. "Wet day, sir," he said. "The mines and the lady's workshop flooded, but the rest of the valley is handling the downpour well. The lady will see you at your convenience. She's in the back parlor with the little lord. Virgil already laid out dry clothing in your rooms."

"Little lord?" I echoed.

"The lady has decided that's how we are to refer to the baby, sir."

"I'll try to remember. Please ask the cook to prepare a large pot of coffee. I'll go see Virgil and get cleaned up."

"Very good, sir. Do you want the coffee in your rooms, or—?"

"In the back parlor, to share with Maran. I hope you have a roaring fire in the hearth."

"If I may, sir, the lady says it is extremely muggy from the rain, but not actually cold inside the manor. She had us bank most of the fires. I suspect you'll feel the same way once you're dry and in fresh clothing."

Twenty minutes later, clean, dry, and dressed in what Virgil called "modest but elegant morning attire," I joined Maran in the back parlor. The large glass doors leading to the garden were closed, as were all the windows. Maran appeared to be sleeping on the divan, half reclined, Aiden in her arms. The tray containing coffee and mugs lay on a table beside her.

Aiden was awake, in one of his quiet-but-lively moods. His eyes darted around the room, taking in each detail as if he'd never seen the parlor before. His pudgy little arms waved seemingly aimlessly. When he spotted me, he smiled, displaying his toothless gums. A bit of drool trickled down one cheek. I bent to kiss his forehead.

"Shh, little lord," I whispered. "Your mother is sleeping."

He gurgled happily and went back to examining the room.

I limped over to the doors to peer outside. Rain had flattened all the rose bushes, and still pummeled down, mostly in vertical sheets, but with occasional sideways blatting as the wind shifted from side to side. I couldn't even hear the rain over the din from the smithies.

"I suspect it will last until noon, perhaps a bit later," said Maran.

I turned quickly. "I thought you were sleeping," I said.

"Just resting, waiting for you." She shifted on the divan, pushing herself nearly upright, and cradling Aiden in the crook of one arm. "Pour the coffee, would you?"

I moved the table closer to her, so she'd have a place to set down her mug between sips without having to lean. Then I poured for both of us, and took a seat beside her. "How long until Aiden can sit up by himself."

"Usually around six months," she said, yawning suddenly. "Why do you ask?"

"Curiosity. I wondered how long you'd have to hold him all the time."

"The longer the better. It helps the bonding process. But the bassinet adjusts. The latching hinge lets him either lie down flat or sit up, depending on how I set it." At my worried look, she added, "Don't worry. He can't wiggle enough yet to tip the bassinet." She smiled fondly at our child. "At the moment, he's basically a lump with eyes and a mouth. And, of course, the other end."

"How long until he can travel? I mean using the dolmens, assuming we can wrap him thoroughly enough to protect from the cold."

"He's still technically a newborn. Mothers in villages use baby carriers and take their infants everywhere they go. He *can* travel, but I'd prefer to wait a couple of months. We have the luxury for extra caution."

"I see. So if it were an emergency, you'd allow it, but otherwise not."

She yawned again, took a large gulp of coffee, and put down her mug. "Grey, why are you asking all this?"

Reluctantly, I told her about Tessa. It took only a few minutes to describe the entire situation, including my prognosis and Tessa's refusal to stay with us.

Maran stood up. "We must go immediately. What's it like upland?"

"Far worse than here. Snow and ice in the north. I don't know about the rest, but Tessa's hamlet had hurricane-like winds overnight, despite being nearly as far inland as we are. It was still raining heavily this morning when I talked to Brand."

She bit her lip. "Not ideal conditions. Can't you—" She waved her free arm in a vague gesture. "—do something? Push the storm back to sea, or at least out of our path?"

"I can't discern upland conditions from down here. I'd have to go outside the valley to see if anything's changed. But my percipience has limits. The only thing I can say for sure is that yesterday, the storm was much larger than my reach. It's far too big and powerful for me to control, although I can produce a temporary calm by countering the rotation with a cyclone of my own. I did it yesterday before moving the altar and finding the underground chambers at the temple."

"You did *what?*" she practically screamed.

"The upper atmospheric winds move circularly. With a tornado going the opposite direction—"

"No, not that. Tell me about the temple and what you found."

"Oh. There are machines—sort of alive—under the temple. I don't understand how, but they can talk. Not the common tongue, but ancient languages. All gibberish to me. I had the chief archivist of the royal library with me. A very nice woman named Selene. She understood just enough to make the machine change languages into one she could translate better. The machine called itself Malmö. I guess that's a name."

"The word is vaguely familiar. I think it's a prehistoric Terran city. Did this Selene woman name the languages?"

"Yes, but I don't recall. Malmö referred her to a book in the reliquary, and I left her overnight so she could read. I hope the next time I see her, she can tell me Malmö's purpose, or teach it to speak modern."

"You said 'machines,' plural. What names did the others use?"

"Only one talked to us. Hundreds of them occupied the small area we explored. There are likely thousands. The passages and chambers extend for miles. The machines we found look like desks or cabinets. Solid, all made of ship's metal. Selene says the best translation for them is 'control surfaces.' Before Selene figured out Malmö was a machine, I thought a person was crouching inside the cabinet."

"And she stayed overnight to continue the conversation?"

"No, just to read. The machines only seem to respond to my

touch. I don't know why. Malmö called me 'Controller.' Selene thought it was a title. I really want to get back there—especially since there may be weapons I can use—but the storm washed away the bridge, and I can't transfer to Center directly. In the meantime, what shall we do about Tessa?"

I was still sitting on the divan, sipping my coffee, but Maran began to pace around the room. The furrow of her brow told me she was thinking furiously. At length, she seemed to reach a decision, and turned to face me.

"As soon as the rain slacks off, we must ride through the dolmen and visit her. I'll carry Aiden under my cloak."

"Is that safe?"

"Grey, you know I'm an equestrian. You may not realize how good I am. I could juggle eggs while galloping bareback and never break a shell. The baby won't be at risk. And if Tessa is as bad off as you believe, it's important to go right away."

"What do we do with Torrey, after . . . afterward? He has no other family. The king has given up hope of finding Lane. He has some friends in the hamlet, but. . . ."

"He'll come live with us," said Maran immediately. "*We're* his family. I won't see him in a foster home or orphanage."

"Ashe suggested a place at court, eventually."

"It's much too soon for that. He's not even ten years old yet."

"There are pages that age, some even younger. I've met several."

"Grey, don't you want Torrey here?"

I hesitated, trying to order my thoughts. "Of course I do, and I promised Tessa we'd take him. But I'm thinking of his future. What would he *do* here? There's no schooling available, no work." I chewed my lip. "I want whatever's best for him, even if that doesn't mean staying here."

Maran laughed without humor. "I can make a homunculus tutor far more capable than anything he has now. And he can learn all sorts of skills by doing chores. He won't lack for opportunity to learn things."

"But can you make friends for him, too? Won't he be lonely, living with just us and your staff?"

"Are *you* lonely here?" she asked.

"I have you and Aiden, and I go upland all the time—but honestly, yes, sometimes I'm lonely." Hastily, I added, "It's not your fault. It's not anyone's fault. It's something built into me. Although I hate crowds and noise, the valley is too tranquil, too uneventful, to fulfill me. I need to spend time with people like Brand or Ashe, and I need to feel like I'm doing something important."

"Have I ever forbidden you from forming friendships?" Her tone was slightly frosty, as if daring me to contradict her.

"No, quite the opposite. But Torrey doesn't have my skills. He'd be trapped in the valley."

"Take him with you on your trips, then. Let him be your squire. He can even work as a page for a season, to associate with children his own age. The important thing, Grey, is that he has a home he can return to. He has to feel he belongs here, so that his outings or apprenticeships or other experiences are forays, not banishments. Emotional security is as important as physical safety, perhaps more so."

"I don't know about squiring—I'm not a knight or even a fighter—but I understand your point. He would love to travel with me, and I think he would enjoy a season or two at court. He more or less asked me to adopt him the last time we spoke."

"He worships you," said Maran.

"That's what Tessa says. I'm not sure I qualify as a proper object for worship. It makes me uncomfortable."

Maran asked, "Do you love the boy?"

"Of course!"

"Then shut up. The hero thing will pass. Before he gets too

much older, he'll start sassing you and disobeying. Let him grow up naturally. It'll be good practice for raising Aiden. But you're thinking too far ahead, borrowing trouble. We don't know how long Tessa has. Right now, his place is with her. I'll make room in my schedule to visit as often as I can."

"Won't that throw off your plans for making the army?"

"Not today, at least. The workshop flooded, and all the hay and other materials were soaked. I can't work again until things dry out and I recover my strength. I made fifty homunculi yesterday, mostly armorers and officers."

"Only fifty? That will yield only a thousand by the end of three weeks."

"These were the hard ones. It's why I'm so tired. I can make nearly three hundred foot soldiers a day. They only need to know how to fight and follow orders. We're actually ahead of schedule. You should stop by the barracks and introduce yourself to the officers."

"Maybe tomorrow," I said. "But speaking of the armorers, couldn't you have put the smithies on the other side of the hills? The racket is giving me a headache."

"It would be too inefficient. They need constant supplies for their work, and the finished products are needed here."

"You know best," I said, sighing. "How may I help the effort?"

"Right now, you can't. There's nothing to be done until the rain lets up. I plan to feed Aiden, think about the machines you found, and take a nap. You should rest, too. We'll ride out as soon as the clouds break."

I stood and put my empty coffee mug beside hers. "I'm hungry. Do you want to join me for lunch?"

"It isn't even noon yet. I'll eat something when I wake up. You go ahead and eat before your nap, dear. I'll set a servant to watch the skies and wake us when the weather changes."

"Okay," I said. "See you later."

Virgil brought me lunch in my rooms, and insisted on changing me from the "modest but elegant morning attire" into a robe and slippers. After I finished eating, I curled up under a light coverlet and fell asleep immediately. *Not even noon yet* was my last conscious thought. The voice of Malmö filled my dreams, always unintelligible, always just beyond reach of understanding.

I woke only when Virgil shook my shoulder. The dreams evaporated, leaving nothing of substance behind. "It's late afternoon, sir, nearing nighttime. The rain finally stopped, but it's still overcast. The lady is waiting for you."

"Riding leathers, then," I said. "And a fur cloak. None of that fancy court dress. It will be wet and cold on our ride."

"Very well, sir. I've taken the liberty of asking the cook to prepare a package of food and wine, in case you or the lady becomes hungry on your trip."

"Good thought. Did you get any reading done the past two days?"

"If you'd please stand, sir, it will be easier for me to dress you." He waited until I'd climbed from the bed, then continued: "Yes, I browsed extensively, but I found nothing on the list you gave me. *A Brief History of Sundering* yielded nothing of new value, except for more details on city and road building, so I abandoned it in favor of books about the monks and ancient religions."

"Nothing about neural interfaces or control surfaces?"

"No, sir. Perhaps if I had access to the strange books you found at the temple, I might find more pertinent information."

"I'll try to arrange it. In the meantime, keep digging into whatever Maran has in her own library."

He gave my cloak a final adjustment, and pointed out that the hood had tie strings. He also suggested a pair of leather gloves.

"Yes, yes, all right," I said. "I'm ready. You've done good work, Virgil."

"Thank you, sir."

I wandered through the corridors toward Maran's rooms, but Hasq met me at the first turning and redirected me to the stables. Maran had gone to await me there.

I hurried out the back door, across the courtyard, and into the stables. The groom held Butter ready for me. Maran, the nursemaid, and a footman were already mounted and ready. I swung into the saddle, and jerked my thumb at the nursemaid and footman. "Why are they here?" I asked Maran.

"The nursemaid is to hold Aiden, in case I need to tend to Tessa with both hands. The footman is to carry lanterns. We have no stars to light the path."

"Good planning," I said.

The homunculi needed no special protection against the weather, but Maran was wearing a cloak similar to my own. She had the hood up, but the cloak slightly parted at her neck and upper torso.

"Is Aiden under all that fur?" I asked. "Can he breathe?"

"He'll be fine. He has furs of his own and a woolen bonnet for his head. If anything, he's too warm. But I dressed him for what's to come."

The groom handed the footman a pair of storm lanterns tethered to a stout horizontal brace, so he could hold both of them with one hand. We set off for the dolmen, I in the lead. Our river had swollen tremendously, but the path beside it remained intact. At the base of the deer trail, I sent the footman ahead to scout the slope. He returned in only a few moments.

"It's all slick mud, sir," he reported. "The horses won't find purchase."

"Then we walk from here, I guess."

We all dismounted, and I hesitated. "Should I ride back to

fetch the groom? I don't like the idea of leaving the horses here alone."

Maran laughed, and slapped her gelding lightly on its rump. It started off immediately, and the other three horses tossed their heads and followed. "Aster will lead them back," she said. "He's the alpha in my herd, and he knows where to go. The others will follow unquestioningly. If I weren't carrying a baby, I'd brave this hill with him; he'd make a gallant effort."

"Can you manage to climb while holding Aiden?" I asked.

"I'll hold onto the nursemaid for support. I'm more worried about your leg than my own balance. You can brace yourself on the footman."

"Right," I said. "Ladies first."

We made our way up the deer trail with much slithering and sliding, but no mishaps. At the turn toward the dolmen, I pushed into the lead, showing the others how to push through the underbrush and enter the circle.

Even before I woke the lights, Maran pulled her cloak tighter against the chill. Afterward, she shuddered in place. "Hurry, Grey. I'll either smother the baby or freeze him to death."

I found a narrow, twisted purple ribbon that led to Tessa. I wound it about my right wrist and stroked it with my forefinger. The doorway opened. "Single file," I said. "Everyone put a hand on the shoulder of the person in front of you, and step forward when I do. I normally emerge in the back yard for some reason. It may be full of water or snow, so watch your footing."

I stepped forward, and blundered immediately into a snowdrift easily half my height. The air was frigid, but nothing as bad as the bone-chilling cold of an awakened dolmen. We plowed our way toward the front of the house, using the lights from the windows and the footman's lanterns to avoid falling into deeper drifts. It was eerily silent.

Torrey was out front, rolling chunks of snow to build a snowman. He wore a fur cap and warm winter coat, and spotted us as soon as we rounded the edge of the house. He sprinted our direction, but immediately after leaving the vicinity of the front porch, he floundered into a drift that came up to his chin. He swam toward us, clearing a path of sorts.

"Grey," he said happily but breathlessly. "You came back! Where's Butter? You promised me a ride." He paused. "Maran? Is that you?" He pushed his way through the remaining piles of snow separating us and tried to give her a hug.

She held him off with one hand. "Easy, there. I'm carrying the baby. We must get him inside immediately."

"Of course," he said. "Grandma will be so happy. Follow me. Solon and Bell taught me how to toss water over the snow to form an ice crust. You'll have to sort of step up out of the softer snow to reach the porch."

Solon and Bell, I recalled, were identical twins, friends he had mentioned in passing when we had first met. I was glad to learn Torrey still had local friends. It must have eased his burdens tremendously.

The edge of the ice crust was crumbly, but the main body, out where Torrey had been constructing his snowman, was a good inch thick. Except for being slick, it made good footing. We made our way to the porch, and Torrey swung open the door for us, yelling, "Grandma! Grandma! You'll never guess who came to visit!" Without waiting for us, he dashed inside.

The footman carefully set his lanterns down on the porch bench, and he and the nursemaid took up stations on either side of the door.

"None of that," I said. "Follow us inside. You're not servants here, you're guests." I gestured for Maran to precede me across the threshold. She gratefully accepted, opening her cloak as she stepped inside the tiny home. A welcome overflowing of warmth struck my face as I followed her.

"Close the door," I told the footman. To the nursemaid, I said, "Help us out of our cloaks and gloves. There's a place to stack things beside the door."

As soon as she was free from encumbrances, Maran carefully unwrapped Aiden's layers of clothing and took a chair at the small table outside the kitchen. Drafts came through chinks in the building from all sides. Aiden opened his mouth and squalled as the colder air struck his face. I asked the footman to build up the fire in the hearth.

"Is he okay?" I asked Maran anxiously.

"Fine," she assured me. "He was startled by all the changes in temperature." She cooed softly to calm the baby and pulled one of his furs up to shield his face and hands.

"Grey? Maran?" came Tessa's beloved voice. "Why did you come at night? Your man Brand brought me firewood, fresh lettuce, beets, carrots, onions, and a leg of lamb, thinking we might get snowed in. But I can't keep the oven lit. Water's coming down the flue and putting out the cook fire."

She was unsteady on her feet, but her voice was strong. Torrey led her gently from the back room to the table, and helped her sit.

"Grey," said Maran, "go fix the chimney."

"You want me to climb onto the roof at night, with only one working arm, and plug leaks without any tools?"

She looked at me serenely. "I want you to go away so I can talk to Tessa. You might as well do something useful."

I signed the footman to meet me by the door. In a low voice, I asked, "Do you have any idea how to fix a leaking roof?"

"I wasn't fashioned to be a carpenter, sir, but the rudiments of roofing are simple. And I won't fall or suffer from cold. Shall I attempt it?"

"Please," I said.

"Torrey," I called. "Do you have any nails, a hammer, planks, or even pitch? A ladder would be handy, too."

The boy rushed to my side. "We have a couple nails and a hammer," he said. "I can put on my coat and help. I've climbed up there before."

"In the snow? No, just fetch whatever you can find. This man will go aloft and see what may be done. You can show me your room and things. The ladies want some privacy."

He shrugged and started putting on his coat and cap.

"What are you doing?" I asked. "I just told you to stay inside."

"The hammer and nails are in the shed," he explained, his tone suggesting I was stupid for not knowing where they kept things.

"Then never mind," I said. To the footman, I added, "The shed is a broken down building without a roof, very near the place we arrived. You might find some usable wood there, even an old ladder."

"Very good, sir. I'll carry the lanterns with me."

He went outside, letting a huge draft of frigid air into the house before he shut the door behind himself.

"Now, show me your room," I said to Torrey.

I had seen his bedroom once before, the night I had healed his left ear, losing my own in the process. But he had been sound asleep at the time, and I hadn't gone there to see his things or talk about his life. He dragged me by the hand through the house, and sat on the edge of his bed. He had a small study desk with a boy-sized chair to accompany it. I turned the chair around, and straddled it.

We stared at each other for a moment, and then I said, "You're not as chatty as usual. How have things been going?"

He twisted his hands in his lap, looking everywhere except at me. I thought of making small talk or telling jokes, but decided to wait him out instead.

"You promised me a horse ride," he said finally. "And you promised to think about what I asked."

"When I have a horse with me," I replied, chuckling gently, "I can give you a ride. In the meantime, unless you want to climb on my shoulders, I can't do much." I let my voice grow more serious. "I have thought about what you asked, and talked to Maran about it, too. We're still thinking things through. How has your grandmother been since my last visit?"

"She wandered off into the rain last night," he said in a very low voice. I had to strain to hear him. "It was my fault, because I was studying instead of watching her."

"That doesn't make it your fault. 'Watching' her doesn't mean staring at her continuously. She probably didn't make any noise when leaving, did she?"

"No, I didn't even know she was gone until Brand and a couple of guards brought her back. She had only reached the end of the lane. Brand said she was looking for her apron, even though she was wearing it. He helped me dry her off and put her to bed."

"That must have been a bit scary for you."

He shrugged. "Not really. She does stuff like that all the time now."

"She seems like herself tonight. She recognized us and spoke normally."

"Every night is different," he said, his tone suggesting resignation, even despair. "Sometimes she doesn't even know me."

"You know that I wanted a housekeeper or live-in maid, right? But Tessa refused."

"I remember!"

"Well, maybe we've reached the point where we have to help her make decisions. Do you understand what I mean?"

He kicked one leg back and forth, his toe just barely scraping the floor, his expression unhappy. "She won't like being treated like a baby."

"This is an important part of growing up, Torrey. You have to learn to give whatever's needed, not only whatever's asked. Does that make sense?"

"I suppose," he said slowly, "but she still won't like it."

Pounding noises from the roof interrupted us. We both glanced up speculatively. I was hoping the footman wouldn't fall. Torrey was probably eager to go help.

I looked around the room after the clatter above subsided. "Where's Zoxo?" I asked. "I thought you kept her in here."

"Wandered off again. I can't find her."

"Reptiles like warm places. I bet she's near the fire, or hiding in the kitchen. Let's go look for her together."

We spent the next fifteen minutes lizard hunting without luck. We ended up in the main room. Tessa was holding Aiden and cooing softly. Maran hovered protectively at hand, in case she needed to rescue the baby. Neither one paid us any attention until we crawled under the table looking for Zoxo. When we emerged, both women were staring at us.

Tessa said, "Grey, look, a baby!"

"I know, Tessa. He's my son, Aiden."

"Maran, why didn't you tell me that?" asked Tessa.

Maran just smiled and said, "Grey, would you watch Aiden for a minute? I want a word with Torrey."

She waited until I took a chair right beside Tessa, my good hand helping to support Aiden, then took Torrey by the shoulders and marched him to the door. "Put on your winter things and wait here for a minute," she told him. "I'll be right back." She wrapped herself in her furs and slipped outside.

Torrey looked at me questioningly. I said, "I've learned it's best to obey her."

He rolled his eyes and started putting on his coat.

The door opened again before he finished, but it was the footman returning, not Maran.

"I've patched three spots, sir," said the footman. "But not well. We should send our carpenter as soon as possible. Many shingles are missing, and some of the supporting timber appears rotted."

"Let's see if Brand can find someone local," I said. "If that fails, we'll send our own from the valley. Is there paper about, so I can leave a note?"

"I'll get something, sir."

Maran opened the door just a crack. "Torrey?" she called. "Come outside now."

She held the door for him, and then entered the house.

I heard shrieks of delight from outside, but couldn't imagine the cause. Still wearing her furs, she came to collect Aiden and rewrap him in his layers of protective garments. I took the cue and went to fetch my own cloak and gloves.

Tessa had nodded off in her chair by the time I got back. I don't think she'd noticed that Maran had taken the baby.

"I think we should leave the nursemaid here," I said.

"Yes, I've already come to the same conclusion. The boy isn't old enough to care for her. I've convinced her—for now, at least—that it's best. I gave the maid instructions. When we have time, we can swap her out for a better fit, but she's more than capable of taking care of Tessa and the house."

She looked at the nursemaid. "Help Lady Tessa into bed, then see about roasting that leg of lamb."

"Yes, ma'am."

"Come, Grey, we're leaving."

I always enjoyed seeing Maran act decisively, although I wished she'd use a different tone when talking to me than when ordering her servants around. Still, she was only imperious when she was sure she'd made the right decision. It made me feel better to have my judgment confirmed. "Okay," I said, as the footman approached with a quill and piece of parchment. "But I want to leave a note for Brand first."

I scribbled instructions hastily, put the note in the center of the table, and straightened up.

Maran and the footman were already waiting beside the door. Once outside, we paused on the porch. The footman picked up his lanterns and held them high. We saw Torrey riding on the snowman's shoulders, whooping and cheering the clumsy, rotund creature as it raced and glided in circles on the patch of ice. The snowman paused to wave at us, then suddenly flipped Torrey head over heels into a deep drift and dove in after him.

"He won't last long," Maran called loudly.

Torrey stuck his head up from the drift, giggling. "I want Solon and Bell to see him! They live just up the road."

"How far?" Maran asked.

"Two minutes each way without snow. Riding on *him*— probably only a minute."

Maran considered the weather, then nodded. "I've left the nursemaid to watch your grandmother, so go show your friends while you still can. They'll never believe you if you wait until he melts. But don't be gone long. It's still very cold, and it's nighttime."

Torrey started to reply, then, with a sudden startled squawk, disappeared under the snow. I suspected the snowman had snagged an ankle and pulled him back down for more play.

Maran turned to me. "I'm ready. This cold air isn't good for Aiden."

I unwound the purple streamer from my wrist, opened the door, and led Maran and the footman through. Once back inside the dolmen, I hunted for the strand I'd used before to go from here to the stables. It came quickly to my hand. "One more step," I told Maran.

A moment later, the warmth of the stables, along with the scents of hay, grain, and horses, enveloped us like a hug of greeting.

The groom looked up and nodded affably, as if people materialized in his stables every day. "Welcome back, ma'am, sir," he said. "Your horses returned without you."

"I sent them to you," said Maran. "We won't need them again tonight."

"Very good, ma'am."

The footman lit our way across the courtyard and then excused himself, presumably to return the lanterns to the groom.

"Hasq!" called Maran once we were inside the manor.

The majordomo appeared instantly, bowing. "Ma'am?"

"I've left the nursemaid behind. Choose another servant to help me with the baby."

"At once, ma'am." He snapped his fingers, and two maids appeared moments later. I wondered if Hasq, devil that he was, had predicted Maran's actions with sufficient precision to have two helpers standing by. Then I realized the servants had probably been standing in alcoves anyway, waiting, as always, to see to our whims.

Hasq issued a complex set of hand gestures. One of the maids came forward to take Aiden, the other to divest us of our winter clothing.

"That will be all for now," I said.

Hasq tilted his head toward Maran. When she did not demur, he bowed and escorted the other servants from the entrance hall.

I turned to Maran, wrapped my good arm around her waist, and kissed her thoroughly.

"Goodness," she said when we came up for breath. "What prompted *that?*"

"It was a nice thing, what you did for Torrey."

"Oh, that." She fluttered a hand in dismissal. "It wasn't much."

"It was still very thoughtful. You gave him some joy in a hopeless situation."

"Well, depending on the weather, the snowman may outlast his grandmother. From what I saw, your prognosis was optimistic. She may not wake from this night's sleep."

Chapter Fourteen

I thought Maran was wrong, but didn't argue. Instead, we ate a quiet dinner together and spent the night comforting each other.

In the morning, the sun came blazing out from behind the clouds. The servants dragged Maran's raw materials out into the fresh air and spread them around to take advantage of the heat. Even the early morning light was strong in our perpetual summer. The officers she'd made the first day took charge of pumping water from the mines and her workshop before we even rose from bed. We took a quick ride around to assess damage. Everything in the valley gently steamed as it dried out, and the officers were busy dredging part of the river beside the manor to protect from future floods.

Maran and I ate a leisurely breakfast, waiting for the sun and her servants to do their work. About halfway to noon, Maran decided enough straw and ragtag bundles of string were ready, and said she was going to resume her work. I asked her if I could watch.

"I work alone, dear," she said, using the kind of voice that brooked no argument. I acquiesced with grace, kissed her good-bye, and set off on my own errands.

I rode Butter to the dolmen and transferred to Tessa's village.

The sun hadn't been nearly as kind here as in Maran's valley. Although the snowstorm had blown over, the sky remained overcast, and the air felt more like winter than autumn. Nothing had melted. The entire hamlet lay under a blanket of snow. In most places, the drifts were thigh-deep for me; in other spots, especially along fences and against houses, the wind had created improbably tall towers that reached far above my head.

Torrey was nowhere in sight. He had told me his school normally started at noon, but I suspected he would have no school at all for a few days. I hoped he was playing with friends and enjoying his unexpected holiday.

By luck, I arrived just as Brand was leaving. I stopped to chat with him on the porch. He had found my note and was on his way to look into repairs, but didn't hope for a quick solution.

"Likely, my lord, it will be several weeks until a carpenter or roofer has time," he told me. "Too many other houses and shops were either damaged or destroyed entirely. Many are quartering with friends or family, or sheltering in public buildings."

"How urgent is Tessa's roof?"

"Compared to others, not urgent at all. Frankly, my lord, this is a poor area. Few homes are free of drafts, or have perfect roofs. Architects would call most of the houses either huts or cabins."

"Would it speed things up if you let it be known that I, personally, wanted Tessa's house repaired?"

Brand hesitated. "Yes, lord, but I should refrain from doing so. Too many others have lost their shelters entirely. It would be unseemly to invoke your authority to aid one whose need is minimal, while others huddle near freezing."

Now it was my turn to hesitate. "I withdraw the suggestion. You are quite correct in your assessment."

"I have duties, lord. May I be excused?"

"Yes, yes, of course. Did your commission and insignia arrive?"

He eyed me as if I'd lost my sanity, but replied with courtesy. "After this storm, lord, it may be weeks before normal movement is restored. The King's Guard cannot begin to clear the roads until everyone is safe. Neither couriers nor merchants can travel in these conditions."

Nodding to myself, I let him go and went inside to see Tessa.

She seemed quick-witted today, even sharp. She remembered having seen Aiden, but not why a golem maid was staying in her house. "I didn't ask for a helper," she said crossly. "In fact, I sent the last one away. Why are you doing this to me?"

"You nearly got lost in a rainstorm the other night," I reminded her gently. "Torrey is too young to take care of you by himself."

"Well, I don't like it."

"I'm sorry, Tessa, but it was Maran's decision. She talked to you about it last night. Do you remember?"

"I do, now that you mention it. Maran insists, does she?"

"Yes."

That brought her up short and stopped her complaints. We shared a pot of tea at her table, talking about nothing in particular for nearly an hour. I finally stood up, saying, "I must attend to other duties. Did you get your roasted lamb?"

"Torrey ate half of it last night, the scamp. I nibbled a bit this morning, and the maid is keeping it warm in the oven for later. She's a good cook, but I'm not all that hungry these days."

"Keep warm and safe," I said. "Tell Torrey I stopped by."

"That's cruel, Grey. You know that Torrey died in Jappa."

I peered at her closely. "Tessa, it was Owen who died. Torrey's fine."

She shook her head emphatically. "Don't twist my words. Owen died. That's what I said."

It wasn't. She was lying to cover up her momentary lapse. I wondered how much of her mid-morning clarity was illusion and fakery. I sighed heavily and took my leave.

I transferred back to Maran's dolmen and selected a strand for Ashe. This time, instead of blundering in or poking my head through the doorway, I tried to re-create what I had done last year while exploring the dungeon. I sent my mind questing through the portal, while my body remained motionless. In this mode, I was like an echo of myself, more ghost than man. Unless I willed it, only sorcerers or mages could see or hear my astral self.

Ashe sat alone in his tent, writing. The large work table now resided somewhat near its original position, but comfortably away from the fire pit. Ashe was enough of a mage to sense my presence, so I let my image solidify a bit. Unsure of his mood, I asked, "Permission to enter, sire?"

"Yes," he said. "I wanted to see you."

"I'll tie up my horse and be right back."

I withdrew back into my body, and, apologizing profusely, tied Butter to the same tree I'd used before. "I'll be back soon," I said soothingly. She nuzzled at my hand. I patted the wide flat space between her eyes and assured her of my love, then left her and stepped through the still-open doorway to materialize in Ashe's tent.

"Your Majesty," I said, inclining my head.

"Stop that," he said. "It's just the two of us." He seemed to have forgotten his former ire and acted glad to see me, going so far as to get up from his table to offer me wine.

I accepted gratefully, and we sat at a smaller table on the other side of the fire pit. "You wanted to see me," I prompted after the silence stretched until nearly a full minute had passed.

"I have bad news," he said heavily. "The snow and ice stopped this morning, but enough has accumulated to shut the roads to anything but the strongest horses."

"Does that mean no rescue party? I'm worried for our friends trapped inside the monument at Landing. They didn't carry much food, and firewood is scarce in that area—especially as they were on a hilltop surrounded by rising flood waters."

"Give me a chance," he said. "I couldn't send an engineering team to rebuild the bridge, but I sent a few stout men—mountaineers—at daybreak with ropes, picks, and climbing gear. Their horses practically swam through the snowdrifts, but they made it. They rigged a rope across the gap, and crossed hand over hand, dangling over the river at great personal risk." He paused, and when he resumed, his voice sounded strangled. "Why did you leave the temple doors open?"

"So they wouldn't be locked in. So they could gather firewood. So the interior lights would stay on."

"That was a mistake, Grey."

A sense of dread rose from my stomach to my throat. I put down my wine glass. "What happened?"

"They had no firewood. They all froze to death, huddled together in a heap as far from the door as possible. Three of the horses died, too, still on their tethers, encased in ice. It's a wonder any of them survived."

"But—"

"You know how cold an active dolmen can get. Add to that the bitter winds from the storm. The entire floor was knee-deep in snow and ice. The mountaineers couldn't even remove the bodies."

He drained his wine and went for a refill. When he came back, he slammed his glass on the table so hard that it shattered. "You killed them."

I moved to clean up the broken pieces of glass, but he said roughly, "Leave it. Selene was a good person. One of the most intelligent and educated persons in my kingdom. I *liked* her; I depended on her. Now she's dead. I'm not saying you're guilty of murder, but you are guilty of carelessness yet again. I warned you about not thinking things through. Did you consider it idle advice?"

"Of course not. I liked Selene, too—and Sergeant Nix. I didn't know the others very well, but I'm sorry they died."

"Dammit, Grey. Why didn't you take them with you? You must have left using the dolmen network. You could have saved them all."

"Selene wanted to stay the night," I said miserably. "She's the one who asked me to leave the doors open, so they could leave and reenter. I thought Nix would find firewood or take them back across the bridge if things got bad."

"You were in charge of the group. You should have told Selene it was too dangerous. You should have had the sergeant carry her if she refused to leave. Dammit all to hell, Grey. You 'thought' this and you 'thought' that, but you didn't *think* at all."

I didn't know what to say, so I hung my head and apologized again.

"There's more," said Ashe evenly. "Kiril died in the night. He never woke from that seizure you provoked. Add another death to your total. I hope you didn't mean for it to happen."

I looked up quickly, meeting his eyes squarely. "I disliked the man intensely, but I didn't want him to die."

Ashe used his sleeve to brush at the tabletop, sweeping the

shards of glass off toward the corner of the tent. He got a new glass, this time bringing the bottle with him.

"Drink," he commanded.

I drained my goblet, and he immediately refilled it. "To Selene," he said, holding up his glass.

I raised my own. "To Selene, and to Nix, and to all who die unjustly."

We finished the toast, and then he said, "There's more."

Horror filled me. What *else* could have happened? He didn't give me a chance to ask any questions. "When you burst in last night," he said, "I was talking to my most senior advisors, the full council. That's why I sent you away again so quickly. They wouldn't be able to speak freely in front of you."

"Why not?" I was genuinely puzzled. "They know I'm your confidant."

"That was the topic. The stories of your misadventures have spread. Your oh-so-innocent mistakes have raised questions. This morning's discovery at the temple only made things worse."

Ashe, I said in mind-speech. *If you have any doubts of me, look into my mind. You know it's impossible to lie with mind-speech.*

I know, he replied the same way. *I've been probing you lightly since you arrived.*

I hadn't felt his mental touch. I hadn't known he was deft enough to read me without giving himself away. On the other hand, I considered him a friend; I hadn't been watching for intrusion.

"Then you know," I said aloud, "that I share all your goals. My loyalty can't be in question. If anything, my passion for lost technology exceeds yours. My wife is killing herself to make you an army. I have done everything you've ever asked of me—including things you didn't know to ask, like restoring your eyesight and saving you from death at your brother's hand. The cost has not been light."

"Your loyalty and sacrifices are not the issue. Your recklessness and lack of common sense are. The councilors accept your help with the Amrhyn problem. They tolerate your exploration of the temple. What they will *not* suffer is your being my heir-in-waiting. If the worst should happen, they won't follow you. And if I fail to heed their advice, they won't even follow me now. I risk a palace coup by continuing to favor you. Do you carry my ring on your person?"

Wordlessly, I drew it out from under my chemise, and pulled the chain over my head. I tossed it on the table. "I never wanted it," I said as it rattled to a stop.

"I know that, and you know that. Do you think it matters? I told you we couldn't afford to have the throne contested, not after the civil war my brother caused. I'm going to give the ring to General Yarval. I can trust him not to stab me in my sleep before Ariel and I have a child."

I did not reply. He had clearly made up his mind, and I didn't want the responsibility anyway.

He waited me out. Finally, I relented and asked, "Is there anything more, or am I dismissed?"

"Two last things," he said. "First, I still value your friendship, and I hope you still value mine."

"Crowns and thrones are toys to my kind," I said stiffly. "I understand their fascination for others, and I even understand the functions they serve, but they don't hold my interest. I prefer not to spend time at court henceforth. If we are to be friends, let us meet away from the trappings of power, the stifling etiquette and proprieties. We can be at ease when alone together."

"Very well, although with the Amrhyn affair still unsettled, I may need you to give reports to the council from time to time."

I ignored that. "You said two things."

"Ah, yes. There's an old man named Larkin. His specialty is

linguistics. He's from Port Abb, on the northern coast. He used to lecture at the university at Halmar."

"What about him?"

"He wants access to the reliquary, and he wants you to be his guide."

"Does he know what happened to Selene?" I asked darkly.

"Yes, but he's undaunted. Larkin is an odd fellow. Willful. Older than dirt. Looks frail, but could probably outrace a horse. Wears tattered robes like a penitent. Completely bald. And more than a little insane. Hasn't bathed in years. Keeps to himself except at academic conferences, where he's usually the most strident voice in any controversy. They'd kick him out, save that he's usually right. If you can stand his ways, I'd like you to oblige him. He knows more about ancient languages than anyone on the continent. But I warn you again, he's *quite* mad. He can't always talk coherently, and his behavior is, shall we say, peculiar."

I shrugged. "It's moot for now. You need to clear the roads and rebuild the bridge. I don't know how a madman can help, but I'll take him on my next trip, when the way is open. Where can I find him?"

"In the brothels. The staff sergeant will drag him out. Come back in three—no, four—days. Wait until I'm alone in the tent, as you did today. And now, finally, you're dismissed."

I stood, swirled the remaining wine in my glass, and quaffed it in one long swallow. "Four days, Ashe. Watch for me."

"Good-bye, Grey," he said softly. "When all this is over—"

I was already gone before he finished his sentence.

Back in Maran's valley, I had nothing to do. I couldn't get to Center and had nothing new to report to either Benlyn or Brand.

Maran remained holed up in her workshop, and Hasq informed me she would not emerge until nightfall.

"Can I help?" I asked the majordomo.

Hasq regarded me gravely. "I don't know, sir. Can you?"

"I meant 'may' I help, as you know damned well."

"If you cannot, then permission is irrelevant, sir. The lady works alone, always."

"The servants go in and out freely. You take supplies to her, bring refreshment, and do other chores."

"We are *part* of her work, sir. She uses us as mercilessly as she uses herself. Do you understand the mechanisms involved in creating homunculi?"

"No, but I want to. It may be something I can learn."

Hasq coughed politely, a synthetic noise meant to convey skepticism. He made no verbal reply. I dismissed him by the simple expedient of walking away.

Virgil, deeply immersed in his research, didn't look up when I entered the library. I let him be; I didn't need anything, and I didn't want to interrupt. I browsed Maran's shelves for a minute, finding nothing of interest. I left as quietly as I'd entered and went to the stables.

The groom was busy tooling designs, an intricate series of swirls, into a leather harness. "Don't get up," I said as he started laying down his work. "I'd like to watch."

"As you will, sir," he said, resuming his efforts.

He had an odd array of tools. I didn't recognize anything by name except for a needle-tipped awl and an oddly shaped triangular knife with a very thin edge. The blade with a wild, flat, rounded edge was new to me, as were the things that looked like forks and rakes with tiny tongs or tines. I asked him to describe his work.

"This is called a swivel knife, sir," he said, holding up an instrument. "One finger holds the blade against the wetted leather to do the incising. The bottom part rotates easily with just thumb pressure, allowing quick and precise changes of direction without ever lifting the knife."

"What's that rounded thing?"

"A head knife, sir. One uses it to cut pieces of leather, or to skive the edges of an already-cut piece. The chief advantage is that it cuts without tearing."

"I see. Where did you learn your trade?"

He tapped his head. "All in here, sir. The basic knowledge at least. I've had years of practice. I could explain each tool and technique, and you'd know everything I know, but not be able to work leather at all."

"Well, carry on. I'll watch for a bit."

His words made sense to me and tied in neatly with other questions I'd been pondering the past month. Ashe had first chided me, then finally rebuked me, for not thinking carefully enough. I resolved to do that now.

First, Maran claimed the muria could not give gifts they did not possess themselves, but she had failed to follow through. Her claim did *not* mean I couldn't have talents of my own, ones not designed or implanted by Qol. Ordinary folk might have children who turned out to be musical prodigies, talented athletes, or consummate artists. The parents, lacking such skills themselves, did not give these things directly. The recombination of genes at meiosis—or in my case, manufacture—allowed recessive or even completely novel traits to emerge. Qol had probably given me second sight and weak telepathy, as well as a brain apt for learning physiology and philosophy. But my control of the god-winds was something entirely my own, an emergent talent previously unknown. As far as I knew, no muria understood how I controlled the weather, or how the god-winds were simultaneously an expression of fate and the result of desire.

Second, all the descendants of Captain Leonais possessed a

degree of magery, although its strength and expression varied widely among individuals. Vastil had understood it well enough to manipulate the Archon's genetic material, enhancing Gaheris to sorcerer-level power. This did *not* imply Vastil possessed magery himself. The types of magic I'd seen displayed by the muria were all, essentially, mental powers: telepathy, much stronger than my own; overwhelming persuasion, if not outright dominance, of humans or nina; and sharing of a single mind across multiple bodies. The only exception I could recall was Vastil's orange nimbuses, the balloon-like prisons he had fashioned to hold Gaheris, two sorcerers, and Nina. Could they have been illusory, or simply a projection to demonstrate the fact of his unfettered control of the captives? I had never seen the muria levitate, control remote objects, cast charms or spells, teleport, shift shapes, or, really, do *anything* that couldn't be attributed to telepathy or extensions thereof. Did they lack 'magic' as I understood the word?

One ability remained unexplained. Qol *made people*. Maran had called us the "children of twilight." We were flesh and blood, alive and self-determining in ways even her most sophisticated golems were not, but we had no human parents. We had never nestled in a womb. I was "born" only two years ago, with a body that seemed around thirty-five years old. Maran had had a youth, but no infancy or childhood. When I had confronted Qol about my origins, suggesting I wasn't a real person, he had said, *All children are made, some more deliberately than others. Why should the method I chose make you any less real?*

As I stood there, watching the groom finish one piece and begin another, I compared his artistry to Qol's. Neither created things out of thin air. Each used pre-existing materials and tools to shape their visions into reality. How Qol accomplished his feats was a mystery, but I suspected we came from stolen human embryos, modified extensively, grown in artificial environments, and decanted at the desired physiological age. Sophisticated technology, combined with an intimate understanding of genetics, explained everything adequately. Qol, like the other muria, had descended from the original terraformers of Sundering. Suppose they, like Justian, had not destroyed their machines, but hidden them away?

My last thought was of prophecy. It seemed to defy cause and effect, the necessary sequencing of events inherent in the universe itself. Did I fool myself with my visions of the future, or did I shape things yet to come so they matched what I expected? Logic told me that predestination was an unreasonable predicate for useful contemplation. If all future events were fixed, making free will and agency merely illusory parts of destiny, then there was no point debating intentions, goals, or actions. Intuition, not logic, suggested my prophecies were real, despite their tail-swallowing nature. Could I float among the myriad possible futures and determine which ones were most likely to occur? If so, that was prediction, not prophecy. Given sufficient information about the positions and motions of every atom in the world, some events might qualify as inevitable. Most events, however, seemed essentially chaotic; even if all the initial conditions and subsequent interactions could be codified, the eventual result might not, in fact, be predicted accurately.

If prophecy had any use at all, why hadn't I foreseen the horrible deaths of Selene and Nix? I was torn between fury and shame at my impotence. How could I possibly share this news with Maran without accepting responsibility?

Dust motes drifted leisurely throughout the stables, rendered visible by the sunlight streaming through the open door. If I picked up each mote, placed it back on the shelf or beam or horse from which it originated, and gave each the same initial impetus that had launched it, would it fall the same way again? I doubted it. I watched one in particular, large enough to track easily by eye, but light enough for air currents to keep it aloft. It wafted lazily back and forth, trending downward, until caught by an updraft. Prophecy never came upon demand; it was a thing of inspiration. Yet I tried to prophesy where and when my selected mote would touch the floor.

No sense of certainty came to me, no ring of inevitable truth. I *willed* the mote to fall, tried to move it downward with telekinesis, directing it to land on the toe of my right boot. A tiny breeze, barely perceptible, made it fly up into the rafters and disappear from sight.

So much for that, then. My bad leg was starting to ache from standing so long. I decided to take Butter for a ride.

Maran! I called in mind-speech.

I'm busy, Grey.

I'm going upland to check the weather.

As you like. Stop bothering me.

I asked the groom to get my mare ready, and went outside to wait. I studied the sky for signs of any residual bad weather. Only a few small clouds marked the otherwise unrelieved blue. The sun was westering, but I still had at least three hours until dark.

Butter whickered and nuzzled my hand as soon as the groom led her out. He had brought me a heavy cloak and lantern, too. I took the cloak, grateful for his foresight, but told him I wouldn't need the lantern.

I patted the mare's flanks and mounted. She trotted out of the courtyard and started toward the dolmen. I used the reins and knee pressure to guide her the other way. I wanted to emerge near the boulder where Benlyn had first caught me, and it was easier for me to retrace my path than find—or create—a new one. We wound gently upward, following the contours of the hills, until the mists enveloped us. I concentrated on our exit point. Butter leaped up the last slope, nearly unseating me. Fortunately, I had developed the habit of holding the reins loosely while resting my good hand on her saddle horn. When Butter lurched forward, I clenched my fist and retained control.

Leaving the mists behind, I pulled Butter to a halt beside the boulder. Winter reigned here, not Maran's summer. The chill air made me catch my breath and draw my cloak up.

Colonial Plain spread before us, but so changed that it was difficult to recognize. Where broad avenues had once wended through the trees, now smooth fields of snow, broken only by upthrust tree trunks, greeted me. The deciduous trees, shorn of leaves by wind and cold, stood stark, black, and naked against the sky, the thinnest branches encased in ice. The evergreens were so laden with snow they appeared as mere conical shapes, bottom heavy and gravid. I estimated that the blanket of snow averaged five feet deep, more or less uniform throughout this part of the forest. The sky was cloudless, but the sun seemed to provide no warmth.

No birds flitted amongst the branches. I saw no deer tracks, or any sign of wildlife. I didn't think it wise to take Butter surging through the snow, because she wouldn't be able to avoid deadfall or roots. Reluctantly, I turned her head and walked her around the boulder in preparation for reentering the mists. Then I reined her to a halt again. Even if I couldn't explore physically, I could test my percipience.

Butter stood patiently while I closed the eyes of my body and extended my mind in all directions, striving for the all-encompassing view I had once achieved. My viewpoint rose through the air until it overtopped the tallest trees. I could see small hamlets spread throughout the forest, miles distant, visible mainly by their chimney smoke. The snow blanket obscured the roads themselves, but I could puzzle out their locations by observing long treeless aisles.

My second sight seemed limited in range, as usual. I could see the immediate vicinity, but nothing farther than ten or twelve miles. I forced my viewpoint higher, but it didn't help. Although my range increased a bit, the edges of what I could perceive were fuzzy and indistinct, blocked by simple distance. The conditions that had once let me soar freely over the entire continent no longer obtained; I suffered neither high fever nor insanity. I didn't think the price for regaining such vision was a good bargain. After all, if I truly needed to see something far away, I could transfer there via the dolmen network.

I started to withdraw back into my body, but paused, struck by inspiration. I retuned my perception to look for life signs instead of buildings or towns. Now I could make out the people moving about within their homes in the hamlets I had spotted. A word of command hovered behind my lips. If I spoke it, I would be able to join with any of the lives I perceived, using their senses to experience their environments, make them move or speak according to my desires. I had accomplished the same state once before, back when power first awakened in me. It had frightened and confused me then; it still did.

I left the word unspoken, but flitted from home to home, examining each bright spark of life with interest. Eventually, I abandoned human habitations and scanned the forest itself. Now I spotted deer, mostly hiding within the shelter of coniferous trees, sleeping, waiting for the snow to melt. I also found rabbits, foxes, raccoons, and squirrels, all dug into dens or nestled deep in burrows buried under the snow. The birds that normally sang and flew among the branches all huddled motionless, feathers puffed out to trap heat, safe in nests or tucked into crotches where major tree limbs joined the trunks. A few had even dug themselves long tunnels in the snow itself, relying on it to provide insulation.

Not far from the dingle where I had thrown down the dolmen, I found twelve sparks, burning like stars to my second sight. *The stone children.* From this distance, their incandescence didn't blind me, but I still couldn't make out their features. They stood in a circle with their hands linked as usual, and didn't seem bothered by the snow or cold. I wondered again about their origin, their imprisonment, and their plans. Maybe they would speak to me if I reached out.

The word of command I had been suppressing finally fell from my lips, but not directed outward toward them; it focused its power on me. Suddenly, I seemed to stand among them, although my body remained on Butter's back beside the boulder.

"Hello," I said. "I'm still curious about you."

I couldn't tell if they looked at me or not; the flames that seemed to serve as their clothing blocked my second sight as easily as if I looked at them with mortal eyes. One of them said, "Your time is not yet come. Remember, we urged you to patience."

"Will you answer some questions?"

"Ask."

"Are you really children? Your sizes and voices suggest it."

"Not as you understand it."

"Then what?" I asked.

"We are waiting."

"For. . . ?"

"Activation or retrieval."

Well, that was jolly. They were nearly as cryptic and uninformative as Nina had been. On the other hand, they were at least speaking to me. Perhaps it was worth continuing the conversation.

"Who imprisoned you?" I asked.

"Justinian Pontifex."

"Justian? *Why?*"

"Ask the wind," they chorused, all of them speaking at once.

"In my experience, the wind never replies," I said. "What do you mean?"

"You woke Malmö from its long sleep. It is only one. You are the imperator. Wake the correct ones, and we will come."

I withdrew into furious thought. They were telling me they were machines, artificial beings like Malmö itself, but not bound to a control surface. Why had they been left outside, when all the other speaking machines had been concealed in passages underneath Center.

"State your function," I commanded. If I were the imperator, the controller, they would have to answer.

"We monitor and wait," said the one who had done most of the talking.

"Reveal your true shapes."

"We cannot. You would die."

At the mere sight? I doubted it. "Explain," I commanded.

"You have already been injured by seeing us too closely. Your cheek will never heal."

"That was a chip from one of the bluestones," I said, remembering the events clearly.

"The proximal cause, but not the true injury. You are vulnerable now in a way you have never been."

"Well, my body is miles away at the moment."

"You are partly in both locations. You only perceive the superficial damage, not the deeper hurt. If we reveal ourselves fully, you will carry even more damage back. We are injuring you even now, just by letting a tiny part of you so near. Look at all the dead animals and vegetation surrounding us."

"I don't understand that at all. My body is back on the horse."

"Comprehension is not required."

So, even acknowledging me as controller, they would not obey. I tried a different tack. "Can you convey me to Center?"

"It is not safe to open the doorway."

"Then how will you meet me there if I wake the other machines?"

"The one named Ramirez will provide the needed security."

That made a kind of sense, even though the mechanisms were utterly beyond my current grasp. I was about to ask them why the sorcerers had fled at their appearance, but they raised their linked hands, flared to an intolerable brightness, and disappeared.

I relaxed my second sight, withdrawing back into myself like slipping my hand into a glove. Butter still stood patiently. I felt my cheek and face thoughtfully. I'd almost forgotten the granite-like scab. It had been part of my face for so long now that no one seemed to notice it. The rest of my face felt wind burned again, and I suspected a mirror would show another false tan. Apparently, even remote exposure to the stone children was sufficient to cause superficial damage. Still, I counted it a small cost for the information I had gleaned.

The sun was nearing the horizon as I urged Butter down into the mists, leaving the frigid air behind. I unfastened my cloak and enjoyed the late-afternoon warmth of the valley. The heavily slanted sunlight threw everything into a kind of sharp clarity, with dark shadows demarcating the edges of everything I saw.

The ride back to the stables was uneventful. I gave Butter and the borrowed cloak back to the groom and went inside the manor house.

"Dinner in two hours, sir," said Hasq, popping up as if he'd been standing by the door waiting for me. "The lady has requested informality due to her fatigue."

"It's not like the first day, is it?" I asked. "I mean, is she all right?"

"Merely tired, sir. She is now tending to the young lord. You may join her in the nursery, or wait until dinner is served."

"I'd like to see the baby before dressing for dinner," I said.

"Very good, sir. I'll alert Virgil to await you in your rooms."

I made my way to the nursery and was delighted to find Aiden had finished nursing. Maran was rocking him in her arms by the window, singing something so softly that I couldn't make out the tune, let alone the words.

"May I hold him, please?" I asked.

She transferred him to my good arm, and I settled into a chair, focusing on meeting his eyes. He stared at me intently, then cooed and broke into a smile.

"I told you he was developing faster than most," said Maran, observing over my shoulder. "He's a good four weeks ahead of schedule. That's why I was singing to him. It will help his language development."

"Language? Do you mean he's about to start babbling?"

"Oh, no, not at all. He'll just make occasional noises when he's happy. I'm imprinting as many different kinds of vocal sounds as I can. He won't remember, but his brain absorbs the patterns and sound shapes. Purposeful babbling comes much later. The social smiling is more important. That's amazing for someone his age."

She moved around and seated herself in another chair, passing one hand across her forehead.

"Tiring day?" I asked, judging her walk and face. "Tell me about it."

"I think you should start," she said. "You're tanned again."

"Oh, well, depending on how you look at it, nothing much actually happened. No grand adventures, no death-defying deeds. Just a lot of talking."

"Did you go to Tessa?"

"Yes, and you were wrong—she's still very much alive. Not doing well, though. She got Torrey and Owen confused while we were chatting, even though it was supposed to be her best time of day. But she was steadier on her feet than last night. I stand by my prediction. She has some time left."

"How was Torrey? Still playing with the snowman?"

"I didn't see him. I assume he was with friends. The snowman may last until spring, given what I saw." I quickly filled her in on the weather I'd observed.

She nodded thoughtfully. "Winter is one of the reasons I created this valley. I abhor winter. But this was just an early and unusually violent storm. Normal autumn weather should return quickly. It will be crisp for several weeks, especially at night, then ease into true winter gradually. Tell me how you got tanned. You are also," she said, leaning forward to pluck at my head, "losing hair."

"Am I?"

"Ask Virgil to collect whatever falls out when he bathes you next, so we can see how much you're losing. It's hard to tell under those braids, but I believe you're thinning at your temples and hairline." She held out her palm to show me the tuft she'd pulled from the top of my head. It wasn't much, and I had felt neither pressure nor pain when she'd yanked it free.

"I lose more than *that* every time Virgil brushes me," I said dismissively.

"From loose ends and snarls," she said. "I think this is something different. Tell me about the tan."

"Mild burn again. Apparently, it comes from exposure to the stone children. They said they were damaging me, just by talking to me. They also took credit for the scab that won't heal."

"They injured you again?" she asked. "I'm not happy about that. Stand up and walk around for me. Move your arms and legs, and then twist your torso and neck."

I handed Aiden back to her so I could obey. I wiggled all my limbs except for my withered left arm, which hung, as usual, like a dead stick.

"Your left leg is dragging slightly, and you're pronating." At my quizzical look, she explained. "Your foot isn't aligning correctly when you step. How do your shoulders and hips feel?"

"Normal for me. But now that you mention it, my neck is stiff."

"Turn your head to either side for me, and lift your chin up and down. Any pain?"

I swiveled my head in all directions. "No pain," I reported. "But the stiffness begins above my jaw, and reaches past my left shoulder. I can't tell if it goes farther, because my left arm is mostly dead anyway. My right leg aches, but it always does. That old tibia fracture healed wrong. Nothing new there. May I sit again?"

She nodded, and I reseated myself, grateful to take the weight off my right leg.

She asked, "Any nausea or vomiting? Any unusual bleeding?"

"No," I said. "Nothing like that."

"Start at the beginning, then," she said. "Tell me everything you experienced."

I related the strange circumstances and stranger conversation, giving as much detail as I could remember.

She stood up and started pacing. "Living machines," she muttered to herself. "Autonomous, mobile, and intelligent. Radiating enough energy to cause skin burns and hair loss. I hadn't thought to see such things—"

"Mobile *now*," I reminded her. "They were trapped in that isolated dolmen until I freed them."

"I think you should stay away from them, Grey. They're dangerous."

"They'll come to me when I wake more machines under the temple. They said it would be safe then."

"Safe for you, or safe for them?"

"Uh, I think they meant safe from sorcerous interference. Safe to open a doorway to Center."

She resumed her seat and leaned forward, her elbows on her knees. "Grey, there are both visible and invisible kinds of energy."

"I know that. The bands and streamers of a dolmen are invisible to most, unless I rouse them to visibility for everyone."

"I was thinking more of something like the sun. It radiates energy to warm the planet and light our days, but it also gives off energy we can't see. The kind that causes sunburns, for example. You and I are immune to normal sunburn, but imagine if you flew one of the starships very close to the sun."

"Wouldn't the ship's metal protect me?"

"I'm talking about quantity and intensity of energy, not a real voyage. I think the stone children are like the sun. The bright light you see is the visible part. They must give off invisible energy, too. *That's* the danger. You must stay away from them as much as you can. I don't know what will happen if they appear alongside the machines at Center. I suspect they'll report on whatever they've been monitoring for three thousand years, but after that. . . ? I can't guess. There's nothing, *nothing*, in the Book of the Ship or other old records about them."

"Perhaps the books at the reliquary will explain," I said. "Ashe wants me to take an old man named Larkin on my next visit. He's supposed to be some kind of expert."

Maran rocked back in her chair. "Not Larkin from Port Abb?"

"The same," I said. "Have you heard of him?"

"I've even met him. He's the scholar I visited in Halmar to help with translations. He was already ancient and very eccentric back then. He'd taken to wearing rags and urinating on students he didn't like. The university had to dismiss him. I was fortunate to catch him on his last day. He told me his home was in Port Abb. Given his age then, I'm surprised to learn he's still alive."

"Fortunate?" I asked skeptically. "He sounds like a horror, much worse than Ashe described."

"Yes, fortunate. He has the keenest brain for ancient tongues I've ever encountered. I think I should accompany you to Center. He may be vulgar and half-insane, but he'll have unparalleled insights and arcane knowledge."

"What of your work here?"

"I need breaks from time to time. You can whirl us home in moments. The only time wasted will be getting there."

I shrugged uneasily. "As you will, but I think it may be dangerous."

"All the more reason for me to go. Larkin and I can help identify the dangers, and help Selene with her reading. Now tell me about your meeting with Ashe. You've been avoiding it."

"It's complicated," I said, avoiding her eyes. "The rain we had down here was much worse up there, causing even small rivers to turn into raging torrents. It then changed to snow and ice. In short, things didn't go very well. I'm no longer a prince of the realm. Ashe took back his ring."

"He didn't blame you for the weather, did he? It wasn't your storm!"

"No," I said, my voice barely above a whisper. "Not for the storm, but for what I did—or failed to do."

"Grey, look up and tell me what happened."

Feeling miserable, I related what the mountaineers had found at the temple. After I finished, we both sat in silence for a long time. Finally, I said, "I think that was the tipping point. The king's councilors already disapproved of me. After Selene, they gave Ashe an ultimatum. He had no choice, but I don't think he really disagreed. He wants you to continue working on the army, and me to continue at Center, but I'm out of politics."

"I won't make him another damned soldier. Not one. He treated you disgracefully."

"Maran, try to see it from his perspective. I do blunder about and make mistakes. He can still like me as a person, but he can't have that kind of chaos at court. It was probably rash of him to select me in the first place, and I never wanted it. He made the best of a bad situation, and I think he made the right choice."

"*You* are free to forgive him. That doesn't control me," she said tartly.

"Will you still make the army? It's not for him, really; it's for everyone on Leonais, including us. The sorcerers need to go. The whole plan was originally your own idea."

"Promise me that when everything is over, you'll settle down and stay in the valley."

"I don't know what will happen at the temple or in the war. I can't make promises, but I can state intentions. I want to be with you, living in peace, raising our son."

"I want a promise," she insisted.

I stood up and leaned over to kiss her forehead. I nearly stumbled while straightening up. A new flash of prophecy overcame me. It only lasted a moment, but was vivid and frightening. "I promise," I said woodenly. I don't think Maran noticed my discomfort, or the change in my voice.

"See you at dinner, then," she said, tickling Aiden and smiling.

She didn't even look up at my departure. She was already singing to the baby again.

Chapter Fifteen

Virgil bathed me, unbinding my hair first. I remembered to have him collect stray strands for Maran's inspection. After the bath, he braided my hair again, put lotion on my face, and dressed me for an informal dinner, just a shirt and slacks. He was clearly unhappy with the situation, but Maran had been the one to request informality, so he didn't say anything to me.

At dinner, Maran was tired, and I was brooding, so we didn't talk much. Toward the end, when the servants brought tea and shortbread, I bestirred myself to ask again about her day's work.

"Two hundred today," she said, "a bit below quota because of the late start, but I'll make up for it tomorrow."

"And these were all foot soldiers, I presume. How well can they fight? General Yarval was worried about inexperience. Put one of yours up against a skilled fighter in light armor. Which would win?"

"Rapier, broadsword, or close-in grappling?"

"I doubt we'll encounter an épée or rapier. I mean hacking with a sword, either short or broad."

She pondered for a moment. "A truly excellent fighter could

probably disarm a homunculus in a prolonged duel. I'm not as skilled with full-tilt battle as I am with fencing, and they get their skills from me. Of course, a mounted fighter always has an advantage against a foot soldier."

"And if one of your soldiers has his arm or leg chopped off?"

"Her arm or leg," she corrected me. "Most of the foot soldiers are going to be female. They're easier for me to make. But that doesn't change the answer. For a leg, she would hop and continue fighting. For an arm, she would try to scoop up her blade and continue with her remaining hand."

"No blood? No pain? No mortal wounding?"

"No, they can feel pressure, but not pain. A spear thrust would just be an annoyance, as would a rain of arrows. Why are you asking?"

"I'm worried about attrition," I said. "If the opposing forces are greater in number than we expect, can they hack your army to bits, limb by limb, and succeed on the field?"

"Oh, that. Well, technically, yes. But remember the dungeon. Each part of the soldier would continue trying to fight. The only ways to kill homunculi is by burning, beheading, or expiry. Perhaps a direct hit with a cannonball would put a foot soldier out of commission; she wouldn't be exactly dead, but she'd be unable to move afterward."

"So your army is essentially invincible," I concluded.

"Fire is the chief danger, and that's your job. They'll have shields to protect against flaming arrows, but the shields won't help against a sorcerer lobbing fireballs. Those splatter, almost detonate, and the flames cling as if made of pitch."

"I remember the dungeon," I said with a slight shudder. "Nina and the stone walls and floors were our main protection."

"So, assuming you can control or eliminate the sorcerers, it's correct to say that no other army could defeat mine, even if we're outnumbered a thousand to one. It's nothing like normal fighting."

She hesitated, then asked, "How are your plans against the sorcerers coming?"

"I still don't know how to neutralize them. I'm hoping to find weapons at Center, or perhaps information about how they acquired sorcery in the first place. I suspect they somehow draw power from the monuments. I believe the blood rites—that practice using human sacrifice they call religion—only augments their power, not grants it outright. Else they'd keep their stone altars and stone knives working at all times."

"That should be your main focus in the coming weeks, then," said Maran. "The human sacrifices will die with them, I hope." She yawned widely. "I need sleep, Grey. Making homunculi, even simple female soldiers, drains me. A part of my own essence goes into each one."

"By all means," I said, rising to hold her chair. I hesitated, unsure if she wanted company. She read my expression and shook her head slightly. She leaned up to kiss me, then patted my shoulder in affection and moved toward the door.

"Maran," I called.

She paused, looking back over her shoulder. "Yes, dear?"

"You once called me 'one of the children of twilight,' referring to Qol's handiwork. You said you were one, too."

"Yes, I recall using the phrase."

"I was just wondering . . . how many others did Qol make?"

She appeared thoughtful. "I've always suspected there were many, but I had no proof until I met you."

"How would I recognize one?"

She leaned on the doorframe, exhaustion evident in her posture, but she paid me the courtesy of pondering my question carefully. "You and I have nearly unique coloration. I don't think Qol is limited to that. You may have no way to tell, without using your percipience. I have some ability there, but nothing like yours."

In consideration of her fatigue, I spoke rapidly. I shared my theory about stolen human embryos, genetically modified, grown using artificial incubation and controlled maturation. "If true," I finished, "could Qol mix muria genes with human ones, creating hauflin in the laboratory rather than by interbreeding?"

She yawned again, trying to hide it with her hand. "I don't think so, Grey. He does *something;* else we wouldn't have our looks or powers. But the muria have mutated so much, I don't think mingling genetic material is possible, either in a womb or in a laboratory."

"Thank you, dear. Sleep well."

"You, too," she replied.

I dismissed Virgil for the night, asking only for a bottle of gin and a glass before letting him go back to his studies.

I drank sparingly, brooding unhappily over my new prophecy. I decided all my previous analysis was trash, about on the level of a first-year university student discovering philosophy for the first time. True prophesying carried with it a conviction of certainty, a sense of inevitability, all paradoxes be damned. Before I realized it, the gin bottle was empty. I stumbled through the hallway in search of more.

Hasq met me only a few steps outside my quarters. He took in the empty bottle, my stagger, and my facial expression, and sent for Virgil to attend me. While we waited, he guided me back into my rooms, pushed me gently onto the bed, and took off my boots.

"Has your despondency returned, sir?" he asked quietly.

"It has never left me."

"Sir, you must not contaminate the lady with mordant thoughts. It will affect her work. Despair is only an emotion. It can be overcome, but not by strong drink."

"Don't get in the habit of being right all the time, Hasq."

He lifted his eyebrows. "Why not, sir?"

"Because it makes your inevitable errors that much more demoralizing."

"I shall take your advice in the spirit it was offered."

I narrowed my eyes. "Was that a deliberate pun?"

"Sir, I have not yet acquired the habit of making mistakes. You may assume my choice of words was premeditated."

I tried to struggle up onto my good elbow, but failed. "You can be an ass. Have I ever told you that?"

"Many times, sir. Ah, here's Virgil. He will take care of you sir. If you must vomit, please try to avoid staining the sheets."

"Dismissed, both of you. I want to be alone."

Hasq bowed and left, but Virgil remained to finish undressing me. I have a vague memory of his adjusting my pillows, then nothing—not even dreams—until morning.

<hr>

I normally slept with the drapes closed, but Virgil must have opened them. Bright sunlight stabbed me in the eyes. I rolled, shielding my face with my good arm, but the relief was only temporary. The door banged open.

"Coffee, sir," said Virgil. "It will help your headache."

"I didn't have one until you opened the door so loudly. Where's Maran?"

"The lady is already at work, sir; she rose at dawn. Hasq instructed me to let you sleep."

"What time is it? Why doesn't this house have any clocks?"

"Timepieces, sir? The lady dislikes them, but I can procure something from storage for you. The sun is good enough for the rest of us. It is nearly noon now."

I groaned. "Help me up, then. Riding leathers today. I'm already late."

"If I may, sir, your errands can wait until you've eaten and had some coffee."

The thought of eating made me ill, but I accepted the coffee and sipped at it while Virgil prepared my clothing. I used the time to plan my day. Since it was already late, I'd visit Tessa first. Afterward, I should take an update to Benlyn. He needed to know the new army's capabilities and limitations in order to plan his campaign. If daylight remained after that, I thought I should go to Draycott, to see if the storm had reached that far south, and to check on Lady Ariel's welfare. Ashe would welcome news of his fiancée. I highly doubted messengers were traveling up and down the coast yet.

I declined the cape Virgil offered. "I don't think it's appropriate now," I said. At his quizzical look, I added, "You must have noticed I no longer bear the royal signet."

"I did notice, sir, but it was not my place to ask."

"It means I'm no longer a prince. If you must dress me in fancy clothes, they should not be regal. I should carry a coin purse from now on. I no longer have the perquisites of office."

"Very well, sir. I'll see to that."

I finished the coffee, grateful that Virgil didn't ask any questions. My stomach still felt a bit queasy, and my headache wasn't gone, but I felt able to face the day. When he brought the purse, a hefty leather bag as large as my fist containing copper, silver, and gold coins, I raised my eyebrows. "This is a rich man's purse."

"Upland, sir, you are still a lord."

I dumped most of the coins onto the bed, making sure I kept only a handful of coppers and a few silvers. "Perhaps, of a sort. But I don't need to carry *that* much. A fat purse is hard to hide. I don't want to advertise my wealth to brigands."

"Of course, sir. I should have thought of that."

"Enjoy reading, Virgil. I'll likely be gone most of the day."

I limped to the stables, collected Butter, and rode to the dolmen. Once inside, I tapped a menhir to wake the lights, and selected three strands, then on impulse, a fourth. I mentally knotted them securely to Butter's saddle, plucked the first ribbon, and urged Butter forward.

With a few paces, Butter carried me through the doorway in the sky, and we emerged in the snowdrifts of Tessa's back yard. Things had started melting; no ice clung to the trees, and the drifts were considerably smaller than before. Butter splashed through pools of water and mud on the way around to the front of the house. From the wind's bite and overall temperature, I suspected the thaw would reverse itself overnight, only to have things melt again the following day. Brand's estimation of weeks before normality returned seemed likely true.

Torrey met me at the door when I knocked, and practically climbed me in order to give me a hug.

"I'm not a tree," I said after setting him down. I rubbed absently at my bad leg. "I've brought the horse, so, assuming there are places to ride safely, I'll make good on my promise today. How's your grandmother doing?"

"Ask the maid," he said, losing his grin. "Grandma won't get out of bed. I even asked the maid to make lemon cakes for her."

"Lemon cakes are *your* favorite, not hers," I said. "Go reacquaint yourself with Butter while I talk to the maid. And don't steal any currying brushes this time."

He went back inside, emerging a moment later with his winter coat, a scarf, and gloves. We pushed past each other in the doorway, and I carefully closed the door against the chill wind.

"Nursemaid?" I called loudly.

She came bustling out from the back rooms. "Lady Tessa still sleeps, sir. I haven't been able to wake her since she went to sleep early last evening. She hasn't eaten anything since your previous visit, although I did get her to drink water and tea before she went to sleep."

"I'll go examine her," I said. "Take my cloak, please. Even with the drafts, it's beastly hot in here."

"Lady Tessa complained of being cold yesterday, sir. I had Brand build up all the fires."

Nodding to myself, I went around the small table, went past Torrey's room, and found Tessa lying in her bed, one side of her face slack.

Stroke? I wondered, scrambling my percipience to check her from the inside out. I saw nothing but the tumor, unchanged for the most part, although new spots showed on her cerebellum. I shook her shoulder gently, and called her name several times.

One eye fluttered briefly. She murmured something unintelligible, and promptly lost consciousness again. Drool leaked from one corner of her mouth.

The nursemaid came into the room and stood beside me. "Sir, I'm no physician, but—"

"Your insights are adequate," I said harshly. "She may last a few hours like this, but I'm not hopeful."

"I'm sorry, sir. I know she was beloved."

"Go fetch Brand," I said. "We need to make arrangements. In the meantime, I'll try to do something to ease her suffering."

The nursemaid scuttled quickly from the room, and I drew up a chair to sit beside Tessa's bed. I rested my good hand on her forehead.

Tessa? Can you hear me? I asked in mind-speech.

She was no mage and had no telepathic skills, but I imbued her with some of my own vitality. She did not rouse, but I heard a very faint reply. *Grey, take care of Owen and Torrey.*

I will, I promised. I could not lend her any more strength—

rather, she was unable to accept it. I felt a fleeting sense of gratitude, then her sleep turned into a coma, and she was lost to me. She still breathed, but with long, alarming pauses.

I sat with her for what seemed like hours, trying to keep her autonomic functions working properly. I don't know how much time actually passed before Brand came in, Torrey in tow.

"Lord?" inquired Brand. "Does she fail?

Instead of answering him, I stood up and guided Torrey to my chair. I picked up his hand and laid it on Tessa's. "You should stay with her," I said.

He pulled his hand away sharply. "She's cold."

"Her circulation is poor. Her heart isn't beating in the right rhythm. But she may be able to feel your hand, so hold hers and sit with her."

I inclined my head to Brand, indicating we should withdraw. The nursemaid took my place at Torrey's side until I should return. Once in the other room, I said to Brand, "I don't know the local customs. Do they hold funerals or wakes? Do they bury their dead, or build pyres?"

"Services are rare here, lord. They bury, most often on family land. Coffins are unknown among the very poor. They simply dig deep graves, usually eight to ten feet. Sometimes people say a word or two, or a passing monk might pronounce a blessing, but they usually just lay flowers on the grave in silence."

"What's the customary waiting time?"

"For the prevention of disease, burial is normally immediate."

"But it's winter," I said. "Or something damned near like it. Her body won't start to turn immediately. Do I have time to fetch Maran?"

"I can douse the hearth in her room and open the windows, lord."

I nodded. "Okay, go arrange a burial site. I'll sit with Torrey until the end, and then bring Maran here."

It felt like forever, but only took a few hours until Tessa died. I left Torrey in Brand's care while riding back to get Maran. Hasq didn't want me to disturb her, but I settled that by walking wordlessly past him and into the workshop.

"You need to come with me, right now," I said as soon as I'd entered.

Maran looked up, her irritation at being interrupted dissolving into alarm at the look on my face.

"What is it, Grey?"

"Tessa died just now. The local custom is immediate burial. Brand's already arranged the grave and is watching Torrey until we return. I think the least we can do is say a few words."

Maran put down her tools and told a servant to go harvest a large quantity of flowers from the garden. "I won't even change. Just give me a moment to wash. I'll meet you at the stables."

"The groom is bringing your gelding here."

"Then I'll be ready by the time the flowers arrive."

I went outside and mounted Butter. I hadn't cried yet, and wondered if I would. The groom arrived with Aster just as the servant came running with a bouquet of roses. Maran emerged from the workshop, her face and hands freshly scrubbed. She vaulted into the saddle, took the bouquet, and asked, "How does this work when we're mounted?"

"Side by side, knees touching. Walk your horse forward to keep in step with my mare. It will only work from within the dolmen."

We rode in silence along the path and up the deer trail. Once inside the ring of standing stones, I pulled at Tessa's ribbon, opened the doorway, and we rode through together. I suddenly realized that once I untied Tessa's ribbon and let it go, I would never be able to locate it again. My throat ached, but still tears did not come.

Brand, Torrey, and the nursemaid stood on the porch waiting for us. The nursemaid wore her usual uniform, but both Brand and Torrey were bundled up against the cold. Torrey's eyes were red, but he wasn't visibly crying.

I lifted an eyebrow at Brand, asking for guidance.

"Just across the field behind you, lord. In what used to be a vegetable patch. Everything is prepared. It's where all the family members are buried."

Except Lane and Owen, I thought, but kept my mouth shut.

"Torrey," I said, "swing up behind me. This isn't the ride I wanted to give you, but we should go together."

He grasped my good hand and pulled himself up. It was the wrong side for mounting a horse, but Butter didn't shy away. She stood rock steady until he settled, then tossed her head and whinnied.

"In a moment, girl," I said softly. I looked at the two still on the porch. "Brand, you can ride behind Maran. Nursemaid, do you want to come, too?"

She shook her head. "I will tidy things here, sir," she said, curtseying.

Brand said he'd jog alongside us. We set off across the field. Once past a copse of snowy trees and bushes, I saw a full complement of King's Guard standing at rigid attention beside the grave mound. Now tears sprang to my eyes. To them, this precious old woman was only a name—if that—and they had no reason to honor her.

Brand took up a position at the head of the mound, while the King's Guard lined up on either side. I swung out of the saddle and helped Torrey down, much the way Benlyn had once helped me. Maran, Torrey, and I stood at the foot of the grave. Tessa, apparently, was already interred. A wholly irrelevant question struck me. How had the guards managed to burrow so quickly through frozen ground and then clean up? I saw neither picks nor shovels. I wondered if the digging party was a separate group. Hundreds of footprints crisscrossed the snow. The area around the grave had been cleared for dozens of feet on all sides. I shook my mind free of trivia, and concentrated on the funeral.

Torrey slipped his hand into mine when Maran bent to lay the roses on the freshly turned earth. I squeezed his hand tightly. Maran straightened with a long sigh and said, "She was a gallant lady. Rest in peace, Tessa. Your troubles are behind you now."

I said, "I loved her. She was kind to me. Rest in peace, Tessa."

Torrey didn't say anything for a long time. Then he dropped my hand and took a step forward, his boots nearly touching the grave mound. "Grandma, please—" His voice broke for a moment; he swallowed and bravely resumed speaking in a normal voice. "Please say hello to my parents and Grandpa and Owen. I love you."

Thinking he was done, I put my hand on his shoulder. He roughly shook me off and said, "Rest in peace, Grandma. I'm sorry if I didn't always obey you."

"She loved all of us," said Maran after a moment, "and we all loved her."

Brand gave a hand signal, and the King's Guard withdrew their swords in a single motion, swinging them high in a final salute. They held the posture for thirty long seconds, then, at Brand's sign, they turned and marched away, their swords still upraised.

We stayed a moment longer, in case Torrey wanted to say more, but he just stood, head down, staring at the grave.

I jerked my chin at Brand, and we stepped to one side. "Your work here is finished," I told him. "We won't be coming back. You need to meet the officers of your army and begin planning your campaign with Duke Benlyn. The king will want to see you, too.

Be so kind as to get the nursemaid. Do you have your own horse, or will you ride behind Maran?"

"I've my own, lord. It will take me a few minutes to fetch him."

"How are the roads here in town?"

"Passable, but not fully clear, lord. Local men have shoveled enough for horses and sleds. The drifts outside town, once one reaches the trees, are still too deep for travel. No couriers are riding."

"Then I've an idea. Take the nursemaid, collect your horse, and meet us at the tavern. Have the innkeeper clear the place. I'll make it worth his while. We'll dawdle, so you can get there first. We could all do with some food before leaving."

"I'll arrange it, lord." He bowed and sprinted back toward the house.

"Torrey," I said, turning back to the gravesite. "I'm minded to fill your stomach. Have you ever eaten at the tavern?"

He shook his head mutely.

"Climb up behind me, then. No—wait until I'm up, and then get on from the horse's left side. Grab my cloak or the straps, not my arm."

"Grey, is this a good idea?" asked Maran. "We have food in the valley."

"Trust me," I said.

At the tavern, a lanky and somewhat surly teenager took our horses. The innkeeper and his wife hovered attendance, welcoming us inside. The common room was empty, and the blaze from the hearth quickly took the chill from our bones. We removed our winter outerwear and settled at a table. The smell of lamb stew was pervasive. I knew I'd made the right choice.

Torrey looked at the stag, fox, raccoon, and wolf mounts on the walls with fascination. The heads stared back at him with glass eyes. His gaze swiveled in all directions. Horseshoes decorated the tops of each door frame, nailed in place. Pieces of a hand plow and other sturdy farming implements hung from the rafters on heavy fiber strings. The rough wood planking of the walls bore lanterns on iron poles, completing the rustic décor. The room felt safe, exactly as I'd hoped.

"Ale and lamb stew for all," I told the innkeeper.

"Is your house wine any good?" Maran asked.

The innkeeper rubbed his hands, bobbing in apology. "My lady, it's swill for soldiers and traders, only good for getting drunk. We brew our own beer and ale, though. Both are excellent."

Torrey said, "I'm not allowed to drink ale."

"Today you are," I replied. To the innkeeper, I repeated my original order and waved him away.

Do you plan to get the boy intoxicated? Maran asked in mind-speech.

No, just put him at ease. He needs food. Look at him. He's in shock.

Aloud, I said, "Torrey, I'm so sorry for your loss. Your grandmother was a lovely and gracious lady. That first night, when we met, she should have handed me over to the soldiers. Instead, she treated me like an honored guest. I liked her very much right from the start and learned to love her."

"I loved her, too," said Maran, putting her hand on Torrey's. "She doted on you and never failed to care for you."

Brand put in, "I did not have the honor of knowing her for very long, but she was always courteous to me."

The nursemaid said, "Last night, before she went to sleep, her last words were about your welfare. She loved you very much."

Torrey took it all in, but said nothing. His deep brown eyes seemed to suck all the light from the room. The adults shared a look and mutually decided to let the silence continue.

When the ale arrived, Brand, Maran, and I each took a tankard. I nudged Torrey. He stirred to pick up his own, staring into its depths.

"Follow my lead," I said *sotto voce*. He nodded, and I raised my tankard to eye level. "To Tessa," I said loudly. "May her memory be a blessing for all time."

The others echoed me, and we all drank—the nursemaid pretending, and Torrey only taking a sip.

"That's called a toast," Maran explained. "It's a way of honoring someone."

Torrey cautiously sipped more ale, then, appearing to approve, took a long draught. He licked his lips. By the time the stew arrived, including fresh-baked bread, he had finished the ale.

We ate quickly, tearing off hunks from the bread loaf to sop up the remaining juices. Torrey said he wanted to offer another toast.

"One full tankard is enough for you," I said.

"Too much, actually," Maran commented.

It will let him sleep tonight, I thought to her, my mental tone stern.

Was this the prophecy you tried to hide yesterday?

No. I thought Tessa had more time. My vision was darker.

Will you share? she asked. *I heard about your drinking last night.*

Maybe later. I'm still processing it.

Torrey raised his hand, calling for more ale. The innkeeper nodded and got up. I pulled Torrey's arm back down and shook my head, telling the innkeeper we'd had enough.

"Are you my parents now?" Torrey asked, his speech slightly slurred.

Maran and I exchanged a helpless look. "Yes," I said firmly.

"You may continue calling us Grey and Maran, but you are now part of our family. That makes Aiden your little brother. Today, you'll get to see the valley."

"Is it really enchanted?"

"Well, it's always summer there. We'll leave this horrid snow behind."

I stood, belched suddenly, and felt embarrassed. But it made Torrey grin, so Maran also stood up and belched. Brand did the same. Torrey swallowed air and forced a burp. But his smile faded quickly, and his face turned glum again.

I told the nursemaid to go find the teenaged stable boy and have our horses brought around. I loosened the tie of my coin purse, worked it free, and tossed it to Brand, asking him to settle with the innkeeper. "Make it worth his while," I said. "We cost him his entire luncheon trade."

I offered my good arm to Maran. "Shall, we, dear?"

"You were right to insist we come here," she said, holding out her free hand for Torrey. "It was just what we needed."

Outside, the air was brisk, but the sunshine was warm. The stable boy slouched around the corner in a few minutes, leading all three horses. I guessed he was the innkeeper's son, or maybe a kitchen helper forced to assist in the stables. He didn't seem to like horses very much, and the horses themselves seemed reluctant until they saw us waiting.

The nursemaid rode pillion behind Brand while Torrey shared my saddle, and Maran rode alone. I got us all lined up, made sure everyone knew what to do, and plucked the purple strand to transfer us all back to the valley's dolmen. Our horses took a few steps forward, and the snow faded like a bad dream.

I untied Tessa's ribbon from the knot on Butter's saddle and reluctantly let it flutter away, watching while it unraveled and faded to nothing. That particular doorway would never open again. I had three strands left—Benlyn, Ariel, and the one I'd added at the last second—the monastery. It was already late afternoon, and I doubted I'd have time for all three trips.

Maran said, "This is home, Torrey. It's only cold because we're inside the stone circle. The manor house and grounds are warm."

I hesitated for a moment. "I should take Brand to talk to the duke. Do you mind showing Torrey around and assigning him servants and rooms?"

"I don't mind at all," she said.

Torrey protested immediately. "I want to stay with Grey!"

Maran and I held a brief conversation consisting only of eye and facial movements. I told her it was fine for Torrey to accompany me, and she said she doubted the wisdom of taking a boy to Amrhyn. In the end, I left the choice to her.

She shrugged. "Do as you will."

The nursemaid got down from Benlyn's saddle and hoisted herself onto Maran's huge gelding.

"This first trip won't take long," I said. "We'll meet you at home within an hour or so."

"I'll have Hasq arrange things for your return," she said. "The seamstress will be working all night, but we can have private rooms ready quickly."

I waited until she was clear of the circle, then told Brand and Torrey to remove their coats, scarves, and gloves. "I know it's cold here, but it's hot where we're going." We left our winter clothing in a pile by one of the menhirs, and I went to Butter's saddle to remove and stroke Benlyn's strand. As before, I checked to make sure he was in a position to receive visitors. He wasn't alone, but only one of his people shared his room. She was a stern-looking woman, with her hair shorn nearly to the scalp. She wore an abbreviated version of the standard uniform, and the Duke himself wore only an unbuttoned white shirt and short trousers.

I turned to the others. "We walk this time. Torrey, put your hand on my shoulder. Step when I do. Brand, tie the horses up outside the circle, then put your hand on Torrey's shoulder.

In a few moments, we were in a line and ready. I stepped forward from the dolmen's chill into the blasting heat of Benlyn's chambers. It felt like putting my head into a smith's furnace.

"Your Grace," I said briskly, using a voice meant to announce us without startling anyone. "Pardon the intrusion. I've brought Colonel Brand and my son. Torrey, this is Duke Benlyn."

The warrior woman reached for her sword, but Benlyn told her to stand down and guard the door. He and Brand clasped each other's forearms and shook cordially. "Good to see you again, Colonel," said Benlyn. "Congratulations on your promotion. We should play chess soon. The Amrhyns use slightly different rules, but it's essentially the same game. I've had to learn all new strategies."

"I would like that, Your Grace. Perhaps I can even win."

"With practice, certainly," said Benlyn. He turned to me. "I wasn't expecting you so soon, Prince Grey."

"Just Lord Grey now," I said. "I've been demoted in favor of General Yarval." I waved to keep him from protesting. "It's a great relief for me and probably better for the kingdom, so everyone wins."

Benlyn took his cue from my brusque tone and didn't ask what had happened. Instead, he turned to appraise Torrey. "And this young man is your son?" he asked, feigning polite interest.

"Yes. Torrey, address the duke as 'Your Grace' at first, then you may use 'my lord' thereafter. Ignore the way he's dressed. It's the custom here, because of the heat."

"Your Grace," said Torrey without any hesitation. "Do you outrank my father?"

Benlyn and I both laughed. "Yes," I said finally. "But we're friends. Don't worry about rank too much."

Benlyn shook Torrey's hand using the same arm grip he'd used with Brand. "Nice to meet you, Torrey."

"Ben," I said, "we only have a few minutes. May I talk to you?"

"Certainly. Do we need privacy?"

"Not for this. I wanted to tell you more about the new army." I briefly summed up the vulnerabilities and advantages of the homunculi, stressing how hard they were to kill and how they didn't feel pain.

The duke whistled. "With an army like that, I could take over all of Leonais. Only fire and beheading, eh? Amazing! Do you still mean to bring five thousand?"

"Yes, along with captains and lieutenants. The colonel will meet with them later today. How did the local leaders respond at yesterday's parlay?"

"Very well indeed. They'll stand with us against the sorcerers, but they want to see your soldiers first. For now, they're officially neutral, except for Dhutori, Viscount Alvishire. He may well fight on the other side. We've subtly cut him out of our discussions, so he cannot betray our plans."

"I don't know either the place or the person."

"Alvishire contains the largest horse- and cattle-breeding ranches; wide, rich, fertile grasslands with rivers, brooks, and lakes. Dhutori is the richest of the nobles, and can outlast any war of moderate length. The region is largely self-sufficient—he can withstand the loss of trade. He also commands the largest private army in Amrhyn, likely five hundred strong, all of them mounted."

"I see. Horses might become harder to obtain. But what of the grain farmers? Will three weeks be too late?"

"The nobility is quietly sending workers into housing near the fields. It will be a near thing, but I think they can harvest as long as the battle is short."

"My hope is to avoid war at all," I said. "But I share your skepticism. I worry that flammable creatures may not daunt the sorcerers. And this viscount, if he commands sufficient forces, could prolong the conflict."

"I think," said Benlyn, "that Dhutori plans deception, probably on both sides. He'd like to see us destroy each other, so he could step in afterward and fill the vacuum."

"My lords! We should discuss deployment and positioning," Brand broke in. "Amrhyn is a very large region. Even five thousand cannot patrol all of it. We must draw the enemy to us."

"I've ideas about that," said Benlyn, turning to Brand. "But you—you're like the army. Are you indestructible, too?"

Brand smiled tightly. "A sword thrust or stray arrow would kill me, lord, as would starvation, drowning, poisoning, or any other mortal peril. I plan to lead the army, not die with them." He turned to me. "Lord Grey, may I stay the night to discuss strategy with the duke?"

"Ben?" I asked. "It's your choice. The colonel can meet with his captains and lieutenants at any time."

"We're leaving this blasted city tomorrow morning, heading south to rejoin my forces on the moors. Will you be able to find me if we leave Parva?"

"My father can do anything!" said Torrey loudly, then gulped and added, "my lord."

Benlyn laughed. "I believe you, lad. So does half the world." He paused, pursing his lips. "We have spare horses. The colonel may stay. If we don't finish our plans tonight, we can talk while riding south."

"Then, with your permission, Your Grace, I'll take my leave."

"Can you teach me that trick of appearing and disappearing?"

"Sorry. It's not something that can be taught."

"Figures," he said.

I bowed and kicked at Torrey's shin to get him to imitate me. Torrey looked confused for a second and then bowed deeply, his hands behind his back.

A moment later, we were back at the dolmen. I went to get Butter, and led her back into the circle. Torrey was already putting on his winter coat.

"You've met a duke today," I said. "Would you like to meet a princess, too?"

He nodded eagerly, and started to climb into the saddle. "Half a tick," I said. "Hold the horse for me while I peek ahead."

I twanged Lady Ariel's strand, and poked my head through the doorway. She was in a tapestried tower room, accompanied by two ladies-in-waiting. Reluctantly, I led Butter back to the tree and refastened her reins. "Sorry, girl," I said. "It won't be long."

I untied Ariel's strand and wound it about my forefinger, then limped back to Torrey. "Ready?" I asked.

"Do I hang onto your shoulder again?"

"Yes, that's the best way."

"Couldn't I just hold your hand instead?"

I nodded, winding Ariel's strand around my wrist. I took Torrey's hand, and together we stepped through.

"Lady Ariel," I said. "The storms were terrible in the north, so I came to check on you."

She looked up, seeming unsurprised to see a man and a boy materialize from thin air. "Lord Grey, how pleasant to see you again. These are the Ladies Beth and Maeve. They are helping me plan the wedding. Of what storm do you speak? The weather has been most agreeable."

"Rain, followed by snow and ice all along the northeastern seaboard, even extending quite a ways inland. We didn't know if it came this far south, because the roads are impassable."

"That," she said thoughtfully, "must be why I've received no letters. Who is this handsome boy, and where is Lady Mint?"

"Lady Mint is busy today," I lied. "The boy is my son." I turned to him. "Torrey, this is Lady Ariel. She is to be queen soon."

"How do I address her?" he whispered.

Ariel overheard and smiled demurely. "Torrey, is it? I'll share a secret. In private, I prefer no titles. That will have to end after I marry the king, but in the meantime, just call me Ariel." She held out her hand, and Torrey went to her immediately. I'd noticed this quality in Ariel before; she could put anyone at ease in any situation.

She handed Torrey off to either Beth or Maeve—I didn't know which was which—and said, "Find him something sweet. I think there is honey cake or toffee shortbread in the outer chamber."

Both ladies-in-waiting escorted Torrey from the room. He cast a backward glance at me for either permission or rescue. I smiled and waved him away.

"Now that we're alone, Lord Grey, do you bring bad news?"

"Pardon?"

"These terrible storms. Is the king all right? Was his tent city destroyed?"

"Oh, no, nothing like that. They are still digging out from under, but everyone at court is well."

"I'm glad to hear it," she said. "I feared the worst when you appeared. But your son surprises me. I thought he was yet an infant."

"The baby is still a baby," I assured her. "Torrey is an orphan whom Maran and I adopted."

"Hmmn," she said. "You're very kind to take in a stranger."

"We've known his family for a long time. He was practically my son already, even before we adopted him. But he's had a long day, and my visit needs to be brief. Do you have letters for me to take to the king? I won't see him for a few days, but I will still outpace any messenger you try to send."

"Yes, I just finished one." She glided to the door and called, "Maeve, Beth, fill the boy's pockets, but bring him back now. Lord Grey must leave us."

She went to her writing desk, sealed a letter with wax, and handed it to me. "Thank you for your courteous thought to check on us, lord."

"Just Grey is fine. I'm even more informal than you."

"Grey, then. Tell the king—no, my letter will suffice."

Torrey came back, his face smeared with honey, his hands sticky. A lumpy packet, likely containing more sweets, bulged from his jacket pocket.

"Ladies," I said, nodding politely. I plucked at the strand, took Torrey's hand, and stepped through the doorway in the sky.

"These are lemon cakes baked with honey, with even more poured on top," said Torrey. I disengaged my hand and wiped it on my trousers.

"I can tell," I said. "I had another errand for today, but it's nearly dark. I'll go tomorrow."

"Can I go with you again?" he asked eagerly.

"Not for this trip. I intend to see the abbess, the lady in charge of the monks. She's reputed to have a temper, and I don't know if she likes children. Besides, Hasq will probably have you busy being fitted for new clothes."

I had him scoop up all of our discarded winter gear and tie it into a bundle on Brand's horse. "We'll walk back," I said. "You lead that horse. Just follow me."

"Okay," he said agreeably. I released the last strand from Butter's saddle, and put the dolmen to sleep for the night.

Once away from the menhirs and down the deer trail, he took off his jacket, careful to keep the packet of sweets from falling. "It's beautiful here," he said, marveling at the river, lake, graceful arching trees, and immaculately maintained lawns.

I led him to the stables, introduced both the boy and Brand's horse to the groom, and then looked at Torrey solemnly. "Are you ready to see your new home? You'll have your own rooms, a personal valet, and dozens of other servants. It may feel strange at first, but you'll get used to it quickly."

"Rooms?" he asked. "Not just one?"

"In the manor house, each of us has a private suite. There are also common areas. You'll catch on."

"What's a valet, and what's that banging noise?"

"The first is a special servant to attend to your needs. He will bathe and dress you, among other chores. The second is the sound of smiths making weapons and shields. I'm afraid it never stops, not even at night. Eventually, they'll finish, and the valley will be peaceful again."

"Is it quieter inside the house?"

"Not much," I admitted. "Are you ready now?"

He nodded. I didn't want to touch his sticky fingers again, but I knew Virgil would soon clean me up. I took his hand and led him across the courtyard to the back door.

Hasq greeted us. "Welcome back, sir. Welcome to your new home, young master."

"Which way to his quarters?" I asked.

"Near your own, sir. Farther down the hallway. His valet will be waiting for him. You'll each have plenty of time to prepare for dinner. The lady has requested to be served in the main dining room at two hours past sunset."

I limped through the corridors, past the library, and toward my own rooms. A servant I didn't recognize stood patiently waiting beside an open door. "Young master," he said, inclining his head to Torrey. "I've taken the liberty of drawing you a hot bath. And the seamstress has tailored some clothing so you can be presentable at dinner. She'll make proper clothes your size during the night."

"A *bath?*"

"Maran's orders," I said, trying unsuccessfully to hide a grin.

"I can wash myself. I don't want some strange man watching me."

"Young master," said the valet. "I am not a strange man. I am your personal servant. Your word is law in this house, second only to your parents' rules. If the lady wishes you to bathe, then bathe you shall, even if I must tie you down and throw hot soapy water at you."

Torrey cast a despairing glance at me. I just shrugged. "Lady Maran rules here," I said, trying to keep my tone light. "I'd dunk you myself, but my own valet would tie me down and throw hot soapy water at me. If it makes things easier, pick a name for your valet. Call him anything you want. If Hasq approves, that will be his name henceforth."

"Skoda!" Torrey bellowed.

"No, it has to be a proper name. Stop struggling and go with the flow. Swimming upstream will just wear you out."

"Do *you* have to take a bath, too?"

"Yep. No choice. You'll survive it."

"Grandma only made me wash once a month."

I wrinkled my nose. "I know. I can smell it. But—new house, new rules. See you at dinner."

"This way, young master," said the valet, leading the skeptical and hesitant boy into his new quarters.

I went to find Virgil, wondering when I had stopped kicking over the traces myself. I decided that I never had; I had just resigned myself to the inevitable and taken the path of least resistance.

I rather thought a bit of rebellion and insubordination was a sign of health in a child. He would grow into his manners eventually, either with grace or not. In the meantime, I found his attitude perfectly appropriate.

Chapter Sixteen

WE MET for dinner at the appointed hour, all of us dressed for a formal evening meal. Torrey's clothes showed no signs of hasty tailoring; I wondered how the seamstress had managed it. He demonstrated none of my reluctance for frippery and formalwear, seeming delighted about everything except the forced bath, and kept asking Maran how he looked.

She smiled serenely, told him he was very handsome, and didn't correct his table manners, even when he lifted his plate to slurp. To me, she shot a mental query: *Has he cried yet?*

Not in front of me.

He can't keep holding it inside. We don't want him turning into you.

I found her comment harsh, but not wholly unjustified. I hadn't shared my two most recent prophecies with her, although she only knew of one. Both hurt cruelly, but I kept them to myself. I maintained mental and verbal silence, sipping my wine and even pouring a child-sized glass for the boy once the meal ended and we moved to the front drawing room. The nursemaid brought Aiden to us. The baby seemed sound asleep, so Maran left him in the bassinet.

"Is that my little brother?" Torrey asked. "He looks different without all the furs and wrappings. Why is he bald? May I hold him?"

I laughed a bit and told him maybe later, when Aiden woke up. "You'll have to fight for him. When he's not with the nursemaid or Maran, I like to rock with him and tell him stories."

"In other words," said Maran, "you get the fun times, and we do all the work."

I grinned at Torrey. "Sounds right to me. What do you think?"

Torrey hesitated. "Does he *do* anything? Can I play games with him?"

"He poops, pees, eats, and sleeps. Sometimes he cries or smiles," I said.

"Torrey," said Maran, "pay attention. For the next few weeks, I'll be busy during the days, and Grey has work. You'll need to continue your schooling, but will still have time for play, including with the baby. The adults will be busy, but the servants will keep you company." She paused, calculating her next words. "Would you like a horse of your own? I've a six-year-old I think would suit you. His name is Rebel, because he resisted breaking for so long. You two should be a good match. He's very fast and high-spirited. He can even do some tricks."

"Are you joking?"

"Not at all. Horsemanship is one of the many skills a young gentleman needs to learn. We'll also give you fencing lessons. You won't be bored."

Torrey blinked rapidly, seemingly overwhelmed. "Yes," he finally managed. "Yes, *please.*"

"Your valet will be your tutor for now, until you need more than he can provide."

"Locke," said Torrey. "Grey's valet helped me pick the name, and Hasq said it was okay."

"A good choice," said Maran, shooting me a dark glance. I just smiled innocently. To Torrey, she said, "The name has historical significance. It's one of the things you'll study someday."

I set down my wine glass and stood to stretch. "I've just remembered that the monks have midnight devotions. That means it's not too late to visit the monastery. I'll make a quick trip to chat with Siobhan and check the weather around Landing."

Good idea, said Maran in mind-speech. *He's too proud to cry in front of you. I'll smother him with kindness until he acknowledges his grief.*

You're not the only one troubled by empathy, I shot back.

She ignored that and said aloud, "Don't stay out too late."

Torrey rushed to give me a hug and then sat on the floor, legs crossed at the ankles, positioning himself between Maran's feet and the bassinet.

I left them there, sure that Maran would know how to get Torrey to talk and start dealing with his feelings. I'd shown him love and support today by proclaiming him my son in front of important people, but that was only foundational work. The rest I trusted to Maran's capable hands.

Vigil met me in the corridors. "Going out again tonight, sir?" he asked. "I've laid out your riding clothes."

I nodded. "How did you know?"

"Hasq suggested it was likely when we were discussing the young master's choice of name for his valet."

"Hasq has elevated observation and intuition to the level of divination. I didn't know myself until just a few minutes ago. Maran seemed to recognize the name you chose. Who is this Locke character?"

"A prehistoric physician, sir. Better known for political philosophy and ideas about empiricism and epistemology."

I grunted. "Good name for a youngster's first tutor. Is his valet up to the task?"

"I think so, sir. They are among the lady's interests, and Locke's works were very influential on later philosophers. We have some of his theses in our library, but I don't believe the young master can read well. He will need to learn many things before approaching complex subjects."

I dressed quickly, retrieved Butter from the groom, and rode up to the dolmen. It was dark, but my percipience worked nearly as well at night as during the day, and Butter knew the route. The path was limned to my mental sight as clearly as if lanterns had been placed every few feet.

I hesitated before waking the monument's lights. I didn't know Siobhan personally, so I couldn't select a strand for her. I would have to search the monastery until I found her. Mindful of Ashe's earlier rebuke, I decided that blundering through the front door and explaining my visit to ordinary monks would be disruptive. Besides, I didn't fancy asking for an audience only to be turned away by functionaries.

I slapped Butter on the rump, sending her back to the stables, then touched a menhir and chose a ribbon leading to the monastery steps. I tugged it gently to open the doorway in the sky and projected my astral self through to investigate. Walls and closed doors were no obstacle to my questing mind. I passed like a ghost through hallways, dormitories, cloisters, and refectories, and then floated up two flights of marble stairs. Most of the upper chambers were empty at this hour, but one held a kneeling woman surrounded by dozens of candles, apparently deep in meditation or prayer. She wore a hierophant's chains, but no other visible symbols of office. Still, I was sure I'd found the abbess. I carefully memorized the room, and withdrew back into my body.

I released the monastery's ribbon, and selected a new one that led directly to the abbess. I tugged on it, took a single step, and transferred from the dolmen into her chamber, twining the ribbon around my fingers as I went.

***

She didn't seem to notice my arrival, so I took the opportunity of going to her balcony and extending my percipience through the darkness. The snow was still very deep in most places, but the sheen of ice had faded, and Ashe's laborers had cleared the major thoroughfares. Looking down at the temple, I saw the doors standing wide open, the interior lights shining gently.

The bridge still awaited replacement. The small river beneath had receded, but the gorge between hills had become a lake. Physical approach was still blocked. I would have to wait for the engineers to build a new bridge, or divert the river to drain the new lake. I wished I had Justinian Pontifex available.

"Who are you?" asked a sharp, querulous female voice. Had her pitch and timbre been lower, I might have mistaken the speaker for Kiril.

I turned from the balcony. "Hello, Siobhan. We've corresponded, and I believe you've met Maran, my wife."

She rose from her kneeling position and faced me, her arms crossed within her plain monkish robes. Her face was ancient, a mass of wrinkles. Her hair, tied behind her head in a ponytail, appeared plentiful and thick but iron grey throughout. Her eyes widened a bit as she recognized me, but then narrowed to disapproving slits.

"Grey," she said, nearly spitting.

"At your service," I said in a pleasant tone, bowing slightly.

"You serve no one but yourself."

"You're wrong," I said, "but we can't control each other's beliefs. What were you doing when I first arrived? It looked like praying."

"I was asking the gods for guidance," she said stiffly.

"I thought the monks didn't believe in gods."

"As an order, we have no official position. As individuals, we are free to believe in a god or gods as we choose. I am a believer."

"I believe in higher powers, too," I said. "The muria, for example."

"False gods," she sneered.

"A god is a god is a god," I replied. "How is one to know? I am pious in my own way, but the gods are remarkably silent. I tried to get Kiril to explain, but his words made no sense."

"Is that why you killed him?"

"He died from a seizure, not from anything I did. Why do you call the muria false? They seem godlike enough for me, and they have the advantage of being real."

"Say 'illegitimate' if you prefer. One believes in the true gods because they are the basis for all morality and ethics. Why else would you object to evil—assuming you do? The laws of humans are an imperfect reflection of the laws of the gods. We detest rape, murder, theft, witchery, and lying—to name just a few sins—not because some king declared them illegal, but because they are inherently *wrong*. All people know this in their hearts. The internalized knowledge comes from extrinsic standards; your conscience, if you will, depends on accepting there is something greater than humanity and human rules of conduct. It comes from your belief in the gods and what they teach us."

"You're talking about psychology, not theology," I said. "Your argument is sound, but not valid. The premises are neither provable nor axiomatic. Yes, most people share nearly universal moral values—but not all. Otherwise, there would be no murder for us to condemn. The murderer may or may not feel guilty; he's just as likely to feel justified, or excuse it as revenge, or claim the victim deserved it. His feelings are irrelevant. Very few actions are inherently right or wrong in themselves. You, for instance, would not flinch at executing a murderer, even though you are committing the same act for which you condemn him."

She was quiet for a moment, and then she shook her head minutely from side to side, her eyes never leaving mine. "If you can't tell the difference between a crime and exacting justice for it, I cannot help you."

"I did not ask for your help in this."

"No, but your every word screams out a plea for spiritual guidance. You choose to express your doubts and unbelief to me. I answer as I am able. If you want to know about dry secular law, you should seek out a magistrate or judge for your puerile challenges. You don't want to memorize *rules*; you want to know about sin and holiness. These are not easy questions, but neither are they as inscrutable as you pretend."

"May I sit?" I asked. "My leg pains me."

"No."

"As you will, then. This is your house, not mine. From this balcony, looking down, I can see the temple. I could shut the doors from here. Could you?"

"I was a hierophant before becoming the abbess. Of course I could."

"Then why did you let those people freeze to death?"

"Is that why you came? Does my inaction trouble you?" she asked. Her tone suggested profound skepticism.

"Mainly, yes. I want to understand you. I find your actions— and inactions—at variance with the compassion and charity monks espouse. I call deliberately letting those people die sinful, not holy. They were innocent."

"I did not call up the storm, nor did I open the doors and violate the temple's sanctity. Those so-called innocents," she said, biting off the word, "bore the penalty of your sacrilege. You blaspheme by suggesting the gods are not entitled to justice when mocked."

I shifted my weight to relieve the pain in my bad leg. "The words 'sacrilege' and 'blasphemy' suffer from the same problem. They each presuppose the existence of omnipotent entities who are nevertheless frightened or offended by simple syllables dropped from human lips. I find the supposition unsupported by empirical evidence, and the entire notion faintly ridiculous. You cannot validate an argument by asserting its conclusion as your first premise."

"So," she said quickly, "you admit to being an atheist."

"It's not a word I would choose, but according to your worldview, it's likely the only term you'd accept. I seek truth wherever it may be found."

"You said 'mainly.' What other questions do you have? The hour is late, and I must lead devotions."

"I want to know why you allowed Vastil access to the Book of the Ship, and why you trust his translations. Surely your own scholars, or even secular ones, would have done the job as well."

"Have you ever tried denying a muria's wishes?"

I knew what she meant. If a muria wanted to compel trust, or exert dominance, humans had no defense. "Yes," I said. "It didn't go well."

"Then you have been answered. Vastil came to us, not we to him. He forbade us to translate more, or to share ancient knowledge. That his work proved useful does not detract from his soulless nature."

"There's another of those undefined and likely indefinable terms. What is a soul, beyond an unsustainable metaphysical conceit? You and I probably believe the same thing—a person's essence, the sum of experience and proclivities, the repository of ethics—but we disagree about the muria. If humans have souls, so do they. They were human once. Have you met any other muria?"

"I have not even met Vastil. He visited the monastery ages ago. Are you through with word games yet? I tire of this."

"Sorry," I said, striving to make my tone calm. "Whether you believe it or not, I come humbly, seeking information. Did you tell Kiril to obey the king?"

"I did. He chose not to listen."

"He told me he and one other hierophant had that privilege. Wasn't it foolish of him to ignore you? You control all the rest of the monks. You could set them against the two upstarts."

She said, "I only intend to set the monks against *you*. Kiril and Anander are irrelevant to that purpose. You may have tricks and magics, but you cannot stand against all of the monks on Leonais."

"Why would I? I am nothing to them. They have no reason to harm me."

"They will after tonight. When I lead devotions, I shall declare you anathema—outcast, pariah, blasphemer. To be killed on sight."

"That's likely your right—" I began.

"It is," she said sternly. "Also my duty."

"—but what sins have I committed to deserve it?" I finished.

She narrowed her eyes, crossed her arms, and took a few steps forward. The candlelight threw odd shadows, making her seem tall and menacing. "You can't be that ignorant," she said. "Blackmail, for one thing. You threatened the starships. When we paid your price by opening the reliquary, you compounded your evil by showing irreverence. You stole sacred books and brought horses—*horses!*—into the reliquary. You moved the altar and went below. I could go on, but any one of these sins alone earns you death."

I hesitated. I knew she was volatile, and our conversation had not gone well so far. But despite our querulous tone, I had only spoken the bald truth. I chose my next words carefully. "Do you want me to repent?"

"No, I want you to die."

Well, that was clear enough. "I don't share your enmity," I said. "Why won't you believe I mean no harm?"

"Experience," she said, her bitterness evident by the color rising in her cheeks.

"One last thing, then," I said placatingly, holding up my palm in what I hoped was a humble gesture of supplication. "I seek your wisdom. After this, I'll leave you in peace."

"What?" she asked.

"I want to know if you believe in prophecy."

The change of subject seemed to surprise her. Instead of an angry retort, she gave my question due consideration. "There have been prophets through the centuries," she admitted. "Many of them are considered saints now, due to their foreknowledge."

"Do any still walk among us?"

"Not of which I'm aware. The gods speak to us through scriptures and prayer. The days of the great prophets seem long past."

"Were all prophets saints?"

"No, many were heretics. It's a holy mystery. Why do you care?"

"Because I am afflicted by prophecy at times," I said softly. "I can offer you two. Call them predictions or premonitions if you want, but I know them to be true. The monastery will be overthrown when the secrets of the temple are revealed. You can't prevent it, and knowing ahead of time won't prepare you."

"So, you threaten us," she said scornfully.

"I didn't mean it that way. I stated a fact yet to come."

"And your other prediction?"

"I will suffer a doom far greater than yours."

"I shall rejoice when that day comes," she said.

I shook my head sadly. "No, you'll be dead by then." I took a step toward her, and she flinched back. But I was only tugging on the strand, and I disappeared from her chamber as inconspicuously as I'd arrived.

I hadn't been gone more than two hours, but Virgil informed me that everyone else was asleep already. "Sir, the little lord and the young master are sleeping in the lady's rooms tonight," he explained. "The nursemaid is staying with them in case the little lord wakes. The young master is on one of the couches. Locke couldn't get him to change into proper nightclothes."

"Did Maran get Torrey to talk?"

"I'm sure Hasq would know, sir. Shall I inquire?"

"No, let it be." I yawned. "I'm tired myself. Lead on, my man. I feel my bed calling me."

I slept very well that night. I suspected that Siobhan's slumber was less restful. Before rising, I buried my right ear in a large pillow, trying to block the sound of the smithies. It was no use. The infernal clanging penetrated the walls of the manor house, scoffed at my pillow's contemptible acoustic insulation, and assaulted my ear as if I deserved punishment. I could also hear shouted orders and the stamp of soldiers marching.

I went to the window, drew back the drape, and watched the officers drilling the first few hundred foot soldiers, marching them back and forth, presenting arms, and singing in unison.

I shook my head. Things would only get worse before peace returned to the valley. Virgil entered, bearing a breakfast tray, while I still watched the soldiers. I turned to him in surprise, smelling the sausages before I heard the door.

"Where are Maran, Aiden, and Torrey?" I asked. "Aren't we eating together?"

"The lady resumed her work at dawn, sir. The young master is with the groom, becoming acquainted with his new horse. Both of them ate long ago. After his morning's play, the young master will begin his studies with Locke."

I knew better than to expect Maran to stop for lunch, but I asked if a midday meal was in the offing for the rest of us.

"Sir, if you ask for it, it shall be done. Perhaps it will give the young master an opportunity to recover from his first school lesson."

"Please arrange it." I paused suddenly, and looked at Virgil in shocked delight. "There's a clock above the hearth!" I exclaimed joyfully.

"Yes, sir," he said, and I thought I detected pride in his expression. "I hope you're pleased."

"More than pleased." I limped over, took the clock down, and examined it carefully before setting it back on the mantel. "Brass gearing, spring driven, no pendulum, needs winding daily," I said to myself. I asked Virgil about its accuracy.

"The smith who found it in storage said it needed minor repair, sir. In the meantime, I'm to watch for high noon and set the hands each day. Dawn and sunset would be better, were it not for the surrounding hills. He says it should be accurate enough if corrected once a day."

"You're a wonder, Virgil."

"So you've said, sir. I'm glad you approve."

"Put the tray down and get my riding clothes. I left a colonel stranded on the moors of Amrhyn."

"Of course, sir."

I ate hastily and made my way to the stables. Torrey was learning how to curry Rebel; all the stable doors stood wide open today, and the groom was teaching him in the bright sunshine. Torrey dropped the brush, ran to me, and begged to accompany me, hanging onto my good arm.

"It won't be much of a trip," I said. "I'm just going to fetch Brand. We'll be back almost before we leave."

His face fell, and I ruffled his hair in consolation. The groom, having heard every word, quickly saddled Butter without needing instructions. He started to prepare Brand's horse, but I stopped him. "It's a very short ride. We can go double."

The groom had to help me mount. The stiffness in my left leg had gotten worse, not better. I hoped the ride would help work out the cramps.

At the dolmen, I stayed mounted, and chose a ribbon for Brand. I was getting so good at using the dolmen without waking all the lights that the deep underground chime didn't even ring. I wondered how long I'd been able to do that. The last chime I remembered had been at Center. Either something had changed, or I just no longer noticed.

I studied Brand's ribbon, trying to divine his location. He was much farther south than I'd expected. They must have ridden hard through the night. I shrugged, plucked the strand, tied it to my wrist, and urged Butter through.

I emerged under overcast skies. The intolerable heat was gone, replaced by an incessant wind from the west that nearly blew me from my saddle. The air hinted at rain, or perhaps only thick fog, yet to come. I turned my collar up and surveyed my surroundings. As far as I could see, the ground rolled in gentle hills, barely more than mounds. A thick carpet of what looked like soft green velvet covered everything. I dismounted to touch the stuff. To my fingers, the grass felt like thick moss, but somewhat bristly and tough, resembling gorse in many ways. The softness was an illusion cast by distance. Even at ground level, the wind was unrelenting and fierce.

Benlyn and Brand, along with over three hundred mounted soldiers, cantered south toward me, their horses thundering. I remounted and waited, my good hand upraised, my cloak flapping in the breeze.

Benlyn signaled his group to stop. He and Brand continued forward.

"Lord Grey," said Benlyn. "I've a letter for the king. Would you bear it back for me?"

"Of course, Your Grace. I've come to collect Colonel Brand, assuming the two of you have finished your talks." I gestured around. "Are these the downs or the moors? And why is the wind so constant?"

"Moors, lord," said Brand. "Although you can't see from this vantage, we are very near the West Ocean. The breeze you feel originates far out at sea. The winds are gentle enough for ships, but once they climb the cliffs and spread out over the moors, they become damp and continuous. Little actual rain falls here, but the area does not lack for moisture. At night, the air condenses into dense fog. Lanterns let travelers spot the stone mile markers. Without them, nighttime passage across the moors is hopeless."

"Thanks for explaining," I said. "It seems a wild and lonely place. I see no homes or spirals of smoke, even in the far distance."

"Shepherds drive flocks of sheep and goats up from the valleys for daytime forage. Horses can eat the vegetation, but only at great need. No one actually lives on the moors, save for a few hermits and religious ascetics."

"Very interesting," I said, trying to hide my impatience. "Ben, may I take Brand now? His captains and lieutenants are drilling the army. He needs to supervise. And, frankly, I'm cold."

Benlyn waved graciously, granting permission. "The colonel has my letter in his coat. How long until you can get it to the king?"

I counted on my fingers. "Two days, if all goes to plan. He is expecting me then. I have another letter for him, too."

Brand dismounted, and handed the reins of his borrowed

horse to one of the other riders. He looked at my saddle with evident distaste, but swung into a pillion position behind me.

"Talk to you in a little more than two weeks," I told Benlyn. "The colonel can fill me in on your plans. Preparations on our side are going well."

"Give my regards to your lady wife," said the duke.

I pulled at the strand tied to my wrist, and nudged Butter to take a few steps. We left the moors behind and appeared at the dolmen.

* * *

"Do you want to ride back, or walk?" I asked Brand. "It's just over a mile. Along the way, you'll find your captains drilling the troops. They took over the grounds beside the barracks, and are now spreading all along the riverfront. I should have thought of bringing your horse for you."

"I'll walk, lord," he said, dismounting. "I've been in the saddle for half a day. My legs could use the exercise. Here is the duke's letter for the king."

I tucked the letter inside my chemise. "Do you remember the way?"

"Lord, I first showed you the deer trail."

"Oh, right, of course you did. Sorry. I'll see you at the manor. Take your time. You're master of your own schedule until the army is finished."

I gave Butter a nudge, and we started down the slope. I let her stretch her legs on the main path, and we galloped back toward the manor house. I reined her up short near the paddock, when she wanted to veer right instead of left into the stables.

"Sorry, girl, I don't know how to exercise you except by riding. I can't even take your saddle off by myself. You'll have to wait for the groom." I pressed with my right knee, and she obligingly ambled left toward her stall, slowing to a proper walk only a dozen paces away.

The groom came to take her reins.

I swung down and said, "She wants to run, or exercise in the paddock," I said. "Can you see to it?"

"All the horses are a bit twitchy, sir. It comes from having to wait out the rainstorm in their stalls, and the noise of the smiths and soldiers. I'm taking each one for a good long run around the lake today."

"Where did Torrey go?"

"Locke called him inside to begin his studies, sir. I believe they're in the young master's rooms."

I nodded my thanks, crossed the courtyard, and entered the manor house. I wasn't surprised to find Hasq waiting for me.

"Sir, Locke asks that he not be disturbed," said the majordomo. "The young master is already unhappy and wants either you or the lady. However, if Locke is to succeed, he must manage the balance between servant and tutor. He is teaching now, and should remain in charge. If you countermand him, his work will suffer. The young master also must learn to juggle Locke's roles. It will take some time for him to understand when he may give orders and when he must obey."

"Makes sense to me," I said.

"Sir?"

"You're right, as usual. Do I need to say it twice?"

"I expected a token protest, sir. Are you attempting to change the nature of our relationship? If you stop complaining when I say sensible things, I won't know how to respond."

"I'm trying to set a good example for Torrey. Think of it as a new phase in our burgeoning friendship." I pulled the letter from my chemise and handed it to him. "Ask Virgil to find a pouch and put this letter inside. There's another letter on my dresser. It should go in the pouch, too. I seem to have become an involuntary courier."

"Very good, sir."

"That will be all, Hasq."

The majordomo left me standing just inside the doorway, wondering what to do next. The past few weeks had been so hectic that I'd barely had time to think. Now I faced two days and nights before visiting the king or Center. For the first time in recent memory, I had no duties to perform, no one waiting for me, and no idea what to do with my leisure time.

I went to check on Aiden, hoping for time in the rocking chair, but the nursemaid chased me out, saying the baby had just gone to sleep. I ended up in my quarters, staring glumly into the mirror at the scab on my cheek. Virgil found me there at lunchtime. "It's noon, sir. The servants are setting out a meal for you and the young master."

I glanced at the clock on the mantel. The hands read half-past noon. "Not so accurate, after all," I remarked.

"It's time to set it, sir." Virgil swung out the glass covering and adjusted the hands. "That should last until tomorrow."

"What must I wear? I hope it's informal."

"Since the lady is not in attendance, you may wear whatever suits you, sir. The young master has chosen bright silks and linens, with supple leather boots and a cape. He seems to favor sashes and hats, too, although Locke persuaded him that hats may not be worn at the table. He sports an épée at his belt, blunted of course. Overall, he seems delighted with the new garments provided by the seamstress."

I couldn't help laughing. "Dress me like him, then," I said. "We'll be ridiculous peacocks together."

When I arrived at the main dining table twenty minutes later, I found Torrey already eating, using both hands and no utensils. "This is delicious," he said around a mouthful of roasted chicken, somehow managing to smile and chew at the same time. His face was as greasy as his fingers.

"A gentleman should wait until all guests are seated before eating," I chided gently. "And the knife and fork aren't decorations."

He neither slowed down nor lost his smile. "Aw, Grey, not you, too. Locke has been riding me all day about how to sit, how to walk, how to bow. It never ends."

"That's one of his jobs," I said.

"Then don't you go after me, too."

"You wanted a father," I reminded him.

That took the grin from his face. "Yes, Father," he said meekly. He put his food back on his plate, picked up the fork, and waited for me to sit.

"I don't really care how you eat. You're enjoying being rich for the first time in your life. I understand. But Maran has expectations. It's best not to disappoint her."

"May I take a bite now?"

"First, wipe your face and fingers, then put your napkin on your lap."

He complied, but continued talking while eating. "I got to ride Rebel today. The groom led me all around the pasture. And Locke says he'll teach me fencing and gymnastics in the afternoons. But not *this* afternoon. We have to go back to my old house. I forgot to bring Zoxo."

"I'll fetch your lizard for you and ask the smith to make a proper cage. You need to stay with Locke until dinner."

He shrugged. "It's better than mathematics and geography. I'm good at wrestling and tumbling."

"I'm sure you are."

Lunch was all too brief for me. I took genuine delight in his innocent wonder at all the new experiences the manor house offered. I found myself more than a little jealous of his boundless energy. He dashed from the room before I'd finished my chicken, without even remembering to say good-bye.

I took Butter to Torrey's old house, using the front porch as my anchor point. I found Zoxo eventually, lying dormant and lively as a brick, beside the cold hearth. Putting her in my pocket, I transferred back to the dolmen and let Butter have her head. We wandered through the pastures, eventually ending up in a long trot around the lake. She seemed much more sedate than this morning, so I assumed the groom had already let her gallop her fill.

The valley's warmth woke the lizard, and I nearly lost her again in a field of oat grass. She bit me when I picked her up, but settled on my shoulder to bask in the sunshine. I dropped Butter at the stables and asked the groom what to do about the lizard until the smith had a chance to make a cage. The groom found a wooden box with a hinged lid, and I gratefully put Zoxo inside.

I carried the box inside and left it in Torrey's rooms, then went to my own quarters, pulled off my risible costume, and took a long nap.

Virgil woke me for dinner, and I chose unrelieved black formalwear to suit my frame of mind. I knew it wasn't fair to inflict my brooding on the others, so I kept quiet. Brand and Maran discussed technical details about the army, which went far beyond anything Torrey or I could understand. They seemed willing to sit at the table forever, although I caught Maran stifling yawns from time to time.

When the nursemaid brought in Aiden to suckle, I caught Torrey's eye and took him into the front parlor. He thanked me for finding and returning Zoxo, and I told him the smiths would eventually make a proper cage. I tried to listen to his jabbering about his exciting day, but was only able to muster polite noises from time to time. At length, I suggested teaching him chess. He learned the moves quickly enough, but seemed to have no grasp of strategy beyond the next move ahead. He asked if chess modeled how real armies fought, and I gave up, switching us to checkers.

Meanwhile, my mind kept turning over past and forthcoming events. I was not half as sanguine about Amrhyn as Maran and Brand seemed to be. The prospect of fighting the sorcerers filled me with dread, and I couldn't keep from replaying all of Ashe's complaints about my recent behavior. Torrey had to prompt me more than once when it was my turn to play, his tone eventually turning waspish with impatience. After one very long pause, while I was pondering the import of the machines at Center, he simply got up and stalked off. I didn't notice he was gone until Maran came to join me, carrying the now-sleeping baby in her arms.

I bestirred myself to look up at her entrance. "Where's Brand?" I asked.

"He declined rooms in the manor and is staying with his captains in the barracks. Where's Torrey?"

"I think he went to bed. He lost interest in chess and checkers."

She seated herself in the rocking chair and pushed the seat gently back and forth with her toes. After a moment, she asked, "He lost interest, or you did?"

I lifted my good hand, fingers spread, then swiped it sideways in a jerk, as if catching her question and tossing it away.

"I see," she said. "Do you want to be alone?"

"I *want*," I said, suddenly passionate, "to know how to defeat the sorcerers. I'm not worried for myself, but your supposedly invincible army could be wiped out in seconds if the sorcerers catch them in a bunch or manage to encircle them."

"That's what Brand and Benlyn were discussing, as you'd know if you were listening at dinner. You can't defend a border by placing your soldiers evenly along a line, because any breakthrough by the enemy means your own army is spread too thinly to race to the conflict in time. Likewise, you don't group your soldiers in one solid lump, because they can't control the flanks—and, as you pointed out, a small group of sorcerers could destroy them all at once. Brand plans to establish independent commands, each led by a captain or lieutenant, each squad having separate goals and able to change tactics without needing new instructions from him."

"So one squad might be destroyed, but the others would survive to attack from behind or the sides?"

"Yes, exactly. Benlyn is working on a way to entice the sorcerers to come to us, rather than our having to hunt them down individually or in small groups. He plans a feint, a show of weakness that will embolden them to muster their army around them. That's when *you* step in, to demolish the sorcerers. Brand's troops can then mop up any Amrhyns fighting on the wrong side."

"But I don't know how to do that," I protested.

"You'll have to learn quickly. Do you still hope to find weapons among the ancient machines?"

"Yes, it's my only real idea for now. Otherwise, I'll have to try rousing the Sleeper again. Ashe won't have that, and I agree with him. It's too dangerous."

"I agree, but I have faith in you. Right now, we need to talk about the army itself. You're right to call them invincible. Against anything but a sophisticated technological attack or against sorcery, they simply can't be defeated. And that's a problem."

"How so?" I asked.

"After the war, we can't keep the army. I've known that since conceiving the original plan, but things Brand reports make it even more critical than I'd thought. Any lord or noble gaining control of them could dethrone Ashe."

"They only answer to you and the officers you made."

"I wish that were true. The officers will take orders from you, Benlyn, Brand, or me, and, by extension, anyone to whom we grant authority. The foot soldiers, on the other hand, are—how to put it?—unsophisticated. Maybe stupid is a better term. Think of them as willing idiots with swords. They know how to fight and how to follow orders. I couldn't make as many this fast while also giving them reasoning powers. The sergeants and warrant officers have just enough brain power to supervise their groups and carry out basic instructions."

"And the foot soldiers obey them. I get it. But don't the sergeants and warrant officers know who has authority to give orders?"

"I built an *army*. They follow the chain of command. Above sergeants come warrant officers, lieutenants, captains, colonels, generals, and civilian rulers, in that order. Each type of soldier will follow orders from a superior. Brand outranks all the other homunculi, but you and Benlyn outrank Brand. If Brand should fall in battle, without you there to take command, they'd follow Benlyn. And if you, Brand, and Benlyn all fall, any noble or petty lord would inherit the army."

I thought it over, remembering Benlyn's comment about being able to conquer the continent. He hadn't suggested it was something he wanted, and I didn't doubt his loyalty to the king, but it was a weakness. "That seems unsafe," I said at last. "Amrhyn has nobles, too."

"I didn't have much choice. The need for fighters was urgent. It would have taken me years to craft an army of Brands. Do you know what the word 'failsafe' means?"

"I think so."

She got up, put Aiden in his bassinet, checked the corridor, and shut the parlor doors. Then she crossed to a writing desk in the corner of the room, and scrawled something on a scrap of parchment. She brought it to me, adjusting the lantern so I had plenty of light.

"*Don't* say it aloud! Just read what I've written here and memorize it."

"It's a nonsense word. Why can't I say it?"

"Memorize it. Don't even move your lips to shape the syllables silently. It's a word of disposal; the key I've chosen for the army's expiry. I told you I foresaw the potential for this problem, so I've built the key into every single soldier, including the officers."

"What does 'disposal' mean in this context?"

"If you stand within a dolmen, wake the lights, and speak the word, the army will literally fall to pieces, no matter where they're located at the time. They'll become straw and rags, leaving empty uniforms behind. At the conclusion of the war, you must do it."

"I'm not the only one who can operate the dolmens," I said. "What if a sorcerer...?"

"That's why you must never say it aloud, write it down, or tell anyone. Have you memorized it yet?"

I scanned the parchment again to be sure. "Yes."

She wordlessly took the parchment and tossed it into the hearth. She waited until it had burned completely, and then used the poker to push around the ashes, mixing them thoroughly with the wood embers.

"You can't wake a dolmen's lights," I said. "If I die in battle, who will speak the word?"

"No one," she said simply. "They will eventually expire, like all homunculi, but I didn't build in an early expiration. I have no idea how long we'll need them. It isn't like my pregnancy, where I knew the end date far in advance. Therefore, dear, I forbid you from dying. Not only are you needed for the war and its aftermath, but I and your children require your presence in our lives."

I got up from my chair and kissed her. After a bit, our embrace became passionate, but before things progressed too far, she pushed me slightly back. "I'm sorry, Grey, but I need to save my strength for tomorrow's work."

"I only have tonight, tomorrow, and tomorrow night before I can—and must—go back to Center. Can't we make love at least once during that time?"

"I'll try, dear, but you simply cannot understand how draining this work is for me. I could barely keep my lids open at dinner. Each new soldier rips out some of my life force. Hasq forces me to eat and drink, and reminds me to nurse Aiden, otherwise I'd forget. It took all my remaining strength to have this conversation with you."

"Okay," I said, letting concern for her erase my own desires. "I'll have to accept your judgment. But if you're going to be this tired all the time, how will you be able to go to Center with me? You said you wanted to."

"Wanting and doing are separate things. I'll accompany you if I can, but right now, I need to sleep. I can't think even a day ahead."

I called the nursemaid to come take Aiden and escorted Maran to her rooms. I dismissed her maid and tucked her under the covers myself. She was sound asleep by the time I finished turning down the lamps.

Chapter Seventeen

My night was uneventful, as were the following day and night. I got to rock Aiden several times, and told him stories about sorcerers and golems. He seemed delighted by my voice, and I didn't worry about what words I used. The only bit of excitement was a brief trip to check the status of the engineers rebuilding the bridge. They were making good progress, although the design and construction showed they intended it as a temporary solution until a proper bridge could replace the old one. It would be ready for crossing tomorrow.

Save for underneath trees or alongside fences, the snow and ice had melted around the king's tent city. I didn't disturb Ashe, but did explore the mud and debris, keeping my hood over my face. I suspected the storm had been of the once-in-a-lifetime type, for I had never heard of, let alone witnessed, such widespread destruction.

Before leaving, I stood at the base of the starships and laid my good hand on the cold ship's metal, feeling the minute vibrations caused by the wind far above. I transferred back to the valley before any monks or King's Guard recognized me.

I rode Butter far into the hills to get away from the banging of the smiths and found a wide, shallow pond nestled on a grassy area between a tor and a steep rise—a tarn, if it were in the mountains —that seemed like a nice place for a picnic. I went back to the manor house, collected Torrey and supplies, and we had lunch together beside the tarn, enjoying the simple meal and peacefulness of our surroundings.

Afterward, I returned him to Locke's care, and spent the afternoon in the library, reading with Virgil. He still studied the classics, whilst I sought out something in modern writing. The best I could find was a book for children that enumerated the birds of Leonais, each name accompanied by a sketch, a description of its song, nesting habits, and preferred habitat. I found it interesting primarily because I was only familiar with a handful of them.

Dinner that night was subdued. Maran was clearly exhausted, dark circles under her eyes, her face haggard. Brand was preoccupied with his battle plans and volunteered nothing. He ate mechanically, methodically, his mind obviously in Amrhyn rather than here with us. When I tried to question him, he barked out, "Strategy and tactics rule in palaces and command tents; logistics rules in the field," as if settling an argument. I let him be thereafter.

Torrey, too, showed signs of fatigue. He had spent the entire afternoon fencing and wrestling, and slumped over his food.

I asked Maran with my eyes if she'd changed her mind about either making love or going to Center with me. She replied aloud, "Be careful tomorrow, Grey," which answered both questions at once.

I slept poorly most of the night, thoughts racing about what I might discover in the morning. I must have finally fallen into a deep sleep, for when Virgil awakened me, I was groggy and out of sorts. I also found Torrey curled up on the blankets at my feet, snoring softly.

"The young master was lonely in the night," said Virgil apologetically. "Locke and I could not console him, and Hasq would not let the lady be disturbed. He settled down when he saw you, so we let him sleep here. I hope you don't mind, sir."

I slid from under the covers without disturbing the boy. "What upset him?" I asked.

"Locke thinks he's worried about your impending departure, sir. I think it was simple loneliness. If you recall, he spent his first night with the lady, and has only slept in his own quarters once."

Although Virgil and I kept our voices low, we were loud enough to wake Torrey. He stirred, rubbed his eyes, and sat up. "Am I going with you today to see the king?"

"Sorry, no," I said. "I'm only meeting the king for a few minutes, then going to the monument near the monastery. It's too dangerous for you. Go back to sleep while you can. I'm sure your valet has a full day planned."

Torrey grumped and muttered, but lay back down. By the time Virgil had finished dressing me, the boy was snoring again. I asked for a vest and an extra-warm cloak, knowing how bitterly cold the monuments could be.

As I was leaving, Virgil hurried to catch up. "The pouch with the letters for the king," he said, handing me a leather case.

"Good man," I said, tucking the case under my otherwise useless left arm. "I would have forgotten."

"Sir, if I may inquire, are you in pain?"

"No," I said. "Just the usual. Why do you ask?"

"Your stride favors your left leg, not your right, sir. And you are holding your neck stiffly."

"I probably slept wrong. Don't worry about it."

"If you say so, sir," said Virgil, bowing.

Butter and I passed through the valley swiftly. I had her wait while I poked my head into the king's tent. He was alone at his desk again, working on papers. The fire pit contained only embers, and he wore a rich, fur-lined jacket. I withdrew my head, told Butter to stay—she knew the drill by now—and stepped from the valley into the tent.

"Good morning, Ashe," I said. "I've brought you letters from Duke Benlyn and Lady Ariel."

"What? When did you see Ariel?"

"A couple of days ago. I didn't know how long the roads would be out of commission, and you expressed some concern. I thought it only courteous to pay her a visit. She and her ladies appear to be doing well. The storm did not reach as far south as Draycott or Lyonmouth. Only the north suffered."

"Kind of you," he said, putting down his quill. He laced his fingers behind his neck, watching me. "I hear you paid the abbess a visit, too. She claims you threatened her. Why?"

I felt him probe my surface thoughts, exerting his soothsaying powers. I wondered why he felt the need. So deftly that he wasn't aware of it, I withdrew my private thoughts behind a mental barrier, and then hid the barrier itself. He scanned what he could, trying to be stealthy and failing. If this was the limit of his magery, it was insufficient. I decided to ignore it and answer his question.

"I wanted to meet the abbess and ask some questions about monkish beliefs and practices. She wasn't much help. She threatened my life, which seems to be the normal ecclesiastical attitude toward me. I said some unwise things in return, but I didn't threaten her. I only shared a few prophecies. She may have taken them as threats. As I said, it was unwise of me."

"Very unwise," he said, still appraising me. "She's declared you anathema."

"I agree. In retrospect, it was a wasted trip. I was hoping she could help me understand what Kiril meant by meditation, prayer, and holiness. Her answers were singularly unenlightening. She could have saved Selene, Nix, and the others, but she *chose* not to."

"What? Why?"

"Sorry, her explanation didn't make sense to me. I'm still as ignorant about religion as ever. It seems to involve a lot of hatred and distrust, which strikes me as a direct contradiction to what they profess." I paused to shrug, then continued: "Maybe only the leaders are bitter. Maybe they have good reasons for it. But our conversation gave me no information about Center."

"Center?" he asked.

"If you recall, that's what Justian called the monument—the chief dolmen—below the monastery. The name appears in the Book of the Ship."

"I don't think you ever told me that."

"An oversight. I thought you already knew."

He pulled his hands down and rested them on the table. "Tell me of your plans for today. I've already sent Larkin and a small squad of King's Guard to await you."

"Thanks. I didn't enjoy the prospect of searching the brothels. My plan is nothing more elaborate than exploring as much as I can, trying to locate weapons, or at least knowledge, for fighting the sorcerers. With help from Larkin, I hope to continue the conversation with the machines. And oh, I nearly forgot—I expect the stone children to show up."

"Really?" He looked surprised. "Why?"

I quickly recapped my encounter with them and shared the conclusions Maran and I had derived from their cryptic comments.

"So they're Justian's creatures, machines like the ones at Center, but left outside for some reason," he mused. "Be wary. They may serve some hidden purpose. We still don't know why

Justian hid most technology away or why the muria wanted to keep it sealed."

"I believe each child serves a particular function. I just don't know the functions yet. Speaking of children—"

"Yes?"

"I'm sorry to report that Tessa died shortly after my last visit with you. Selene's medications and herbs never made it, so I don't know if they would have helped. Brand's commission and insignia didn't arrive either, but I've explained things to both him and Duke Benlyn. Maran and I have adopted Torrey. You can stop sending money to their hamlet, and reassign the teachers you sent. Maran is seeing to the boy's education now. If he ever desires a position at court, or even a season serving as page, he'll be ready."

"I'm sorry to hear about Tessa," he said. "I didn't know her well. I'd like to see the boy, perhaps when this Amrhyn business is over. Would Maran allow visitors in the valley?"

"If she or I escort you, then certainly. Otherwise, you'd never find it."

"I was asking permission, Grey."

"Oh. Consider yourself invited. We'd be delighted to entertain our friend. Hasq may suffer a nervous breakdown, but he'll arrange everything."

"Who's Hasq?"

"Maran's majordomo. Something between a chief butler and a drill sergeant."

"I look forward to meeting all the strange characters in the valley."

"Then, with your permission, I'll withdraw. I'm afraid my horse is waiting untied, and she doesn't like dolmens much."

Ashe shuddered. "Who does? Thank you for bringing the letters. Let me know what you and Larkin discover."

I plucked the strand, stepped forward, and vanished from the tent.

Butter had wandered, but not far. She stood, shivering beside the tree where I usually tied her reins. "Good girl," I said. I led her back within the circle of standing stones, sorted through the strands for one leading to the foot of the bridge, tied it firmly to Butter's saddle, and rode through.

A captain and squad of four awaited me. Larkin was performing somersaults in what remained of the snow. The King's Guard studiously ignored the old man, who chose that moment to try walking on his hands. His thin, tattered robe fell down, exposing his genitals and pale, spindly legs.

"Lord Grey," said the squad leader. "I'm Captain Kwan. We've been expecting you since dawn."

I acknowledged his salute, and then turned my attention to the old man, who had fallen over, chuckling to himself. "Larkin, Lady Maran sends her greetings. I believe you know each other. I'm Grey, her husband."

"Barren Maran," he cackled. "That's what we used to call her. Only cerebration for consolation."

"You helped her with some difficult translation work, and she is a mother now."

He rolled over to sit up, legs akimbo on the muddy ground. He stuck his tongue out at me, then seemed to become fascinated by his kneecaps. Ashe had told me Larkin was completely bald, but that wasn't quite true. He had bushy grey eyebrows and tufts of what looked like white ferns sprouting in a semicircle around his lips. Similar stuff—I suppose I had to call it hair—grew from his nostrils and ears. While I watched, half in bemusement, half in horror, he tried to insert his left heel into his mouth.

I glanced away. "Captain, is this normal?"

"Lord," said Kwan sadly, "this is somewhat improved. After

dragging him from the brothel, we had to tie him over a saddle just to get him here. Then one of us needed to stand with a drawn sword blocking the bridge to keep him from running inside. He . . . *sang* . . . to us during the ride. I won't repeat the lyrics." The captain's ears flamed red.

"I see," I said, wondering what Ashe had gotten me into. Couldn't the king have sent a more coherent scholar? I turned back to the old man. "Larkin, can you understand me?"

"You haven't said anything yet, impudent fool. How can I understand nothing? It's a contradiction in terms."

I took a deep breath. "I intend to enter the monument, go into the chambers beneath, wake the living machines, and converse with them. Will you come with me and translate? The machines do not speak the modern tongue."

He stood up immediately and began capering. His gyrations took him very near Butter, and he stopped for a moment, his hand on the reins, one eye locked on my face, the other roaming freely. "Are you Hamlet or Macbeth?" he demanded.

"I don't know those names," I answered.

"Of course you don't. How could you? It doesn't matter. But you're one or the other. Either way ends in tragedy, but taking different paths, la, la, la."

"Lord Grey," said Kwan sharply. "Is he sane enough to help you?"

"I have no idea. Let's go inside and find out."

At my words, Larkin scampered on all fours behind the guards and then suddenly stood to run across the bridge, disappearing inside the temple before anyone had a chance to react. The guards and I raced after him, slowed only by having to cross the bridge single file. Once within the circle, I slid from Butter's back, handed her reins to the captain, and told him to maintain guard here. "You may see lights, or hear noises," I said. "Try to ignore them. If you sense danger, run—don't try to rescue us. Your main job is to make sure I'm not disturbed."

"As you will, lord," said Kwan and began arranging his squad. I noted with some amusement that he faced two of them outward, while he and the other two faced the temple doors. I had a feeling that Ashe had told them both to guard me and to guard *against* me. Human soldiers were the least of my worries right then. I shrugged and left them behind to maintain their posts.

Inside, I saw that the workers who had made the temporary bridge had also cleared the temple floor. I was glad I didn't have to see Selene's corpse, or Nix's.

Larkin was lying on his stomach, bare feet up in the air arching so his heels nearly touched his back, head propped on one elbow, reading one of the reliquary's strange metal books.

"What did you find?" I asked.

"Recipes for lentil soup," he said. "The lucubrium is below. Go look for a stewpot."

"Mad," I muttered to myself, "completely mad." I didn't see how he'd be any help. But he heard me, lurched to his feet, and threw the book across the room in sudden anger.

"Sanity is depravity, vanity is profanity, but audacity is concave! If a thing said to happen cannot be distinguished from a thing that did not, it's not a thing at all. You should know that, Hamlet. Ask better questions."

I sighed. "Why lentil soup?"

He danced in circles, the light streaming in through the great temple doors reflecting off his bald pate. "Why *not* lentil soup?" he sang in a high, quavering voice. "Distinguish the relevant from the important, else your father's ghost will never rest." He stopped suddenly, standing as still as a man frozen in time. Only his eyes moved, seemingly independent of each other, scanning the room, the altar, the stairway, and finally me. "Oh, you poor child of twilight, the last act comes, and 'the rest is silence,' according to the Bard. Qol's son, what do you truly seek?"

I strode forward, grabbed his thin shoulder, and shook him violently. "What do you know of the children of twilight or of Qol? What are you saying?"

He came back to life under my grip, wriggling free, leaving part of his tattered garment in my hand. His callused feet slapped on the marble as he dashed for the stairwell. "Come, bring your fractured face. Investigate, interrogate, and communicate! All converse is perverse," he called over his shoulder.

The old man knew *something*. His madness might prevent him from speaking coherently, but his babblings might reveal important snatches of information, and he might be able to help translate.

I made my way down the steep ladder-like stairwell. The doors at the bottom were still open. Larkin was nowhere in sight. I edged past the doors, and the ubiquitous indirect lighting came on. I followed my earlier path toward the cabinet-desk machine that called itself Malmö. When I saw that Larkin was not in that particular chamber, I went back into the corridor and called for him.

The old man answered from what seemed a very long distance. I tried to follow the sounds, but quickly got lost. The walls and floors had no markings or labels, and all the metal rooms and hallways seemed alike.

I found him eventually, urinating on one of the cabinets. "Larkin!" I cried.

"Designed by and for humans, but not a toilet in sight," he said. "What's an old man to do?"

I ripped off more of his rags, leaving him bare-chested. I used the filthy old cloth to wipe up the urine, and looked for a place to put it. I ended up kicking it into the corner of our current chamber. If Larkin felt the cold, he gave no sign. Underneath my cloak and heavy vest, I was shivering. Nevertheless, courtesy demanded I do something. "Do you want my cloak?" I asked.

"Cold is bold, chill a thrill. Do as you're told, or do as you will."

I took that as an oblique way of saying yes, so I loosened the clasp, worked off the cloak, and handed it to him.

He promptly used it as a rug, sitting cross-legged and staring at the machines with one eye, me with the other.

"What, no offer to duel? Perhaps you are Macbeth after all. Tomorrow and tomorrow and tomorrow, the silent creep of your brave words will bring me to tears. Touch the machines, and resume your heart's hope, else all signifies nothing."

Having no idea what he meant, although it seemed one of his more rational speeches, I placed my palm on the surface of the nearest cabinet. Immediately, lights glowed softly, embedded within the top surface. I said, "Hello?" and a mellifluous voice spoke in gibberish.

Larkin listened closely, and then shook his head. "More," he commanded. "More machines, more languages."

I obligingly walked around the chamber. More than half the machines did not respond to my touch, but at least twenty of them did. I stood in the midst of them and called, "Hello?" loudly. A mélange of voices replied all at once; I couldn't make out any words.

"Can you teach them to speak modern?" I asked Larkin, who was currently out of sight, but presumably still using my cloak as a cushion.

He stood up, did a handstand on one of the surfaces, then a backflip, somehow vaulting himself to the top of another. "Wrong room, wrong womb, wrong tomb, wrong doom. All gloom, I presume. They told me where to go. Follow!"

I retrieved my cloak and went into the corridor. All the surfaces blinked to darkness as I exited. In moments, Larkin rushed past me and ran down the corridor, sticking his head into each chamber for a moment, and then withdrawing to inspect the next. All the rooms were mysteries to me, but Larkin seemed to be searching for something specific. I did the only reasonable thing I could: I followed him.

"Surprise! The prize, or so I surmise!" he yelled suddenly. "Come in, come in. Touch the machines, tickle their beans, and puncture their spleens!"

I entered the chamber. Although I had not awakened the monument's lights above us, either to my second sight or to human eyes, this room swam with streamers, bangles, ribbons, strings, and stars. They wove in and out, forming a pattern too complex for me to decipher. The effect was hypnotic, nearly hallucinogenic. I saw only three cabinets, one of them malformed —or no, purposely formed in a different shape. Instead of being a boxlike lump of a desk, it was a hollow tube, open on one side, like an ancient tree trunk. It rose seamlessly from the floor and merged with the ceiling, flaring out at either end, but perfectly cylindrical for most of its height.

"Can you see the lights?" I asked Larkin softly. He was standing beside the cylinder, stroking it with loving fingers.

He turned his head just enough for his left eye to swivel my direction. "There are no lights, except from the walls."

I touched the surfaces of the two normal cabinets and was rewarded by telltales springing to life from deep with each desk. "Speak!" I commanded.

Two deep voices, one martial, the other melodious, responded immediately. The first one seemed strident, the second dulcet, but I couldn't understand anything they said. I cast a despairing look at Larkin. "Either translate or teach them modern speech," I pleaded. "If you don't know what they're saying now, you can request other languages."

"Having no fetter, I can do better!" he crowed, and stepped

into the hollow cylinder. He looked directly at me with both eyes for the first time. "I have been alone and insane too long. I yield my burden to you now. Don't thank me."

He closed his eyes, spread his arms wide, and enunciated loudly and distinctly: "*Accipe me! Vos postulo ut manducare cor meum!*"

A bright light flared, and all the ribbons and bangles swarmed to fill the cylinder. They flowed out again, and the brilliance faded. Larkin was gone, the cylinder empty.

"Larkin!" I called, "Larkin!" I feared the worst, but hoped he had merely used the dolmen's power to transfer elsewhere.

"Larkin is within," said the martial voice from the farther of the two cabinets. "We have consumed his mind, as he commanded."

I whirled to face the two cabinets.

"Where?" I demanded. "Give him back."

"He was too damaged to survive the merger," said the nearer voice. "He is no longer an independent entity. Only his knowledge remains."

"Identify yourselves."

"Ramirez online," said the first.

"Anceron online," said the second.

"What about Larkin's madness? Wouldn't he contaminate you?"

The machines conferred with each other in a rapid series of tones and clicks that I presumed was a language as artificial as their own lives.

Anceron said, "There is no perfect translation between Latin and what you call modern speech. He ordered us to take him and 'eat his heart.' We did not consume the parts of his mind you call madness. We only absorbed language and history."

"History? Then check your records. Who are Hamlet and Macbeth?"

"Locating . . . located," said Anceron. "They are names of prehistoric stage plays, also the titular characters of each."

"What did Larkin mean by addressing me by those names?"

"Unknown. By inference, he may have been attributing the characters' personalities or actions to you."

"How did each character fare?"

"Each died at the end of his play."

"I want to sit down," I said, rubbing my forehead with my good hand. Another life lost, this one by his own actions, but still my fault. If I hadn't brought him here, if I hadn't asked him to translate, if I hadn't let him rush into the room ahead of me. . . .

The floor beneath my boots bulged, making me leap backward. The bulge became a rod, growing, extending upward, and finally flowering on top into a mushroom shape.

I gingerly seated myself. The chair shaped itself to my buttocks, then hardened in place. The control surfaces were within easy reach from here.

"Anceron, state your function," I said.

"I coordinate and facilitate transfer and location services."

"Explain."

"I find things and move them from place to place."

"Do you mean the dolmen network? Is that why this room is full of streamers and ribbons?"

"I find things and move them from place to place," Anceron repeated.

Okay, leave that for later. It's not the right question.

"Ramirez, I know your function is defense. The stone children told me about you. Do you also manage offensive weapons?"

Ramirez said instantly, "The words are known, the meaning is not. The syntax entails a contradiction. Explain 'stone children.'"

"Living machines, like you, but mobile. I call them stone children because their voices sound young to my ears and because they spent three thousand years encased in stone. I've never actually seen their bodies. They surround themselves with a blinding light."

"A self-directed intelligent mobile unit is an automaton. The automata are primarily monitoring devices," said Ramirez. "They observe and report."

"They said they'd come here once you were awake. They also said they were dangerous to human flesh. They damaged my skin more than once, and suggested deeper injuries."

"They have not reported in three thousand years. They may be malfunctioning."

"Can you open this monument for them, without letting sorcerers follow?"

Anceron said, "Once Ramirez raises a tuned noetic field, I can transport them here. Locating . . . locating . . . located. Their long immobility damaged their power shielding. The radiation levels exceed human tolerance."

"Simplify. What does that mean for me?"

"You would burn to death."

"Then don't do it!" I practically screamed. Regaining my equilibrium, I turned my attention back to the other machine, who had only partially answered my question.

"Ramirez, describe your offensive capabilities."

"Main systems offline. Ballistics, explosives, and ordinance unavailable."

"Explain."

"I cannot supply offensive capabilities. Remote nodes nonfunctional."

"I need weapons. Can you fit me with a neural interface and give me something portable? I need to fight sorcerers in Amrhyn."

"You have twice used the plural noun 'sorcerers.' Unknown referent."

"Humans who control supernatural powers. They can generate lightning from their fingertips and throw fireballs."

"Syntactical error likely. Query: Do you speak in metaphor?"

"No, dammit. Real people, real supernatural powers, real theurgy. They live in Amrhyn, a region on the southwest coast of the continent."

Anceron said, "Locating . . . locating . . . located. They have neural implants, and draw power from the monuments. By definition, the supernatural is not observable or subject to analysis."

"You can damned well see the lightning and fireballs," I snapped. "If it's not supernatural—or magic, or theurgy, whichever word suits—then it's a good imitation. I don't care what you call it. I want whatever they have."

"You are a controller," said Ramirez. "You operate the monuments directly. No interface is required."

"The stone children called me imperator, which I recognize as another word for controller. But in modern speech, 'imperator' is singular. You imply I'm one of many. I'm not sure I *am* a controller. I can't project their types of force. I can't even defend myself from such things."

"The automata must be recalled, so their accumulated observations may be integrated," said Anceron. "I will bring each one back separately, and absorb it. You should leave the room. The walls will provide sufficient shielding for brief exposure."

Ramirez said, "Noetic field in place. Proceed."

Anceron said, "Command function incomplete. Human imperative required."

I sort of understood their plan, but had no idea why they were waiting. "Do I need to do something?" I asked.

"Trace the blue circle on my surface counterclockwise, then again clockwise. Immediately press the red square and leave the room."

"Won't you become inert again if I leave?"

"The function you initiate will persist until your return."

Shaking my head in wonder, I followed Anceron's instructions. As soon as I reached the corridor and stood with my back to the wall, twelve incandescent flashes, quickly snuffed, cast their glares into the corridor. After the last one, I reentered and resumed my spot on the stool.

"Well?" I asked.

"Still assimilating. The data store is quite large," said Anceron.

I turned to Ramirez while waiting. "Tell me about imperators and controllers."

"They are synonymous in this particular context, as you surmised."

"Why do you think I'm one of them?"

"You are here," said the machine.

"I left the doors open. Anyone could have walked in, gone down the ladder, and found you."

"The noetic repulsion field is sufficiently strong to prevent that."

"You mean the aversion everyone feels around dolmens?" I asked.

"The proper term is monument, not dolmen. Noetic means telepathic in this context."

I leaned back on my stool. "If by telepathy you mean mind-speech, then why didn't you just speak to me directly? Why fool around with all these languages and absorb poor, mad Larkin? The stone children—the automata—spoke colloquial modern."

"They never spoke to you."

"The devil they didn't!"

"All of your conversations with them were noetic. The speech seemed 'modern' to you because that is your native tongue. Your brain interpreted it as speech."

"Why didn't you do the same?"

"We lack the interfaces designed for mobile intelligences. Our interfaces are designed for verbal and tactile input."

"This is fascinating, and I want to learn more about it—someday. For now, I need to know what it means to be a controller. Why can the sorcerers do things I cannot?"

"Assimilation complete," said Anceron suddenly. "I can now assist. Those you call sorcerers are highly attuned to destructive energies. They not only bear implants, but they have studied the monuments extensively. Your own inexperience limits you."

"Why don't I need an implant thing?"

Anceron and Ramirez spoke to each other in the same tones and clicks they'd used before. After the briefest of pauses, Ramirez said, "Unknown."

Anceron said, "I can disconnect their monuments from the network."

"Will that stop what I call supernatural powers?"

"No, but it will prevent them from using the network for transportation and remote visualization. I can lock out those specific functions."

"Do it!" I commanded.

"Locating . . . locating . . . fifteen independent nodes and two clusters located. Disconnection complete."

"Only in Amrhyn, right?"

"The automata provided the geographical information required. Only the region you call Amrhyn was affected."

On impulse, I asked, "Are there monuments in Avermorn?"

"Unknown referent."

"The northern of the two continents on this planet."

"No," said Ramirez. "The architects created no monuments there. The inhabitants destroyed our remote sensory equipment."

I thought I understood, but for confirmation I said, "Meaning you can't go there or even see what's happening."

"Correct."

"Okay, never mind. I still need weapons."

"Main systems offline. Ballistics, explosives, and ordinance unavailable."

"You said that before," I snarled. The machine intelligences were compliant and helpful, but seemed to have certain inherent limitations. I could spend a year questioning them before getting a useful reply.

"What does 'offline' mean? Can these 'main systems' be repaired?"

"Offline means inoperative, unreachable, or disconnected. Repair by qualified technicians may be possible, if replacement parts and tools survive."

"What is Center's function?" Before they could ask, I added, "I mean this monument. It is unlike all the others."

"I coordinate and facilitate transfer and location services," said Anceron.

"I monitor and maintain noetic fields," said Ramirez. "I also control access to this location."

Not terribly well, I thought. The hierophants and I could open the doors, and a team of horses was sufficient to move the altar blocking the stairwell. On the other hand, what I thought of as "magic" was required to open either the main exterior doors or the smaller doors at the foot of the stairs. If Ramirez recognized me as a legitimate controller, it made sense that someone able to manipulate a dolmen's energies would be granted entry.

I stopped my mental rambling, and doggedly went back to the main question. "If you cannot supply weapons, and if the only edge the sorcerers have on me is knowledge, then teach me."

Anceron said, "The automata believed you already have the requisite knowledge. You refer to it as the Sleeper."

"That's *too* much power," I said quickly. "I need a hand-held weapon, or just the ability to do what the sorcerers do. If you can't teach me yourselves, perhaps the other machines here can. I spoke briefly with the one called Malmö, although it lacked modern speech at the time." I paused thoughtfully. "I assume all the machines down here can speak modern now?"

"Correct," said Ramirez. "Most consoles are either offline or decoupled from the systems they were designed to control. But among those still operable, all knowledge is shared."

"Consoles?" I echoed. It sounded to me like something a mother might do for a distraught child. I didn't recognize it in this context.

"A word for the control surfaces and the functions they supervise."

"So," I said, feeling dispirited. "No weapons."

"Correct."

"What about ships that can fly through the air? The old books mention machines called 'flitters.' Are they offline, too?"

"Locating . . . locating . . . not found," said Anceron.

"Can you help me *at all?*"

"I can enhance your ability to manipulate the monuments," Anceron said. "The energies you call 'streamers' or 'ribbons' need not originate at a monument's physical location."

"How?"

"I can embed control fibers in your brain. You would then only need to conceptualize a location and desire transportation. The request would be relayed to me, and I would effect the transfer."

"You're joking!"

"Step into the booth," Anceron instructed. "The embedding will only take a few seconds."

"By 'booth,' you mean that cylinder where you killed Larkin?"

"It has many functions. You will not be harmed."

Uneasily, I got up from the stool and watched in fascination as the floor reabsorbed it. *More motion without moving parts,* I thought. *Like the books upstairs, designed to last forever.* I took a hesitant step toward the cylinder, then with a deep breath, stood inside it.

The floor shook suddenly, so violently that it tossed me from my feet, threw me from the cylinder, and laid me out face down on the floor.

"What the hell?"

"A minor geologic instability. This structure is not in peril."

"Did I cause that by getting into the cylinder?"

"No. Surface shale and limestone realigned over granite bedrock, releasing deformation pressure. Event occurred five miles from this structure, radius small, effects localized."

I rolled over, sat up, and climbed to my feet. "You mean an earthquake." Compared to the ones I'd experienced or caused, it was very small. "Are the starships still standing?"

"Landing vehicles unaffected."

"So it was just the ground shaking a bit, right in this area?"

"Correct. Reenter the booth."

I did so, with even more reservations than before.

All the bangles, stars, streamers and ribbons in the room flew toward me, each one striking the center of my forehead before disappearing. I felt nothing. By the time the room had emptied, I saw replacements spring into being.

"Just think of a place?" I asked, stepping from the cylinder.

"Correct."

I visualized Captain Kwan holding Butter's reins.

"Invalid conceptualization. Location does not exist," said Anceron.

Okay, then, just Butter. I tried again, thinking of her silky mane and patient face. A moment later, I was standing beside her, staring into her eyes. Kwan was not holding her reins. I glanced around and spotted him and his squad galloping across the bridge. I looked up the hill, and saw the toppled pillars of the monastery sliding and rolling ponderously down the hillside. As I watched, the monastery roof collapsed, the walls fell inward, and a shower of dust and debris ascended skyward.

Well, I'd told the captain to run at the first sign of danger. I couldn't blame him for obeying. I looked again at the bridge and noted that it swayed and rocked alarmingly. I urged Butter to a trot, slapping one of the monoliths as we went past, and we made it across just before the bridge fell into the gorge.

From the far side, I used the wakened lights of the dolmen to shut the small doors at the foot of the stairs, then also the great outer doors of the temple. I reined Butter to a halt, concentrated on the stables in Maran's valley, and requested passage.

Chapter Eighteen

I fell straight down a good five feet, landing on my heels and tailbone. Butter had not transported with me, and I was at the dolmen, not the stables. I cursed Anceron thoroughly, and then realized it had likely been my own fault. I had not visualized taking the horse with me.

I rolled to my feet and concentrated on Butter, picturing myself standing beside her. At my sudden reappearance, the mare spooked and reared. I finally calmed her, remounted, and tried again.

She suddenly stood calmly within the stone circle, although I had been visualizing the stables. Perhaps this was the closest Anceron could take me, due to the valley's enchantments. I knew that I, myself, could wake the dolmen and select a strand for any location within the valley from here, but I suspected the dolmen was as far into the valley as Anceron could reach.

I dismounted and slapped Butter on the hindquarters the way I'd seen Maran do with Aster. Butter turned her neck and looked at me reproachfully.

"Go home, sweetheart," I said. "Find your stall."

She tossed her head and walked off. I stood beside the king stone until she'd made it through the thickets and found the deer trail, then stepped outside the stone circle myself, put the lights to rest, and tried getting Anceron to transfer me back inside the circle. Nothing happened, even though I could see my desired destination right in front of me. I visualized other spots in the valley with the same results. I tried locations outside the valley and repeated the experiments. Again, nothing happened. Finally, I stepped back within the circle, careful not to wake the lights, and pictured the steps of the citadel in Jappa. A pair of workers, carrying a heavy wooden beam, cursed and stumbled as they tried to dance sideways out of my way. I looked around, picked a building in the city at random, and transferred there. I briefly visited the starships, then Tessa's front porch, and finally Benlyn's former bedchamber at Parva. All transitions were smooth and effortless.

I concentrated as hard as I could, including every detail my memory could provide, on the front parlor of the manor house. I found myself inside Maran's dolmen.

So, it was clear the interior of the valley lay beyond Anceron's reach. But from here to anywhere, or from anywhere to here, worked fine. And once outside the valley, I could go from place to place without reentering a dolmen. Unless I needed something from the valley, the multiple-strand trick would no longer be necessary. I fixed the rules in my head, intending to ask Anceron the next time we talked.

The sun was already far west of noon. I must have spent most of the day at Center without realizing the passing hours. I needed to report to Ashe and had no time left for experimentation.

I didn't know how to ask Anceron to let me peek ahead, so I woke the dolmen, selected Ashe's ribbon, and projected my astral self through. He was outdoors this time, talking with his generals. He noticed me from the corner of his eye, nodded almost imperceptibly, and made the sign I'd seen Benlyn use when asking his guards to wait.

I hung in the air, invisible to everyone but Ashe, until he dismissed the group and went into his tent. I waited a few more seconds, and the pages and servants I'd expected came hurrying out.

I released the strand, re-solidified beside the king stone, and let Anceron transfer me to the tent's interior. Ashe was pacing, waiting for me.

"Ashe—" I began, but he cut me off immediately.

"More earthquakes, Grey?" he asked angrily. "We felt the tremors, and I've sent riders in all directions to find out what happened."

"Only a small one," I said meekly, "and not my doing. The machines said it was natural. The center of it was on the far side of Landing from here, but I don't think the effects reached the town itself."

"Is the temple all right?"

"The machines assured me it was, but. . . ."

"Speak up, man. But what?"

"The monastery collapsed."

He narrowed his eyes, and again I felt his mental finger probing inside my skull. "How bad was the damage?" he asked.

"More or less complete, from what I could see. I doubt anyone inside could have survived. Captain Kwan and his squad should be returning soon, but the temporary bridge gave way. The entire area around the monastery shook so hard it knocked me off my feet."

"You're telling me it's just coincidence that Kiril and Siobhan each died after threatening you?"

"Yes," I said. "And since you're reading my thoughts, you know I'm telling the truth. I thought we'd agreed to grant each other privacy."

He grunted, releasing my mind. "You have no idea how upset the monks will be." He went to the tent flap and called. He issued rapid instructions, pulled the flap closed, and resumed pacing. "I've sent work parties to the monastery to search for survivors. At least tell me you found the weapons we need. Was old Larkin helpful?"

"Larkin sacrificed himself to teach the machines modern speech. He was sane enough to know how to command them. I couldn't have prevented it, since I didn't know what he was saying. I've closed the temple doors again, to prevent any further accidents."

Ashe stopped pacing and sat at his worktable, posture slumped. "I knew the old man was mad, but he was also brilliant. You say he committed suicide?"

"No, he sacrificed himself in service to our cause. The machines *absorbed* him and the stone children. Larkin's plan worked. The living machines took language from him and assimilated the observations of the stone children." I paused and then asked, "May I sit?"

He glanced up and gestured irritably at a chair. I seated myself, grateful to take the weight off my bad leg. "Center," I said, "is both more and less than we'd hoped. All the machines that still operate are sentient. They can answer questions, once you puzzle out how to ask things properly. They mostly seem designed to control other machines, but say the other machines are no longer working."

"So, they're useless," he said.

"For us, right now, yes. For the future, not at all. They contain all of the ancients' knowledge, and thanks to Larkin and the stone children, they have updated their information to include modern speech and recent history. Imagine if you had a book that could explain itself as you read it. Academics will be able to regain technology in mere decades, not multiple generations."

"What of weapons against the sorcerers?"

"All nonfunctional. But the machine calling itself Anceron was able to disconnect all of the Amrhyn dolmens from the network. The sorcerers can no longer spy on us, or even travel using the dolmens."

"But you, you can still use them?" he asked with sudden interest.

"I don't know if I could travel there. Anywhere else, yes. Those dolmens are locked, like the one in Maran's valley. The machines didn't grant me any special kind of control."

I wondered, as I said it, if that was true. I could either go back to ask Anceron or I could experiment. I didn't fancy showing up in an Amrhyn dolmen, however. The risk was too great.

"What of their sorcery itself? The fireballs and such?"

"Undiminished, I'm afraid. We still have no way to fight them."

"Report all this to the duke. It may affect his plans."

"Of course," I said. "I'll also keep Brand informed."

"Then go away," said Ashe. "If your description of the monastery is accurate, this place will soon be swarming with outraged monks." He lifted a hand quickly. "I believe your story," he said, "but the monks will not. They already distrust you, and think your excursions inside the reliquary are sacrilege."

"You've been inside, too, Ashe," I pointed out softly. "Beware mobs. The anger of the common folk lies just beneath the surface. Kiril demonstrated that, and you were the instrument of his imprisonment."

"I've already made plans to increase security."

"Good," I said, and promptly disappeared.

I recapitulated my conversation with the king for Duke Benlyn, and he took the news better than I'd hoped.

"I want you to start bringing the army through in small groups immediately, no more than two or three hundred at a time," he said. "I'm going to dress some as field hands, and have them start harvesting. That will bring the sorcerers running. If they can't use magical transportation, they'll have to come on horseback. Can you supply a map of where they are now?"

"I don't even know where we are ourselves."

He turned to gesture outward, and I noticed with distaste that he was wearing his pistol. "This is the industrial city of Stoling," he said, "where most of the grain shipments are processed. Alvishire, the viscount's domain, is just north of here, and the bulk of the fields lie to south and east, stretching nearly to the moors. How did you find me without knowing where I was?"

"I found *you*, Your Grace. I can only travel to places I already know, or to persons themselves. I can't draw a map for the sorcerers. Assuming they're clustered around their dolmens—a proposition that used to be likely, but may no longer obtain— there are only seventeen places they could be, but they've likely scattered. Since I don't know any of them, I can't travel to them."

I studied our surroundings. The sun was still high in the sky here, and no clouds interfered with the light. We stood on a balcony overlooking a mass of housing to our left. To our right stood tall silos and many buildings. I guessed they were mills or workshops. "Do you want me to bring soldiers here to this balcony?" I asked. "It seems . . . small. Is there a landmark outside of town I can use, or a barracks?"

"Our staging area is to the west, between the city and the sea. Can you take the soldiers there?"

"Not unless I've been there myself."

"You said a person was as good as a location. What about a horse? I can leave Snuffles at the staging area with an open space around him. After the first trip, you'll know the location, and I can rescue my poor horse from landmark duty."

"That should work," I said. "I've done much the same with my own horse. When do you want the soldiers? How many groups per day?"

"As many as you can manage, as soon as you can. Just leave a space of time between each hundred or so. My captains need to distribute the influx, so they don't end up standing on each other's feet. There's plenty of room, but as the numbers grow, so does the time it takes to assign each group an unused spot. Don't start until tomorrow morning, though. I have to ride there first, to prepare the area, leave Snuffles, and alert the captains what to expect."

"Okay," I said, "but Ben, you'll likely be sacrificing the soldiers you send to pretend to be field workers. A single sorcerer could easily destroy fifty or a hundred golems. They burn quite fiercely."

"So do crops. The sorcerers will only attack with fire if the soldiers group together away from the grain. We may lose some soldiers, but they're an essential part of the feint. We need to spend as many as needed—no more—to draw all the sorcerers out. If they think the soldiers are field hands, they'll come without much caution, planning to attack the hands in their quarters at night. I hope to ambush most of them, with crossbow fire from multiple sides. That will likely cost even more soldiers, since ambushes don't always work. Once the remaining sorcerers are grouped, we'll pincer them with the main army. The nobles are wavering, and they won't contribute troops until they actually see your army. The viscount's spies have discerned we plan a major offensive, but are still unaware of your army's nature. I think Dhutori will stay out of things until he knows which way the wind blows. If you could tell us how many sorcerers to expect, and their likely routes, we could plan better."

"I see," I said. "I'll go back to Colonel Brand and explain. I'll also start lining up the troops for transfer starting at dawn your time.”

“Bring the colonel and his officers with the first group.”

“Fine.”

“Bide one more moment,” he said. “I’ve another letter for the king.”

I waited while he went inside. Privately, I thought his plan wasn’t bad, but unlikely to succeed unless I could help neutralize the sorcerers. It was true that a single crossbow bolt would kill, assuming it struck in the torso or head. But how many ambushes could he pull off successfully? The sorcerers might have lost travel through the dolmens, but they might still be able to communicate with each other using mind-speech. The first ambush could well end up being the only one.

When Benlyn returned with the letter, I bid him farewell, visualized Maran’s dolmen, and transferred back home.

I didn’t want to walk, so I woke the dolmen and used it to transfer yet again, this time into the front parlor of the manor house.

***

It took remarkably little time to bring Brand up to date, once a servant managed to fetch him for me. I received him in the parlor. Benlyn’s strategy was apparently one of the many contingencies they’d sketched out as possible approaches, so he already knew the basics. He told me he’d have all the officers and foot soldiers ready for transport by dawn.

“After breakfast,” I corrected him. “Dawn comes sooner here than in Amrhyn, and the duke doesn’t want us before dawn.”

“Is he encamped at Stoling, lord?”

“He himself is in the city, but I gather his troops are outside of town.”

"Very good, lord. I'll make the arrangements."

Hasq entered the parlor as Brand was leaving. "The lady and little lord will be with you at dinner, sir," he said. "The young master is resting in his rooms. Do you require anything while waiting for them?"

"A good long bath," I said.

"I shall have Virgil waiting in your rooms, sir. If I may say, you seem in much better spirits than before. Did your errands today go well?"

"Many discoveries and surprises—some of them good. I didn't find what I sought, but I learned a lot. Tell me, how is Maran doing with her work? I've lost track of the days. Will she finish on time?"

"Well ahead of time, sir, if she keeps her current schedule. I estimate she has ten days of hard labor ahead."

"And the armorers? I can hear them working. Are they equipping each new homunculus as it emerges, or making all the helmets and shields first, with swords and spears to follow?"

"Sir, Brand asked for the former regimen. Although it is less efficient, the smiths are arming each new soldier fully before working on the next."

"Excellent."

"May I ask why this is good, sir?"

"Brand is going to do a staged deployment, not a massive assault. I'll be removing fighters daily until Maran finishes. Each must be ready for combat upon delivery. With luck, we may avoid full-scale war. Even without luck, the campaign is likely to be much shorter than I'd anticipated."

"You have no doubts of winning, then, sir?"

"Far fewer than this morning, but of course I still have doubts. We don't know if we'll only have to fight sorcerers or if we'll also have an army of commoners to defeat. A troublesome viscount may enter the fray, but we don't know on which side. Brand's plans may fail. Benlyn's small troop of riders may be insufficient. A thousand things could go wrong. But I'm hopeful. I'm still missing a few small, but vital, pieces of information. Oh, and I have news for you personally."

"Sir?"

"The king intends to visit after the battle. Have you had royal visitors before?"

"No, sir."

"Well, Ashe is easy to please. He'll find the manor house and grounds delightful. He may stay a few days or just for a meal and a tour. Can you handle such indefinite plans?"

"Of course, sir. I'll have the maids and footmen begin cleaning immediately."

"Hasq, the house is always spotless. Your standards exceed the king's."

"And if he steps in horse manure, or sits upon a chair whose cushion is stained, sir?"

"He won't notice either one. He's been living in a tent lately."

"Nevertheless, sir, I must begin work immediately."

"Hasq, you have at least two weeks!"

"That should suffice, sir, but only if I begin now. Do you need anything else?"

"Can you tell me how to defang sorcerers?"

"I'm afraid not, sir. I wasn't aware they possessed fangs."

I looked at him askance. "I was speaking metaphorically. Tell Virgil I'll be in soon. That will be all for now."

He bowed and left me in peace. I decided to visit the nursery to see if Aiden was awake. He was, so I leaned over his bassinet to make eye contact, produce silly noises, and contort my features into ludicrous shapes. He gurgled happily at me, and reached in my general direction. His stubby arms had insufficient reach and coordination to touch me until I lowered my face right beside his own. We were still staring into each other's eyes when the nursemaid bustled in to change him.

I went to my rooms. Virgil had my bath waiting, but no new information from his research. I told him of the impending royal visit, and he seemed most impressed, but also somewhat skeptical.

"How will he reach the manor, sir? The valley is hidden."

"I suppose I'll have to go upland and lead him down," I said, luxuriating in the hot water.

"Will he not then learn the mechanism, sir?"

"I think only Maran can provide the capability. I'll have to lead the king back up, too."

"The young master went upland today, to study herbs with Locke."

"How the devil did Locke navigate the mists?"

"He did not, sir. The young master did. Locke merely provided the desired destination, and then followed the young master in both directions."

"He shouldn't be able to do that," I said. "I thought only Brand, Maran, and I could find the way in or out."

"Sir, the unicorns at the little lord's birth, plus the one who visited by herself, needed no guidance. The lady implied the muria could do the same."

I swiveled my head to stare at him. "The nina are a special case, and I was alone with Maran when we talked about the muria."

"I was waiting attendance in the hallway, sir."

"Hasq told me you don't listen to private conversations."

"We normally don't, sir; or rather, we listen but fail to remember. We must listen in case we are called."

"But this time you remembered. I find that somewhat disturbing."

"Sir, please don't be distressed. We only remember things that might pose a danger to the household. Your discussion of the muria caused Hasq to send servants to scour the hills, looking for signs of infiltration. He reported the results to the lady immediately. I'm sorry if we failed to tell you, too."

"What did the searchers find?"

"Nothing, sir. If, as the lady suggests, the muria visit here in secret, they leave no sign behind, no boot scuff, no hoof print, not even a broken branch."

I relaxed. "That's all right, then," I said. "And well done. But it leaves the mystery of Torrey's unexpected knowledge. I'll ask Maran about it at dinner. Rinse me off, please. It's nearing mealtime." At that moment, the clock above the mantel chimed noon. Virgil apologized, saying that the smith didn't have the proper tools to fix it. "Never mind," I said. "Just get me out of the tub and ready for dinner."

As soon as I was presentable, according to Virgil's standards, I went to collect Torrey. He jabbered continuously on the way to the dining room, nearly gabbling in his haste to tell me everything he'd seen and done recently. I finally had to lay my good hand on his shoulder and say, "Settle down, son," before he subsided.

We only had to wait a few minutes for Maran. The servants laid out a sumptuous feast, and one of them quietly informed me that Brand would not be attending. Maran, although even more fatigued than the last time I'd seen her, had taken the time to have her hair arranged and don a sweeping formal gown.

"You look beautiful," I said, giving her a kiss on the cheek before we all took our seats.

"Thank you," she said.

"We seem to be missing one. Where's Aiden?" I asked.

"Sound asleep. I left him in the nursery."

One of the servants poured wine, but hesitated over Torrey's glass, looking to me for a signal.

"Half a glass," I suggested. "Another half after eating, if he wants it."

"Hasq tells me you're making excellent progress," I said to

Maran by way of starting the dinner conversation. "He says only ten more days."

"I'm looking forward to a long rest afterward," she said. "Perhaps a week-long nap."

Torrey laughed, but I just nodded thoughtfully. "You deserve any comfort you choose," I said. "Benlyn asked me to start transferring troops tomorrow morning. I should empty out the temporary barracks quickly, and then I'll only have to keep up with your output until the end. If I go at Benlyn's top speed for receiving them, I can probably take a thousand a day. That would let me move the whole army in five days—but I won't try. Better to meet the duke's immediate need, and then spread the rest over our remaining time. I'm glad I don't need to worry about rations, else I'd do nothing but travel back and forth forever."

"Tell me about Center," she said. "Did you find any weapons?"

I quickly filled her in, not omitting Larkin's tragic death, and the not-quite-so-tragic but likely death of Abbess Siobhan. I finished by relating my audience with the king and subsequent discussion with the duke.

"So, in summary, you got the machines to talk, the duke has a mad plan, and you still have no weapons against the sorcerers."

"That's about it," I said, "except that the duke's plan isn't necessarily crazy. If he can catch the sorcerers off guard, and if they can't communicate with each other using mind-speech, then he has a good chance of catching most of them."

"They'll have to take the bait," she pointed out. "They might attack the nobles instead."

Torrey broke into our conversation. "Machines are things like levers, plows, winches, pulleys, water pumps, and wheeled carts. How can they *talk?*"

"These are living machines," I told him. "Much more complicated than a cart, but with all the workings hidden inside.

They look like cabinets or desks, but all one piece. They can't move from their chambers, but they can hold intelligent conversations—well, with me they can."

I caught Maran's eye and warned her to silence with my look. I asked Torrey, "Tell me about going upland today. Is that your first time since coming to live with us?"

Maran started violently, but kept her peace.

"Locke wanted me to study some plants, but he called it a botany lesson."

"Yes," I said, "that would be botany. But how did you find your way?"

"I just kept going up, until it got all misty. That last hill, Grey —how do you manage it? I had to use both hands and feet."

"It's very hard for me, which is why I prefer to ride, or use the dolmen. Once you were upland, how did you find your way back down?"

"I slid, mostly, which got Locke all upset because I ruined my trousers."

I looked at Maran blankly. *Well?* I asked silently. *Has the valley's enchantment failed? I thought you were the only one who could teach the way.*

I thought so, too, she thought back. Aloud, she said, "Hasq!" very loudly.

"Yes, ma'am?" said the majordomo, stepping into the dining room.

"Send three servants upland. The destination doesn't matter. Just out of the valley and then immediately back."

"Ma'am, we cannot—"

"Just have them *try*. Report your results as soon as possible. In the meantime, ask Brand to post armed guards around the manor and grounds."

Her tone left no room for reply. Hasq disappeared from the room almost as quickly as I could have transported out.

Torrey was a member of our gestalt, I reminded her. *Perhaps something of that remained after the dungeon.*

Maran regarded Torrey gravely. He kept turning his head from one of us to the other. "Did I do something wrong?"

"No, sweetheart," she said after a moment. "Just something unexpected. We'll sort everything out quickly. Eat your dinner and try the wine. I think you'll like it."

Torrey shrugged and went back to his meal. I'd been so busy talking that I hadn't taken my first bite yet, although both he and Maran were nearly finished.

"Weapons," Maran reminded me.

"I've been thinking about that all day," I said. "I keep coming back to how Vastil imprisoned the sorcerers back in the dungeon. I have no idea how he did it, but I want to learn. I don't think I have his kind of power, but I might be able to slow the sorcerers down long enough for Benlyn and Brand to fill them with arrows."

"Can the machines at Center help?"

"They don't seem to know anything about the muria, and they're true philosophical skeptics—they believe anything supernatural is outside the bounds of study."

"Then where will you get the information?"

"From Avermorn, of course. That's where the muria are."

Maran put her napkin in her lap very deliberately, her eyes never leaving mine. "Torrey," she said softly, "please go to your rooms."

"But I haven't finished eating!"

"The servants can bring you whatever you want. The adults need to talk. Go now, please."

Grumbling, Torrey got up and stalked off. Maran waited until he was gone, then asked the house servants to leave, too. "Close the doors behind you," she said. "I'll come out if I need anything."

I assailed my food, head down, avoiding her gaze. When I finally looked up, she was still staring at me.

"Did the machines deprive you of sanity?" she asked quietly. "Let me know, so I can plan appropriately."

"You don't like sarcasm from me; I don't like it from you. And it isn't called for. I can't get to Avermorn itself, except by ship, and —assuming such a trip is even possible this late in the year—it would take weeks."

"Then what did you mean?"

"Ego-free mindfulness."

"Which is?" she asked evenly.

"Meditation, I think. The Ketlan said Avermorn was a state of mind as well as a place. I intend to achieve the proper state of mind so I can talk to them again."

"They are . . . children. What could they know?"

"They're *muria* children. They knew how to restore my eyesight, and I suspect they knew how it would serve me. I can't operate the machines by percipience alone; only real eyes can see the control surfaces. This leads me to believe they not only foresaw the 'future need' correctly, but might be inclined to help."

"A thin hope. You have no idea what they might do. They may have had some other purpose in mind and be enraged that you woke the machines at Center."

"Possibly," I agreed. "Do you have a better idea? Center can't help. Any ancient weapons and tools are unavailable or inoperable."

"What if muria adults answer your summons instead of the Ketlan?"

"Then I'll ask them, I suppose."

"I won't allow you to try within my valley. I don't want muria here."

"So I'll go upland."

"No. If the valley has lost its protection, I want you beside me to defend the manor."

"You literally have an army on your front porch," I said. "A cripple can't help."

She sighed, picked up her wine glass, and pushed back from the table. "When do you intend to try?"

"Tonight. If I have no success, I'll keep trying. We have ten days. A very busy ten days for both of us, but ultimately futile work if I cannot obtain weapons."

"Finish your dinner," she said, voice heavy with resignation. "I'll await the report from Hasq."

An hour later, I was at the stables, dressed in my warmest cloak, asking the groom to saddle Butter for me. "Send the footman with that double-lantern thing," I added. "It's cloudy tonight. I'll need him to light the way for Butter."

Upon reaching the dolmen, I left the mare with the footman, and asked him to wait for me. I stepped within the circle, and let Anceron transfer me to the boulder above the valley. It was as good a spot as any, and it was where I'd met the Ketlan before.

The snow had mostly melted here, too, although patches still lingered in sheltered nooks where the sun couldn't reach. I pulled my cloak tightly around me and stood with my back against the boulder.

The eyes of the body were nearly useless in the dark, so I closed them and scanned Colonial Plain with my percipience. I could see every rock, leaf, footpath, and woodland creature for miles, but no sign of the Ketlan.

I composed my mind, trying to emulate what Kiril had described. I needed to want without wanting, desire without specific goals, and empty my mind of all thoughts, especially of myself, while yet retaining a heightened state of mindfulness. I even walled off my percipience, so the outside world would not distract me.

After two full hours of earnest non-effort and relentless non-thought, I decided Kiril had either been lying or deceiving himself. Either way, he'd been full of skoda. The only things ego-free mindfulness brought me were pain in my feet and leg and a rising sense of inadequacy.

I opened the eyes of the body as well as my percipience. A half-circle of unicorns stood regarding me gravely. Their horns were invisible, and they did not change position when I took a step forward. Had they not been so dainty, so uncannily beautiful, I might have thought them horses.

"I didn't call *you*," I whispered. "Why are you here?"

I got a faint sense of mirth in reply, so muddled I wasn't even sure it was an emotion at all. What I felt immediately after was an overwhelming desire to touch them. Their horns blared into visibility, and they reared, not in honor but in challenge. They whisked their tails in unison, whirled, and trotted off through the trees, each heading a separate direction. I knew then what had happened; they had discovered me standing in utter silence and thought to lure me into a chase with their glamour. I knew better than to follow. If I did, I would wake the following day, miles away, with no memory of the chase, only a lingering sense of great loss.

Resisting them brought tears to my eyes, but I forced myself to stand still until they were long gone.

"Beautiful creatures," said a quiet voice to my left.

I whirled to find the Ketlan girl regarding me, her eyes solemn, even grave. It was so dark now that without my percipience, I wouldn't have seen her at all. She wore the same brief singlet I remembered, but without the flowers tucked behind her ear. Her bare arms and legs seemed unaffected by the cold. She was veiled, however; I saw only the girl, not the muria. She had none of the unearthly beauty, none of the indefinable eldritch quality she had shown before.

"Yes," I agreed. "The nina are a blessing, in whatever form. Ulat's doom was cruel."

"The alternatives were worse," said the girl.

"Thank you for giving my eyes back. They were very useful. I'm surprised you came. I had just given up for the night."

She neither shrugged nor nodded. She said nothing.

"Do you know what I need?" I asked.

She reached one hand toward my face, her fingers touching my left cheek. I felt nothing save for a brief stir of wind, and wondered if she'd actually made contact. "I am dreaming now," said the girl. "I often follow the nina in my dreams. Your needs intrude. We do not dream the way humans dream."

"How do you dream, then?"

She smiled, letting her mask fall for just a second. Suddenly, she was a young goddess, no taller in stature, not even different in shape or features. Yet I knew I would not be able to remember the way she appeared now. Like the nina, her glory was something human minds could not retain.

Just as suddenly, she seemed like a mortal girl again. "We drift in our dreams, either among the memories of the five or across the mortal world, following our fancies. You did not call me. You interrupted my journey."

I wanted to learn more, but my exigency would not permit distractions. "Can you help me?" I asked. "I need to fight an unknown number of Amrhyn sorcerers."

"Avoid them," she suggested, her eyes roaming the forest. I supposed she was looking to regain her dream by finding the nina, but she might have been thinking anything at all. I could not reach her mind.

"I cannot avoid them," I said. "Can you teach me to make a prison of energy like the one Vastil used last year?"

"Qol gave you odd proclivities. Your inclination should tend toward self-preservation, not toward a battle you cannot win."

"Nevertheless, I'm *asking* for your help. I'm begging."

She seemed to look at me again, although her gaze simultaneously focused elsewhere. "Qol's child, even if I were minded to aid you, I could not. I am still Ketlan, straitly bound by the five from direct intervention in human conflicts. I have already done what may be done for you."

"Do you have any weapons at all? Anything I could use?"

"Nothing apt to your hand," she said, and I thought a hint of compassion flickered across her face. "My time is more than a decade in the future. Many Ketlan delay their choice until Aiden matures. I can offer you only one last thing. When your doom falls, some Ketlan will comfort you and let you dream with us."

My blood turned suddenly cold. Did she know of my prophecies? "I intend to thwart my doom," I said stiffly, "and Aiden is none of your business."

"Qol's child, have you ever found your maker to be kind?"

"He seemed to care for me," I answered. "I've only met him twice. Both times, he treated me with courtesy and compassion."

"You mistake tolerance for approval, and civility for charity. If Qol graces you with a third meeting, you may see more clearly. Now my dream continues, and I shall not tarry. I follow the threads of ancient memories."

"Wait!" I called, but she was already gone. I concentrated on what I could remember of her features, and asked Anceron to transfer me. Nothing happened. I rather thought the girl had not been physically present at all,

No help from the muria seemed forthcoming, and a veiled threat took the place of the hoped-for weapon. I resigned myself to fighting the sorcerers using only the powers I now possessed.

Anceron took me to the dolmen. The footman still waited with the lanterns. I mounted, and we walked back to the stables.

We passed dozens of guards along the way, and two more stood with drawn swords by the back door.

Hasq met me immediately. "The lady requires your presence in the back parlor, sir."

"Okay," I said, and followed the corridors dispiritedly. Maran was waiting on the divan, but as soon as I entered, she sprang up.

"The valley's enchantment is broken," she said. "The three servants I sent were all able to exit and return. I went to the monument to try to fix it, but it no longer responds to me. We're vulnerable to anyone who stumbles by."

"Can you still make homunculi?"

"Yes," she said, then added, "at least I could all day."

"Then we'll post guards. I can even ask the king for help. I can ask the machines what's wrong with our dolmen. It still provides you power, and I used it for transportation today. We can survive until we find an answer."

"You don't understand," she said, breaking into tears. "The valley is shrinking. I can feel the edges evaporating."

I didn't comprehend the ramifications of that, but I recognized that the valley was more than a place to Maran. It was her retreat, her fief, her fastness, her entire world. And it was crumbling around her.

I decided to keep my own bad news to myself for now.

Chapter Nineteen

I was up and out the door long before the sun rose. I went to the dolmen and transferred directly to Ramirez and Anceron in their chamber below Center.

Immediately after bringing the control surfaces to life, I yelled, "What the hell did you do?"

"Rephrase query," said Ramirez.

"Our dolmen isn't working properly. It no longer hides our valley, and the valley itself is shrinking in size."

"State the monument's designation," said Ramirez.

"They have names?"

"Each has a designation number. To investigate a problem, I need the designation."

"I have no idea. The bloody things don't have labels. When you messed with the dolmens in Amrhyn yesterday, you somehow changed ours, too."

Anceron's surface lights changed, and a map of the continent appeared where the whorls and lines usually glimmered. "Touch the monument in question," it said.

Tiny spots of white light dotted the map. I started at Halmar-by-the-Sea, traced my way to Landing, and followed the road Benlyn had used to take me through the forest. I assumed that our dolmen, like the manor house, was a constant reference point, even though the boundaries of the valley were fluid.

I had once scanned for dolmens and knew, in general terms, where all the ones on Colonial Plain should be. Maran's was not among them. I thought I'd need to transfer to each dolmen and identify Maran's by elimination. Then I had another idea.

"I can't find it on the map," I said. "But when I visualize a monument, and you send me there, can you follow me and identify the monument?"

"Yes. Privacy override required." The map disappeared, replaced by a large yellow circle. "Place your hand within the circle."

I did as requested. "Okay to go?" I asked.

"Proceed. Tracking system engaged."

I visualized Maran's dolmen, mentally desiring to be there. The familiar broken bluestones rose around me for a moment, then flickered and faded. I was back in the chamber with the machines.

"Monument identified. Analyzing functionality. Analysis complete. The monument's power supply is dangerously low. Attempting to reroute. Failure. The monument requires a technician with replacement parts."

I didn't need the messages translated. I didn't know what a "power supply" was, but I understood the concept of exhaustion.

"How long will it last?"

"Power draw exceeds normal limits. Query: Is the monument being used for purposes other than travel and communication?"

"Yes," I said impatiently. "We use it to create a barrier, a kind of misdirection that prevents humans from perceiving its location and the area around it. Additionally, my wife uses the monument's power to create golems—homunculi—temporary people, not made of flesh and blood. Uh, it also keeps the weather in a kind of perpetual summer."

"Understood. At the current rate of draw, the monument will cease to function entirely within twenty-five days."

"How can we prevent that?"

"The monument requires a technician with replacement parts in order to continue operating at its current rate."

"What happens if we reduce the rate?"

"The monument will eventually replenish its potency from solar power."

"Sunshine?"

"Correct."

"When I visualize somewhere in the monument's vicinity, like the manor house, you always send me to the monument itself. And I can't transfer out unless I'm standing inside the monument. Is this related to the 'power supply' problem?"

"No. An external agent has locked the area surrounding the monument."

Maran, I thought. She'd once disconnected the dolmen completely, and then reconnected it, but keyed it to my genetic material. "Don't worry about the agent," I said. "We anticipate the extra power needs for only another ten days. But during that time, I'll have to transport a lot of people—the homunculi I mentioned —from the monument to Amrhyn. Does the monument have sufficient energy for that?"

"If I facilitate the transfer, the monument's power is not used."

"So I can move as many people as I want without weakening the monument even more?"

"Correct."

"Good. I have a few more questions. First, if we finish the extra power needs within ten days, will the monument resume its other functions—hiding its vicinity and keeping the weather controlled?"

"Yes, but not immediately."

"How long?"

"Unknown."

"Your best guess, then."

"Weeks to months, assuming the monument's power consumption returns to levels before the current surge."

"Not what I wanted, but good enough. Next question. You can move anyone on the continent anywhere, right?"

"Given coordinates and permission, yes."

"Can you locate the sorcerers in Amrhyn? The ones we discussed before, with neural interfaces. The ones I said performed supernatural feats."

"Yes. Their implants distinguish them from other humans."

"How many can you find?"

"Locating . . . located. Thirty-two," replied Anceron.

Only thirty-two? That was better than I'd hoped, but still far too many.

"Can you transfer them into a volcano or the middle of a deep lake?"

"Such an action would cause their life functions to cease."

"Yes, that's the general idea. I want them dead."

Ramirez said, "Offensive action forbidden except by command of a weapons officer. You lack authorization."

"Okay, I get that," I said excitedly. "You can't kill on my command. But could you kill to defend me if I were in imminent danger?"

The two machines conversed briefly in their odd machine language.

"Yes," said Ramirez. "If Anceron cannot transfer you away, you may authorize lethal force in your defense."

"Your function, Ramirez, is defense. Can you defend me?"

"Main systems offline. Ballistics, explosives, and ordinance unavailable."

"So you've told me many times," I said. "That leaves Anceron's 'transfer and location' services. Suppose I forbid being transferred to safety. Can you follow me wherever I go and, if I'm attacked, transfer the attacker away at my command?"

"Yes," said Anceron. "Privacy override already established. Until you terminate the function, I can trace your position."

"I don't want any mistakes here. Your judgment may not agree with mine. Can you hear me speak aloud when I'm not here?"

Ramirez said, "I can establish and maintain a noetic link, similar to the one you currently use for personal transport. Speech is not required. You would have to think the command. Anceron cannot be authorized to act unless commanded through the link."

"Do it," I said.

"Done," said Ramirez.

I turned my attention back to Anceron. "If I command you to transfer an attacker, where would you send the person?"

"Sufficiently far to eliminate your personal danger."

"May I specify a lethal destination?"

Anceron said, "Default defensive actions require a nonlethal response. I would transfer the attacker to a safe distance from you."

"What if that puts another person in danger?"

"The destination algorithms would detect the collision and redirect the transfer."

I paced back and forth, thinking desperately. The weapon I needed had been here all along; I just hadn't known how to ask for it. I still didn't know the correct commands. I was glad to learn the machines wouldn't wield their abilities wantonly or irresponsibly, but I wished Justian had left me an opening. Only thirty-two of them. I could dispose of the whole lot within the rules currently described, but only by sending them somewhere that wouldn't kill them. I really, *really*, wanted them dead.

Perhaps a remote destination, one sufficiently far away that they couldn't escape to trouble us again. Alfheimr, the island in the middle of the West Ocean, would work. They could throw fireballs at each other until they died naturally. The problem was that I couldn't visualize it for Anceron. I had spent my entire life near other people, or at least near enough that a dogged bunch of sorcerers could walk their way out of the wilderness.

"Show me the map of monuments again," I commanded.

The map appeared on Ramirez's surface this time, perhaps because my pacing had led me in his direction. I studied the map, looking for remote locations. I finally spotted one that might do. The island I found was at the tail end of an archipelago that spiraled away off the continent's southernmost tip. I put my finger over the white dot. "Is this location inhabited?"

"Locating . . . locating . . . no human life found. The monument is functional, but not in use. The island is named Stormwind on the earliest survey maps."

"Could you send all my attackers there?"

"Yes."

"Record Stormwind as the destination, then. When—if—I give the command, that's where I want the attackers to go. Can you disconnect Stormwind's monument from the network?"

"Yes."

"Once disconnected, can you still send my attackers there?"

"Yes."

"Do it!" I commanded gleefully.

"Done."

"Thanks," I said, and promptly returned to Maran's valley.

Maran was still eating breakfast. I burst into the room, and explained both the changes in the valley's properties and my solution for dealing with the sorcerers.

"How long until my enchantment starts working again?" she asked.

"The machines couldn't say for sure. Weeks to months, depending on how much power you draw from the dolmen. We can live in a smaller space in the meantime and use guards to protect ourselves. Once you finish making homunculi as fast as you can, the dolmen will begin to heal."

"Good morning, Father," said Torrey.

I whirled around. He was sitting at the table across from Maran, quietly eating. In my excitement, I had overlooked him.

"Good morning, Torrey. Sorry, but I can't stay. I need to start transferring soldiers. I'll be at it all day."

"Grey," said Maran, "what if sailors discover this island, or the sorcerers make boats?"

"I plan to ask the king to quarantine the location. The island is far off the coast, anyway. I don't think a bunch of old men can make seaworthy boats or rafts. Benlyn told me the currents are deadly. Unless they can magically swim or grow wings, they'll be trapped."

"Good riddance," she said vehemently.

I nodded my agreement, then remembered I hadn't told her of last night's encounter. "I met the Ketlan girl again last night. I don't think my meditation did the trick. It was just luck."

"Did she agree to help?"

"No, she was asleep, chasing unicorns in her dreams. She wasn't even there."

"Can you explain that better?"

"No, not really. She's muria. What she said didn't make much sense."

Are you withholding? she asked in mind-speech.

Nothing important, I answered. *I'm just late.* It was partly true, because it was well past time to meet Brand.

I gave her a kiss, then impulsively, I went around the table and kissed Torrey's forehead. "Be a good boy," I said. "I'll have more time to spend with you once all this is over.

A long line of soldiers started at our front doorstep, spiraled through the lawns, and extended as far as I could see. I got Butter from the groom and rode alongside the line until I reached the base of the deer trail.

Brand and his captains and lieutenants waited for me there. I presumed the lesser officers and sergeants were shepherding the line.

"We begin," I said. "I can't fit a hundred into the dolmen at once. I think twenty is the limit. There just isn't room. How many soldiers are waiting to go today?"

"All of them, lord."

"I'll take as many as I can while daylight holds. Let's start with your own group. Will the others follow my orders once you've gone through?"

"Lord, each soldier knows you, even if you haven't had the time to meet them individually. You are the lord of the valley. They'll follow you through fire if you ask."

"Let's hope it never comes to that. Tell them to keep the line tightened up, heel to toe all the way. I'll want a constant supply ready to go."

I took Brand and his three captains first, visualizing Snuffles as my anchor point. The sun had barely risen above the horizon, but all three hundred of Benlyn's soldiers were standing outside their barracks, watching for our arrival. I took a good look around, fixing the place in my memory.

"Take the duke's horse, and keep this area clear. Move quickly."

"Yes, lord."

I waited until they had untethered Snuffles and led him away, then transferred back. This time I took twenty, telling them to run clear. By the time a hundred had passed through, the dolmen had grown frosty. I waited a few minutes, then started the next hundred.

By the time I reached a thousand, the frost on the dolmen had turned to icicles, and I was both exhausted and elated. The process was routine by now, and I barely had to think about what I was doing. I told the remaining soldiers we were done for the day. They saluted, and prepared to stand in line until tomorrow. I'd forgotten just how simple golems were to manage. No need for food, drink, rest, or any other distraction.

I spent the early evening playing checkers with Torrey, then we ate dinner together as a family, and the whole routine started again the next morning. It only took me two more days to catch up with Maran's output. After that, it would be three hundred a day until she reached her goal. Counting on my fingers told me seven days remained, or just over two thousand foot soldiers. Plenty of time to rest up; plenty of time to pay overdue visits.

I took Torrey with me after I transferred the next batch of three hundred. I stole him from under Locke's nose after lunch, and we set off for the dolmen. Torrey had learned to ride Rebel well enough to walk his horse side by side with my own. When we reached the deer trail, I had Butter take the lead, and Torrey had no trouble urging Rebel to follow me up the steep slope.

We tied the horses to my usual leaning tree, entered the circle, and transferred to the staging area west of Stoling.

Torrey was surprised by the change in climate, but even more confused to see the sun directly overhead when only moments before it had been afternoon. He had studied geography, but he hadn't connected the sun's motions with time of day until experiencing it himself.

Rank after rank of homunculi stood in the blazing sun, apparently on display. A few of Benlyn's riders cantered back and forth down the lines, escorting richly dressed visitors, but most of the camp was quiet. As we walked past the ranks in search of the duke, each soldier stiffened and saluted. Torrey was agape; seeing all of them in one spot, armed for battle and standing at attention, was overwhelming. I had to admit to myself that they looked imposing, even though I noted several had slashed uniforms, and one was missing a leg. I tried to count them, but quickly lost track. Even standing in ranks five deep, the line seemed endless.

Brand spotted us before we'd gone too far astray and ran out to meet us. The duke's quarters were officially in Stoling, but he happened to be bivouacking here today, as he often did. Brand led us back the way we'd come, around a stand of trees, to a collection of lodgings. I presumed this was where Benlyn's riders stayed, because they were milling about, holding mock horseback battle sessions. Their uniforms differed from the standard army outfit worn by the golems; each fighter's breastplate carried the ducal seal emblazoned in the center.

"How many horses does the duke have?" I asked.

Brand chuckled. "This is Amrhyn. We have over six hundred."

I whistled in appreciation. "That's two for each rider, isn't it?"

"I'm teaching the homunculi captains to fight from horseback, but yes, nearly twice. The extras are spare mounts or pack horses. Here—this barracks. The duke will be inside. I'll leave you to it."

The barracks door had a man standing at attention, one to each side; to all other appearances, the lodging seemed identical to the others. I nodded politely to the guards and knocked on the door.

"Enter!"

Torrey followed me inside. Windows without glass or shutters provided plenty of light, but Benlyn had two lanterns lit and was standing in front of a large map, studying it intently. He looked up, recognized us, and his face lit with a smile.

"Lord Grey!" he boomed.

"Your Grace," I replied. I stepped on Torrey's foot lightly, and he quickly repeated my greeting.

"I'd offer you chairs and refreshments, but I have neither to hand. I use this building solely as a workroom. Did you bring a reply from the king?"

"Your Grace?"

"To my last letter, man. Surely the king wrote in response."

"Ben, I'm sorry—I've been so busy that I forgot to deliver your letter."

The duke's welcoming smile faded a bit, but he regained his composure quickly. "No matter. I've another to send. You can deliver both at once."

"Of course," I said. "Does the army meet your expectations? I'll have the remainder delivered within a week."

"Meet my expectations? Are you joking? They're amazing. You missed the big show yesterday and again this morning. All the Amrhyn nobility rode in to inspect them. They were skeptical when they saw most of the foot soldiers were women, until they sent their best fighters to challenge them. Each Amrhyn fighter was quickly disarmed. So the lords threw spears and launched volleys of arrows. The golems just stood there and maintained their fighting stance."

"I noticed one homunculus was missing a leg."

"Ah, that would be Prince Quert of Voland. He's not really a prince, but no one is willing to take the title away from him. He rightfully considers himself the finest horseman in Amrhyn. He insisted on doing battle himself. He managed to lop off a leg with his broadsword before his opponent dragged him from the saddle and balanced on one foot, holding the prince's own sword against his neck. After that, there were no more question from anyone."

"So all of the nobles have sworn fealty to you?"

"They fell over themselves to swear. All except Viscount Alvishire, of course. Dhutori has been parading his own army around in a display of strength, and he has spies everywhere. We're still trying to hide the nature of your army, but he's bound to find out soon. Too many other nobles have seen them."

Torrey stirred restlessly at my side and tugged at my arm. "May I go watch the riders practice?" he asked.

I nodded. "Don't wander off. I'll collect you soon."

When the door had closed behind Torrey, Benlyn continued. "We've already snared five sorcerers. The plan worked beautifully at first. They came at night to burn out the field hands, and your army filled them with crossbow bolts from the trees on either side. That took the fight right out of them. But they've caught on, so I've withdrawn the feint. Their last attack was two nights ago, just one sorcerer, and he managed to set three villages afire and destroy all their crops. He escaped without injury, even though I had a squad in the area. I think it was to demonstrate their abilities; the villages were not strategically important."

"That leaves twenty-seven sorcerers," I said.

He smiled grimly. "You've managed to track them down? It would have been useful to know their travel routes. We could have ambushed them along the way. But if you know where they are now, we can set new traps."

"It's somewhat complicated. They won't fall for another field hand feint. I believe they can communicate mind-to-mind over long distances, so they all will know to avoid similar situations. We need larger bait, something they can't ignore, something that will make them band together."

Benlyn creased his forehead. "Do you propose a direct offensive? We know where their main army is encamped, but with twenty-seven sorcerers to defend it, a frontal assault is not likely to succeed—unless you've figured out how to defeat them."

"I'm focusing on the bait, not the tactics," I said. "For you to draw them into battle, I'll have to be there myself. I'm the bait, you see. I can't fight them effectively if they stand behind the lines and throw fire and lightning at our soldiers, or if they split up. I need them to attack me directly as a group."

He laughed. "You want us to mount you on a pole and carry you into battle like a flag?"

"Ben, be serious. I need you to engage the enemy with sufficient strength that the sorcerers will feel compelled to come to their defense. The pincer movement you described before sounds good to me, but I'm not a military man. I'm not trying to give you advice. I'm telling you what I need in order to remove sorcery from the field. At some point, yes, you might as well hoist me on a standard. But until then, I'll be hiding as much as possible. I'm not very brave."

He stood with his fists on his hips, staring at me. "You want me to commit enough force that the enemy brings out its most formidable weapon—the sorcerers—and then stand aside and let them rain lava on you?"

"Essentially, yes. After the sorcerers are gone, my job will be over. The rest is up to you."

"And if you fail?"

"Then those twenty-seven sorcerers will rule Amrhyn," I said.

"High stakes, Lord Grey."

"Yes. I don't have a better idea."

"I'll talk it over with Brand and our captains. We considered the kind of assault you propose, but discarded it in favor of several smaller battles." He rummaged through a mass of papers on a side table. "Here, my letter to the king. He should get it today, if possible."

"Your Grace," I said, bowing.

Outside, I found Torrey watching two mounted soldiers swinging swords at each other, their horses throwing up tremendous clouds of dust as the riders jostled for position.

"Are those blunts?" Torrey asked me when I touched his shoulder.

I squinted. "I don't think so."

"Is that, well, *dangerous?*"

"Very much so. Stay far away. Those horses are trained to fight, and the riders have them in high spirits. Would you like to meet the king today?"

I don't think anything less would have torn Torrey's eyes from the mock battle. "Yes!" he cried joyfully.

We transferred back to the valley's dolmen. I woke the lights. "Be right back," I said, selecting a ribbon that led to my rooms in the manor. I kept hold of the strand, stepped into my bedroom, picked up the letter from the dresser, and returned to the dolmen, all in one breath.

"One more second," I said. "I need to see if the king is alone."

I searched the ribbons for the one that led to Ashe and projected my astral self through. Ashe sat at a small table inside his tent, huddled with a few advisors. He noticed me and started to dismiss the councilors. I faded back to the dolmen and released the strand. "Ready?" I asked.

Torrey nodded, and I visualized the tent so Anceron could transfer us.

I tossed Benlyn's letters on Ashe's table. "From the duke," I said. "One from just now, the other somewhat delayed. Apologies. The delay was my fault."

"Your Majesty," said Torrey, bowing. I suppose Locke's lessons were beginning to take, because Torrey's bow was graceful and to the correct degree.

Ashe raised his eyebrows. "Torrey? You've grown! I was sorry to hear about your grandmother."

"I'm nearly ten now," Torrey replied, forgetting to add "sire" to his statement. He said nothing about Tessa, a behavior I'd come to expect. He never wanted to talk about his former life.

"Grey," said Ashe, "tell me how things are going in Amrhyn."

"I suspect the duke's report will be more thorough than anything I can say, but the lords and nobles have mostly committed to fighting on our side. From what I saw, he already has sufficient strength to win—Brand's army, his own troops, and the nobility's forces. And we might need to hold some soldiers back anyway."

"Oh?" Ashe gestured to the chairs, and we all sat.

"You once complained about Maran's valley being invisible. Currently, it's not. Maran wants guards until she can reestablish control."

"What happened?"

"The machines explained we were using too much power while making the army. Things will go back to normal before long."

Ashe sat back in his chair. "What size force do Benlyn and Brand control already?"

"Over three thousand homunculi, about three hundred mounted troops, and whatever the nobles bring to the field. That number may be in the duke's letters. We had planned two thousand more homunculi for the colonel, but I want to withhold five hundred."

"So many? It seems excessive."

"Maran's valley has no proper borders or roads. It encompasses a vast area, so we'll need guards posted in the hills to watch every direction."

Ashe shook his head. "You have household staff. They can guard you. I want every fighter possible at Brand's disposal."

"A hundred, then? Just to keep Maran happy?"

"I'll let you keep twenty. The King's Guard can patrol the area."

"But—"

"I've decided. Twenty soldiers, plus your current staff, no more. That ferocious storm destroyed too many crops. We no longer want Amrhyn's grain, we need it, else easterners will starve this winter."

"As you will," I said, yielding to his authority. "Did the abbess survive?"

"No one in the monastery survived. Falling masonry crushed many monks on the hilltop, along with a group of pilgrims. It was a disaster. I've assigned a large number of my own laborers to help the monks clear the rubble."

"And the town of Landing itself?"

"Rattled, but not demolished. One very old building's roof collapsed, and several townspeople hurt themselves by falling down. It could have been much worse."

I cast my mind back to my conversations with Kiril. What was the name he had mentioned? Amandor, or maybe Anander. The second one sounded right. "With Siobhan gone, will Anander become abbot? He was Kiril's equal, I think."

"I don't know. The monks will decide. Why do you care? You're to stay away from the monks and anything monkish from now on. You're anathema, remember."

"I was hoping their new leader might be more . . . sympathetic . . . to our cause."

"That's my problem, not yours. I want you to focus your energies on Amrhyn. Afterward, when we're sharing a meal at your manor house, we can talk politics. Speaking of which . . . I must get back together with my advisors now. I've kept them waiting too long already."

"Should I wait for you to write a response to the duke?"

"Good idea. Go show the boy the camp. Send my advisors in as you leave. I'll send a page to find you when the letter is ready."

We stood, bowed, and did as instructed. Torrey was awed by the size of the tent city, but unhappy about his audience with the king. "He didn't act very friendly."

"Kings are like that, especially when busy. But he remembered you and was glad to see you. Not many commoners are invited to sit privately with him."

We wandered a bit, but only ten minutes passed before one of the jauntily dressed youngsters ran up with a sealed letter. "For the duke from the king," he said with an air of supreme importance.

Torrey reached to take it, but the page deftly evaded him and presented the letter to me. I tucked it inside my chemise, invoked Anceron, and transferred back to our dolmen.

As we rode back to the stables, I told Torrey to blame his absence on me. Locke would otherwise devise punishments for skipping school. He asked me dozens of questions about the places we'd visited and the people he'd met. I tolerated each query and gave duly considered answers, while thinking he had indeed grown. Not in the way Ashe meant, but in mental stature and poise. The laughing, bubbly child I'd known was evaporating before my eyes, revealing the beginnings of a serious-minded young man. He still had plenty of childhood left, with time for games and play, but I could see the incipient adult in his choice of questions, and his thoughtful absorption of the answers.

At dinner, Maran—initially outraged that the king would only allow her to keep twenty soldiers—grumpily agreed they would probably suffice, especially since the valley's physical size was shrinking by the hour.

"Six more days of this," she said. "I'm sorry I ever suggested the idea. Benlyn would have thought of something else."

"On the contrary," I said. "Amrhyn is bigger and more divided internally than we ever knew. A large army may be the *only* solution. But that reminds me of an errand. The king gave me a letter for the duke. I should deliver it tonight."

"Go ahead, if you must. Dinner's nearly over anyway."

I excused myself and went to find the letter. Virgil had likely placed it on my dresser when he outfitted me for dinner.

I materialized on the balcony outside the duke's quarters in the city of Stoling. The balcony was empty, but the doors to the interior apartments stood open.

Benlyn was entertaining nobles at a dinner party. I stood quietly just inside the balcony doors until he noticed me and excused himself.

"King Ashe's reply, Your Grace," I said formally, handing him the letter.

"I'll read it later," he said. "Will you join us at the table?"

"Thank you, Ben, but I'm needed at home."

"Then step outside with me for a moment."

I followed him out onto the balcony and listened while he spoke in a low voice. "This isn't for general dissemination," he said, "but we've discussed your idea extensively. Our scouts report that the enemy is digging in and building fortifications at their current location, indicating the sorcerers are willing to wait, forcing us to go to them. They may have spies among us, or may have come to the same conclusions you did. They hold the high ground in the area and don't lack for supplies. Their encampment is too large for us to encircle. We outnumber them, but not by much. Our best guess is that they want to start and finish the war in one battle. Since that was your plan, too, it doesn't bode well. It means they don't fear us enough."

"What will you do?"

"They've practically forced us to follow your idea, but we intend several days of skirmishes—all while holding the golems back."

"They're your most capable fighters," I objected.

"Our best hope is that they still don't know the kind of opposition they'll face in a real battle. We want to keep that a secret for now. The skirmishes are designed to draw out as many as possible, without provoking the entire army, hoping for attrition on their side. We'll also be attacking their fortifications with cannons. The nobility and my riders will provide the initial fighting force, while Brand positions the golems. The minor lords will move their fighters to the flanks."

"What does this mean for me?"

"I don't know until we see how they respond to provocation. But my best guess is that by the time you bring the last group of golems, the main battle will already have started. The sorcerers and you will get the big confrontation you both seem to want."

"Okay," I said. "I'll check with you or Brand daily, after I bring each group through."

"Good man," he said, clapping me on the shoulder. We were already speaking quietly, but he lowered his voice even more. "Let me ask you a theoretical question. We know what happens if you fail, but not what happens if you succeed. What will the golems do if we win the war?"

"They'll follow Brand's orders," I said. "They can maintain the peace, or maybe help with reconstruction. They're not trained for it, but they could probably help with the harvest, too."

"Interesting. What if Brand falls in battle?"

"Then they'll follow you," I said. "They're army, and you outrank Brand."

"Could I command them to fight Viscount Dhutori if the need arises? He's still holding back, refusing to commit to either side."

"I suppose," I said slowly, vaguely disturbed. "They'd be conflicted, because Dhutori is titled. That kind of rank counts, too."

"But they'd fight him—or any other target—if I demanded it?"

I wondered where he was going with this. I felt no need to tell him about the word of disposal I intended to speak after the main battle. Any ideas he had about using the golem army afterward would be bootless, since the army would expire all at once. I glanced away, thinking quickly. It was good to learn he had plans for after the battle, because that meant he had confidence in the outcome. On the other hand, his "any other target" wording made me wonder how high his ambitions rose. Did he mean to fight the king, or was I just being paranoid? I looked back at him. He was staring at me with an odd intensity, waiting for my reply. I decided to answer exactly what he asked, no more. "As long as the army stands, they'll follow orders from the highest-ranking person present. Military rank supersedes titled rank." I didn't bother adding that Maran and I surpassed any other level of authority.

"That's good to know," he said, smiling broadly. "That's very good. Now I must get back to my dinner guests. These damnable people are suspicious by nature. They'll think we're plotting something."

"Yes," I said, thinking they'd be right to worry. I kept my misgivings to myself and matched his smile. "With your leave, I should go home."

He nodded permission and stepped back inside. I had Anceron transfer me to the valley.

For the next six days, I collected the newest batch of soldiers, delivered them to Brand, took letters to the king, took responses back to Benlyn, then sat with the duke or one of his officers to get updates on the situation before returning home. It was annoying to endure challenges and pass checkpoints inside the valley, but I put up with it, knowing it was a temporary nuisance. Maran deployed her guards and staff cleverly, making sure they were able to monitor and thwart each approach to the manor house. She kept Torrey inside at all times, which frustrated the boy.

I, personally, didn't see the need for such extreme measures. No bandit or brigand even found us, let alone tried to attack. Several times, I spotted mounted units of the King's Guard ranging openly through the hills surrounding us, a highly visible deterrent to any mischief. The valley itself continued shrinking, until eventually only the stretch of land between the manor house and the dolmen remained. Gone, the lake. Gone, the river, save for a single stream. Gone, the grain fields. Gone, the outbuildings, mines, and private hills. I would have found the process frightening, had I not known it would begin reversing itself once Maran finished her work.

Each day, fewer and fewer of the golems remained in the staging area. Brand was moving them stealthily into position or having them cut down trees to fashion ladders, ramming logs, and catapults. Meanwhile, Benlyn pursued his opening moves.

The sorcerers' army, most of them not professional soldiers, fell for Benlyn's gambit many times. They sent large sorties out to chase squads who attacked on horseback while cannon fire provided cover and distraction. The cannons blasted their wooden fortifications and gates to splinters. Before each attack, Benlyn sent archers under cover of darkness to lie in wait. After a sortie passed the hidden archers, the attackers would wheel their horses and pretend to charge, stopping just short of engagement. The archers rose from gullies, or from within thickets, and loosed their arrows, catching most of the defenders in the back. The riders then easily rode down anyone left alive and protected the archers with their shields during retreat.

Far more defenders than attackers fell. The skirmishes went heavily in Benlyn's favor for several days. The tactic would not have worked against experienced soldiers; at least five hundred of them died chasing riders who couldn't possibly have breached the gates. Then, finally, someone with authority inside the encampment forbade future sorties.

The numerical advantage was now clearly ours, especially as I was adding three hundred new warriors each day, and the nobility were summoning soldiers from far-flung corners across all of Amrhyn. Even the pettiest hedge lord mustered at least twenty-five fighters, and Quert, the self-styled Prince of Voland, commanded nearly four hundred from his own household.

The enemy's encampment lay south of Stoling, on a flat area with mountains at its back. Gullies and canyons, many of them significantly deep and treacherous, protected the front. The encampment itself was set back from the canyons a ways, leaving a small battlefield between the enemy's gates and our access points. Every time we knocked down a barricade wall or tower with cannon fire from afar, the defenders rebuilt it. Some approaches avoided the canyons on natural stone bridges; all of Benlyn's forays had followed those routes. But the stone bridges were few, and insufficiently wide to allow an army to march against the fortifications. Attackers would need to scale the canyon walls using ladders and siege towers to approach in strength.

I couldn't help with any of this, and it sounded to me as if the enemy had an overwhelming advantage simply by having chosen a good spot. But both Brand and Benlyn seemed undismayed, saying that escalade—ladder assault—would be no problem for the golems, since they didn't need protection against arrows from above. The ramming logs and siege towers were for golem use, too, with the humans holding back to use the catapults until the enemy's walls were breached. They could then attack on horseback. Brand and Benlyn also said the advantage of position was an illusion, since the enemy had no way to retreat except through the mountains at the rear.

I absorbed as much information as I could from them and used my percipience to infiltrate, invisibly gathering information on the defenders' positions and equipment within their encampment. Otherwise, I was no use until the sorcerers took the field themselves.

On my last trip, I brought my three hundred fighters only to find the staging area nearly deserted. A corporal briefed me while his squad led my new soldiers southward.

Benlyn had sprung his final feint just before dark yesterday, getting riders close enough to fire flaming arrows into the wooden fortifications. Then, while the defenders struggled to keep the blaze from spreading, he wheeled up the catapults and began lobbing gigantic stone balls over the walls. He let the defenders think this was his major offensive, with a show of nearly two thousand riders whooping, jeering, and lining up in formation as if to attack. What the defenders didn't know was that down in the canyons, under cover of darkness, the golems silently and swiftly scaled up toward the walls. By daybreak, the golems had broken through in dozens of places, and the riders began their attack in earnest.

The war had begun.

Chapter Twenty

I had Anceron transfer me to Brand's side. He didn't notice me at first. We stood on a slight rise, well to the east of the fighting. I shielded my eyes with my good hand, trying to make sense of the tumult. Across from us, to the west, Benlyn sat astride his great warhorse, surrounded by the ducal troops.

I coughed, and Brand whirled. "Lord Grey, I have been expecting you."

"What do you need from me?"

"At the moment, lord, nothing. The battle is underway. We lost two cannons overnight when their breeches exploded, killing fifty of our troops, but it's all infantry work now. Thus far, our plan holds."

The great mass of mounted fighters followed a wall of golems marching in twenty columns, each column two hundred fighters deep, directly toward the center of the defenders' main army. It was an overwhelming show of strength, especially considering it left over a thousand other golems free to scale the remaining walls and attack the enemy's flanks. Nothing like a main gate remained.

The golems had not only knocked it down, but had thrown the pieces into the canyons.

The defenders first shot volleys of arrows, but the golems didn't slow or fall, and the riders were out of range. Still not understanding the nature of their attackers, the defenders drew swords, hefted spears, and charged. Unfazed and barely damaged, the golems slew everyone who came at them. Their slow march into the enemy's encampment proceeded unchecked.

It was uncannily like the vision I'd had in the forest pool—but like most of the visions, it was both incomplete and not wholly accurate. No sorcerers stood within the enemy ranks to throw fireballs or lightning.

If the sorcerers did not begin helping soon, the golems by themselves would wipe out the entire defending army within the next few hours. The defenders had lost their frontal defenses entirely, relying solely on hand-to-hand combat to survive. They had no good way to retreat. Benlyn's victory seemed not only inevitable, but also already nearly complete. The carnage among the defenders was horrific. I didn't need to extend my percipience to hear the screams as each warrior fell. As the golems continued to advance, step by inexorable step, their captains slowed their march and spread them out laterally, so they wouldn't become encircled after pressing through into the wider battlefield beyond where the gates had once stood. I honestly didn't see the need. Even from where I stood, I could see the defenders breaking rank and running toward the mountains behind the encampment. A few of them cast down their arms and surrendered, but the majority simply fled.

If the sorcerers' army could reach the mountains, they could find passes to let them escape, or even tunnels in which they could hide. I quickly scanned the mountains with my percipience and found what I feared: Innumerable passageways and mineshafts honeycombed the rocks.

"Brand," I said. "Those mountains are full of tunnels and mines. The enemy's retreat isn't blocked at all, not the way you'd hoped."

He didn't take his eyes from the field, but he said, "This is not a rout; it is a tactical feint on their part. You should examine the mountains more closely. We have prepared for a retreat into the mines, should they become desperate enough."

I sent my percipience soaring, flying through the mineshafts, exploring each passage, and emerging atop the peaks. There, contained by rocky walls, hidden from human view, a large and deep lake nestled among the mountains. Golem workers had delved a tunnel beneath, following a natural crack in the supporting stone. Even as I watched, they were filling the crevasse with burlap sacks of black powder.

"Did you find it yet?" Brand asked.

I withdrew back into my body. "Do you mean to flood the mines?"

"Only if necessary. The Amrhyn nobility would rather preserve the mines and equipment. Those mountains are a great source of wealth and material. If that lake pours through, it will take years to pump out the tunnels and resume work."

"Does the enemy know of the threat?"

"Likely so. This is why I believe their current retreat to be a pretense. They won't run into those tunnels unless forced. But I like to plan ahead."

"This was all your work?" I asked, impressed.

"The main assault was the duke's responsibility; I am in charge of contingencies. But the captains down there are running the war. Watch closely, now. Something is happening."

Brand was correct. The fleeing soldiers split into two groups, one going right, the other left, revealing a shimmering round shield of energy in the center. Within the sphere stood all twenty-seven sorcerers, blue-robed and blue-cowled. The soldiers rejoined ranks, forming a semicircle behind the bubble, weapons bristling outward.

The sorcerers paced forward, and I saw their mouths moving. They were chanting, I guessed. The first fireball flew out from within their shield, and two golems began to burn. More followed in quick succession, each one a green flare that detonated against the golems. The entire front row was now aflame, and shreds of golem bodies flew into the air. The god-winds began fluttering around me, restless, eager to churn.

"That's my cue," I said quickly. "I should take you to safety. Where do you want to go?"

"To the duke. Good luck, lord."

I didn't waste time talking. I transferred both of us to Benlyn's site, and then quickly returned to where I had been standing. I let the god-winds grow from a small spiral on my right palm into a tornado that completely surrounded me. The winds howled and shrieked, rising to a deafening roar, but it was calm in the center. I visualized the space between the sorcerers and the burning golems, and commanded Anceron to transfer me.

I materialized directly between them, facing the sorcerers. I suffered conflicting impulses. The wall of wind enclosing me would deflect arrows easily, but probably not sorcerous attacks or a well-aimed crossbow quarrel. I wanted to protect the homunculi and the riders behind me, but if I widened my gyre to affect the army backing the sorcerers, I would end up pushing our own forces off the battlefield and into the canyons. The golems wouldn't be hurt, but the human riders and their horses would all die. Already, my tornado had raised so much dust and debris that I doubted I could signal our captains to retreat. On the other hand, if my own army couldn't see to obey me, the opposing army couldn't see to aim their crossbows. I closed the eyes of my body to protect against flying grit, and used percipience to see through the wildly rotating winds. I had to suppose the sorcerers had a similar ability.

While I stood in indecision, a sorcerer launched a fireball directly at me. It seemed to arch lazily in my direction, but I knew that was just an illusion generated by the adrenaline coursing through my veins. Only my sense of time's passage was affected; the fireball's speed was undiminished.

Anceron! Transfer him!

The sorcerer who threw the fireball promptly vanished, but his deadly missile still flew toward me. I raised the tornado's velocity to a scream, but held the diameter tight, wrapping my body in a cloak of wind. The winds caught the fireball and whipped it around behind me. Four more sorcerers tried the same kind of attack, with the same results. They seemed to understand all at once that their number was dwindling, and huddled to come up with a new strategy.

This gave me a chance to turn my attention skyward. Heavy dark storm clouds scudded across the heavens, blotting out the sun. Rain began to fall, picking up intensity and turning into brick-sized hailstones. I hoped the riders behind me would rush away to safety, but I had no way to check on them. The golems would no doubt simply halt in place until an officer ordered them to move. No hail fell within the sorcerers' sphere of protection, nor on me, but it devastated the semicircle of soldiers behind the sorcerers. They tried to use their arms and shields to protect themselves, but eventually fell, pummeled by rock-hard hail, until each skull caved in.

I risked a quick glance behind me. Many of the riders were fleeing, but nearly a third of them had fallen to the sudden death from the sky. The golem army stood passively. The hail was strong enough to drive them to their knees, and it was causing damage, even though it did not quench the fire of the ones already alight. I saw one after the other slowly crumple to the ground. I couldn't help them right now. I still had twenty-two sorcerers to outface.

I raised my right fist and brought it down in a sudden, savage gesture. Lightning exploded from the sky in coruscations that would have blinded me had my eyes been open. It struck the sorcerous defense shield and glanced off, blasting a hole several feet deep into the ground. Again and again, I brought down my first, but only succeeded in making more smoking craters.

Within their bubble, the sorcerers neither cringed nor retreated. They seemed to be studying me with curious speculation, as if I were a puzzle to solve rather than a threat.

In a way, they were probably right. Neither I nor my storm could touch them, and I had few powers left to add to the mix. They had obviously concluded that attacking me directly was unwise. The energy required to maintain both my personal tornado and my monstrous hailstorm was beginning to tell, although I hoped they didn't know that.

Reluctantly, I loosed my hold on the clouds, and let the world's winds drive them away. In a few minutes sunshine returned, and we stood at stalemate, I within my protection, they within theirs, neither one of us able to attack.

I tried mind-speech. *I killed two of you last year, and set the nina upon you.* A small exaggeration couldn't hurt. *Five more of you have perished today.* A direct lie, but they couldn't know. *Do you really mean to stand against me?*

The reply came back quickly, seeming to originate from one sorcerer who stood slightly in front of the others. *We know who you are, thunder god.* I heard the name *Grey* echo in his head, and I wondered how he knew what people called me. *I am Cevak*, he continued, *the rightful ruler of all Amrhyn.*

The peoples of Amrhyn dispute your assertion. You only rule by intimidation and violence. I do not recognize your claim, I thought back, hoping to goad him or the others to attack. Anceron would only protect me from direct and imminent danger, and a standoff didn't count. I was half-worried that Anceron might decide my tornado gave sufficient protection.

We can hear your thoughts, Cevak said. *Who is Anceron?*

I frantically raised the kind of mental barriers I'd used to keep Ashe out of my head, hoping they would work against sorcerers, too. I left open only the narrow channel that permitted mind-speech and trusted they could not use it against me.

My thoughts are my own, I declared.

Evidently so, he admitted. *We number twenty-two. You are only one. You will tire eventually. When your winds fail, we will kill you and retake Amrhyn.*

I had no reply to that. He was likely correct. Even if I transported myself away in time, they would remain to make short work of Benlyn's coalition. I was tiring quickly; exhaustion threatened to end the stalemate, even if they did nothing further.

We can wrest the winds from you, thought Cevak. Behind him, a dozen sorcerers raised their hands in that curious crooked gesture I'd seen before. Blue lightning crackled from their fingertips.

Anceron! Transfer them! I commanded, but nothing happened. I soon understood why. They directed their lightning around me, not at me. They were trying to cancel my rotations by creating their own going the other way. I knew from my own experiences that it was a good tactic. I strove to maintain the speed and strength of my shield winds, but I could tell it was a struggle they'd eventually win.

I raised my right arm again, hoping that the golems still standing would be able to see and obey. I gave the signal I'd seen the drill sergeants use to mean *forward march*. Nearly instantly, the golem army surged forward. Those who could no longer walk crawled. They stepped over the burning front ranks, or shoved them roughly aside. In moments, at least two thousand golems stood abreast of me or just behind, waiting for orders.

My cylinder of protective winds was beginning to fail. I couldn't penetrate the sorcerous shield, but maybe I could bury it. It had worked with Gaheris in the dungeon, although he had lacked the sphere of protection Cevak and his fellows projected.

I hated using the homunculi so callously. Maran's words flitted through my mind: *You might be better off thinking of them as garden shovels.* It had seemed harsh then, and it still felt wrong now, but I had little choice. I gave the attack signal, pointed at the sorcerers, and simultaneously let go of my tornado and let Anceron transfer me back to the slight rise on the northwest side of the canyons, where I'd left Brand with Benlyn.

I bent over, my good hand on my knee, to catch my breath. When I looked up, Brand, Benlyn, and Benlyn's mounted troops were all staring at me, some with admiration, most with something approaching frank terror.

"How fares the battle, Lord Grey?" asked Benlyn calmly, setting the tone for his riders. "Had I realized how deadly you can be on your own, I might have devised a different strategy. It's difficult to see from this vantage, but their numbers seem diminished. Why did you leave the field?"

"A brief tactical retreat," I said, still striving to control my breathing. "I fought them to a temporary stalemate, but I can't penetrate their sorcerous shield. Your strategy, Ben, was a good one. We would never have drawn them out to fight directly without a serious threat to their defenders."

"All of whom now seem either dead or incapacitated," said Brand. "Along with a goodly number of our own soldiers. Would it not have been better to send you against them alone? Your last instructions in the field are spending homunculi recklessly."

I gave him a withering look. "I know. I had little choice. I'm worn out. I'm hoping they survive long enough to weaken the sorcerers. Their theurgies must have limits. Each fireball must cost them energy. I hope the golems can weaken them enough for me to breach their shield. I need time to regain my strength and figure out my next move."

Benlyn said, "Without their envelope of magical protection, the sorcerers cannot withstand an onslaught of arrows. A single crossbow bolt can take down a vulnerable sorcerer. Meanwhile, the golems burn. The smoke now obscures the battlefield. The toll among them must be horrific."

"The same might be said of me," I said, "The toll has been horrific, and a stray arrow would suffice to take my life. I can't go back until the sorcerers weaken. Their leader, Cevak, seems pretty damned sure of himself."

"What then do you propose?" asked the duke.

A sudden spate of coughing prevented me from answering immediately. After I'd cleared my lungs, I said, "I don't know yet."

As smoke from the burning golems drifted our direction, most of the riders' mounts shifted uneasily, stamped their forelegs, and neighed in distress. Many soldiers coughed as I had. Only two horses remained unmoved—Benlyn's great warhorse and Brand's mount. Another rider soon brought his horse under firm control and urged it forward to join us.

"Lord Grey," said Benlyn. "Meet Prince Quert of Voland."

"Your Highness," I said, guessing at the proper title.

"Lord," said the prince, "My arbalests don't miss, and if I lead, they will follow. At your back, we could fire at the sorcerers without endangering you. If the duke's assessment is correct, incoming quarrels are no longer a worry."

"What's an arbalest?"

"An expert with the crossbow," Brand murmured.

"Thank you, Prince," I said, "but even if you took the field, you'd have to climb your way over the piles of burning soldiers to get close enough. And if the sorcerers' shield protected them from my tornado, lightning blasts, and hailstones, I think your crossbow bolts would fare no better."

"What then do you propose?" repeated Benlyn.

"A quick consultation. Be right back."

I visualized Ramirez and Anceron in their chamber, and let my awareness of the battlefield fade away.

I touched each machine to bring forth the interior lights. The familiar glowing patterns soon arose, seeming to float just beneath each machine's top surface.

"Ramirez online."

"Anceron online."

"Listen, fellows—" I began

"We do not possess gender," said Ramirez, interrupting me.

"His speech is colloquial," said Anceron. "It is meant to be inclusive."

"Imprecision leads to ambiguity," Ramirez objected. "From which of us does he expect a response?"

"Shut up, both of you, and listen. I don't care which one of you answers me, as long as the information is helpful. Anceron, thank you for transferring the five sorcerers. Did they end up on Stormwind, as planned?"

"Correct," said Anceron.

"The remaining twenty-two of them were attacking me, too. Why didn't you transfer them at my command?"

"They posed no imminent threat. Your defenses were sufficient."

My surmise had been accurate. The machines might be intelligent, even sentient in their own peculiar way, but were hampered by literal interpretations and strict rules of behavior.

"Explain the shield they employ."

"Unknown referent," said Ramirez. "Describe."

"They are surrounded by a shimmering envelope—at least to my eyes, it shimmers, somewhat like the rainbow on a soap bubble. From within, they can launch attacks. But projectiles and strong winds cannot reach them while they stand inside the bubble. Anceron could transfer some of them out."

Ramirez answered. "They draw monument energy through their neural implants. You lack the vocabulary for a more precise explanation."

"Can you—either of you—or any of the machines down here —neutralize the shield?"

"I can deactivate their neural implants," said Anceron. "The process is destructive. Subsequent repair requires a technician with replacement parts."

"How did they obtain the implants? Do 'technicians' with the proper tools live in Amrhyn?"

"Unknown," said the machines in unison.

Anceron added, "Logic suggests the correct answer is yes, but I am unable to locate inactive neural devices."

"Deactivate their implants now," I commanded.

"The process is destructive."

"Meaning it would kill them?"

"Correct. Remote deactivation would cause an explosion. Operation forbidden. Only an onsite technician with the correct tool can remove or deactivate an implant without causing harm to the bearer."

It's what I expected the machines to say. They couldn't fight my battle for me. I paced, thinking furiously. Then I suddenly looked up, a new idea dawning. "Measure the size of their shield," I commanded. "What is the diameter?"

"Locating . . . located," said Anceron. "The field energies are not static in nature. The size fluctuates. The shape approximates a hemisphere."

"Estimate the size for me," I said.

"The median diameter observed so far is one hundred feet. Shall I continue monitoring?"

"No, that's good enough. Can you transfer a group of soldiers to within the shield?"

"Only if they accompany you."

Fair enough. "Can you identify the homunculi in Amrhyn? They're surrounding the sorcerers at the moment."

"Located," said Anceron instantly. "Many of them are inoperative."

"Yes, well, I suppose that's true," I said. "Can you transfer them elsewhere? They are not living beings. Your rules shouldn't apply."

"Only if they accompany you."

I had been afraid Anceron would say that. "Okay, here's what I want. First, transfer me near to the homunculi, close enough that you can transport them, but far enough from the sorcerers that they won't have time to react. Can you do that?"

"Visualization required."

"Don't send me yet," I warned and concentrated on picturing the rear of the golem phalanx. "Will that location let you remove me and all the homunculi?"

"Yes."

"Then this needs to be quick. After you send me through, I'll immediately visualize a new destination. Once you have the picture, transfer the entire group without waiting for a command. Can you do that?"

"Yes."

"Begin the procedure now."

I found myself behind the main golem army. Smoke billowed from in front of me, thick, dark, blinding. I coughed, shielding my face with my good arm, and visualized the staging grounds on the outskirts of Stoling.

Without any sense of transition, the homunculi and I sprawled on the hard-packed dirt outside the barracks area. I found a golem captain, told him to work on saving as many soldiers as possible, then bowed my head and visualized myself standing next to Brand again.

Brand, Benlyn, and Quert were exactly where I'd left them. Only a few minutes had passed. I watched with them for a bit. The smoke from the battlefield slowly lifted, and I could see the fallen soldiers on both sides, as well as the shimmering and apparently undamaged protective bubble surrounding the sorcerers.

"The smoke clears," observed Brand, apparently speaking to Benlyn. "The homunculi no longer burn." He squinted, and then added, "They do not even occupy the field. Lord Grey reveals a new tactic."

"Yes," I said loudly, "he does. The golems were in the way."

Brand looked around, spotted me, and leaped off his horse, tearing a blanket from his saddle roll. "Lord Grey, you are ablaze!" He wrapped me in the blanket and slapped at the flames until he had extinguished them.

Only my cloak and my left arm seemed damaged, although soot covered my entire body. I thought, quite irrelevantly, that Virgil would be shocked to his core. My left arm and its claw-like hand were nearly useless to me anyway, and I felt no pain. I thanked Brand for his quick action, and turned my attention to Quert.

"Assume your archers have their weapons ready, but are

disoriented. How rapidly can they locate their targets and fire, and with what accuracy?"

"What kind of disorientation, lord?"

"There are twenty-two of *them*," I said, jerking my thumb at the sorcerers. "The sorcerous shield is large enough for me and twenty of your archers. I can't risk taking more, since your fighters will need elbow room. If all goes well, we'll appear within their protective shield about a dozen feet *behind* them. Your archers must find their marks and loose within seconds. Otherwise, the sorcerers will incinerate them—and me—where we stand. When we arrive, it will be sudden, like tripping over a hillock, and it may still be difficult to see through the remaining smoke."

"Arbalests, then, not archers. At close quarters, we can be sure of head or heart shots. I will lead the party myself. Since the targets outnumber us, all should carry two loaded and cocked crossbows, one in their hands, and the other at their belts, ready for use. The secondary crossbows may be cranked ahead of time, but the arbalests will still need several moments to fit the quarrels and locate new targets."

"Can you be sure of getting all of the sorcerers?" I asked. "You won't have much time, and we'll only have the one chance."

Benlyn leaned over in his saddle and put his armored hand on my good arm, squeezing my shoulder firmly. "No plan is flawless, nor can success be guaranteed. Yet your scheme is simple and has the element of surprise. It should work." He straightened up and looked at me oddly. "You told me you weren't a brave man," he said. "Yet you propose to lead a task force within feet of the sorcerers. Before I approve the effort, I must know if you speak from confidence or from desperation."

"Both, Your Grace. A little of each. It's either this or let them escape, which only means doing it all over again."

Benlyn considered that, then nodded. To the prince, he said. "Assemble your arbalests. Make sure each knows what to expect and what is required. I'm minded to keep you back, however. Your courage is not in doubt, but I shall need you after the fight. Amrhyn is still bitterly divided internally, and each noble who has sworn fealty may be required to prevent more war."

Quert cocked his head. "You are my liege lord. I bow to your wishes."

"Then see to it," said Benlyn.

In short order, Quert had his team armed and ready. The arbalests, all seasoned men, had grim faces. I arranged them in a semicircle, their backs to the sorcerers, and stood behind them. "When we appear, the enemy should be directly in front of you, but facing away," I said, raising my voice to make sure each man could hear me clearly. "Don't wait for orders. Fire as quickly as you can, reload, and take out any left standing."

They all nodded. I glanced back over my shoulder to fix the position clearly, then bowed my head and visualized the location for Anceron.

Two men stumbled, confused by the unexpected transfer. The others loosed their crossbow bolts immediately. Fifteen of the sorcerers fell on the instant, the backs of their heads nearly exploded by the short-range deadly quarrels. Cevak was among those to escape the initial attack, and he whirled, blue lightning already springing from his fingertips, aimed directly at me.

Anceron! Transfer him!

Cevak didn't have time to look surprised before he vanished. His last strike caught me on the left side, searing my face and arm. Anceron had transferred him before his theurgies were at full strength, and I had had a moment to turn partially away. The blue lightning jolted me, but did not do much damage. The other sorcerers didn't even get a chance to turn. They seemed confused by the sudden violence and disappearance of Cevak. Quert's men launched their secondary attack and slew them before they understood the danger. The shimmering bubble popped and evaporated.

I transferred us all back to Benlyn's side.

"Report," commanded the duke.

"Your Grace, Amrhyn is yours."

Chapter Twenty-One

Duke Benlyn dismounted and gave swift orders to his captains. "No quarter," he said harshly. "Tend to any of our soldiers who may be saved, then go through the encampment and surrounding area to locate wounded or fleeing enemies. Search the mines and tunnels. Everyone who fought on the sorcerers' side, man or woman, dies today. The victory must be unambiguous, quashing any hope of resurrecting resistance to my rule. You may spare those under fifteen years old—provided they yield and agree to swear fealty. I will show mercy."

The captains saluted and scattered. I thought Benlyn's orders were ruthless and unnecessarily cruel, but I also understood the principle of not leaving enemies at one's back. I found the aftermath of the battle anticlimactic, as though it had been an inevitability we merely needed to wait to happen.

"Lord Grey," said the duke, commanding my full attention. "You have been injured."

"Nothing serious," I said. "A lashing from Cevak, just the beginning of a true blast. It probably looks worse than it is." I spoke with false bravado. My entire left side, from boot tip to scalp, felt numb. I had to put most of my weight on my bad leg just to stay upright.

"Have a medic examine you anyway. Your face looks half-melted from here. Battle adrenaline does strange things to one's perceptions."

"I'll have it looked at," I promised, thinking I'd prefer to trust Maran's staff than a bunch of field medics who specialized in cautery and amputation.

Benlyn nodded approval and continued, "The lords and nobles will gather in my apartments in Stoling. We will join them for a victory feast. What did you do with the bulk of the golem army?"

"I left them at the staging grounds, with instructions to put out the fires and save as many as possible."

"That was well done," he said, "but a goodly number remain in the canyons or surrounding terrain. What will they do now that the war is over?"

I turned to Brand and gestured for him to answer.

Brand said, "I'll send officers to collect the strays. They'll respond to recall trumpets. They can march to the destination of your choice."

"Send them to the others for now, and tell your captains to set a watch. Those soldiers, sadly diminished in number as they are, still represent the single strongest fighting force in Amrhyn. Now that there can be no sorcerous interference, they would become a doughty weapon in the hands of the wrong commander. Do you need to stay with them yourself? I'm mindful that their first allegiance is to you, not to me."

"No, Your Grace. They will follow my orders, as I follow yours. I will ensure they only obey the two of us."

"Then see to it, Colonel. Meet us in Stoling."

Brand nodded, wheeled his horse, and rode to locate his captains. After he'd gone, I turned to peer closely at Benlyn. He seemed unmoved by our triumph, displaying neither surprise nor pleasure. His face was unusually thoughtful, and I detected a hint of uneasiness in his expression.

"Ben," I said diffidently, "how did you know to prepare a victory feast? We might easily have lost. It was a very near thing. And what of the crops? Shouldn't harvesting be the first priority?"

"The field workers are already in place, and carts and wagons fill the roads in anticipation. The workers will begin at first light. Some of them may still have time yet today. At least two hours of sunlight remain, but it will take time for messengers to carry word. The grain fields are vast. As to the feast . . . it made more sense than not. The cooks have been working since dawn. I had little doubt you and Brand's army would succeed."

"You flatter us, Ben."

The duke laughed heartily, but it had a somewhat hollow sound. "The alternative was to assume you would fail. Which outlook would have served us better?"

I lifted my shoulders in a helpless shrug. "It was a very near thing. I was neither pessimistic nor optimistic. I was just terrified. It hardly seems possible it's all over now."

"Have more faith in yourself, man."

Benlyn rested his hand on his pistol as he turned to Quert. "My lord prince," he said with excessive formality and a forced grin. "If you would dismount and yield your horse to the care of your lieutenants, my friend Lord Grey can spare us the tedious ride back. Come stand at my side."

Quert climbed down slowly, looking much smaller once he was off his horse. He was also bow-legged. I wondered if he had been that way since childhood or simply shaped by too much time in the saddle. He, too, wore a pistol at his belt.

"Will the balcony do, Ben?" I asked.

He nodded, and a moment later, the three of us stood outside his apartments, fresh air at our back, and the welcoming smell of roasted meats drifting from within.

"I'll never get used to that," said the duke. "Are you sure you can't teach me the trick?"

"Sorry."

Benlyn gestured for Quert to precede him, and we left the balcony. The servants, having had no word of our victory or imminent return, started violently. Benlyn curtly told them to expect other guests to arrive over the next several hours, and ordered a bottle of wine for the three of us.

The duke and the prince settled at a side table near the balcony doors, but I remained standing.

"Ben, I should tell Ashe what happened. My wife, too, will want word."

"Go ahead," he said, "but don't stay long. You are the guest of honor tonight. Have those burns treated, too."

I inclined my head and had Anceron transfer me to the valley's dolmen.

I wanted to talk to Maran and get a change of clothing before visiting the king. It was already full dark in the valley, but someone had thought to place lanterns all along the path from the dolmen to the manor house. Something about the valley was very different, but I couldn't tell what. Finally, I realized that the smithies had finally gone silent. I could hear birds again. I limped home, passing through multiple checkpoints of mixed King's Guard and Maran's twenty soldiers, and entered through the front door.

Hasq greeted me, tsk-tsking at my appearance, but behaving cordially enough otherwise. "When you did not return this morning, sir, the lady became upset. I shall inform her of your arrival while you change. She is in the front parlor with the little lord and the young master." For once, I didn't want to argue with him. I left soot on everything I touched on the way to my quarters.

Virgil took one look at me, and ran to start the bath.

"No time for that. Just wash my face and arms, and get me into clean clothing. I need to visit the king and go back to Amrhyn yet tonight."

"Very good, sir," he said. He fetched a basket before undressing me. Each article of clothing went into the basket, sending up tiny puffs of dirt and soot, despite the gingerly way he handled the garments. Even my boots went into the rubbish. He laved my entire body using a lot of cold water, strong soap, and many cloths, complaining that a bath would be more thorough. He then slathered my damaged face and arm with burn ointment. Eventually, he had me clean enough to don new clothing.

I made my way to the front parlor. Maran sprang up from her chair at my appearance, and I hugged her tightly. Torrey stood back, hesitant, until I reached with my good arm and pulled him into our embrace. Aiden gurgled quietly to himself, his lively eyes scanning the room continuously. I bent to kiss the top of his head, then turned back to Maran.

"Sorry I couldn't get word to you," I said. "It was one of those days. Benlyn started the attack last night, and it was in full swing when I arrived. They needed me to stay."

"How did the army perform? How long do you think the campaign will last?"

I laughed, realizing I hadn't laughed properly in weeks. "It's over. Your army was everything you promised, and the sorcerers are either dead or on that island I told you about."

"You were injured," she said, scanning me critically. "What happened?"

"My left arm got scorched, and I have superficial facial burns on the same side, but it doesn't hurt. Virgil put ointment on it."

Maran reached up to rap her knuckles on the scab covering my left cheek. It sounded like a tiny hammer hitting granite. "I think your old wound may have saved you. It acted like a helm's cheek guard. I'm glad we never had it excised."

I had my own thoughts about that, but kept them to myself. The burns were the least of my worries. My entire left side felt stiff and awkward, almost as if it no longer belonged to me.

"You defeated an entire army *and* the sorcerers, and only got singed?" Torrey demanded incredulously.

"I and many, many others defeated them. Brave fighters from Amrhyn wanting independence, your mother's army, and superb command and planning from the duke and the colonel. You may call me a hero if you want, but only until morning. My head is big enough already."

Torrey puffed out his chest as if sharing my glory. His eyes shone. I ruffled his hair.

Maran smiled at me, too, but her expression was thoughtful. "You haven't spoken the word of disposal yet," she said. "None of my energy has returned, and the valley still suffers."

"I wanted to wait until I was sure they wouldn't be needed," I said. "And the machines said it would take weeks or months for the valley to return to normal."

"Yes, but I reabsorb the energy I put into each homunculus when it expires. I can barely stand upright—I want that vitality back. Please say you will join us for dinner. You look utterly exhausted."

"Sorry," I said. "We'll hold our own celebration another day. Tonight, I must report to the king, then return to Amrhyn for a victory feast. Benlyn made it clear my presence was mandatory."

"Stay and tell us about the battle," Torrey begged.

Maran nodded her agreement, but acknowledged my look of

resignation. "Don't get too drunk at the feast," she said, giving me another kiss. "I expect you to be functional in the morning. And, as soon as Amrhyn is secure, speak the word and let the army expire."

"I shall," I promised.

I wondered if, now that the valley's enchantment had weakened, Anceron could transfer me from here. I closed my eyes and concentrated on the dolmen. Nothing happened, so I limped wearily back and stood beside the king stone within the circle. I flicked it with my thumbnail to wake the lights, and began sorting through the strands.

Ashe's ribbon came to me in moments. I peeked through. He was alone in his tent, lying under a thick comforter on a narrow cot, seemingly sound asleep. I released the strand to conserve the dolmen's energies, and had Anceron transfer me.

The only light in the tent came from two tall tapers held by an ornate cut-glass girandole on the worktable. "Ashe," I said quietly. When he did not respond, I said, "Your Majesty!" quite loudly. He still didn't stir, so I crossed the tent and shook his shoulder gently.

He groaned and opened his eyes, taking a few moments to focus.

"Grey?"

"Yes. I bring news from the Duke of Amrhyn. Ben has now obtained fealty from all but a few lords, and he rules the region in your name. The sorcerers and their army have been defeated."

"The golems worked?"

"Exactly as hoped. A great many succumbed to fire, but most survived. They are unexcelled fighters. No merely human army could stand against them. Without their sacrifices, I would not have been able to challenge and defeat the sorcerers."

"The sorcerers are gone?"

"Sire, how much wine did you drink before bed?"

His tone became tart. "Too much, obviously, but I get the gist. Tell the duke I'll expect a full report. Congratulations on your victory. I look forward to hearing every detail from your own point of view—perhaps when I visit your valley. The duke's report will be dry as a year-old bone. Tell him to start writing anyway. I guess I have work to do." He got up, shivered, and pulled on a thick fur cloak. He moved to the desk and began shuffling documents.

"Congratulations to you, too, Ashe. It was your foresight to send Ben long before conflict erupted. Reaping and harvesting are commencing even as we speak. The grain will reach your subjects before winter."

He peered at me blearily. "It's nighttime."

"Not in Amrhyn. The sun sets later there."

"What of the horse trade?" he asked. "When may I expect new animals?"

"A troublesome viscount may delay things, but the duke can handle him. Ben expects me to return for a victory celebration. I probably won't get home until tomorrow morning."

"And your wife's valley?"

"Still unprotected, but your guards are helping watch for danger."

Ashe looked at me sharply. "The King's Guard are actually inside the valley now?" he asked.

"Yes," I said. "At first, they only patrolled the hills. Now, they're helping protect the manor house itself. Thank you for providing them."

"Then go," he said. "Enjoy your victory. Send in a courier before you leave. I'll need one immediately." He turned his attention back to the pile of papers on his worktable.

I went to the tent flap and called. General Yarval and several other officers responded immediately. They had been standing beside a nearby fire pit, and seemed unnerved to see my head poking out from the king's tent.

"He wants a courier right away," I said.

Yarval nodded, his expression suddenly blank and unreadable. I noticed with some discomfort that several monks were among the group surrounding the fire pit. Firelight glinted from their chains of office. Hierophants, then. Their faces were exceedingly easy to read—unbridled hatred for me. I would have to find some way to make peace with them, but now was not the time.

I faded from the tent and reappeared on Benlyn's balcony.

Benlyn and a dozen richly dressed nobles, both men and women, were laughing uproariously, cheering and toasting each other. Ale and wine flowed freely, with servants bustling to keep flagons and glasses full.

"To the man of the hour!" Benlyn shouted when he spotted me standing quietly on the balcony.

"The man of the hour!" shouted several others. I suspected half of them were already drunk, and the night would become raucous quickly. I sighed to myself and entered the apartments when Benlyn beckoned.

A servant pressed a wine glass into my good hand as Benlyn guided me to a chair near the head of a large dining table. I made a show of sipping when they toasted me again.

"Is this everyone?" I asked when a break in the noise gave me a chance to speak.

"Only half," said the duke. "Food will be served later. For now, drink."

I noticed that his wine glass emptied very slowly, as if, like me, he only tasted the wine instead of gulping it down. I thought it was the proper behavior for the new ruler of Amrhyn and silently raised my glass to him. He winked at me and pretended to drink.

Several of the loudest lords and ladies dragged him away, and I found myself sitting at the table alone. Each noble whose eyes crossed my gaze made a show of coming up to congratulate and thank me, but no one stayed at the table with me. New guests arrived every few minutes. One of the young men in a serving uniform decided to attach himself to me personally and stayed at my side, whispering the names of all those who greeted me. I promptly forgot each name.

When Prince Quert of Voland showed up, the entire room cheered. He bowed gracefully and made his way to a sideboard to obtain a flagon of ale. "The *real* hero," I overheard someone say. From the way Quert accepted everyone's praise, I concluded that history would likely leave me out of the story. The party's noise grew overwhelming. I got up from my seat and went back to the balcony, closing the doors behind me. It was quieter out here, but not enough. I studied the city, intrigued by the way the setting sun made various structures glow. I guessed our building to be three stories high, made of stout, seasoned wood with a kind of brick cladding that seemed decorative rather than functional. From the noise, I estimated that Benlyn's apartments occupied the entire top floor. Directly beneath me, riders kept appearing; they seemed to talk briefly to someone I couldn't see, then disappeared into the gloom again. I supposed they were delivering reports and then carrying orders back. Eventually, they stopped. I guessed it was either too dark for couriers, or they had nothing left to report.

Someone opened the balcony doors. The racket from within had risen during my brief absence and now blasted onto the balcony like an assault. I turned and found the young man who had attached himself to my personal service. "Lord, food is being served," he said.

"I'll come right in." I took one last glance at the city. A large group of riders bearing torches approached from the west. I supposed using torches was one way to allow travel at night, especially within a city where cobbles covered the streets. Reluctantly, I turned away and went to join the celebration.

Servers had brought in more tables, lit candles and lanterns, and were going around the room laying out food and utensils. I estimated nearly four dozen guests, and wondered how Benlyn could afford such a feast. Then I remembered he was the acknowledged lord of Amrhyn and would likely collect the costs from his liegemen and women.

Benlyn stood at the head of the main table. I quietly took my spot beside him. The duke banged loudly on the table, setting all the utensils rattling and the wine glasses wobbling. "Silence!" he bellowed.

The noise gradually faded away, and the guests seated themselves, looking at him expectantly.

"Tonight we celebrate the independence of Amrhyn," he boomed. "In thrall to sorcerers no more. Those who wished our country ill are dead. Raise your glasses with me. We drink to the brave men and women who sacrificed their lives to liberate our country."

"To the army!"

"To the dukc!"

"To free Amrhyn!"

Glasses and tankards rose and fell, and everyone cheered. I neither drank nor raised my voice to join the chorus. Benlyn took his seat, and I followed suit. While he urged the nobility to continue drinking and shouting, I leaned over, cupped my hand around his ear, and said, "Ben, is this wise? They treat you like their king."

He laughed, leaning close to reply. "Let them celebrate. Talk is just talk."

I nodded, still feeling uneasy. *To free Amrhyn?* Did Benlyn mean to forsake his allegiance to Ashe?

Brand entered. Alone among the guests, he had not changed from his uniform into finery. He saluted, and held the posture until Benlyn noticed him. The duke stood, waving Brand to the head of the table. Eyes swiveled to follow his progress, and table talk died down to a murmur.

"Report," said Benlyn. "Let everyone hear!"

"The homunculi are secure, Your Grace," said Brand. "Over a thousand were lost. The rest are battle-ready. I have set them to repairing their armor and uniforms."

"Did you instruct them as I asked?"

"Yes, Your Grace. They recognize your authority and mine. No aspiring insurgent may command them."

Benlyn picked up his wine glass, and turned to the room. "To the golem army!" he cried. "Amrhyn is invincible!"

Everyone toasted. Benlyn grabbed Brand's shoulder and brought him close in a hug. "To Colonel Brand!" he shouted. "The golem commander!"

This time after the toast, Benlyn threw his glass over his shoulder. Everyone followed his lead. The tinkling sound of shattering crystal filled the room, and a few lords cheered, then everyone became utterly still, watching the duke intently.

"I thank you for your sacrifice," Benlyn told Brand. I saw the sudden motion, but was too late to stop it. Benlyn's dagger thrust sharply up through Brand's abdomen and found his heart.

Before Brand hit the floor, I raised the god-winds and blew out all the candles and lanterns. The only reason to murder Brand was to take sole control of the golem army. With it, the duke could challenge Ashe for the throne in Jappa. But Benlyn had seen my power unleashed today, and I strongly suspected he would either take measures to enlist my aid or, failing that, ensure I didn't interfere with his treachery. The sudden darkness gave me a moment to think. An ominous metallic double-click told me he'd already made up his mind.

I visualized the street outside the building and transferred, the bang of Benlyn's flintlock pistol still ringing in my ears. I had escaped by only a breath. I had been sitting at the table, so I arrived on the street in the same posture. I immediately fell over backward, rolled with the impact, and regained my feet.

The riders with torches were still arriving. They numbered over two hundred by now. Among them rode one in fancy dress clothes; the others all wore uniforms, the ducal seal glaringly absent. I smelled the strong and unmistakable odor of pine tar. The man in fancy dress brought his horse alongside me. I still held the god-winds under tight control, but none of the riders appeared to be carrying bows or holding drawn swords, so I relaxed my guard a bit and focused on the leader.

"I suppose you are Dhutori, Viscount Alvishire?" I asked.

"The same. And you, fellow?"

"That depends on your intent. Did you bring hundreds of soldiers with torches and pine tar so they may swear fealty to the duke?"

He knew that I already knew the answer, so he just smiled grimly. He snapped his fingers, and one rider dismounted, drawing his sword. "Kill him quickly. Don't let him squawk and raise the alarm," ordered the viscount.

Virtue should not be mediated by conscience the way vices are, but I hesitated, pondering Brand's murder, Benlyn's unexpected betrayal, and the viscount's intent. As Benlyn had feared, Dhutori had held back his forces until there was a clear—but weakened—victor. Now he could take Amrhyn in one simple act of mass murder. I knew the duke's treasonous plan to control the golems was hopeless, yet his guests did not deserve to die in flames. I am often burdened with convoluted moral quandaries, but this one seemed easier to solve than most.

I let the god-winds rise, knocking back the advancing soldier and blowing out all the torches. They tried to relight them, but by then I'd summoned enough rain to make the effort futile. I gasped with the effort; my powers were waning rapidly after today's ferocious expenditure.

I grabbed at the viscount's foot, and let Anceron transfer us both to the staging area outside of town. Snatched from his saddle, the viscount fell five feet to the ground. I kicked his sword away. A golem captain hurried up and saluted me. "Hold him, but don't injure him," I instructed.

I closed my eyes, visualizing the upper room where Benlyn and his guests were likely still fumbling in darkness. I appeared beside Benlyn, grabbed his collar, and transferred us to where I'd left the viscount. While Benlyn was still recovering his balance, I plucked the pistol from his belt and threw it as far as I could.

"Arm them equally, and let them fight," I told the golem captain.

My storm back in the city did not reach this far. The sun's fading rays allowed stars to start appearing overhead. I could easily see the hatred between the duke and the viscount.

"I command you to defend me!" yelled Benlyn. The golems did not move, except to offer swords to him and Dhutori and then step back. Brand had neglected to tell the duke that, to the golems, only Maran ranked higher than I.

"Grey!" called Benlyn. "Don't do this!"

I smiled gently. "Ben, if you win, you may call yourself duke or king. I don't care which. Dhutori, the same goes for you. But in either case, the winner *will* honor the agreements with King Ashe. Civil war *will* cease. The nobility *will* stand united. Don't make me come back to Amrhyn to enforce it, and don't test my resolve. I'll either kill you myself or set Cevak free."

Calling upon Anceron, I transitioned from the staging area to Maran's dolmen, leaving the two leaders to duel over the rule of Amrhyn. The transfer was rough; it not only took longer than usual, but I twisted my ankle upon arrival. I wondered if Anceron was weakening, or if our dolmen was losing power more rapidly than anticipated.

I flicked one of the menhirs with a thumbnail to wake the lights, and everything seemed normal, so I stopped worrying. I stood in the center of the circle and spoke the word of disposal Maran had made me memorize. Without my presence to countermand Benlyn, the golems would obey him. I couldn't allow that. As the word left my lips, the dolmen immediately grew brighter. I couldn't see much, but the air crackled, and fat sparks burst from the king stone. I knew that back in Amrhyn, the entire golem army dissolved into tattered rags and lumps of straw, leaving only empty uniforms behind. The vitality of each golem flew back through the dolmen and thence to Maran. I felt a fleeting sense of joy from her, then nothing more. I waited until the energy transfer had completed, and then the dolmen put its own lights out. The menhirs became just big crooked stones, and they seemed to loom toward me. I felt an urgent need to leave the stone circle.

I slithered down the deer trail, favoring my ankle, and found the road. I started limping tiredly back toward the manor house.

It was nearly pitch-black on the path; clouds covered most of the sky. I was grateful for the line of lanterns, yet they were insufficient to keep me from stumbling. I tried to bring my second sight to bear so I could see in the dark, but my awareness didn't flow out from me as it usually did. I thought I was just tired from an extremely long and arduous day.

A soft and melodious voice said from right beside me, "Second sight is a rare and fickle gift. Once lost, few ever regain it."

I stopped and turned. The eyes of the body were of limited use, but they were all I possessed just then. I squinted. An old man with scraggly white hair stood beside me. The lanterns revealed he was barefoot, and he wore only an unassuming homespun robe of brown wool. The robe's hood was thrown back, but his head was bowed as if he were studying his feet. He kept his hands tucked into the folds of his robe.

"Who are you?" I asked. He didn't seem threatening at all; quite the opposite—his presence radiated peace and comfort.

"Qol's child, I shall walk beside you."

He looked up at me briefly, and I caught a glimpse of pale skin accompanied by a twinkling flash of sapphire-blue eyes catching and reflecting the lantern light. His features were ordinary, showing none of the radiant beauty I'd come to expect from the muria. Yet I had no doubt of him.

"You are one of the five," I said without any hint of question in my tone. "I thought Ulat forbade interference in human affairs."

"I do not interfere. I only walk beside you."

"Why is your power veiled? Which one of the five are you?"

"I am Bastion. Did you know that Qol is the youngest of us all? Betimes, his youth leads him astray, and his aspirations blind him. He hazards great risks in lofty hopes of even greater rewards. He is not gentle with his children."

Under other circumstances, I would have welcomed learning more. In a few short words, Bastion had given me more insight into Qol and the muria hierarchy than had all my prior experiences. At that moment, though, I wanted to know why one of the five had revealed himself. The muria did nothing by happenstance. There was a reason for Bastion's presence, and I meant to learn it. "Why are you here?" I asked. "Why do you remain veiled?"

"I veil for your comfort and am here simply to walk beside you. Do you want me to leave?"

Oddly, I didn't. I found his quiet voice and mild manner

compelling, overflowing with compassion and consolation. He exerted no power of persuasion; I sensed he would abide any choice I made. He may have read my mind, or simply my posture. "Good," he said. "Let us walk together. The path is not long."

I resumed limping toward the manor house, following the chain of lantern lights. I came across the first empty uniform after a few minutes. I didn't need anyone to tell me why. When I had spoken the word of disposal, *all* of the homunculi Maran had made for the war expired at once, including the twenty posted here in the valley. It was foolish of me to have thought otherwise. I counted nineteen more empty uniforms until I perceived a member of the King's Guard standing watch.

"My lord!" the guard exclaimed, lowering his sword when I drew near enough to be recognized. "We did not expect you until tomorrow."

I said nothing, but moved to push past him. He put a hand to my chest to stop me. "Please wait," he said. "I'll get others and torches to light your way."

"It's dark, but I can see well enough," I said.

"Lord, I have orders. Please wait here." He stayed just long enough to make sure I'd stopped, and then turned to run toward the manor. Something about his behavior was off, unsettling. With a rising sense of alarm, I started to dash after him.

Bastion held out his arm to stop me. "It is already too late. You cannot change what has happened. Know that I am with you. The path is darker than you fear, but you need not walk it alone."

The devil with that! I twisted away from Bastion and began running. Of course, my injured ankle and bad leg betrayed me at exactly the wrong moment, and I found myself on my knees, blood seeping from the palm of my good hand.

I levered myself to my feet and tried to run again. A shooting pain all down my left side, from head to foot, brought me up short. I must have injured myself in the fall. I fought to control my breathing, and pushed on until I reached the stables, Bastion walking silently beside me.

The torches outside the stables revealed a long row of bodies. All of the house servants were laid out, their heads neatly severed from their bodies. *Only fire and beheading*, Benlyn had summarized when I described golem vulnerabilities. But this wasn't Benlyn's work. I now knew some of the content of the letters I had carried back and forth to the king. Ashe had planned this slaughter using Benlyn's information. I wondered if they had worked in concert or if each was unaware of the other's betrayal.

The heavy scent of fresh blood told me that not only the servants had been slain this night. Using one of the courtyard torches, I peeked inside the stables, and withdrew immediately, dry heaves choking me. Butter, Aster, Rebel, and all the other horses were dead. I looked at the manor house in panic. If they would kill the horses. . . .

Before I reached the back door, a squad of King's Guard came in formation, moving at a fast jog, each bearing a torch in one hand and an upraised sword in the other. Behind them rode a mounted guardsman. I recognized Captain Kwan. His face was impassive and implacable.

"I'm sorry, lord. You weren't supposed to see this. King's orders. It was to be fast and painless."

"My family!" I gasped. "My wife!"

"Unharmed, lord. Calm yourself," Kwan said. "Accompany us to the front of the house."

Maran! I shouted in mind-speech. *Maran!* I tried to raise the god-winds. No gust came at my call; not a leaf or stray bit of straw moved. I turned to Bastion in despair. "Do something! Enchant them. Blind them. Use your power!"

"I will walk with you," he said. "Only you can see or hear me tonight."

Kwan looked at me sharply. "Lord, to whom do you speak?

Did you bring an army of golems with you?" He signaled and four of his guards ran to check behind me. The rest grabbed me by the biceps and marched me around the manor. More torches and more guards met us.

Maran stood holding Aiden in her arms, her back to the manor house. Torrey hovered in front of her, bravely holding his épée against a group of experienced King's Guard, daring them to come closer. The guards were trying to disarm him. They seemed torn between amusement and exasperation. Torrey pinked one on the wrist, and suddenly their tolerance ran out. One of the guards smashed the hilt of his sword against the side of Torrey's head, and the boy collapsed onto his back. The guard raised his sword high, point facing downward at Torrey's chest.

"Hold," commanded Kwan. "The king said only the man, woman, and babe. The boy is not our concern."

The guards thrust me roughly past Torrey, so that I stood at Maran's left side. Firm hands held our shoulders from behind, forcing us to face Kwan together. Maran shifted Aiden to her right arm, and took my good hand, holding it tightly.

I tried to scan Torrey to assess injuries, but had trouble focusing my percipience. I couldn't see anything beyond what my mortal eyes showed: a trickle of blood at his temple and slow but regular breathing.

"Again, lord, my apologies," said the captain. "You were to be taken by quarrel tomorrow. The king did not want you to see this."

I commanded Anceron to transfer the four of us away, picturing Tessa's front porch. Nothing happened. In absolute desperation, I reached for the Sleeper, but although I could sense its tremendous power, I could not reach it. I even called out for Qol for help. My mind-speech echoed hollowly inside my skull, unable to escape.

Bastion stepped over Torrey to stand beside me. "Qol's child, your second sight enabled your other abilities," he said. "You must face this moment."

I ignored him, "Kwan, why? *Why?*"

Kwan unfolded a parchment and had one of the guards hold a torch so he could read. He scanned it quickly, and then apologized to me again. "Lord, this was to be read aloud after you were slain. The king didn't want you to use your powers to evade justice."

What powers? I'm just a cripple at the moment, I thought bitterly. But Kwan couldn't know that. "Aren't you afraid I'll do so now?" I asked.

"It is well known that you exhaust yourself after using your powers. Since we are still alive and you have not yet disappeared, I conclude that you can neither harm us nor escape. It saddens me, lord, to see you in such straits."

"Then why plan an ambush to kill me with a crossbow bolt tomorrow?"

"Prudence, lord. You would have had the night to recover, had you returned when expected." He cleared his throat and began reading the parchment aloud:

"That you murdered thousands of innocents upon and beside Justian Bridge; that you destroyed Justian Bridge itself; that you caused massive earthquakes slaying thousands more; that your earthquakes destroyed the citadel at Jappa and many other buildings; that you conspired with muria and living machines; that you desecrated the temple at Landing and many other historical monuments; that you used the dolmens for personal benefit; that you threatened to destroy the starships; that you killed a hierophant and an abbess; that you cast down the monastery, killing hundreds more; that you failed to repent your crimes or swear fealty to the crown; that your wife crafted an army of unnatural creatures; that you consort with such creatures daily; that you, your wife, and child are not human and wield unnatural powers; that you, through callous disregard, allowed the deaths of

Selene of the royal library, Sergeant Nix of the King's Guard, Academic Larkin of Port Abb, and many others; that despite your services to the crown, you nevertheless act without restraint or wisdom; that your continued arrogance and refusal to acknowledge the rights and privileges of both nobles and clerics causes unrest; for all these reasons and more, I, Ashe, King of Leonais by right of blood and acclamation, do hereby sentence you and your family to die, lest you wreak more havoc upon the world."

A long silence fell after he finished reading, and then I said, "Is that all? I did most of those things either on the king's behalf or at his behest. The rest were accidents or beyond my control. I deny the charges."

"I did not write this parchment, lord; I only read it aloud by the king's command."

"Captain, I treated you well. The king's decree is unjust, unfair, and untrue. Refuse this madness. I will sort things out with the king."

Kwan shrugged. "It's not my place to second guess His Majesty. If I were to have an opinion, lord, it would be that the king believes you have become too powerful. No place on the continent is safe from you, and you have not bent the knee. Your wife, likewise, does not acknowledge the king's suzerainty, and she wields unnatural powers. The babe?" He shrugged again. "I don't know. His Majesty likely believes the child will inherit your powers. Let us not draw this out, lord. The king urged action tonight, while your wife's enchantments are yet uncertain."

"Maran," I said urgently. "I spoke the word of disposal. Reform the valley around us."

She didn't look away from Kwan and the guards, but she bit her lip. "I've tried. Our monument still doesn't respond fully. I have some vitality back, but not enough. I can shield you and Torrey, but that would leave Aiden and me unprotected. I can shield us, but you two would be unprotected. Can't you transfer us away?"

I shook my head, trying with all my might to raise the god-winds or summon Anceron. The effort made my veins stand out. My heart labored, faltered, and took up an unsteady beat. I screamed aloud, bursting the scab on my cheek and spilling what felt like fire all down my left side.

"Still you conspire and protest," said Kwan sadly. "Lord, this is unseemly." When I only glared at him, he signaled his soldiers. "The man first."

Kwan's squad pushed me forward, tearing my hand from Maran's. One guard hefted a large broadsword, and held it ready. Bastion, invisible and inaudible to everyone else, moved to stand at my right side. "This is not the end you fear," he said. "It is the end you dread."

I turned my head to look at him, but had no chance to ask questions. Kwan gave the order, and the guard with the broadsword swung.

He aimed for my neck, a quick, clean kill. Because I had turned sideways, looking at Bastion and trying to reach behind to regain Maran's hand, I didn't see the blow coming. The blade belled loudly and bounced off my neck.

I couldn't turn my head back, or even speak. My jaw was immobile, as was my entire left side.

"Your doom falls," said Bastion. "I will stand with you until the end."

I could only see with my right eye, and I still turned partly away from the executioner. He swung his sword again and this time it broke in his hands with a jarring shudder. He cried out and dropped his weapon. I didn't feel the blow. I pleaded with my eyes for Maran to rescue us, and extended my good hand toward her.

"What sorcery is this?" demanded Kwan. He signaled for

other guards to dispatch Maran and Aiden. They moved swiftly, their blades glittering in the torchlight.

"I'm sorry, my love," she said. She gritted her teeth and disappeared. At the same moment, the manor house fell to pieces, as if only her will had ever upheld the walls. The stream slowed to a trickle and stopped.

I knew what she had done; she had partly reformed her enchantments, but only for herself and Aiden. She had insufficient power to include Torrey, me, or the remnants of her valley. The guards could search forever without finding her.

Bastion stepped around to my left side while a new guard approached my right. Kwan gave the order, but it was already too late. The petrification of my left side had spread to consume my entire body. I could no longer move, no longer see, no longer feel, no longer hear. I stood frozen in place, half-turned, one hand extended in a beckoning gesture. Just enough of my percipience remained that I could vaguely sense my immediate surroundings. My second sight was truncated, nearly useless, limited to vision only. I could only perceive things in a twenty-foot radius. All my other powers had deserted me.

I watched Bastion's silent departure. I watched as soldier after soldier tried to strike me down, all their strength and weapons useless. I watched them march away in failure. Finally, I was alone with Torrey's unconscious body. Zoxo crawled from the ruins of the manor and clambered slowly up to perch on my shoulder. I watched until Torrey regained his senses. He stood up groggily, touched my outstretched hand for a long moment, plucked the lizard from my shoulder, and then wandered away dejectedly.

And so my long years as a statue began. Softly, gently, the first flakes of snow drifted down to settle on my shoulders. Maran's perpetual summer had finally failed.

About the Author

Jeffry Dwight is an author, editor, musician, pencil artist, poet, programmer, and father of two sons. He was born in Illinois, and currently lives in the suburbs of Dallas, Texas. In 2014, he received the *Kevin O'Donnell, Jr. Service to SFWA Award* from the Science Fiction & Fantasy Writers Association. Of himself, Dwight says, "I hate writing, but love having written."

Dwight's brief book of poetry, *Phantas*, and his immensely popular collection of short fiction, *Mortal Dreads*, are available from Amazon and most other retail outlets.

In addition, Dwight authored or co-authored multiple textbooks on programming and Internet technologies, as well as writing several articles for technical journals. Before that, he worked in social services among developmentally disabled and abused/neglected children and adults. All of these experiences inform his storytelling.

Dwight is a self-taught singer-songwriter who plays keyboards, guitars, drums, and several other instruments. His style covers ballads, jazz, and 70's soft rock. His songs are available on YouTube, Amazon, Spotify, Pandora, iTunes, Apple Music, and other services. You may listen for free on most platforms, or purchase the albums in MP3 format from Amazon.

Explore more creative works by Jeffry Dwight:

Short Fiction Collection:

Mortal Dreads: https://books2read.com/u/bMYZwk

Amazon Author Website:

https://www.amazon.com/Jeffry-Dwight/e/B000APBJWS

Music on Amazon:

All Jeffry Dwight results: https://amzn.to/3rAeOYM

All Jeffry Dwight Album results: https://amzn.to/3rxUI16

Albums:

Changes: https://amzn.to/3iJuuov

In My Right Brain: https://amzn.to/3rvRZp0

Vintage: https://amzn.to/3kSBRMN

YouTube Channel:

YouTube Links:
Changes: https://bit.ly/2V7L8G3
In My Right Brain: https://bit.ly/3y6IkYl
Vintage: https://bit.ly/3kSEo9L

THE SUNDERING SAGA

Book 1, *My Manufactured Soul*:
    https://books2read.com/u/38y05O

Book 2, *Monument at Landing*:
    https://books2read.com/u/3G5DLP